Fractured Shadows

K.A KNIGHT
KENDRA MORENO

Fractured Shadows.

Copyright © 2022 K.A. Knight & Kendra Moreno, all rights reserved.

No part of this book may be reproduced in any form or by any electronic or mechanical means, including information storage and retrieval systems, without written permission from the author, except for the use of brief quotations in a book review. This is a work of fiction. Any resemblance to places, events or real people are entirely coincidental.

Written by K.A. Knight & Kendra Moreno
Edited By Jess from Elemental Editing and Proofreading.
Proofreading by Bookish Dreams Editing.
Formatted by Mallory Kent.
Cover by Logan Keys.

Shadows save us all...

PREFACE

I was born in the Shadow Lands, a place between darkness and light
Good and evil.
Between the Dead Lands and the Gilded Lands.
It's also where I died, but let's start at the beginning, shall we?

To understand the Shadow Lands, you must know two things. One, women have no rights and we belong to the men. Two, monsters exist and haunt the darkness at our borders. We are all that stands between darkness and light.
When that darkness begins to creep closer, however, not even the light can penetrate the shadows.
My name is Cora, and I was twenty years old when I was sacrificed to the dark to hold back the shadow's reach.

CHAPTER ONE

Father's yells wake me from a nightmare plagued sleep. Flipping onto my back on the straw mattress, I scrub at my eyes before pushing back my sweaty golden hair. I let my arm flop back to the lumpy mattress as I stare at the wooden ceiling of our little shack. With a groan, I force myself to sit up before Father comes storming in here to demand his breakfast. Ignoring the hunger pains tingling in my belly and the weakness in my sore limbs from hours of labor yesterday, I look at my older sister's empty bed and narrow my eyes.

She is getting sloppy at sneaking out now and not even trying to hide it. If Father finds out, he will brand her as a whore, or worse. The beating would be horrific.

As usual, I hurry to dress in my scratchy wool tunic, worn socks, and boots and then open the door before shutting it softly behind me. Father spins, and I meet his enraged eyes before dropping mine to the floor submissively, not wanting him to think I'm challenging him. I learned that lesson early on, even if it's bitter.

"There you are. You're late. I have to eat before work!" he screams as Mother stands at the old wood burning stove in the tiny kitchen, which also doubles as our eating area. While she's used to his wrath, she's also terrified of him, just as every female in this village is afraid of the men in their lives. Grinding my teeth, I nod and scurry to the kitchen to help her get breakfast ready as he sits in the scarred wooden chair at the small table, watching us.

"Where is your sister?" he finally barks. Practice has me continuing to chop vegetables for the broth without hesitating.

"She went to work early," I lie, my back tensing as I feel his gaze on me. I hope he believes me. If not, I'm in for a beating, which I really don't want today, not with how long I have to work in the fields. Besides, it's getting harder and harder not to hit him back.

Foolish, I know.

It would be a death sentence if I did. A woman striking a man? It's a sin.

Unheard of.

Against the law.

We are property to be punished in any way the men in our life deem fit. We belong to our fathers and brothers until we are married off, and then our husbands keep us obedient and meek.

He finally grunts, and I hurry to serve him his oats. Standing with my hands behind my back, I watch as he eats like an animal, wolfing it down. When he's done, he throws the bowl at me and stands. I barely catch it before it can clatter to the ground. Seeing his protruding belly causes me to wrinkle my nose in disgust. His once white shirt is stained brown in places and stretched to its limit around his robust frame. His once brown hair is now graying at the temples and receding, and his plain brown eyes are surrounded by lines from being narrowed and angry all the time. His nose is wide, and his face is even rounder than his belly. His once strong muscles have turned to jelly from years of drinking and eating, yet he's still stronger than me.

He's still tougher than my mother and sister.

I bow my head like I was taught by Mother and wait for him to amble out of the skewed wooden front door, which he slams behind him. When he's gone, I blow out a breath and wipe the table. Mother silently hands me a cracked bowl with a small, nervous smile. Her dull green eyes are lifeless, the fear in them permanent.

She might have been beautiful once, but the years of abuse have worn her down. Her hair is thin and lifeless, a graying, dull version of my own golden strands. Her eyes were once as bright as the emeralds we saw when royalty visited, but now they are dull and empty. Her tanned face is marked with years of age and fear, and her willowy frame is weak and hunched.

Taking the bowl, I sit heavily on the floor, since I'm not allowed to use the table, and throw back the watery soup. All the good food is eaten by Father first, and we only get the leftovers. It's barely enough to live on, especially when he gets drunk and eats all of our supplies, which happens most days. Once I've eaten, Mother has a small bowl of what is left. Staring at her, I beg her to look at me, to speak, to do something other than this mundane routine she survives in, but as usual, she eats and begins to clean, ignoring me like I am not here.

Once upon a time, just like in the fairy tales she read to me about heroes defeating monsters, she would talk to me, smile, laugh, and play when Father was gone.

Not anymore.

Now, we are just two ghosts in this shack.

I don't even say goodbye as I hurry to the door, sliding a stale slice of bread in my pocket for Kai, my sister, so she won't go hungry. I would be lashed for it, but I do it anyway and shut the door softly behind me, looking around at the gray, foggy streets of our village.

The Shadow Lands.

The shadows from the Dead Lands—hence our town's name—echo across the land here. Fog rolls in from that darkness and spreads across the fields. The early morning sun struggles to pierce it, refracting on the dew decorating trees and plants. I shiver in the brisk morning air and wrap my arms around myself, as if that will shield my thin frame. My head turns like always to take in the glow in the distance, where the sunlight hits the castle in the Gilded Lands and burns brightly throughout the day. The night and day difference between that and the

Dead Lands is not lost on me. On one side of us, it is nothing but darkness, and on the other side is nothing but gold and light.

As for us?

We are the shadows of both.

The fields where we grow and tend our crops stretch farther than the eye can see over the rolling hills. The granary is farther down near the cornfields, the windmill barely visible in the distance just over the small stone bridge. There used to be more housing and farms beyond that, but they are abandoned now, the families dead. After all, that's the only way out of here. Nobody from the Shadow Lands goes into the Gilded Lands, where the rich, like the king, live. And the Dead lands? Well, that's a story for another time.

Pushing forward, I drop my head to brace against the breeze, gritting my teeth as I shiver harder.

I spot the cannery workers, town hall personnel, and the school staff hurrying to their jobs—all male of course. Females aren't allowed in any positions of power. We aren't even allowed to attend school, which I once got mad about. All Father would say was, "Women don't need to know how to add or read, just how to serve and please." Furious at his words, I snuck in dressed as a boy. The beating I received once they found out I had been going to school for weeks was worth it.

Now, I'm the only female who knows how to read, apart from Kai, who I've been teaching in secret. The other women here are either so beaten down into their position or too young to care that we have no rights. Men can do whatever they want, like the easy jobs that keep them warm and fed and stop their bodies from breaking, while women are made to bathe them, cook for them, farm their foods, and make their beds.

To say I don't fit in would be an understatement. Kai once asked me why I don't just let it be how it is, because nothing will ever change, but I can't accept that. I refuse to live this way until I eventually die or am killed by a husband I don't want. There has to be more.

My eyes once again turn to the Gilded Lands I can see on the horizon, the huge houses and palace mocking me as I stop and stare. Do women have rights there? More than us? I know they don't work but are expected to keep house, or that's what I heard from Kai, but she could be full of shit. And the king... Well, everyone knows he keeps concubines. He comes every year and selects the prettiest young women from our people and takes them away, never to be seen again. Kai and I make sure to act dumb and be covered in mud every year, even our teeth, so he won't pick us.

We all know serving and dying in the Shadow Lands is better than being at the king's whims.

A noise has my head jerking the other way, and my breath stills in my lungs as I peer into the darkness that's so close, I can almost feel the wildness rolling from it. Standing between us and the Dead Lands, between us and the monsters that live beyond, is magic—pure magic. It's the last of its kind, and the only magic left in the entire land. The barbed vines sometimes slither and move, interlocking and tightening the wall that stretches far into the sky. No one knows what is beyond, as no one has lived to tell the tale, but we all hear the monsters.

And we all know the hunt.

"Cora!" a familiar laughing voice calls.

Shaking my head of the disturbing, gloomy thoughts, I turn back to see my sister racing toward me across the bridge. No doubt, she spent the night in one of the abandoned farmhouses with her boyfriend. He's a good man, even if I don't believe there are many. He is kind to her, feeds her, and doesn't seem to have the same proclivity for hurting women as the rest of his gender. He still believes we have our own places and women shouldn't be allowed to do certain things, but I guess as far as prospects go in the Shadow Lands, he's a catch. He's also handsome and successful as a trainee professor at the school, so he will look after her and make sure she never starves—if he can get the blessing from my father.

For now, they sneak around, and I've never seen my sister so happy.

She skids to a stop before me, her face flushed and eyes glowing with joy. Her lips are curled in a permanent smile that warms my heart, and her hair is slightly mussed.

Although she's older than me, she's shorter by at least five inches. Where my hair takes after our mother's, hers takes after our father's. Her thick brown hair falls in waves to her hips. She's curvier than me, with large breasts that always attract men and wide hips my father has called "child birthing hips." It's no wonder why every man here vies for her attention and why she thrives on it. Mischief glints in her eyes as she turns and walks by my side. I shorten my stride so she can keep up without panting.

"Have a good night?" I grin, nudging her shoulder.

She giggles and looks around before lowering her voice. "Yes, he's going to ask Father for my hand."

"That's great news!" I exclaim, taking her hand and squeezing. "Truly, sister."

"Yeah?" she asks nervously. "I know your feelings about marriage." She drops her voice to badly imitate me. "About tying yourself to one person for the rest of your life with no goals or aspirations—"

"Shh." I grin, rolling my eyes, because I did say that. "I know what I said, but I'm truly happy for you. You've always wanted to be married and have kids, and he's a good man."

"He is," she replies dreamily, making me fake gag, and she giggles.

"Make it quick though. Father is getting suspicious, and I'm running out of lies." I turn and walk backwards as she stops at the cannery, where she works. "Oh, and here." I toss her the package of food, and she cups her mouth.

She hoots. "You are incredible, Cora Black!"

"And make sure you never forget!" I yell back equally as loud, ignoring the disgruntled looks and whispers from the men walking past.

Laughing, I hurry across the dirt paths and into the fields, knowing I'm probably late for work, as always. The warmth and joy I feel over my sister's happiness keeps me upbeat though, even as the sun beats down on me while I gather crops. I don't stop until lunch, when I break to have some water and stale bread that's passed out by the watchers who maintain the field. I sit alone in silence as I nibble on it. My eyes drift to the Dead Lands beyond before the whistle blows and I'm back to work.

FRACTURED SHADOWS

∼

By the time the sun sets, my back is aching something fierce and sweat beads on my brow. They pushed us hard today since the gift to the king is due—an offering from the Shadow Lands in which he takes nearly all our crops and has his pick of our girls. I'm used to hard work, and the muscles on my body are proof of it, but exhaustion weighs heavily on my shoulders as I drag my feet home. I want to collapse in bed, but I'll have to wash in the cold bucket outside and make the evening meal for Father first, which makes me groan out loud.

I'm so tired, I barely notice the wide-eyed looks or whispers until I reach our shack, and then I turn, my brow furrowed, to see nearly everyone watching me.

This is very unusual, and a bad feeling pangs within my heart, nearly making my empty stomach cramp and roll. Without waiting for someone to tell me what's going on, I push into the shack, my heart racing and mouth dry.

My first sign that something is terribly wrong is that my sister is sitting at the table. She is never allowed to sit there. The second is that she is sobbing, even as she tries to keep silent. Mother is staring into space, completely checked out.

And Father? Father looks almost gleeful.

"What's wrong?" I croak out.

"I-I have been chosen for the hunt," Kai sobs. "I am to be the sacrifice."

My whole world crumbles as I meet Kai's grief-stricken, tearful eyes in which she silently begs me to save her from the Dead Lands and the monsters waiting to consume her.

Hopelessness pours from her as our hearts break in sync.

CHAPTER
TWO

I stare into her eyes, into the pain there, and I feel it ricocheting through me. My sister, my strong, vibrant sister, who is so deeply in love, about to be married, and start the family she always wanted. She's the girl who never did anything wrong, followed the laws—unlike me, who broke them—and who has never even been punished...and it was all for nothing.

She is to be sacrificed to the monsters to appease them.

For the hunt.

I know the girls are chosen at random, but anger—no, fury roars through me. Not her! Anyone but her! My eyes flick to Father, who is smirking at me. Even though Kai would marry well and bring in a good dowry, being chosen for the hunt will offer him a lifetime of gold and food. He will never have to work again, and our family will be looked after.

Well, just him.

No.

I must say it out loud, because his eyes flash in warning, but I rush to Kai's side, drop to my knees, and take her hand, searching her eyes. I'm practically begging her with my gaze to tell me what to do. Even though she's older and supposed to protect me, it's my job to protect her.

"No, not you, Kai. There must be a mistake!" I shout, whirling to Mother. "Help her!"

She's not listening. Father is through with my outburst, however, so he grabs my hair, making me cry out as he drags me into my room and kicks the door shut behind him. The last thing I see is Kai's heartbroken eyes as her shoulders shake from the force of her sobs.

Swallowing, I look up at my father. "Do whatever you have to do. Punish me, kill me, but please save her!" I get to my knees and beg—the only time I ever have and will. "Please, Father. We have never asked you for anything, so please save her. You know she's the best of us."

"She will honor our family and her king. It is a gift to be chosen," he snarls, his belt sticking as he pulls it free from his pants. Terror for a different reason fills me, but still I surge ahead.

"Please—"

"Enough, girl! You will learn your place. With your sister gone, you'll marry well and fast. You will honor us. Enough of this disobedience I've let you get away with. It will stop now, with this."

His belt lashes across my skin, but it barely causes any pain, not when my heart is already broken and my soul is ripping apart at the thought of losing my sister.

He stops at five, a blessing from him, and when I glance down at my thighs, I see they are simply red and stinging, the skin unbroken. He kicks open the door and storms out of the shack, no doubt to get drunk. With my head bowed forward, I let the tears break free.

I scream and rage, hitting my fists against the floor until they bleed.

I am angry at the world.

Angry at the king.

At our father.

At everyone.

FRACTURED SHADOWS

KAI and I huddle together all night. I hold her and kiss her head, stroking her hair. I sing to her, tell her stories, and assure her it will all be okay, and when she finally falls asleep, I stare down at her pale, grief-stricken face that's twisted, even in her sleep.

I can't let her do this. She'll be sacrificed to the Dead Lands, and we all know what will happen. I will lose my sister. She is the only good thing in my life, the only reason I haven't given into my desires, set fire to this entire place, and run away into the lands beyond.

She's my hope, the one pure thing in my existence.

I'm her younger sister, but I always promised to protect her.

"It hurts," Kai whimpers, curling into me, her young face streaked with tears as she shakes from the pain. She was lashed today for asking a question she shouldn't have. One lash was all they managed before I stepped before her and took the punishment. Even now, my back smarts from the lashes.

"I know," I whisper softly so Father doesn't hear and punish her further for crying. Scooping the healing paste I stole from Father from the container, I slather it across the slash on her back, not wanting it to scar or hurt. There's none left for me, but that doesn't matter as long as she's okay. "It's okay, Kai Bear, it will stop hurting now." She cries harder, and I wrap my arm around her. "Shh, no. No one will touch you again, not ever. I will always protect you."

She lifts her tear-stained face, and her big eyes lock on mine. "Promise?"

"Promise," I murmur, holding her tighter.

Staring down at her now, I can't help but remember my promise to her. "I'll always protect you, remember?" I whisper, kissing her forehead and lingering there. "Even from this." Slowly, I slide out from under her, tuck her in, and then brush her hair out of her face. "I love you, sister. Earn this life for me and be happy. Get married, have a family, and give them hell." Swallowing back everything else I wish to say, I force myself to stand.

I want to wake her and say goodbye, because I already know what I'm going to do, but I won't. That's selfish and will only hurt her more. She can't be given a chance to protest, and I will keep my promise to her.

Stepping into the other room, I find Father and Mother waiting there. I nod at them, and with my chin lifted, I leave the shack. I hear them scrambling to follow me as I start to walk. The sun is rising, and I know the king's men will be coming for her. I'm lucky I don't have to wait long, or my courage might die.

The soldiers walk toward me with the king's symbol emblazoned proudly on their chests, their faces hidden behind the black masks they wear. Their bodies are encased in the same black stretchy material, and they wear batons at their side alight with technology—not magic like they would have us believe.

I wait with my hands at my sides, and when they stop before me, I swallow a deep breath and glance back to my mother and father. "Look after her," I snarl at Mother, and then I look forward. "My name is Cora Black. I am volunteering for this year's hunt." I hold out my hands and wait.

"Cora!" my mother yells, but I ignore her.

"Girl, what do you think you are doing?" Father roars, even as a guard steps forward and binds my hands before tugging me after them. They don't care who will be sacrificed, only that it's someone from the Shadow Lands.

A meaty hand lands on my shoulder, and I whirl, kicking Father back. He falls to his ass, his shocked face turned up to me as I sneer down at him. "You are a weak, stupid man who made a brave, fearless daughter, and she will survive this. You make sure of it, or I will come back and haunt you." With that, I whirl again and march after the soldiers, just as I hear Kai screaming after me.

Luckily, when I glance back, Father catches her sprinting form and holds her as she screams for me. Her hand is outstretched, her voice cracking with anguish. I turn away before I cry, not wanting to show weakness. I ignore the gazes of the others watching, their expressions ranging from sad and knowing to happy.

None of it matters. She is safe.

Let them do whatever they want with me.

I am led into the edges of the Gilded Lands for a single day and night. They keep me locked within a brick building, clearly not wanting me to run away—not that I will, because it means my sister's life. Even so, I pace the cell I'm in. There are no bars, and the door is unlocked, but it's still a cell, a pretty one, with a huge bed covered in fabrics softer than I've ever felt in my life. There's an actual bathroom with a working shower, and despite my fear, I wash away years of grime, soaking in the warm water. There are creams and brushes and pretty clothes, not to mention food and entertainment, all enough to make a gilded prison for a woman.

I make the most of it, knowing I will be dead tomorrow.

I stare at myself in the mirror, after using all the creams and putting on a soft silk slip. I look like a stranger. My hair is wavy and luxurious from the oils. My eyes pop from the tinted creams glittering with gold. My ribs poke through the shift, and my hips are boney, but I can't do anything about that. I look older, I conclude, the day aging me.

Turning away, I collapse onto the bed, but I can't sleep.

My mind runs through what will happen. I've seen it every year as I was forced to watch like every other Shadow Lander. A girl is sacrificed to the vines and the monsters beyond. It's an old ritual from before the current king's reign to keep back the surge of the monsters that would kill us all. Every year, one woman is sacrificed to keep the evil at bay. At least, that's what they claim.

I am to be that woman.

I am destined to die.

At least it will be on my own terms.

CHAPTER
THREE

The morning came far faster than I thought it would. I expected time to inch by as I remained awake and stared at the shadows cast by first the moon and then the sun as it rose slowly into the sky, casting light inside the prison I found myself in, but it didn't. I should be terrified, but I'm mostly just resigned to my fate. If this is how I die, then so be it. At least Kai will be safe.

At least I've done something good.

At sunrise, the guards arrive, bearing trays of food I'd never be able to eat. The meal is lavish, complete with meats I'd never been able to sample in the Shadow Lands. My father would never have allowed us to eat so well. Trays of fruits and pastries follow the meats. There is so much food, it could have fed my family for a month with more to spare.

Those in the Gilded Lands live far differently than we do in the Shadow Lands. To have so much food…

I can't even imagine.

I force myself to eat, to sample it. Once I've picked through things and eaten until I can't anymore, it appears as if I've hardly made a dent in it. Knowing I'll need it, I wrap some of it in the cloth napkins provided —*such waste*—before stashing them in a little pouch I can wear beneath the silk clothing they gave me. I don't have many options. I would have preferred pants and a shirt rather than the thin slip they've given me, but I understand I'm not meant to survive.

What better gift than a prettily wrapped one?

No one knows what happens to those who are chosen for the hunt. None of them ever return, so we assume they die, but for decades, it's all we have known. We're told that it's the way of things, and that every year, a young woman from the Shadow Lands would be chosen by random and sent through the barrier. After that, there's no other information.

I'll be in the land of the monsters, but I'm just a human.

My chances of survival are low, I know that, yet I can't seem to muster up any fear, only peace.

They come for me as the first bells toll. Normally, that sound would signify that the first shift of workers was due at their workstations, whatever that may be. Today, they have an ominous tone, a signal that the hunt ceremony is about to begin.

I have just barely enough time to hide the pouch around my body before six guards burst through the doorway. I'm tough and determined when I want to be, but they are armed with swords and brute strength. With my too thin frame, I wouldn't stand a chance right now. I'm weak, and I hate that.

Suddenly wishing that I focused more on gaining strength in the past months than rebelling against my father, I thank whoever is listening that at least my thin frame makes it easy to hide the pouch beneath my shift. There is extra room, thanks to my boney hips and shoulders, so I'm able to stash food and a knife inside. I don't know how much the knife will help, but at least it's something. Better a small knife meant for fruit than no weapon at all.

Stepping from the gilded prison and into the streets, I take in all those lining the edges. All of Shadow Lands is required to come witness this desperate parade, this sacrifice, to keep the monsters at bay.

After all, what's one woman to save everyone? I see the relief written in their faces that it's not them, along with the fear that one day, it might be.

I've never wished for the monsters to tear through the Gilded Lands more than I do right now. What chaos would that create? What was this world like before the barrier existed? I'll never know, not truly, not as I'm being marched to my death.

The barrier isn't a wall in a traditional sense. One would think it would take stone as high as you could see to keep monsters out, but it takes something more than that.

It takes magic.

The barrier between the Shadow Lands and the Dead Lands is nothing but a wall of thorns and vines, intertwined so tightly, you can't see through them. They are taller than I am, perhaps twice as tall, but it doesn't seem like enough to keep out the worst of the monsters. I don't even know what they could be, but I can only imagine they are gruesome, horrifying creatures. My brief weeks in school had shown me a few of them, some of the worst, but I'd been ripped from that freedom too soon to learn what I needed for this.

I'm stopped just before the barrier and made to stand in front of them, staring at where the opening appears every year like clockwork. There's no need to guess when the vines will open to allow a single woman to pass. It's scheduled religiously, and every year, we're forced to attend. Last year, I watched as Beatrice had been shoved into the other side without mercy. She cried, screamed, and begged the king to stop the madness. I felt terrible for her, but like everyone else, I just stood there and watched the vines close on her terrified voice. Unlike others, I stood there and listened to the sounds of the monsters screeching their excitement over a new hunt.

I won't give them the satisfaction of begging or crying. I'll walk across that line willingly with my chin held high. Not a single tear will fall from my cheek—that I can promise.

Kai is standing off to the side with my father and mother. Mother looks as empty as she always does, her eyes focused on the sky rather than her daughter who's about to be offered to the monsters. She'd rather disappear inside her mind than face reality. It's too late for my mother, but it's not for my sister. She still has a chance at happiness. She still has a shot to live.

Our eyes meet as I look at her. Her face is swollen and red from her own tears, but she meets my gaze without flinching. Her mouth moves, forming the words, "I love you," so that she won't be reprimanded for speaking out.

I hold my fist over my heart, telling her that I love her and that she should be happy. Kai would never survive in the Dead Lands, but me? I'm going to survive if it's the last thing I do.

At least I'm going to try.

When the king appears with his group of concubines, it takes everything in me not to snarl at him. Fat with gluttony and coated in gold and jewels, the king seems to rub his richness and status in our faces. When everyone bows to him, I remain tall, my chin tipped up. The king's eyes land on me. Before this, I would have been put to death for the slight. Now, I'm being put to death in a different way.

The joke will be on him.

The concubines, who are gathered submissively around the king, watch me curiously, a mixture of Gilded Land girls and Shadow Land girls deemed far too pretty for the likes of us. They are all young, too young, despite there being plenty of women of age. The king's eyes trail over Kai, who stands with my parents, and his brow rises, but my shift and clearing of my throat draws his attention back to me and away from my sister.

Those of us from the Shadow Lands appear so different from this king dripping in jewels, it's disgusting. I was just like them only yesterday—dirty and beaten down, eyes hollow and empty, and treated no different from livestock—before I was dressed up to be thrown to the monsters.

This was our fate, but now my fate has changed, and I won't waste it.

"Every year, we commemorate the day we were gifted freedom from the monsters in the Dead Lands," the king says loudly, the hushed crowd going still at the looming threat. He towers above us on the wooden podium, breaking the backs of his soldiers who are holding it up so no speck of dirt can touch this godly king. No one will interrupt the king unless they want to die. "This year, we have a volunteer." He looks at me again and narrows his eyes. "Let the monsters tear her apart and show her how we handle defiance in this world."

Bravery has me replying. That, and the knowledge that I won't be hurt before being offered for the hunt. I need to be intact for such games.

"Cowardice is how you handle it," I spit out. "Only a coward sits in his gilded castle dripping in gold while his people starve."

The smile that pulls at his lips drips with malice. "May your offering bring us a prosperous year." They are words that have been spoken many times before, every year, and always with the same careless tone.

"May the crown on your head break your neck," I respond.

I don't know where the bravery comes from. Perhaps, with my death on the horizon, I've realized just how doomed I am, so everything I've ever wanted to say comes to my mind.

Looking out over the other Shadow Lands people, I say, "We were meant for more than this." I meet the king's gaze head-on. "We were always meant for more than to bend and break under your rule."

I get no more time to sow my seed, no more time to practice my newfound bravery. The bells toll again, and the magic of the barrier begins to move.

The thorny vines begin to move, almost vibrating with the preserved magic. The inky black spiked tendrils slither open, revealing a human-sized hole.

My chin never dips, even as I stare at the darkness beyond.

CHAPTER
FOUR

Terror threatens to clog my throat. My resolution not to beg or cry is nearly destroyed when the darkness on the other side consumes my vision.

The king chuckles, no doubt seeing my wavering conviction. "Nothing to say now, I see."

Glancing at the fat bastard, I bare my teeth at him like a feral animal. "Fuck you."

The guard on my left shoves me forward, telling me he'll happily push me inside due to my disrespect of the king if I don't walk willingly. Leave it to the guards, the prisoners in the Gilded Lands, to think themselves better off than we are. Just because they are treated a little better doesn't mean they aren't also prisoners of this world.

Tugging down the hem of the silk slip I'm wearing, I take a halting step forward. The people around me, my people, watch me with various expressions on their faces. Some look unbearably sad, while some look gleeful at my demise. I've caused enough trouble over the years to make many of them, especially the men, happy about this outcome, but I don't care about any of them.

I take another step, slowly moving toward the gap. I know I only have so long, and once I'm on the other side, the magic will sense it and the vines will close behind me.

The darkness before me is terrifying, but something about it also calls to me. Perhaps some sort of death wish makes it easier to take another step, and then another, and then another. I hold my breath as I become even with the vines, almost expecting something to jump out and attack me. I know that won't happen. Whatever magic made the barrier means that the creatures can't attack while the hole is open.

I glance to the side and see my father there, his disdain written clearly on his face. Despite my sacrifice bringing the family gold, he doesn't care. I've somehow won, somehow gotten the upper hand over him, even if it's with my death. That thought makes me smile at him, and it only seems to anger him more. What a worthless man.

Kai stands beside and slightly behind him, fresh tears rolling down her face. As I step across the barrier completely, her face is the last thing I see as the vines begin to knit back together. They move like snakes, slithering between and around. Before I'm hidden from view completely, I mouth, "I love you," knowing she'll be heartbroken at this outcome.

But she'll be okay. She'll be happy, and that's all that matters.

The moment the vines close completely, what little light streamed in from the Shadow Lands disappears, leaving me standing in the darkness for long minutes as I wait for my eyes to adjust. The oppressive darkness makes me shiver, along with the chill from the lack of sunlight. Once my vision adapts, I realize it's not completely pitch-black. There's just less light filtering in through the trees here, as if the forest is meant to be this way. I stare at the twisted and gnarled trees, at the way they form shapes that should be impossible for a tree to make. Thick green moss grows on them, coating them until they are almost fuzzy with it. There is so much black here, so much animosity. The ground, also black, sinks beneath my feet like sludge. There is no color anywhere, only shades of black.

I peer up at the sky, but it rolls with shadows, and there's a scent, like rotting flesh. I nearly gag before I slow my breathing and swallow back the bile. When the sickness passes, I blow out a breath, pull the small bag from beneath my shift, and drape it over my shoulder, wearing it as it should be. This is it. This is what I'm faced with now. I have no choice in the matter.

I'm tempted to turn around and try to climb over the barrier, but I know the magic won't allow me to. The barrier prevents anything from crossing, or at least that's how it's supposed to work. I only know what they have told me.

The darkness beckons me forward, so trying to hold on to the same bravery that had me spitting obscenities at the king, I begin to move deeper into the darkness. Something howls in the distance, and I pause, but when it doesn't get closer, I keep going. They hadn't given me proper boots. I'm wearing soft slippers that match the slip, so when I step on a branch wrong, I curse at the sharpness of it.

I groan at the sting, knowing I've probably cut my foot open, but I can't stop here and check it, not until I've found somewhere safe to settle—if there is such a thing here. I don't know how badly I'm bleeding, but I can feel the moisture staining the slipper. I'll have to fashion something better for shoes soon. Perhaps make some sort of better clothing too. This isn't the proper attire for survival.

The noises reach my ears a moment later, as if the magic of the barrier muted them all. One moment, the world is silent around me, and the next, the sounds of a forest reach my ears. The hums of the insects come through first, and while they are not threatening, they lend to the dangerous atmosphere with their clatter. It isn't the insects that have fear trickling into my throat, however.

It's the other sounds.

Hoots, hollers, growls, howls, and deep, reverberating snarls echo through the trees around me as if welcoming me to their home. It's more like a welcome to the dinner table, I think, as I take precautions to move as quietly as possible. Unluckily for me, I've never been light-footed. Kai had been better at sneaking about. I'm far better at making a racket and waking the entire village.

I'm unsteady on my feet as the cut begins to burn and ache, but I have to keep going. I have to. If I stop, I'll be a sitting duck, and I need to survive. I have to, for Kai, and then when I do, I'll return and start a revolution that the Shadow Lands severely needs.

A big fuck you to the king.

The sound of a stick breaking to my right has me freezing and jerking my head in that direction. I wait, searching for the source, but when nothing immediately attacks, I ease forward again. My heartbeat is so loud, it's echoing in my ears. I pray that the monsters in this forest can't hear it, but it's a foolish hope.

They are monsters, so of course they can hear my heartbeat and smell my blood.

Realizing my mistake, I hiss in a breath and rip a thin strip from my silk shift. I swiftly ease off the slipper and wrap up the cut, trying to staunch the bleeding as best as I can. It's pointless now since the slipper is dotted with the blood. What a fool I've been!

Still, nothing immediately comes out of the darkness, so once I've wrapped it well enough, I move forward again. This time, I pull the small paring knife from my bag and hold it in my hand just in case.

I won't be a gift wrapped in a pretty bow for the monsters.

I won't accept my fate.

I won't go down without a fight...

CHAPTER FIVE

Keeping my eyes peeled, I lighten my steps as I make my way through the darkened forest, trying to stay as quiet as possible and draw as little attention as I can. I see the shadows shifting, and I swear at one point, I even see glowing eyes peering through the leaves of a thorn bush.

I don't see them, but I can feel their eyes watching me, assessing me, hunting me.

When the forest suddenly stops, I almost weep in relief.

I linger in the tree line, peering at the land before me, getting my first glimpse of the Dead Lands. What I see has me equally shocked and wanting to flee in terror, yet something inside of me unfurls at the rugged, uncluttered scenery before me. The darkness calls to a darkness within me I didn't even realize I had until today.

Before me is marshland. Boggy grass and mud stretch as far as I can see, the water a deep black. The grass is dying and brittle, almost obscured by a foggy mist that spreads across it as if it's an ever present feature of the marsh. Swallowing, I look to the horizon, where I spot huge, jagged mountains. The dark sky obscures the true height of them, but I can see their silhouette like a threat stretching into the sky.

That's where I will go. There is no other feature on the horizon I can use to pinpoint locations, and it's better than nothing. There might be a cave there, or even some kind of shade for me to hide in

Rolling my shoulders to ease the tension, I take the first step out of the trees and into the wide-open expanse of the marshland. My feet sink deep, and I have to drag my feet up and out, stepping quickly to avoid sinking. All the while, my eyes dart from my path to the exposed area around me. I am careful not to fall into any water, but I also try to watch my back and sides in case I'm attacked.

My spine stiffens, my neck prickles with awareness, and the hair on my arms rises in response. The deeper I step into the fog, the more my panic seems to grow, and then I hear a musical laugh.

Spinning, I peer into the fog that seems to have swelled to obscure my tracks and what's behind me, but I manage to spy the edge of the trees through the shroud. There, I spot a clawed hand gripping the bark of a tree like a symbol of doom. When the laugh comes again, those claws slash at the wood, leaving behind deep grooves before disappearing back into the darkness.

Okay then.

"Let's hope they don't like water," I mutter as I turn back and hasten my steps. The more I walk, the deeper I seem to be sinking, and at one point, I'm up to my knees. The mud slows my steps until I'm dragging myself forward with my hands and feet. Mud covers my cheeks, where I wipe my face. My legs and hands are heavy with the sludge, making me feel as if each step adds more weight. I claw at it, gritting my teeth as things wiggle inside of the black slop, but I'm determined to keep going. Every now and again, my eyes drift to the horizon and lock on the mountains to ensure I'm still heading in the same direction.

Sweat beads on my head and neck, trickling down my spine. My energy drains, and I'm exhausted after what feels like hours have passed, but when I look back, I've hardly made any progress at all. Great. The monsters might not have to kill me, because the marsh will do it for them.

Shaking my head of the despair that seems to fill me, I force myself to keep moving. To keep my spirits up, I start to sing softly to myself. I cycle through old nursery rhymes and songs of my people, and with each one, I urge myself forward, faster and faster, even as the sky seems to darken further.

Just when I'm about to give up hope and collapse in exhaustion, the mist lifts, allowing me to clearly see for the first time. The rapidly darkening sky makes it hard to see far, but when I squint, I can just make out a structure not too far off.

At the sight of it, hope and adrenaline course through me, and I practically run, despite the mud still caking my body. I push myself faster, desperation filling me. After I slide to a stop before it, however, all that hope comes crashing down.

I should have known nothing whole exists here, nothing that's not destroyed.

The stone structure of what was once a house is leaning to the left with a hole through one side, which I slip through, and most of the roof is missing, so hardly enough cover is left behind. The floor is now nothing but mud as rain suddenly begins to pour down through the gaping holes, cascading inside like waterfalls.

It's just one room with a single door to the right, but there is a triangle of roof left over the old house. Hurrying toward it so I can get out of the freezing cold downpour, I huddle under that area. The floor is dry if not hard and stony, but I have a wall to my left and right as I move into the corner, hiding in the darkness. I wrap my arms around myself as the temperature seems to drop just as rapidly as the rain came, leaving me shivering and wishing for even the threadbare blanket of home. Burying my head into my knees so just my eyes remain uncovered, I curl up and watch the rain bounce on the floor.

The storm lasts for at least two hours, but just as suddenly as it came, it stops, leaving me freezing, wet, muddy, and peering into the almost complete darkness. I know there's no point in heading back outside. I won't be able to see anything or anyone coming for me. The monsters could walk right in front of me, and I wouldn't see them.

So it looks like I'm spending the night here. Sighing, I push back my hair and rub my hands together before blowing into them to retain some heat. I can't feel my toes, legs, or arms, and I know I need to find heat soon or I'll die. Luckily, when I was young, I used to play with one of the boys whose father was a hunter. He taught him all the tricks to survive in the wild, hoping his son would someday become like him. The friendship ended when he realized he was supposed to hate women and not be friends with them, but the lessons remained.

Finding two dry rocks, I collect as much debris and wood as I can, and in the shadows under the roof, I make a little pile. Striking the rocks together, I manage to light it after a couple of desperate tries. I blow on the tiny flame and fan until it grows. The flames pierce the darkness, making me wince until my eyes adjust, but the heat? I almost cry as I move as close as I dare, wiggling my feet and hands before it, trying to get feeling back into my limbs.

When I'm warmer, I lay out my shoes, which I had taken off to survive the bog, to dry before cleaning the cut on my foot and rebinding it as tightly as I dare. Only then do I settle down to eat. I nibble, knowing I need to ration what little I have, since I don't know when I will find anything edible here. After I've eaten, I move out from under the shelter, cupping my hands in the puddles to wash my hands, face, and legs, watching the mud run down them as the moon pierces through the building. Once I'm feeling a little cleaner, I move to a different puddle, one not churned up by my movements, and drink as much as I dare. I know it might make me sick, but I can't survive without water.

I stretch my arms and legs and wander around the room, searching for anything useful. There's old, cracked furniture that might work for kindling in what seems to be a small kitchen in the back corner, and while searching through cupboards, I find an ancient, smelly waterskin. Crinkling my nose, I hurry to wash it at least three times. It still smells, but it should be clean enough to use. Filling it, I drink more before topping it up and melting back into my corner. I huddle before the fire and fight the exhaustion settling in my body now that I have shelter, heat, and water.

I need to stay awake in case the monsters find me. I know I'm too close to the wall to take in my surroundings, but when my eyes slide closed, burning from exhaustion, there is no fighting it anymore.

I fall into a deep, dark sleep filled with reaching claws and howling creatures.

∼

Something is nudging me to wake, my consciousness flaring as my mind screams at me. Then it comes again—a scream. It's close. Jerking upright, I look around. The fog has rolled back in, wrapping around me like a chokehold. The fire is still magically burning, and that screaming howl is closer now. Crawling as quickly as I can toward the fire, I cover it in dirt, extinguishing the flame before holding my breath, and then I wait. My fear only grows as more howls sound around me, as if they are circling me, until they slowly fade.

Blowing out a breath, I settle back into the corner, curling into myself to retain my heat. Leaning my head on the cold wall, I try to fall back asleep, knowing it's useless to fight it. I need to be well rested to survive what is to come when the sun rises—if it ever does here.

I'm between wakefulness and sleep, where nothing quite seems real, when I feel a hand stroke over my foot. I freeze, awareness slowly filling my body, and that's when I smell something sweet, musky, and definitely other. It's like ale and darkness. All I can do is smell it, and then that hand comes back, stroking along my skin.

For a moment, I want to keep my eyes squeezed shut, as if that will save me, but I know it won't, so I force them open. When I come face-to-face with a monster, I scream.

It—no, *he* is crouched before me, his head tilted to the side. His bright red, almond-shaped eyes are locked on me. His skin has a bluish tint to it, with a darker area around his lips, which are almost midnight. His eyebrows are raised, and his claws hover above my leg. We just stare at each other as I seal my lips together in terror, unsure what to do.

His hair is black and plaited to the side, exposing pointed ears. His left ear is pierced with what looks like a bone, and fangs poke over his plump lips. His face is similar to that of a human's, but more angular and sharp. It's hard to tell anything about his body, but he's definitely male, and he's watching me as if he's starving. When his lips part, flashing those huge fangs, I burst into action.

Kicking him back, I grab my stuff and race from the ruined building. His laughter chases me, almost halting me with the teasing lilt of it. The deep, masculine sound reverberates around my body, almost calling to me like a siren's song, urging me to go back and give myself to him. I shake the urge from my head and run faster. I can't see where I'm going in the dark, so I stumble and fall but get back up and move faster once I do.

His laughter chases me the whole way. Water and mud splashes across my body, my slamming heart louder than my footsteps, but I can still hear him. It's as if he's keeping pace with me in the dark. That mocking laughter makes me grit my teeth as I veer left to try and lose him and those creepy, red glowing eyes and fangs.

I see the wooden bridge before my feet hit it. It's old and rickety, and it creaks as I race across it, but just as I think I'm safe, there's a crack that breaks through the night. I skid to a stop in horror and glance down just in time to see the wood splinter and snap beneath me. There's no time to move. I swallow my scream as I plummet to the water below, some sense telling me not to give away my position to every monster in the vicinity.

The icy black water I crash into steals my breath and my fear. When it closes over my head, I can't even tell which way is up or down. I kick and swim, trying to reach the surface, my lungs screaming for air. Panic makes me inhale as the water swirls around me, alerting me that I'm not alone. Something slimy and rough slides against my legs, and my mouth opens on a scream, forcing water into my lungs just as I burst through the surface—only to see that red-eyed, blue monster crouching on the edge of the bridge, grinning mockingly at me. His hand is held out toward me as I cough up the water I accidentally inhaled.

"Take it if you don't want to be eaten alive, human." He nods behind me, and I turn to see the water churning as something that looks like fins breaches the surface. Without another thought, I swim over and put my hand in his.

The warmth of his palm surprises me, and when I look up, my hand clenched in his, I know I've made a terrible mistake.

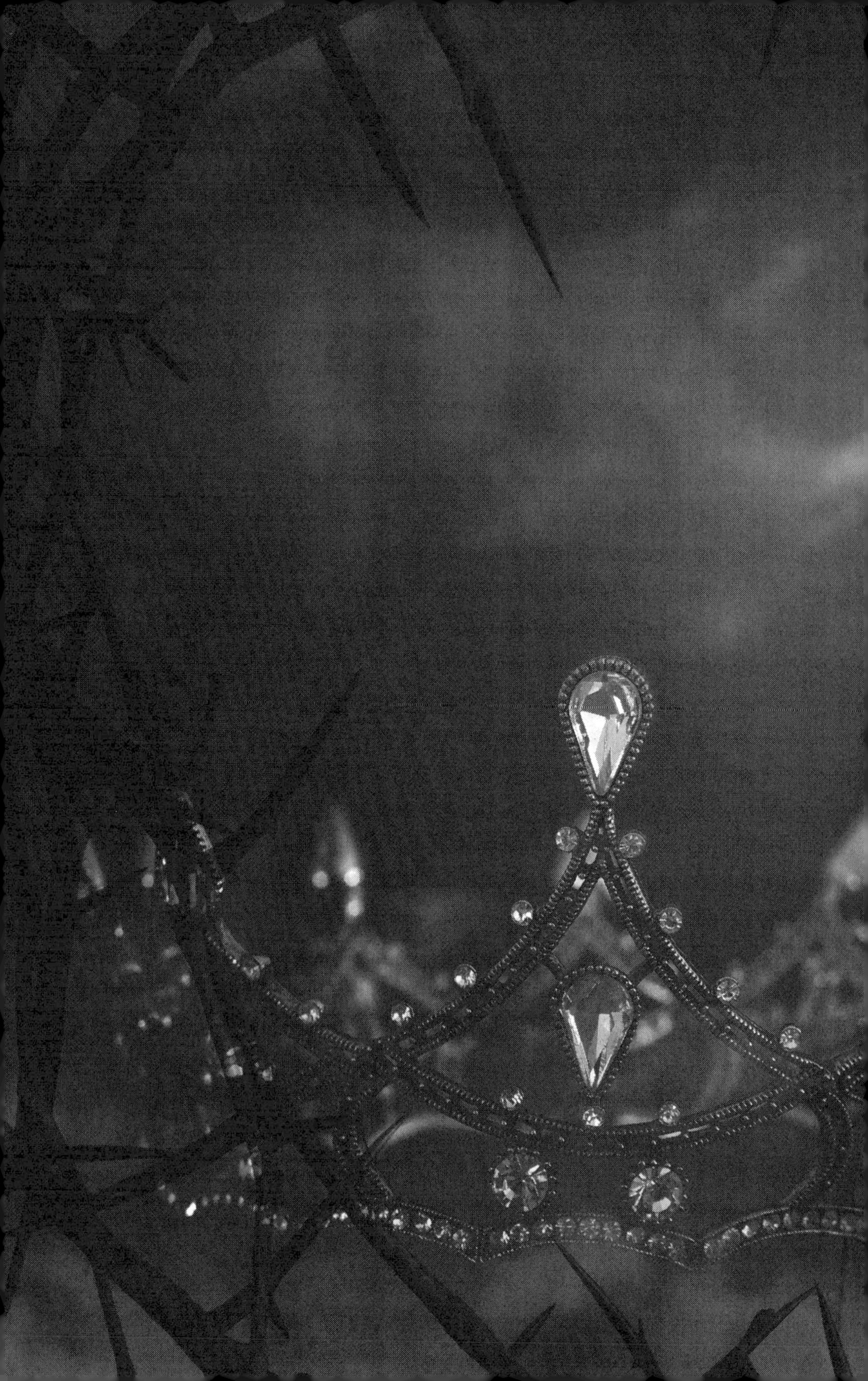

CHAPTER SIX

He hauls me from the river, the weight of the water almost dragging my dress off me, but he doesn't put me down on my feet once I'm clear. With one hand, he effortlessly tosses me over his shoulder and begins to run. My body bounces on his shoulder, and for a moment, I just freeze in shock before I start to kick and punch.

I slap his back and dig my nails into his skin, attacking him any way I can. He just laughs, but when I manage to kick his groin, he grunts, slides to a stop, and flings me down on the ground. I scramble to my feet, breathing heavily. My hair hangs around my shoulders in wet tendrils, and I'm sure I look like a drowned rat. Blinking away the water from my lashes, I back away from him, unwilling to turn my back on the clear threat.

He bares his fangs at me. "That wasn't nice," he hisses. His voice is smoky, deep, and sexy. Just the sound of it has my nipples hardening and my legs clenching. It has to be some sort of magic.

It has to be.

He notices, and those mocking red eyes narrow as he chuckles. "Your dress is see-through, human," he points out, and I look down, my cheeks blooming red as I wrap my arms across my chest to hide my breasts. "No, don't hide on my account. I was enjoying the view," he drawls, his voice sliding across me as he prowls after me.

I walk backward as he walks forward, eyeing him warily. I notice his fangs seem to have grown and his eyes appear to be glowing now.

"You want to run again, Goldie. I can see it in your eyes." The grin on his face shouldn't be attractive.

"Goldie?" I rasp out, my voice cracking from the water.

He tilts his head like an animal as he watches me hungrily, no doubt imagining eating me. "Your hair, Goldie. You can run, but it didn't work out so well for you last time, and I would just chase you again." He shrugs like it doesn't matter to him what I do or say. He's almost nonchalant. Is he teasing me?

I think he is.

That blue bastard.

He hasn't attacked or eaten me yet though, but that doesn't mean he won't. He's definitely not what I expected. I expected mindless, ravenous monsters, not smooth-talking blue men who are well-built. His chest is bare, and his thick legs are encased in leather pants which are tucked into boots, but his arms and chest are broad, the ridges of his abs a darker blue with dark hair leading to the low-slung pants. His arms bulge with muscles, and something glints through a midnight blue nipple...something metal.

"Keep looking at me like that, human, and when I catch you, I won't just drain you, I'll fuck you," he warns, and that gets me moving with a squeak. I turn and race into the darkness. The sky is lightening enough to allow me to see, but it's still not enough to consider it day.

His mocking laughter sounds behind me again. "Run, little human, run swiftly on your feet, for when I catch you, I'll eat you like the tastiest treat."

He lets me run. I feel him chasing close behind, his breaths wafting across my hair, but he never catches me. No doubt this is all just a game to him. He's teasing me, since I know he could easily catch me, and yet I keep running, even as the sky lightens enough for me to see the end of the marshland up ahead. I put on a burst of speed and skid onto solid ground, stopping with my hands on my thighs as I pant, unable to run anymore. When I look up, he's standing before me, staring at me with his lips twisted in anger.

I jerk back, but he doesn't reach for me or attack, so I relax a little. Reaching out, I finally see it. There's a barely perceptible barrier standing between us. Magic? Probably. This place is filled with it, and this monster doesn't seem to be able to cross the barrier.

"You don't want to stay in there, Goldie. Come back, and I'll keep you safe," he purrs, prowling along the barrier as he tosses me a salacious wink. "You'll die over there. In here, I won't let them hurt you."

"Sure, you'll just eat me," I scoff.

"Oh, but you'll like it," he promises, licking his lips as he eyes me. "You'll like it a whole lot. You might even thank me."

"Screw you, Blue." I flip him off and, ignoring his taunts, turn and walk away from the fanged blue man.

I know I'm not safe anywhere, but with him, I'm definitely not safe—not my organs or my body, since he seems to want both.

"I'll see you soon, Goldie!" His voice carries to me, and I shiver at the promise in his words.

I'm really hoping he won't.

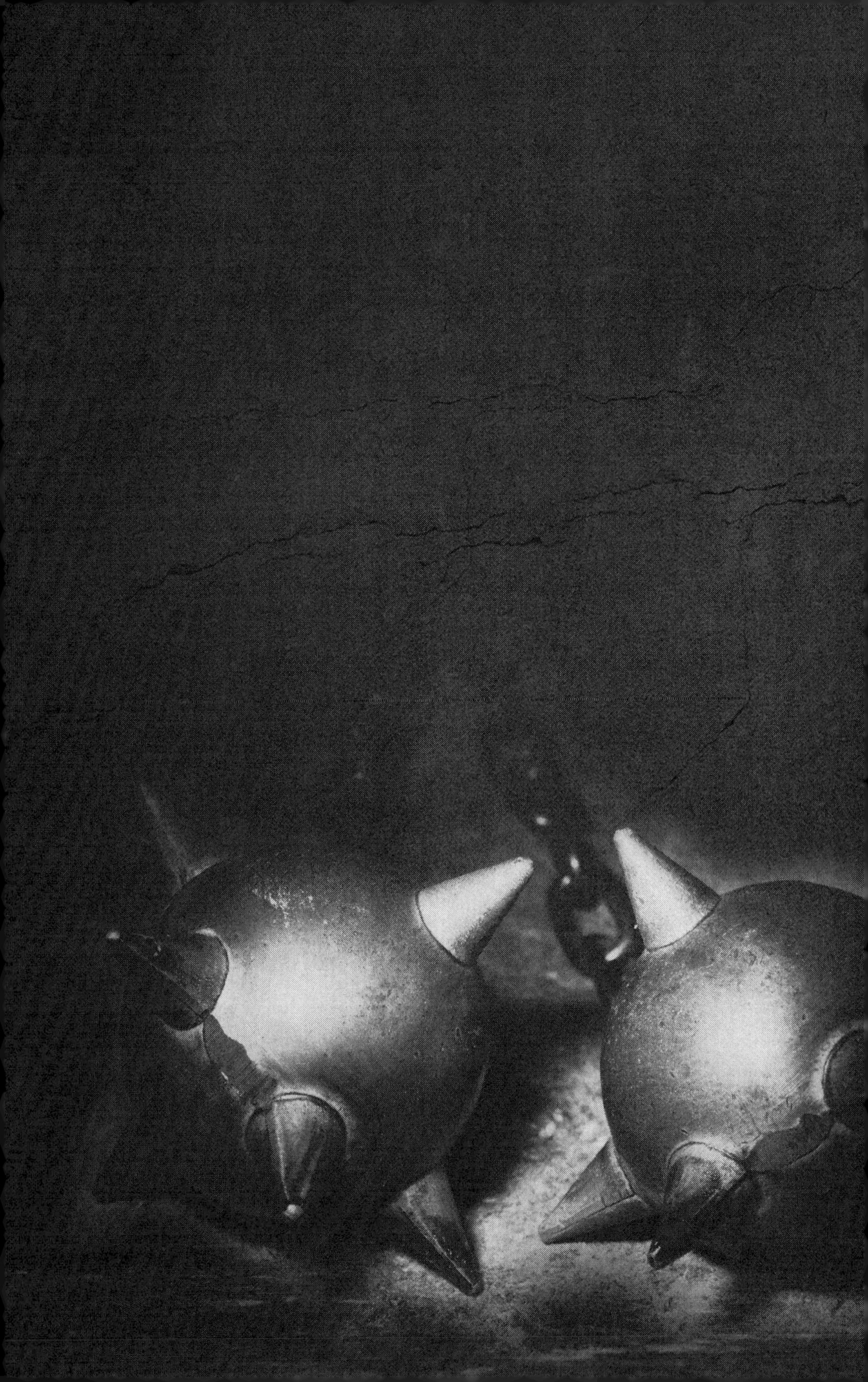

CHAPTER SEVEN
GRIMUS

The beast at my feet rasps its last breath, its body mutilated by my crudely forged morning star. There are three more just like it lying around the area—beasts with no sense, no control, nothing—and now they will literally be nothing but food for the lichen and insects in the soil. The three direhounds were as ugly as they come, always hulking, slobbering creatures. Although they are called direhounds, they no longer resemble a hound at all. They are larger than many things and missing patches of fur along their coat, their teeth poke out of their lips at strange angles, and their eyes, when open, are nothing but red pools. They aren't gentle pups.

Their bite is much worse than their bark.

Luckily for me, I don't take too kindly to being bitten on the leg.

I glance down at the bite in question. It's shallow enough, nothing that will cause any sort of hindrance in my patrol, but it's an inconvenience for sure. I'll need to take time to dress it later. Too many monsters in these lands are called to the scent of blood. They will find no easy meal when they find me, and some small part of me wants them to come, eager for a fight, but I know it's better to continue my patrol without the added complication.

After all, what order am I keeping, really?

Still, some part of me demands I travel through the Dead Lands, killing anything that dares to come across my path with malice. There are no rules here, no laws, except for not crossing into territory that's not your own, and that doesn't get you any sort of punishment—it just gets you dead.

As I wipe my morning star along the coat of the nearest direhound, preparing to continue the path that I follow each night, the hair on my arms rises. Strange. I haven't felt such a tingle in…I don't even remember when. Not long after the hair rises, I feel a deep, thrumming pulse.

A call that begs me to follow.

One as familiar as the weapon in my hand.

Beautiful, enchanting, wild…*magic.*

There shouldn't be such a strong call here in the Dead Lands. There is no such creature within these lands that harnesses such rare power. Not even the fey wield such wild magic in their veins. Too many decades spent locked behind those blasted thorn walls have dampened most of the magic here, so it doesn't make sense that I'd be feeling such a call now.

Unless there's something new in the Dead Lands.

Perking up at the thought and with curiosity dragging me forward, I holster the morning star at my back and straighten. The bite is nothing, barely a flesh wound, but with the call of the magic, I don't tend to it as I should. Instead, I take a step in the direction of the call.

What sort of creature could leak such power? What creature would dare to in a land where beasts and monsters hunger for a taste?

Following the bite of magic in the air, I travel along the edges of the marshlands, tasting the air like so many other creatures are likely doing right now. Whatever is bold enough to flaunt its magic, it'll be dead within hours if it doesn't dampen those waves. I should turn around and ignore it, but I can't deny that I don't also hunger for a taste of that power.

I'm no better than the beasts I reside with.

It's easy to follow the trail, to understand that it's a beacon more than anything. I want it. *Reak*, do I want it, the familiar guttural curse flowing audibly from my lips. I don't even know what it is, but my hunger only grows the closer I come to the power. What a strong monster it must be. What a mighty foe.

And then I see it.

Not it, her.

Rising out of the fog before me like the stars I haven't seen since the Shadow Lands were cut off and we picked out our territories, a female claws through the mud of the marsh, desperation on her face. When she glances behind her in panic, I see what she runs from. The dark fey hovers at the edge of my territory, not daring to cross into my domain, despite not knowing how near or far I am. Wise of him. But really, he's learned too many lessons.

He can't pursue her, not without risking my wrath, so he hovers on the edge of the territory, calling to her as she bends over on hands and knees and catches her breath. Even from here, I can feel her exhaustion. How long has she been running? What did the dark fey have the opportunity to do?

If she stays there much longer, more monsters will come. I can't imagine she'll move with the exhaustion rolling off her in waves. She'll just lie down and die right there. Her humanity is an ache in my bones, and humanity is all the same.

Weak, docile, worthless—

I stare with wide eyes as she shoves herself up on shaking arms, gets one leg beneath her and then the other, and straightens to her full height. Despite her weakness, she doesn't sway. She doesn't bend. She raises her chin and takes a step forward.

And then another.

Respect for this small human female rises within me as she continues forward, entering my domain as she forces herself through the fog, despite everything she's encountered so far.

Intrigued, I turn to follow her as the taste of wild magic bites at my flesh.

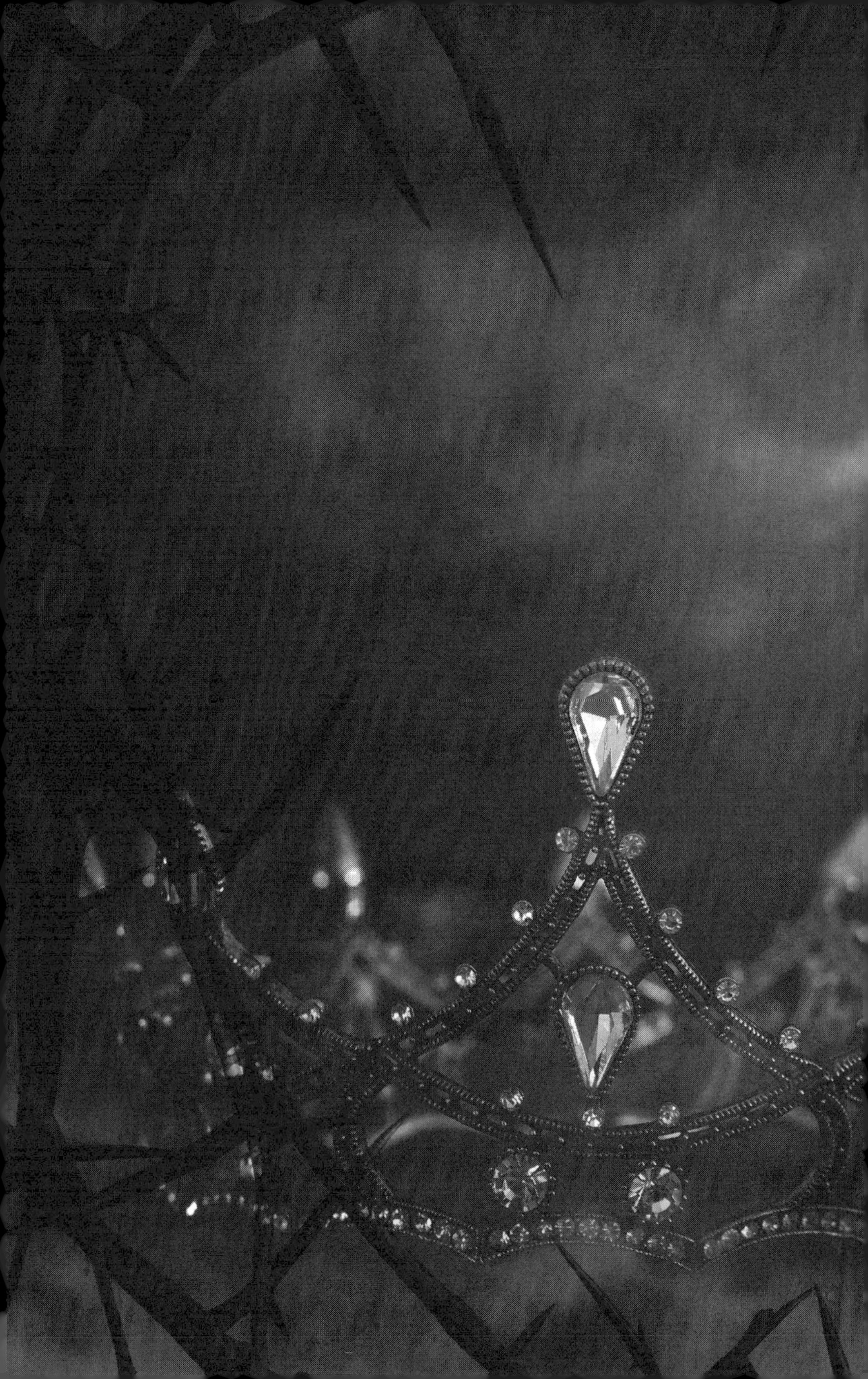

CHAPTER EIGHT

Something is following me.
I don't know what it is or if it's a threat, but I try my best to appear strong, despite the exhaustion clawing at my limbs. Lack of sleep and pure terror have sapped my strength in a way I haven't felt since my first time in the fields. Then, I'd barely crawled home as well. My first day spent working fourteen hours in the fields as a six-year-old drained me in a way nothing should. I'd only made it halfway through the door then and had suffered my father's anger at leaving the door open, but now I have no place to hide. There are no more houses that I can see, no caves or crevices. I'm just walking into a dark forest, the trees a combination of dead limbs reaching for life and trees that are still alive but host to strange fungi coating their bark. Some of it glows.

Some of it reaches toward me as I pass.

It seems like everything in the Dead Lands wants to eat me. For a moment, hopelessness nags at me before I push it away, unwilling to allow myself to give up.

I don't know where I'm going. I can't imagine there are better things than the strange monster in any direction. I'll continue to stumble forward, desperate for a safe space, until I find it or something eats me.

My chances aren't great, but I'm determined to survive and return to the Shadow Lands.

Somehow.

In the Shadow Lands, we don't have trees like these. The trees we do have are thirsty things always reaching for the sun. They regularly lose all their leaves, and we think they are dead until they sprout new foliage the next season. It's as if even the plant life is suffocated by the shadows of the Dead Lands. The Gilded Lands, however? I've heard they have golden trees, as well as trees that never lose their leaves and stay green year-round.

I've heard they even have flowers there in an array of colors.

In the Dead Lands, there are no flowers, not in the traditional sense. The fungi almost seem to serve that position, glowing slightly in the darkness of the trees overhead. I don't dare touch the trees as I stumble through them, keeping my distance as much as I'm able.

The feeling that I'm being followed grabs my attention again, and it takes everything in me not to turn and look over my shoulder, both afraid I'm losing my mind and of what I might see.

Something howls in front of me, and I freeze, the mud on my legs and arms cracking as it begins to dry. I'm leaving behind a trail of mud as I walk, so I'm easy to track. Maybe it'll mask my smell a little and hide me from the worst monsters.

My foot is still sore from where I cut it, but the slippers I managed to save through the marsh were never meant for survival. The longer I walk, the flimsier they become. I can feel a small tear in one, the beginnings of the material failing. Soon, I'll be having to walk through the Dead Lands on bare feet.

The howl echoes again, this time farther away, and I blow out a breath. It's going away from me, not coming closer. That thought has me relaxing. I let down my guard for a split second to gather my bearings and prepare to continue forward—that's my mistake.

A man appears in front of me, peeking from behind a tree trunk so I can only see his torso and face. He's handsome, strikingly so, with skin that shimmers in a way I've never seen, as if jewels are trapped within his flesh, and white hair hanging around his shoulders. I blink in surprise. The more I stare, the more I realize his skin isn't true skin at all, but iridescent scales. Pointed ears peek from his hair, and the hand he curls around the tree trunk sports sharp nails, but I don't immediately stumble back. I'm a sucker for a pretty man. Or I blame the exhaustion. Either way, I just stare at the glimmering man.

When he doesn't immediately speak, I clear my throat. "It's impolite to stare," I say, because that's what I should do. I know nothing about this...man. Chastising him probably isn't the way to go.

He smiles, revealing sharp teeth, particularly two extremely sharp fangs like the mean old snake I accidentally found in the field when I was working. It tried to bite me, and I have the distinct feeling this man wants to do the same.

My eyes widen as I gulp.

"Food that insults me," he purrs, and even his voice is sensual, smooth, and silky, like wrapping me up in the softest furs. "How refreshing."

"Not food," I reply, taking a step back, but I'm stopped by something large. I reach behind me, feeling what seems to be a tree trunk at first, only to realize it's...warm. Frowning, I glance behind me to see a white, scaled body. No, not body. Tail. A fucking tail that's larger than my body. It shimmers just as the man does. Only then do I truly realize the trouble I'm in.

Gasping, I turn to run, only for the large white body to move so quickly, I can't track it. It curls around me before I can take two steps, wrapping me in shimmering coils to keep me still. They don't squeeze, not yet, but I know he's capable of crushing all my bones.

A snake man.

"Let me go!" I snarl, beating at the snake body as if that will help. He's massive, and when he uncurls from the tree and comes around to face me, I see what I missed before—his achingly human torso meets with the body of a snake. He's another monster.

He chuckles at my struggle as if this is just some big game. "Squirm all you like, firefly. It only makes you more tender."

I stop struggling, stubborn to the core, and bare my teeth at him. "Let me go, or I'll carve you into strips and have snake for dinner."

He throws his head back in laughter, roaring his amusement. I hate to say that even that sound is beautiful. As far as monsters go, he's far more beautiful than anything I might have imagined. His scales are white, his skin is a smooth cream where his torso is, and the only flare of color on his body are those magnificent eyes.

"Intriguing little firefly, aren't you?" he muses, tilting his head as he comes closer. The coils around my body don't budge as he moves his upper body closer, studying me as if I'm the oddity here. "What magic flows from your flesh." He hums under his breath, a sound that does things to me in a way it shouldn't. I'm about to be eaten, for fuck's sake, and here I am, wet for a monster.

"Let me go, and I'll show you just how intriguing I can be," I purr, purposely making the words sensual, and his eyes flicker at the innuendo. Of course I don't mean them, even if he's so fucking beautiful, it would be a shame to carve him up.

He reaches up, and I jerk away from him. I have nowhere to go, wrapped as I am in his coils, so I only manage to jerk back a few inches before his sharp nails cup my chin and force my eyes back to his.

Those brilliant golden eyes are slit like a snake's. It shouldn't surprise me, but I still stare into them in a trance, as if he can actually hypnotize me. I reach up and wrap my fingers around his wrist, planning on pulling him away from me, but once there, once I feel the warmth, I linger.

What the fuck is wrong with me?

"Such fire in your eyes," he murmurs. "Your own kind threw you to the monsters. It's such a shame." He leans closer. "With that fire, you could have been a queen."

"You could let me go," I say, blinking and feeling as if I'm clearing some sort of fog from my brain. "You could let me walk right past."

His lips tilt up. "But where would be the fun in that?"

He leans in then, as if he's going to kiss me. I can't decide if I want him to or if by doing so, he'll kill me with some sort of venom I'm not prepared for. Some small part of me wants to say damn the consequences and see what this beautiful monster tastes like, but another part of me sees it for the bad idea it is. Still, I can't pull away.

"Such intoxicating magic in your veins," he purrs, his breath fanning across my lips.

I blink dumbly. "What?"

He doesn't get the chance to answer. Another presence enters the forest, and at first, I worry it's the teasing monster again. I jerk in his hold, even as his lips curl up in annoyance.

"Nero! Release the human!"

The booming voice echoes around us. Only then do I realize how silent the trees are. There are no animals, no wind. It's as if the two predators have caused the forest to tuck into its holes and hide.

The monster, Nero, blows out a puff of air and straightens, but he still doesn't release me. "She's the annual offering, Grimus. You cannot possibly be claiming her for yourself."

I twist, searching for who this Grimus is, but I can't see him in the darkness he stands in. Clearly, Nero can, or else he wouldn't be speaking to him.

"It matters not what I plan to do with her. I've allowed you to remain in my territory only because you cause no trouble for me." The owner of the voice, Grimus, steps from the darkness, and my eyes widen at the sight of the monster before me. "Are you starting trouble now?"

Nero sighs. "I was just going to play." He glances at me. "I wasn't going to eat her." At my narrowed eyes, he grins, revealing those sharp teeth once more. "Unless she asked me to."

Despite the wetness between my thighs, I bare my teeth at him, which only serves to bring back his amusement. Slowly, the white scales uncoil from around me, dropping me back on my feet as he pulls away. I sway slightly but refuse to fall in front of these two monsters, especially since this newcomer could be saving me to kill me himself. He certainly looks like it.

"Don't look so sad, firefly," he purrs. "Perhaps we'll play again."

"Fuck you," I spit out.

"Oh, I intend to." The way he purrs the words has me clamping my thighs together, but there's another threat in the area now, and my eyes trail back to the monster standing on the edge, his arms folded across his chest in a way that only highlights how fucking massive he is.

I've heard legends of beasts like him, read a story in my short time in school about them, but I never thought I'd see one in person. Standing a few feet taller than me, the minotaur, Grimus, is intimidating, and it's as the snake moves away completely that I realize I've just been handed over to yet another monster. His jet-black hair hangs around his shoulders, highlighted by the massive horns on his head. His face and body are humanoid, but his features are reminiscent of a bull's. Though he's clearly half man, half bull, it does nothing to take away from his looks. His skin is a soft gray, making his bright orange eyes glow in the darkness.

I dart to the right, much to Nero's amusement, but the minotaur is faster than I expect. Before I can move into the darkness, strong hands clamp around my waist. I screech and fight its hold as it lifts me into the air. I kick and punch, giving everything I have left to give.

Nero laughs. "Good luck, firefly." He slithers into the darkness, disappearing like a ghost.

My leg makes contact with the minotaur's thigh, and he grunts. "Settle down, little one. If I wanted you dead, you would be."

I still, my heart beating so loudly in my ears, I know every creature within a mile radius can probably hear it. Once I stop struggling, Grimus sets me back on my unsteady feet. I have to grab his arm to keep my balance, but I release him quickly.

Turning, I stare up at the monster before me, at the gold glinting in his nose and the horns curling from his head. If not for the fear in my blood, I'd have realized right then how beautiful he is, but in the way of warriors. Dressed in armor, with a large weapon strung on his back, blood splattered across the worn emblem on the breastplate, he is a sight.

"Why did you help me then?" I ask once I catch my breath and my heart slows. I take the opportunity to take a step back, and his eyes follow the movement carefully, as if he expects me to try to run again.

"I don't know." He shrugs. "But you aren't safe here. If my brethren scent you, which they clearly have" —he gestures in the direction that Nero disappeared in— "they'll kill you for what's inside."

He turns, as if he's going to leave.

"Wait! What's inside? What do you mean?" I ask, taking a step after him. My instincts tell me I'm safer with him than I am alone in the forest. He hasn't tried to hurt me, not yet. It could all be a trick, but my instincts are telling me it's not. He clearly wants nothing to do with me, but why save me? I take the chance. Unlike the blue flirt and the white snake, he doesn't lie and he doesn't seem to want to eat me alive.

He looks at me, his eyes trailing from my feet to my face. The lingering gaze makes my toes curl inside my fraying slippers. Okay then, maybe he does.

"Your magic, human," he says. "They can sense your magic."

CHAPTER NINE

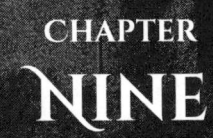

"Magic? I don't have any magic." I chuckle, despite the situation. Even the word coming from my mouth sounds absurd.

He snorts, a deep rough timbre that sounds more animal than man as he peers down at me. His nose ring glistens in the low light, and his dark eyes watch me intently, seeing too much. His body blocks me from a chilling wind, nothing but pure heat pouring from him until I find myself stepping closer, needing that heat, that warmth he seems to provide. He frowns and steps away, making me wrap my arms around myself as the wind swoops in again.

"You're the hunt, I'm guessing?"

"Yes, lucky me, right?" I mutter, shivering again. "Not that I'll survive long enough to be hunted. I have no idea where I am or where to go. I need shelter and warmth, and I'm so...lost." I hate that tears fill my eyes, so I dash them away quickly, jerking my gaze from the monster. I don't want his pity, or worse, his amusement.

As the awkward silence stretches on, I start to turn on my heel and walk away when he suddenly sighs. "You're in my land. Mine and my brethren's." His voice is slow and unsure, and I don't turn around, worried he'll stop talking if I do. "To the east is the Dread Sea. You can walk the forgotten beaches and be safe. Just avoid the water at all costs. Many big monsters avoid going there due to it. To the west is nothing but the Murder Lands. It's where the fights are and the strongest, vicious beasts dwell. They'll eat and kill anything. Beyond them all to the north is the mountains."

"I saw them." I turn, almost gleeful when he nods.

"There isn't much in the way of shelter or anything to eat here." He grins, flashing big sharp teeth. "They don't call it the Dead Lands for nothing. You could make a fire, but then it will attract predators, which could kill and eat you. Otherwise..." He shrugs. "The hunt never makes it this far inland, never past the marshland. If the tree nymphs at the border don't get them, then usually the fey do in the marshes."

"The fey—the blue guy?" I ask, and he huffs.

"Him and his people, though he's certainly the most annoying. Just avoid going east too far or west too far or north—"

"That's everywhere," I point out, swallowing when new fear arises. I knew I wouldn't survive here, but to hear it so plainly? What's the point of running and fighting if there's nothing to fight for? My shoulders slump in defeat at the thought.

"Pretty much, human," he grumbles before turning and starting to walk away. I know I'll lose him to the darkness, and that's when an idea strikes me. He seems willing to help me. Maybe I can make a deal with the monster?

I never thought I'd hear myself thinking that, but here we are.

I hurry after him, only tripping once, and when I reach his side, I'm out of breath. He doesn't slow, doesn't even spare me a look as I practically sprint to keep up with his strides.

"You could help me," I begin, making him snort and stomp his hooves harder into the slippery mud as he storms through the trees. I find myself forgetting about the snake man, Nero, and the danger around me. Instead, I focus on the minotaur as I hurry to keep up with him. "You could. You're obviously strong and capable and don't want to eat me, that's a plus." He continues to ignore me, and my voice starts to get desperate. "Without you, I'll die."

"Not my problem," he snaps.

"Can...we..." I wheeze, "stop while we talk?" I beg, and when he finally stops, I bend over, placing my hands on my knees. "Fuck, you're a fast son of a bitch."

"Go back to your destiny, human, and leave me to mine," he says, and then without waiting for me to catch my breath, storms off again.

Fuck.

I hurry after him, ignoring my shaking, exhausted legs and aching lungs. I manage to keep up, jumping only slightly at the howls that seem closer and the sound of monsters. In fact, I draw closer to his back as we walk, as if he will protect me.

Which he probably won't.

He zigzags, shooting me looks as if he's trying to dislodge his annoying human stalker, but I just grin and speed up after him, much to his annoyance.

The ground soon changes from spongy to solid, hurting my aching feet. They start to drag, and my shoulders start to droop when he slows. I feel his eyes on me, and a moment later, he veers left. There's a huge boulder that towers above us, and he circles it. Swearing under my breath, I hurry around it, expecting him to jump out at me or to have disappeared, but I find him crouched on the ground there with a bag and weapon at his side. He starts to dig in the dirt. Curious, I tread closer and watch him. I take the opportunity to lean into the boulder, resting for a moment, when I realize he's building a fire.

"Sit before you fall," he orders without looking at me.

Eyeing him curiously, I drag myself closer and sit heavily, my side to the boulder as I wrap my arms around my legs and pull them into myself. I shiver from the cold, my head drops to my knees in exhaustion, and my eyes burn from lack of sleep, but I fight it, watching him as the fire blooms to life. He deftly feeds it before he sits back and pulls something from his bag. With sure fingers, all while his eyes search the area, he threads what I realize is meat onto a skewer and props it above the fire. Soon, the delicious aroma of cooking meat reaches me, perking me up. My stomach rumbles, reminding me of how hungry I am and how the food I brought with me got ruined in the water while running from the fey.

He doesn't look over. He completely ignores me in favor of watching the surrounding area as the meat cooks, his hand hovering near his weapon at all times. I take the time to study him.

He really is beautiful.

Ripping the meat from the burnt skewer with his clawed fingers, he shoves as much as he can into his mouth, chewing quickly before biting at more and ripping it off. Juices run over his lips, chin, and hands. He's messy and slightly arousing as he eats. I watch him sadly. I know I'm pouting. My stomach growls loudly, and he looks over at the sound. He freezes, his mouth partially opened from chewing his next bite, as he holds the rest of the skewer protectively in one hand. I try not to look pitiful, try not to look like I'm asking for food he was hard pressed to find himself, but my stomach growls again, and I curl into a tighter ball.

Sighing, he hands what's left on the skewer over, grumbling under his breath. I want to protest, to ask if he's sure, but I'm too hungry to be polite or to eat like a lady—not that I assume he will care since he won't even look at me. He just starts feeding the fire again. Holding the skewer in both hands, I dig my teeth into the meat and rip like he did before chewing. It's tough, tougher than I'm used to, but the taste isn't half bad. It's almost spicy without being overpowering, and after one bite, I devour the rest. I rip into it like an animal. When I'm done, I look up to see Grimus watching me with amusement. Smiling guiltily, I wipe my mouth with the back of my hand and hand the skewer back.

"Thank you," I tell him softly.

He just grunts before handing over another one I didn't even see him cook. My eyes widen as I start to protest, but he just shoves it into my hand. Sliding half the meat off, I hand it back and we eat in silence, sharing the last skewer. Once he's eaten, he gets up and storms off without a word. I stare, open-mouthed and terrified. My eyes dart around the suddenly dark, scary area, but just as I'm about to call out, he comes back. A horn of some kind is in his hand. Without looking at me, he thrusts it my way and turns to grab his weapon, sitting heavily as he begins to clean it.

I almost cry once more when I see the clear water in the horn. Sipping it carefully, I watch him. I wonder why he's helping me when he made it clear he didn't want to.

"Thank you for the food, for the water. Just...thank you. This is the kindest anyone has ever been to me," I admit.

"Anyone?" he asks, his hand stilling on his weapon.

"Anyone," I confirm. "My people aren't exactly... Never mind. Just thank you."

He doesn't reply, and I find myself slumping to my side, curling up around the horn. I watch the flames dance as the heat seeps through my chilled body. When his voice comes again, it's softer, but his words make me flinch.

"You'll be dead soon, human. I won't get attached to you. In the morning, you will go."

"But what if I survive?" I ask, watching him as he starts to clean his weapon again. It's scarred, used, and stained. Unlike the pretty swords of the king's men, this is a real weapon forged to kill, to cleave. He clearly takes good care of it.

"No one survives here but monsters," he responds.

I push myself up on an elbow, watching him pleadingly. I hate myself for the weakness, but I need him. I know that. I'm not stupid or overconfident enough to think I'll survive here without protection. It's a land filled with monsters and death. If I want to make it back to my sister, I'll make as many deals with the devil as it takes. "Then help me."

This time he doesn't outright deny it. Instead, he stills, his gaze going to the small fire. "And what's in it for me?"

"What do you want?" I reply automatically, sitting up excitedly and crossing my legs. He glances over at me, running his eyes across my body, and I gulp. I hope he won't ask for that, even as a dirty, traitorous part of my body clenches at the idea.

"Magic. I want a taste of that wild magic inside you," he finally grits out, as if he can't believe he's making the deal to begin with.

"My magic… I mean, sure." I nod rapidly, lying to him. I have no magic, so he'll be disappointed, but if I fulfill my end, he has to his, even if he's wrong about me.

"I see you don't believe me, but I can feel it," he purrs. "All the hunt women have it, but never as strong as you. Never this wild and this untamed. It's like a beacon."

"Magic doesn't exist where I live anymore," I reply, confused.

"It does. It's just hidden and locked away, but coming through the barrier unlocked it, and now it flows through you so strongly, it almost hurts to be this close."

"If it unlocked coming through the barrier, you must have some here," I say, my confusion only growing.

"Once." He nods. "Now, it's corrupt and rotting our land. The more we go without the pure, uncompromised magic, the more our minds degrade and the eviler we become. We'll become nothing but the monsters your people named us. Most have given into the madness, which is why they kill the women of the hunt to get to their magic."

I blink in shock. "I didn't know any of that," I admit honestly. "The only thing I know about magic is that we used to have it across the lands, and then the barrier came and it disappeared."

"Along with the truth it seems." He snorts. "But tonight is not a night for a history lesson. So fine, little human, I'll make you a deal. I'll help you. I'll escort you to safety, and keep you fed and warm until we make it to the old palace of kings, across the shores of the Dread Sea, through the mountains, and to where the old king lived. In return, you will let me taste your magic when I need to stop my mind from deteriorating further. Deal?"

I have no idea what this palace is or who the old king is, or why he thinks I'll be safe there, but I'm not about to annoy the only monster willing not to eat me.

"Deal." I grin, sticking out my hand.

He eyes it warily before putting his heavy, huge one in mine. I shake his rapidly, and he snorts as he pulls away. "Now get some rest. You look half dead. I'll keep watch. Sleep, human, you're safe from the monsters."

I nod, curling back up, and as I'm drifting off, I swear I hear him speak once more...

"Just not safe from me."

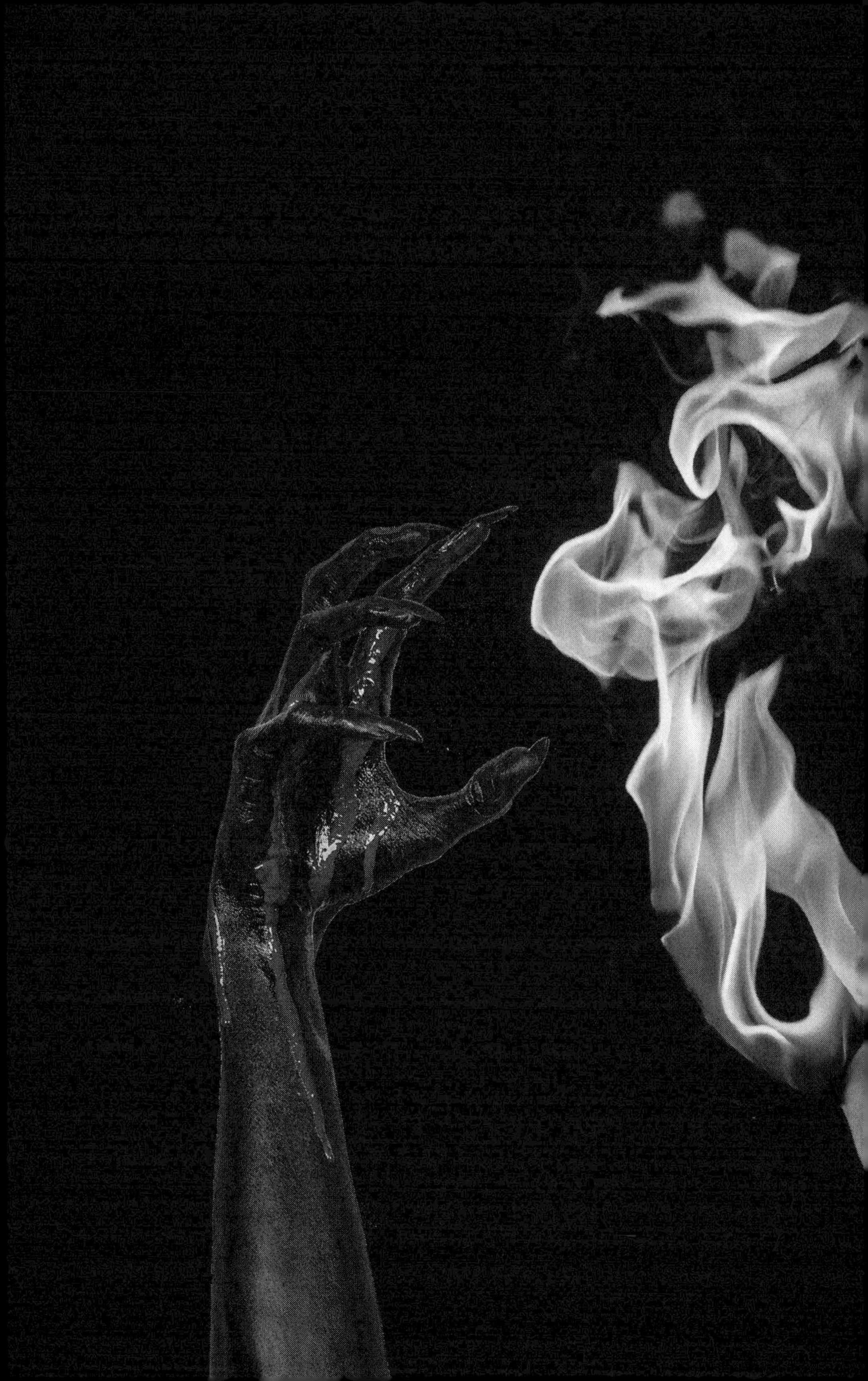

CHAPTER TEN

BRACKEN

The little human sleeps soundly with her new minotaur bodyguard. Grimus the Grumpy Bastard is hard to hide from, but I manage because I'm that good. I watch from the shadows as she wakes up, and he feeds and waters her like a little pet. I never knew the minotaur had it in him to make a deal with the human.

I always thought he was too dumb.

Good for him though. Maybe I'll follow his lead, since it seems to be working. I'd been so close before she ran from me, which I can't even believe. Why run from me and into that? Maybe she isn't as smart as I gave her credit for, but I can't stop myself from following them as they set out toward the Dread Sea. I'm curious where they are heading, but I stay in the shadows, slinking silently after them.

Watching, listening, and biding my time.

He'll kill me if he realizes I'm on his land and following him, but I can't resist the wild magic that pours from the human like a glimmer in the air. She intrigues me in a way nothing has in far too long. Not just because she survived this long and made a deal with a bull, but because she almost looks...happy to be here.

Strange little, golden creature.

The hours drag as we traipse over the land, but I can be patient, and it pays off when she excuses herself from her bull bodyguard and slips behind some trees to relieve herself. Smirking, I drop to the ground and slide through the trees, climbing one close to her destination. When I see her basically stop below me, I laugh and drop down to the ground.

She screams, but instead of running, she cocks back her arm and punches me square in the face. Pain blossoms across my nose in a way it hasn't for so very long. I wasn't expecting the fight, and I stumble back at her hit, shocked. I stare at her as my nose bleeds, and she stares back equally as shocked, as if she can't quite believe she hurt me at all.

The roar that splits the air vibrates through the ground and into my feet.

The ground shakes as the trees wither in fear, and then Grimus is there. He pulls Goldie behind him, and with one meaty fist to my stomach, he sends me flying back into a tree. Pain blooms along my body, this time in my spine as it connects with the hard bark at my back. My slide down the tree would almost be comical if not for the pain. Groaning, I flip to my feet, just barely dodging his other attacks as he tries to kill me for daring to be here.

Laughing to enrage him further, I slip through his legs and guard, taunting him. He's big and a good fighter, but I'm faster, and he soon tires as I chuckle at him. When he turns, snarling, I know I've pushed it too far, so I step back with my hands up.

"If you want to make it to the palace, you will need me," I call out to him and her, knowing she's the brain.

"Grim, wait!" she calls as he barrels toward me. Stilling before me, nostrils flaring, he waits as she hurries over, putting her back to him as she watches me with a narrowed glare.

"Good bull," I taunt.

"Give me one reason why I shouldn't let him eat you," she demands, her arms crossed.

Feisty little thing, isn't she? Prodding my nose, I find it's not broken, but she drew blood, something no one has been able to do for centuries. Impressive. I will have to stop underestimating Goldie.

"Because I have a deal with the orcs in the pass, Goldie. The pass you need to get there. Without me, you'll end up roasting over their fires." I grin, leaning into a nearby tree like I have no care in the world, like there isn't blood dripping from my nose.

Grimus freezes, watching me carefully. He knows the fey have a lot of deals all over the lands, and he's weighing his decision. He was probably just going to storm in there and kill them, which wouldn't go over well or be the smartest course of action. The orcs are necessary, if not absolute brutes.

"So let's make a deal, Goldie." I grin, winking at her.

"A deal?" she snaps.

"Yes, a deal. You made one with bull boy there, but he can only get you so far. Together, we can get you to the palace."

She glances at Grimus, who's glaring at me, and sighs. "What do you want?"

"The same as him of course—a taste of your magic."

"Wait there. Do not move or I'll hit you again," she snaps and whirls to face Grimus, lowering her voice to talk to him. She doesn't realize my hearing is excellent, clearly, but I pretend to give her privacy, even as Grimus watches me with thinly veiled hatred.

Is it because I'm taking his human from him, or because he genuinely just hates me? I don't know, nor do I care.

"What do you think, big guy? Can we trust him?"

"If the fey gives you their word, they will keep it to the death. I don't trust him, but I trust his promise," Grimus mutters to her as I watch with a smug grin, knowing they have no choice.

Or so they think.

He's right—us fey never make promises or deals because we are duty bound until death to complete them, but I'm willing to make such a deal to get close to her, even if I'm telling a lie...or a half-truth.

"And do we need him?" she asks.

He grinds his teeth as he glances down at her. "The orcs and I don't exactly get on. It would be helpful to have a way through without fighting them all."

"Fuck." She sighs and glances back at me. "Fine, deal, but if you so much as annoy me, you're gone, understood?"

"Of course, Goldie," I purr, licking my lips. "Shall we get started then?"

If only the little human knew just what she gave me and how she would be mine before she reaches the palace.

It isn't the orcs she needs protection from, but me.

CHAPTER
ELEVEN

Grimus hadn't once told me exactly how long the journey to the old king's palace would take, but I'm starting to suspect he doesn't actually know. Not because the journey is super treacherous—it is—or because it's a hard thing to guess at, but because of me. After a few hours of walking through the trees, it becomes increasingly apparent that I'm the reason we're moving at the pace he's set. When he first appeared and saved me from Nero, I had to run to keep up with him. Now he moves ahead of me at a normal pace, as if he's making his strides purposely slower to appease me. I should be grateful for the change, but I find it only makes me feel guilty. He's helping me, and the best I can do is keep up this mediocre pace.

Bracken, in contrast, is almost slower than I am. It's not because he physically can't move faster, but because he's constantly distracted by his surroundings. One moment, he'll be walking behind me, making lewd comments about my ass, and the next, he's climbing a tree to grab a flower. The third time he does the tree thing, I watch him scale the trunk as if it's nothing more than a ladder. If it were me trying to climb the thing, I never would have made it to the top. The fey simply climbs up, plucks the flower, and lets go.

I jump when he falls to the earth in front of me, the flower in his fingers as he straightens and meets my eyes. Grimus finally stops to see what Bracken is up to. Eyeing the flower warily, I look between him and the blossom that should be beautiful but feels sinister.

Kind of like Bracken.

"For you," Bracken announces, pushing the flower a little closer to me.

I stare at the flower, taking it in. The petals are a strange, waxy burgundy color, with many of them springing from the center. It almost looks like a mix between the daisies I once saw a woman from the Gilded Lands carrying and a duster. At the center of the petals is a bright green circle that looks toxic and is pinched together as if it's a mouth. Carefully, I reach toward it, only to jerk my hand back the moment that circle opens and a thin tongue darts out in an attempt to wrap it around my finger. Tiny teeth flash before the circle closes again.

"I don't want that," I snarl, stepping back. "It tried to eat me."

Bracken grins. "Ah, yes. Banty flowers are carnivorous, but I find the best way to deal with things that want to eat you..." Bracken looks down at the flower before flashing me a wicked grin and taking a bite of the thing. The tiny screech it makes brings goose bumps to my arms. "Is to eat it first."

"Would you stop messing around?" Grimus grunts. "We're already moving at a snail's pace."

Stepping around Bracken as he continues to munch on the carnivorous flower, I try not to think about feeling his eyes on my back. Despite the general creepiness Bracken gives off, there's also something... intriguing about him. Some part of me wants to learn more, and some smaller part is interested in the looks he keeps throwing my way, as if he's undressing me with his eyes.

Which I suppose isn't too difficult, considering what I'm wearing.

The slip I'd been given before I was thrown across the border is worse for wear. The thin fabric is still holding up, but it's now stained and dirty, and the hemline is torn in some places. The slippers I'd worn across are barely scraps of fabric held on by my hopes and dreams. Before long, they won't be useful for anything at all.

An hour later, I'm driven mad by Grimus' silence and Bracken's mutterings. Neither seems interested in talking to me, but if I don't speak up, I'll go mad.

"Have you always watched the hunts die?" I ask suddenly, clearly directing the question toward Grimus.

He glances at me over his broad shoulder, his nose ring glinting in the light. "None of the hunts in my memory have made it as far as you did before we met," he says. "I've only been lucky enough to see a handful of them, and rarely have they been left alive."

I stare at his back when he turns forward again. "Have you ever been the one to kill a hunt?"

Grimus pauses mid step, but he shakes himself from whatever makes him freeze a second later and keeps walking. It's as if my question surprised him, as if it's something he doesn't want to speak of.

"Why would you ask that?" he says.

Behind me, Bracken giggles, as if he knows the answer. When I glance back at him, he grins at me, flashing those sharp teeth again.

"Curiosity," I reply, turning back to Grimus. He purposely doesn't look back at me, as if he doesn't want to see my face. "By your reaction, I take it you've killed at least one."

No answer.

"Two?"

"Stop asking questions you don't want to know the answer to, little human," he finally grumbles.

My brows furrow. "I have a name you know. You can stop calling me 'little human' like it's some great insult. How would you feel if I called you little bull?"

No hesitation. "Call me whatever you want. I don't care."

"Asshole it is then," I grumble. "So if you've killed other hunts, why not kill me?"

Grimus doesn't answer, but Bracken does. He prances forward and dances around me, gleefully singing, "Because you taste like pure magic, Goldie. Pure, pretty, raw magic. And it's better to keep you alive than waste it in a second by death."

I narrow my eyes. "You think to put me in a cage?"

Bracken grins, reaching out to stroke along my jawline. A dangerous part of me keeps me still, keeps me from pulling away. "Oh, Goldie," he purrs. "You were born in a cage." He leans closer as if he's going to kiss me. "We all were." Then, with a slightly senile giggle, he prances away into the trees, off to do whatever fey like him do.

I'm so focused on watching his path, I don't watch my step well enough. There's nothing left of the slippers on my feet, so when I step on a stick wrong, it slices into my foot, and I stumble on a gasp.

"Ow." I grunt, reaching for the nearest tree to lean against. Before my hand can touch it, Grimus is there, his large hand around my wrist, keeping me from touching it.

"The tree has thorns," he explains, and then his nostrils flare. "You're hurt."

"It's probably small," I reply, holding my damaged foot off the ground. "I can keep going."

"It's not whether you can keep going," Grimus retorts before he glances around us. "Most creatures in the Dead Lands can smell blood from miles away. It's better to wrap the wound than continue forward, leaving a path for any monster to follow." He looks around again. "We'll stop here for the night."

Shame fills me, as does more guilt. "Are you certain? I can keep—"

"We stop here," he interrupts, leaving no room for argument. "I'll build a fire. Sit down on the log."

I frown but do as he says, taking a seat on the log and lifting my foot over my knee. As he goes to work building a small fire, I gently peel the ruined slipper from my foot, realizing just how little is left of the thing. Apparently, I'd long ago walked away what was left of the fabric, and the only things on my feet are the thin soles and the elastic that held them on. As I pull off the slipper, the tear in the sole becomes apparent. No wonder the stick hurt.

It went right through.

My feet are dirty, and when I go to wipe away some of the dirt, Bracken reappears holding a canteen of water and a scrap of fabric.

"Where did that come from?" I ask, narrowing my eyes. My only answer is a sordid grin.

Grimus keeps his eyes on me as he pulls items from his pack and begins to roast them over the fire. The smell of cooking meat fills the air again, and my mouth waters. I don't know what sort of creature we're eating, but I won't ask in case it's something that will turn my stomach. It's best to eat and enjoy the food while I can.

I go to work cleaning off my foot as best as I can, revealing just how deep the cut is. My foot feels warm to the touch when I clean away the mud and debris, and I worry it'll get infected. Still, I don't have much choice but to keep going. The best I can do is clean it and keep moving. Hopefully, the wound won't worsen.

"Here," Grimus grumbles, thrusting a bit of meat toward me.

Before I can reach up to take it, Bracken whistles and tries to grab it. Moving too quickly for me to follow, Grimus jerks the meat away and throws his fist toward the fey. The crack echoes around us as Bracken falls back on his ass with a grunt.

"That hurt," Bracken mutters, reaching up to his bloody nose. His blood isn't red like mine is. It's black. "That wasn't necessary."

"You can catch your own food," Grimus scolds, holding the meat toward me again.

This time, I take it swiftly, the grease and juices running down my wrist as I bite into the larger chunk of meat. I expect Grimus to cook more for himself, but instead, he kneels in front of me and inspects my foot.

"What are you doing?" I ask around a mouthful of food.

He doesn't respond. Instead, he leans in and prods my foot, sending a jolt of pain up my leg. I watch as he reaches into his pack and pulls out a jar of something. He carefully scoops out whatever is in it and gently smears it across my foot. I nearly choke on the food in my mouth.

Even kneeling before me, Grimus' horns make him taller than me.

He's a glorious creature when he's standing, but seeing him kneeling before me makes something inside me wake up. When Bracken shifts to my right, I glance at him. There's a sparkle in his eyes, as if he knows how I'm feeling and can sense my arousal at having such a large warrior at my feet.

Fuck. This is bad.

Clearing my throat does nothing for the rasp that Grimus either doesn't pick up on or doesn't acknowledge. "What is the stuff you put on my foot?"

"Althaea officinalis," he murmurs. "It helps with inflammation and heals." He grabs something from the pack and tears whatever the fabric is, making a thin strip that he begins to wrap around my foot. "This should keep anyone from following your trail."

When he's done, I flex my foot and marvel at the comfort of it. "Thank you," I say softly, meeting his eyes.

"I'll make you something that can work in place of these scraps of material." He holds up the tattered slipper and tosses it away. "You humans have such soft flesh."

Bracken eases closer. "The softest."

Grimus scowls at him. "Back off, fey." To me, he says, "Get some rest while you can. I'll take the first watch." He stands and moves away to take a seat at the fire, beginning to cook his own meat. The scent of cooking food fills the air again, and I wonder why my blood would attract more monsters than the smell of food.

Unless it's the magic Grimus mentioned.

But that's silly. I don't have any magic.

Nodding, I ease myself to the ground and lean back against the log, tilting my head back until I'm looking up at the trees overhead. Strangely, the trees here are almost more beautiful than the withered, struggling things we have in the Shadow Lands. As if, in between two places drawing power, there's nothing left for those of us in the middle.

My eyelids fall of their own accord before I can even fight to stay awake. Somehow, I'm able to sleep, and I know it's because of how safe I feel near Grimus, which is ironic considering I'm in the company of monsters.

Perhaps I don't mind the monsters who dare to keep me alive.

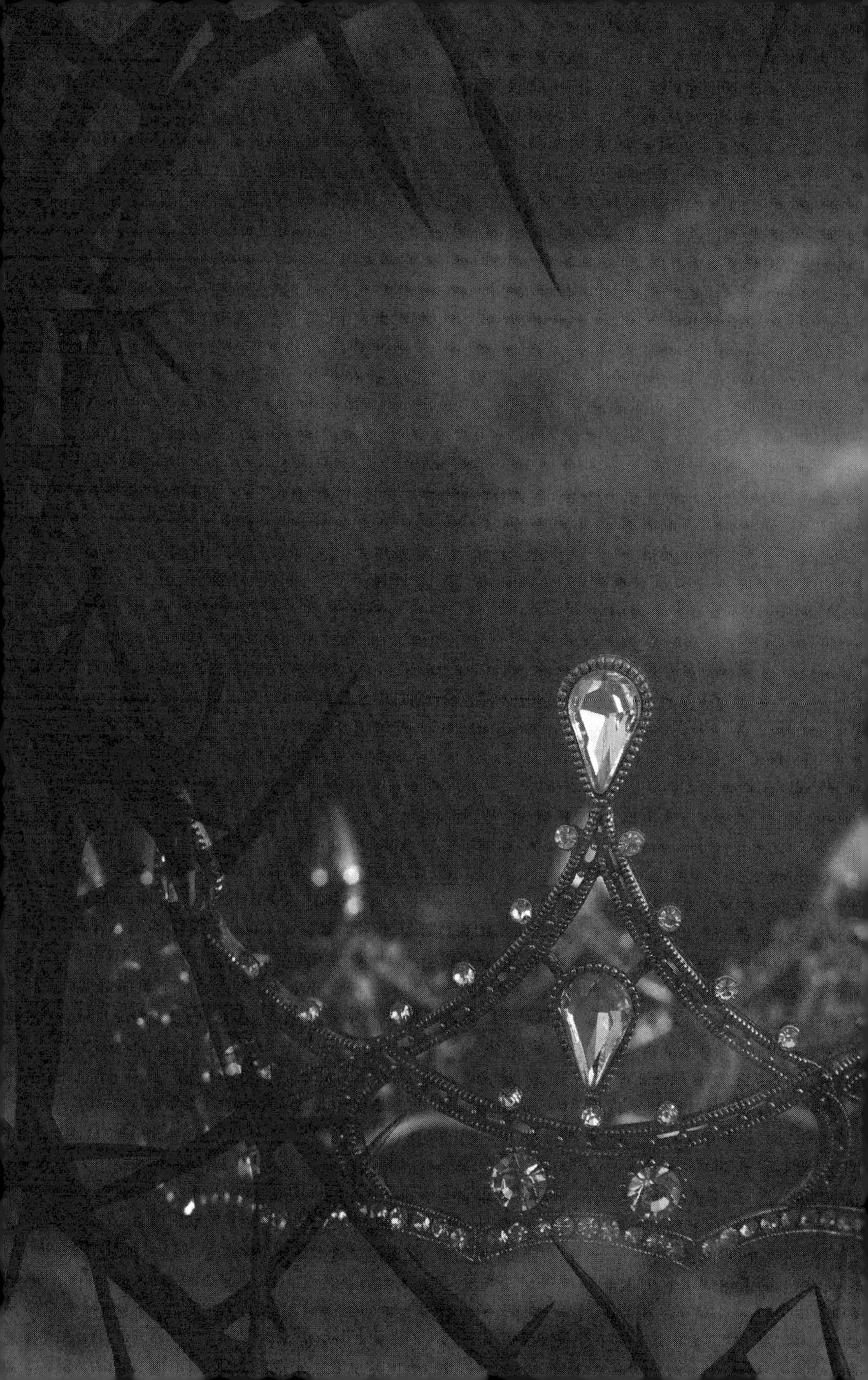

CHAPTER
TWELVE

My dreams are filled with images of the cruel king and monsters slipping from the darkness to eat me. At one point, though, those monsters turn into sensual creatures that make me want to be eaten. It's with that awareness hovering in my mind that I awaken, the memories of those dreams making my face flush bright before I acknowledge my surroundings.

It takes me a few seconds to realize I'm not looking up into the trees, but into a pair of golden eyes. I panic, intending to scramble backward, but I'm stopped by the log I managed to lodge myself against in my sleep.

"What the fuck are you doing?" I hiss, shoving at Bracken as he hovers over me. "And how long have you been staring at me?"

"Oh," he sings, "about an hour. You just look so pretty when you're sleeping."

"That's creepy," I tell him, but he still doesn't move from his position. "Why are you staring at me?"

"I'm hungry too." He sighs, tilting his head to the side in a way that makes his hair fall like a curtain around us. It's almost romantic, if not for the way his eyes dip down to my body.

"So then go eat," I snarl, pushing him again. This time, he eases back a little.

He grins. "I drink blood, Goldie. Are you volunteering?"

I pinch my lips. "Definitely fucking not." I shove harder, and he finally moves away enough for me to see Grimus sleeping farther down the log. "Grimus," I say, and he doesn't move. "Grimus!"

He startles awake and looks over at us, his eyes first on me and then Bracken. "What the fuck are you doing?"

"He's trying to eat me," I reply.

Grimus rolls his eyes and stretches as if he's unbothered by it. "Go find something to eat, fey, so we can get on with our journey."

Bracken winks at me and stands. "Just know, Goldie, when I'm out there drinking blood, I'll be thinking of you the entire time and the way your magic will taste on my tongue as you moan in pleasure." He strokes a finger down my collarbone, and I jerk back in annoyance.

"Don't," I warn. "I'm not some fetish."

"Oh, but you are, Goldie," he replies. "Oh, but you are." Then he disappears into the trees.

"He's a real piece of work, isn't he?"

Grimus shrugs. "He's old. The magic in the Dead Lands is tainted now. I'm honestly surprised he's still able to form a coherent thought."

I frown. "How old is he?"

"Older than I am," Grimus answers. "That's as much as I know."

I stare off into the trees again, curious, but when Bracken returns, wiping a bit of blood from the corner of his lips, I decide not to bring it up. Not yet. Especially when he looks at me with heat in his eyes and I have to clench my thighs.

Grimus hands me a pair of rough slippers. The material is hard and strong, and it will probably cause blisters, but they are thick enough to protect my feet. I don't understand where the material came from until I realize Grimus is missing a bit of his leather armor on his shoulder.

"Thank you," I murmur, and he shrugs as if it means nothing, but it means far more to me.

We continue our journey through the forest, Grimus leading the way and Bracken taking up the rear when he isn't dancing around and frolicking up trees. Every now and then, he darts into the darkness, only to return with some dead creature that had been stalking us. Whatever hesitation I had about Bracken disappears as more and more dead creatures and smaller monsters are placed at my feet. Despite his ulterior motives, he's protecting me in his own way.

Hours later, when the humidity is high enough to make me feel as if I'm choking on heat, the ruins of some sort of structure rise from the foliage. I stare at the abandoned building in awe and confusion. The walls look like they were once more civilized, very much like those in the Gilded Lands. Soon after, more buildings appear, their stone walls left for nature to reclaim. It's almost beautiful in a haunting sort of way.

"What is this place?" I whisper. The aura around us makes me feel as if I should be quiet. I don't know why.

Grimus hardly glances at the buildings. "An old city. I don't know what the name of it was. Monsters don't hold much merit for names of ruins."

"Blaenau," Bracken supplies. "This city used to be called Blaenau."

I glance back at him at the same time Grimus does. "You know it?"

"I was here before the wall was sealed, Goldie," he answers, his tone sounding as ancient as his words. "I was here when the old king united all the races and made a deal with the humans to keep the peace." He turns his head and points to a building with barely any walls left. "There used to be a tavern over there that sold the best soups."

"What happened?" I ask, frowning. "If the old king united everyone, how are we now as separate as we can possibly be?"

Grimus snorts. "They don't teach you your own history across the wall?"

I clench my fists. "Women aren't allowed access to knowledge at all," I answer. "But not even this is taught to the men, or else I would have heard of it, at least in passing."

"The women aren't allowed..." Grimus pulls in a long breath and falls silent, choosing not to address my admittance.

Bracken, not sensing the discomfort in the air, continues his story as if no one had spoken, his mind a million miles away with his memories.

"Humans betrayed the king," he says. "Though there were treaties, humans always wanted more. They saw the magic we wielded and wanted it for themselves. War broke out. There was so much death in those days. Finally, the human king put up the barrier, blocking off our magic in a way that corrupted our land and those of us who reside here." He tilts his head. "We aren't held to the same timeline as you, Goldie. Some of us are eternal."

"Unless I kill you," Grimus mutters.

Bracken smiles as if Grimus said a particularly funny joke. "Unless the minotaur kills me," he corrects.

Sadness overcomes me at his story, at the true history. I shouldn't particularly trust Bracken, but his story rings true in my mind. I'd been up close to our king. Though he's not the same one who betrayed the monsters, he possesses enough cruelty to do such a thing. Those in the Gilded Lands will do anything to keep their wealth and power, no matter who they step on to do so.

"Have any of the monsters ever tried to cross the barrier?" I ask, following Grimus as he keeps walking. My eyes fall over to the remnants of the tavern Bracken had mentioned, the temptation to stop and allow him his nostalgia strong, but we have little time for reminiscing.

"The magic of the barrier is unstable, but it's effective at keeping us back."

"The magic bites," Bracken adds helpfully. "I once saw a naga try to cross and be flayed alive by the magic. However, it grows more erratic every day, draining more and more, until we'll all be nothing but ash."

Although he says the words cheerfully, there's a prophecy in them, as if he knows his fate and sees it coming.

"But you have no magic left?" I ask curiously. "Grimus said—"

"Grimus is not all knowing, Goldie," Bracken cuts me off. He holds up his hand between us, and as I watch, flames erupt from his palm. They are small at first before dancing into a flame big enough to roast a bit of meat. I watch as it flickers, the tips of the flames green in color, tinged with magic. "I was alive during the collapse," he murmurs. The flames take the shape of some beast wearing a crown that looks suspiciously like a minotaur. I watch as it raises a sword in the air before the image explodes into a fiery butterfly, flapping its wings as it dances around Bracken's palm. Wonder strikes me, and I find myself reaching toward the flames. When I touch them, they are cool. They don't burn me, but the butterfly continues to dance before landing on the back of my hand. As I watch, it explodes into sparks and disappears completely. Only then do I realize I've essentially laid my hand in Bracken's.

His fingers close over mine, but I'm not scared. Some instinct, despite our beginnings, is telling me to trust the fey. Either I've lost my mind, or my instincts have grown stronger. I don't really know, but I don't pull my hand away.

"Your magic is..." I can't find the words. There are none that fit.

"You have your own magic, Goldie," he purrs. "You just have to learn how to harness it." He wiggles his eyebrows. "I can do the same thing with blood. Would you like to see?"

Somehow, his words bring a smile to my face, and at my expression, his eyes widen. "Maybe later," I respond. "For now, let's get to the mountains."

Bracken blinks and then willingly releases my hand after a final, lingering touch. "Yes," he murmurs. "Yes, to our next destination."

As I turn back to a thoughtful Grimus, I swear I see the very tip of a pearlescent white tail out of the corner of my eye, but when I go to follow the movement, there's nothing there. When Bracken doesn't rush off into the trees, I assume there's no threat and keep walking forward.

This time, Bracken stays just a little closer to my back, and Grimus doesn't stray as far. Something in me shifts, and I find myself truly smiling while traipsing through the Dead Lands.

As if my clock isn't ticking.

As if I'm not in a realm of monsters.

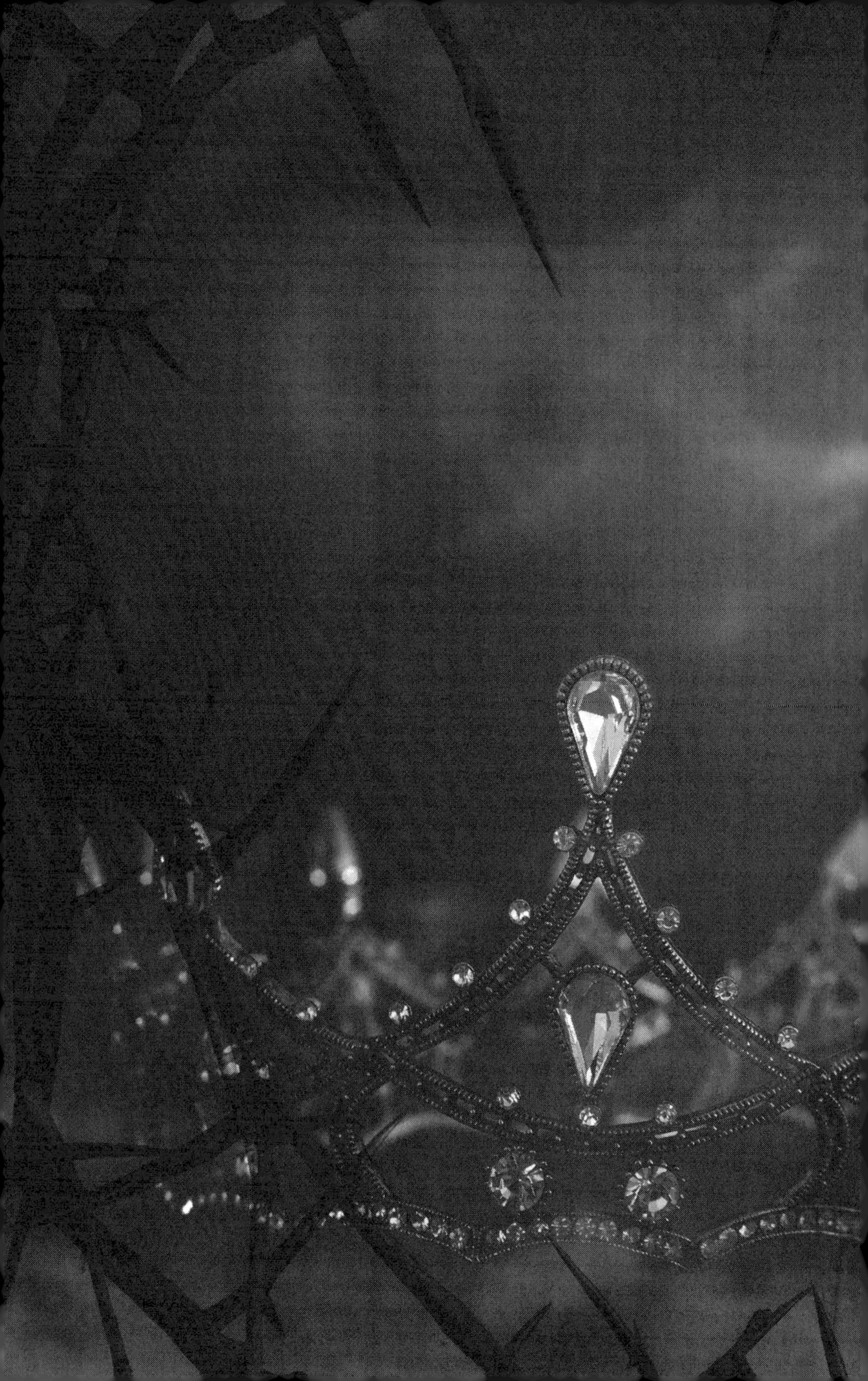

CHAPTER
THIRTEEN

We walk and walk some more. The trees never seem to end, but Grimus appears confident about the direction we are traveling, which is good because I have no idea, and Bracken...well, is Bracken. I swear if he spends any more time staring at my ass, the dress will have a hole burnt through it, though I wouldn't put it past him.

"Bracken!" I hiss when I feel his hand sliding under my dress, but just as I'm about to threaten to chop off the offending hand, my eyes widen as I see the blob of fur barreling straight for me. "Grim!" I scream and duck. I don't even see my minotaur bodyguard move, but he's suddenly before me, backhanding the creature away, and that's when I realize it's a wolf.

A wolf mixed with a man.

Saliva-covered jowls vibrate with a growl from a snout seemingly stuck on a human face. The thing has two wide, red eyes above the snout. Furry wolf ears sprout from black hair that seems to grow into fur on his humanoid body, which is naked. Two oddly bent legs and longer than normal arms ending with bleeding claws complete its ghastly appearance. Grim stomps his feet at the creature, and the wolf howls before diving back at him.

I scream, even as Bracken grabs me and hauls me away from the fight with a sigh, both of us watching as they meet head-on.

"Aren't you going to help him?" I shout.

"He has this," he drawls in a bored tone.

I turn back in time to see more wolf men launch themselves from the trees. My eyes widen as I watch him fight against impossible odds. He cleaves two in half before ripping one into pieces, but more pour from the woods, drawn by the howls, and not even his fury can hold them all back.

Not even my minotaur can take on a full pack, though he's determined to try.

"He's going to lose! Help him!" I implore Bracken, wishing I could assist, but I would only be a hindrance.

"Fine, Goldie, but what do I get for helping him?" Bracken flashes me a satisfied grin.

My eyes dart back to the fight to see more joining in. "Now isn't the time for negotiations."

"It's the perfect time. Better hurry, Goldie, if you don't want to see your monster buddy torn to shreds." He chuckles, not the least bit bothered by the wolves' death cries and Grimus' roars.

"What do you want?" I shout, eyes darting back to the fight again.

"A kiss. That's all, Goldie—one sweet little kiss," he purrs.

"One kiss and you'll help him?" I ask, watching the scene in dawning horror. The wolf men are crawling all over my huge minotaur, ripping into him as he fights, but as he kills one, another appears.

"One kiss, that's all, Goldie," he promises, holding out his pinky. Muttering about what a bad idea this is, I hook my pinky through his and lift onto my toes, kissing his lips chastely.

"You call that a kiss?" He groans. "A true kiss, Goldie, or Grimus there is as good as dead."

I shut him up by grabbing the back of his head and hauling him down to me, slamming my lips to his. I kiss him hard, his mouth opening on a groan as I sweep my tongue in, tangling it with his. I ignore the heat pulsing through my body and the moan that escapes my lips, never mind the way my body falls into his as if seeking more of him. My hand tunnels into his hair, gripping him tightly. He groans and grips my ass, hauling me closer, even as a flash of pain has me freezing. His fangs cut into my lip, and I taste blood, my blood, and so does he. Going wild, he sucks my lip, the pulse of pain and pleasure making me moan before I force myself to pull back.

Chest heaving, I stare at the fey. His eyes slowly blink open as if he's drugged, and he lifts a trembling hand to his bloodstained lips.

"I was wrong," he rasps out. "That kind of magic won't just get you killed, it will get us all killed. I'm ready to die just for another taste," he whispers before swallowing and coming back to himself. "But a promise is a promise. Hey, wolves! You don't want him. I'm much tastier, I promise!" he calls as he dives into the fray.

I watch as Bracken plucks them off the big guy and tears into them with fangs and claws, ripping out their throats before clawing them apart and moving onto the next. All the while, he laughs and taunts them, enjoying himself, but one of the creatures he throws away isn't quite dead, and it starts crawling toward me, snarling, despite the fact its legs are ripped off. Panicking, I look around as I back away, but then Grimus grabs it with one hand while fighting four others. "Oh no you don't," he mutters and throws it so far, it disappears into the horizon.

Fuck this. I refuse to cower here. I grab a blade from Grimus' side and keep it in front of me as I crouch low in case any come near me. When one does, I slash and stab, screaming as I do, until I'm just slashing repeatedly, letting all my anger out.

At my people.

At the laws.

At my father.

At my mother.

At the whole world.

Suddenly, my hand is grabbed in a tight grip, and I blink dumbly. Bringing myself back, I see Grimus holding my hand and watching me with an arched eyebrow. That's when I realize the wolves are all dead and I was still swinging. "Oops." I grin guiltily. A smile tugs at his lips before he cleans the blade and hands it back to me, even though I expected him to keep it.

Touched, I hold it close and look around at the cut up, dismembered bodies of the wolves.

"What was wrong with them?"

"Magic," Grimus mutters, "corrupted them mid-shift. Being stuck between their animal side and their human side drives them mad." He narrows his gaze on Bracken. "I didn't need your help."

"Sure, big guy," he replies as he winks at me. "The blood will draw others soon. We should move."

Despite his annoyance, Grimus agrees, and we hurry away from the scene. The taste of the fey still lingers on my lips, and I don't hate it, which terrifies me.

～

Hours later, after stopping for a break, we reach Grimus' destination—the shores he had told me about.

He was right—it's empty here. The blackened grass suddenly turns into sand dunes and hills, and when I reach down to run my hand through the sand, it almost cuts into my skin, the grains hard like diamonds. I don't touch it again as we trek along the dunes. My eyes go to the empty stretch of beach, forgotten like this whole land. There are remnants of houses and boats on the beach, with washed up wood and sails scattered across it all, but when I glance out at the churning black sea, what I see is even worse.

There's a wooden sailboat out there, crashed up against a huge rock. The sails are broken and blowing in the wind, and the side is caved in as if something massive got out...or got in. I don't look any closer at it. Instead, I focus on not falling as I trudge behind Grimus, but I can't help but ask about it.

"What did that?" I inquire, jerking my thumb at the ship.

Grim follows my gaze and grunts. "You don't want to know, little one. Trust me."

He's probably right, so I don't ask again, but my eyes go to the water, wondering what monsters linger there that are big enough to rip boats apart.

We walk along the water for a while, the scenery rarely changing. More and more boats are broken across the ocean, clearly old human vessels, and for a moment, I can almost imagine what these lands used to be like before humans ruined it the way we ruin everything. Slumping in sadness, I look into the distance, across the rolling lands, and there, obscured by darkness, are the mountains we are heading to. They are too far to reach today or even tomorrow, so when Grimus finds an old fishing hut and suggests we set up camp, I almost drop to my knees in gratitude.

It's a one-room hut, but it's mostly still standing, and the roof is intact. Despite the lack of windows, it's almost cozy. After eating the food Grimus feeds me, I watch as he and Bracken move to the water and quickly wash off. My eyes track the water on their bodies before I force myself to check on my foot, and when they return, I have my strange, new pervy instincts under control as we all hunker down to rest.

As quickly as they hit the ground, they are both asleep.

Not me.

I lie here, staring at the ceiling, too pumped up from everything that has happened. My hand lifts in the dark and traces my lips, remembering how that kiss felt. It was unlike anything I have ever experienced before, lighting me up from the inside out until I needed more.

Stupid, I know.

Dropping my hand in annoyance, I'm just about to flip over when I hear a strange noise. I sit bolt upright and peer into the darkness. I wait for the others to wake up, but they don't. I wait to hear it again. It doesn't take long for the sound to echo through the air for a second time. Hesitantly, I stand, my eyes going to the door that leads out to the beach. I'm not dumb, so I take my knife and stop at the door, peering through the cracks between the old wood, looking for what made that noise. I'm in full reach of my monster protectors, but then I hear it again, and something about it seems almost...pained.

I shoot them both a look to find them sleeping. They need their rest, especially with all the creatures they had to fight today, so I ease the small door open and take a step out. When the sound comes again, just as pained as before, I march out onto the sand, trying to appear threatening as I wander along the shore in search of what made the noise.

Grim said no monsters ever dared to come here, so I should be safe, right?

The noise comes again, and my head jerks around in search of it until I face the dark water. It's coming from those waves, and despite the fact that my heart pounds in fear and I know how stupid it is, I take a step forward. I find my hand convulsing without my will, dropping the blade so that it falls into the wet sand, blade down. My feet lift without my orders and draw me toward the dark waves as if I'm under some sort of spell. I wander to the edge, the water cold around my toes, and without making the decision to, I surge forward. I walk deeper until the water dances across my shoulders, my hands out to my sides as I tread water when the waves lift me. My eyes remain glued to the water, and I can't even force myself to blink, as if I'm in a trance I cannot break.

But just as suddenly as the sound that lured me out here came, it stops, and I blink as if I'm waking up from a dream. When I realize I'm in the water, I turn quickly, desperate to get back to the shore before I find myself in danger. Where is my knife? I don't even have the knife!

I see it before I even make it a few feet toward the shore.

A tentacle snakes out of the water before me, and just as I scream, it wraps around my body and drags me under, leaving me choking as water rushes into my mouth. Eyes wide in terror, I flail as I hit and kick the slimy tentacle pulling me through the water. My lungs ache, screaming at me like they are about to burst. Darkness dances at the edges of my vision from my fading consciousness rather than the darkness of the water. My limbs fail me, and I know I'm drowning.

Despite my aching lungs and my body screaming at me to open my mouth, my eyes widen when I finally see what the tentacle is attached to.

I stop fighting, though there's not much fight left in me as the burning in my lungs grows worse. A huge octopus, like the ones I saw in the books during my short time in school, bigger than any I've ever seen or heard of, looks me in the eyes as it pulls me close like I'm prey.

Which I am.

I'm going to die and be eaten by an octopus.

What an idiot.

Just as my eyes threaten to slide closed and give in, something dark and huge cuts through the water. I can barely make out the creature through my rapidly declining vision, but I see the second creature come up behind the octopus and grab it, ripping it away from me.

I find a fight deep inside of me I didn't know I had and propel myself to the surface. I'm weak, and my kicks don't do much, but I'm not so far from the surface that I can't reach it. Kicking as my lungs threaten to explode, I finally break through the waves with an audible gasp and choke on the water still in my lungs. My vision is fuzzy, but I force myself to swim toward the distant shore. I'm in danger here, and I need to get out. Despite the peril, I can't help but look behind me as I swim, noting the massive tentacles churning up the water as the fight carries on. There are more than I can count, and they are bigger than the boats I saw in the water.

Yeah, fuck that.

I turn and swim as hard as I can with my weak limbs, still gasping for air and trying to ease my burning lungs, but the tide is rough and water splashes in my eyes, making it hard. My limbs are already exhausted, and I go from keeping myself above the water to barely able to take a breath as I begin to sink. I start going under again, the exhaustion too much after the fight beneath the waves. As I gasp for breath, the water around me turns red with blood, and something achingly soft wraps around my waist. It's huge, big enough that I'm cocooned in it, and lifts me above the waves again.

A tentacle, different than the last, appears as I'm lifted from the water and pushed toward the shore. I feel it slide gently around my body as we move, the water dripping from me as I'm lifted up and out of the ocean completely. The shore comes close fast, as if the creature carrying me toward it propels itself through the water far easier than I do. Just as suddenly as it curls around me, it unfurls, and I'm sliding along the soft texture, the suckers gently touching and releasing as I find myself on the sand again—well, technically wood.

The tentacle places me on the broken ship bow nearest the small hut, leaving me gasping as I drop to my knees and try to come to my senses. I watch as that massive appendage slides back into the water, disappearing beneath the dark waves. I start struggling to my feet to attempt to climb from the ship and call after it, panicking that I didn't get to thank the creature that dared help me, when the beast rises from the water.

Eyes wide, I stare at the towering monster.

A kraken.

A fucking kraken saved me.

Red in color, the creature stares at me with large, slitted eyes. Its body is so much like that of the octopus but larger than any ship. As I stare at it, it seems to study me closer, the red skin shifting between beautiful colors as if unsure which one to choose. It doesn't attack or rush toward me. It just lingers there in the waves.

As quickly as the beast rose before me, it swiftly melts away. Water splashes down from its body, so I have to cover my face and eyes against the stinging droplets, and when I drop my arm again, there's a man standing before me. Balanced on the edge of the ship, his eyes as dark as the ocean he swam in, he watches me closely. I have to drag my eyes up high to meet his. He must easily be eight feet tall, with muscles that make my mouth dry and tan skin that almost glimmers like he's the moon reflecting on the waves. His hair is dark and moves in the breeze like his tentacles did, curling around his head. His eyebrows slant down, and his pink lips curl up as he watches me. Then my eyes drop lower, and I realize he's naked.

I cover my eyes, but I can't help peeking through my fingers, because nestled around a very huge cock are tentacles. They are small, almost like an extension of his cock, and I can't seem to stop staring as his cock hardens. I've never seen anything like it before.

"Didn't anyone ever tell you it was rude to stare, *measma*?" His voice is loud, rumbling like water crashing on rocks and just as silky, and my eyes dart back up to meet his amused gaze.

"Tentacles. Tentacle penis," I blurt out.

Great going, Cora, really.

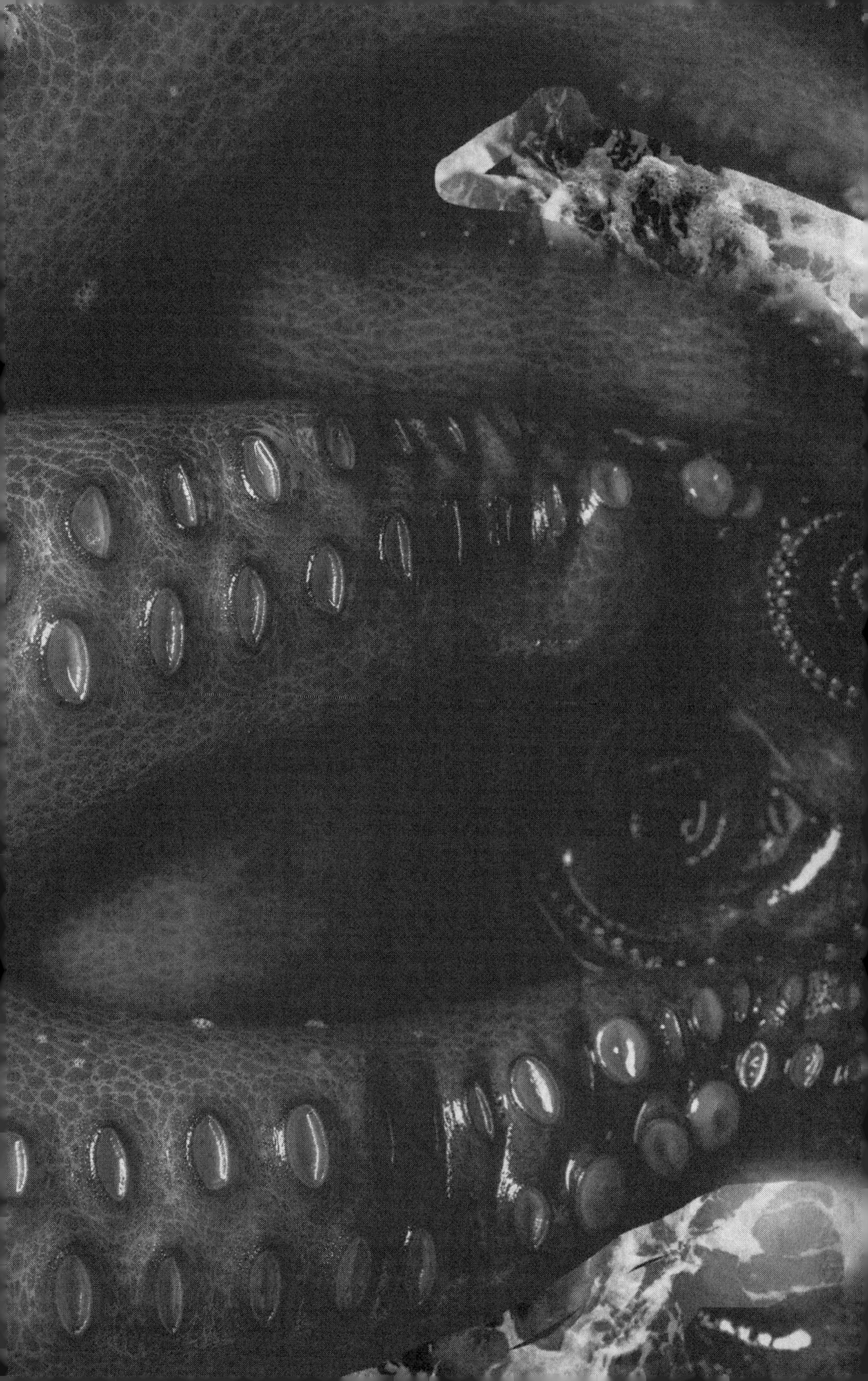

CHAPTER
FOURTEEN
ZETROS

I can't help but laugh at her obvious embarrassment, her cheeks heating as she slaps her face and mutters to herself. When she seems to gather herself, she drops her hand.

"Sorry about that. It, er…just slipped out. I meant—Fuck, okay. I mean, thank you for saving me and all that, er…Mr. Kraken."

"Zetros," I respond as I step down onto the wood of the boat so I am closer. I hate humans. They are responsible for my kin's death and for ruining the water, the place I grew up in, and yet I can't find it in me to hate her. There's something different about her, and I am drawn to her like I am the water. I sense no greed or destruction, only curiosity, and when she wandered so willingly into my water, I couldn't resist a touch.

I even went so far as to save her from someone I tolerated before he attacked her. He's dead now, so it doesn't matter, but I cannot control my curiosity about the little human. I wander around her when she comes close, picking up her wet hair, which is the color of the gold resting below my water. Her eyes are bright and curious, and her skin is pale and so smooth, I ache to touch more. She's tiny compared to me, but that magic…

I inhale deeply, seeing it swirling through her.

"Sure, because no monster has easy names. I'm Cora, Cora Black," she says, interrupting my musings, and I stop before her, making her crane her neck back to meet my gaze. Her mesmerizing eyes slip lower for a moment, tracing my skin like a physical touch, before jerking back to my face.

I grin. "Well, Cora, Cora Black, you are welcome. Now, what are you doing in these lands, *measma*?"

"Erm, I was the hunt."

I tilt my head curiously. Through the years, I have heard about the hunt, but never before has a human made it this deep into my lands. I haven't laid eyes on a human female in centuries, and certainly never one this beautiful. She shines as brightly as the jewel I call her. "And you've made it this far?"

"I'm trying to survive. I made a deal." She shrugs sheepishly.

That makes my eyebrows rise as I follow her gaze back to the shore, where I finally see a minotaur pacing, almost puffing smoke, and a bored, curious fey. Interesting. They are not characters one would usually see together, but when I look back at her, I understand why. She drew them together. She is a curiosity, but I already feel the webs of obsession taking hold, not just for the magic, but for the woman who stands before me totally unafraid. I catch not one whiff of fear from her, when only moments before, she was overcome by it before I saved her. There's only interest, which I inhale deeply as I watch her.

"What kind of deal?" I find myself asking.

"They can, um, taste my magic if they get me to the palace and safety," she replies as if she's unsure, smiling meekly.

I laugh. "Those two? Oh, then you're so fucked, *measma*."

"I guess." She sighs as if only now realizing how much so.

"Want to make another deal, *measma*?" I ask without meaning to. I haven't left my home for centuries, and never voluntarily before that, but for her, maybe I will, because this is the most entertained I have been in ages.

My cock pulses in agreement, hardening once more. My stilma, my tentacles as she called them, wiggle in anticipation of locking onto her skin and tasting her, right between those delectable, pale human thighs and the warmth she hides there with silly garments I never understood the need for.

"No offense, but can you even be on land? Don't you, like, need water?" she inquires, making me grin once more—a foreign reaction. Even before our lands died, I was as sullen as they came. I was always withdrawn, but that was because of the humans here and what they did to us.

To me.

"I like water, it's true, and I couldn't shift on land with my large body, but I'm a fighter even in my weaker form—this one, which seems to please you. So what do you say, human? A deal?" I step closer, desperate for another whiff of that intoxicating aroma, and I'm not disappointed. My eyes close on a groan. "You smell delicious."

"Not weird at all," she mutters. "What is it with monsters sniffing me?"

"Because we can smell every inch of your delectable cunt," I reply, making her eyes widen. "Now, Cora, stop hesitating. A deal or not, because I do nothing for free."

Lie. For her, I would, but I find myself liking this deal idea better. It would make her indebted to me, which I can use as an excuse to get closer.

"Fine, deal," she mutters, and before she can even scream, I shift once more and grab her. She closes her eyes and lips as I dive back into the water. She's as smart as she is beautiful. This time, I keep my tentacle above the water, like a boat holding her up as I cut through the waves. I show off for her and the others on shore, revealing all my power. She smiles in delight as we rush through the darkness.

Once on shore, I put her safely on the sand and shift back until I stand behind her, grinning at the fey and minotaur. "I guess we will be working together."

"We leave you alone for two seconds, and you almost die and make a new friend, Goldie. You are a busy little human." The fey smirks at her.

She flips him a finger, which I don't understand, and he looks at me. "Sorry, I don't do anything with tentacles."

I raise my eyebrow at him. "I only fuck females," I mutter, not understanding why he chuckles. Clearly, I am not in on the joke.

"He's with us now, so let's get moving. I can't sleep here anymore," Cora mutters at them. The minotaur watches me warily, obviously understanding the threat I am, but he nods his head at her, his eyes moving across her body as if to check for injuries. I watch those orbs soften before filling with heat and kindness. Even the way the fey watches her is hungry—not just for magic, but for her body.

Interesting, and she doesn't exactly seem like she is against it.

I smell the desire pouring from her, and so must they. My grin widens.

Oh yes, this sweet little jewel will be mine, like no other human ever has been. Not in the way they once owned me.

Monsters, as they called us, were an oddity even back before the wall. The humans fucked the pretty ones for our magic or for a wild story to tell their friends. We were ordered by the king to pleasure them, left with no choice if we wanted to survive. Even to this day, I bear the scars of what they did to me in those dark years.

My measma is not like that though. She wants us, monstrous sides and all, and the kindness in her eyes tells me she would never enslave those she cares about.

"You are collecting quite an array of monsters," the minotaur grumbles unhappily.

He's stoic, protective. The fey is a flirt and almost clingy, reaching for her constantly. I want to as well, needing to feel her skin again, but I'm very aware of our size differences and how easily I could hurt her.

"You should sleep." I lift my eyes to the sky. "I will keep watch while you all do. I was slumbering when you called to me, so I do not need to rest."

She glances back at me, her eyes softening as she smiles, and it's like a physical blow. I stumble back, and I know without a doubt I would do anything to see that smile directed at me again.

"We'll find another place to settle down," she replies, her smile still brightening her eyes. "Thank you, Zetros."

The way she says my name nearly makes me come undone, but I nod and follow the strange group farther along the beach, farther from my home.

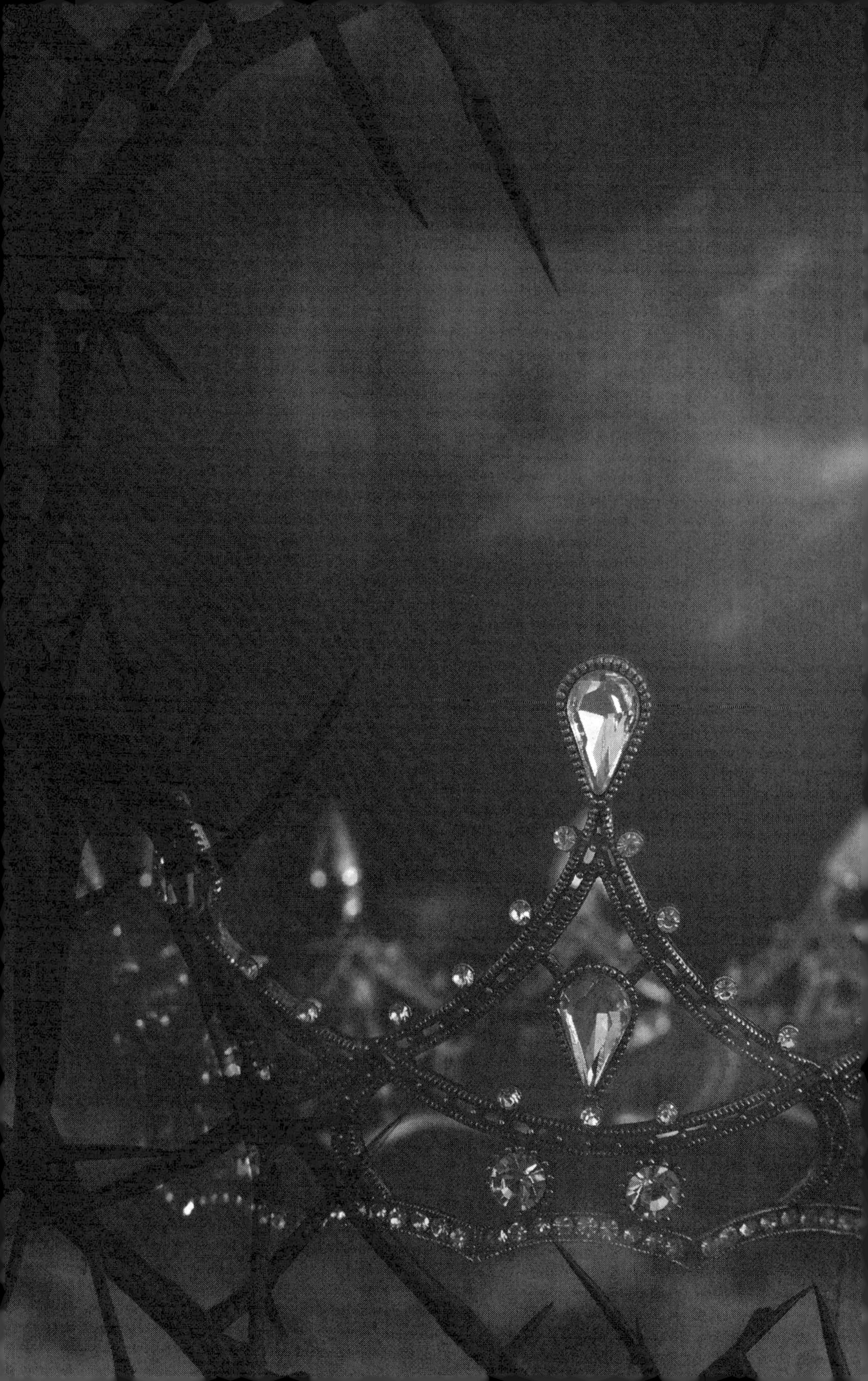

CHAPTER FIFTEEN

The blisters on my feet are almost welcome after the shredded slippers, but at some point, I start to slow yet again. I've never been more aware of my humanity as I am surrounded by these monsters. Every single one of them moves around me as we walk, one in front, one in back, and one on the side, and I can't tell if they are protecting me or checking me out. Bracken, to his credit, is very open about his appreciation. Zetros is more coy but still open with his admiring glances. Grimus, on the other hand, mostly pretends I don't exist. If not for his constant care and appeasing grunts, I'd think he hates to be here.

Sometimes, though, when Grimus looks at me, his eyes soften, and I realize just how much he doesn't hate it. Maybe he's even starting to like me...not that he will ever admit it.

The mountains are beginning to loom closer on the horizon, but after another day of walking, it's clear we're still not going to make it any time soon.

"There will be at least another day of walking," Grimus says, backing up my thoughts. He looks at me, sees the exhaustion in my limbs, and adds, "Perhaps two."

It reminds me again of how much I'm slowing them down, my human legs forcing me to move slower than the three of them likely can, but I can't feel too much guilt. After all, they are choosing to be here due to the temptation of whatever magic resides inside me.

If only I knew how to feel or use the magic. I still almost don't believe it's in me like they explained. Surely I would know if I had magic, but they are so sure, so adamant, it does have me considering...

"There's a natural spring about a ten-minute walk to the west if you'd like to stop there," Zetros offers. "If my memory serves me correctly, there should be a small palace in the midst of it. If there are no other monsters calling it home, it would be a good place to rest."

"A natural spring," Bracken repeats, as if searching through his memory. "The one the naga priestess used to reside in?"

"The very same." Zetros looks in the direction he spoke of, his eyes haunted. "I once spent time there."

Grimus frowns and looks over his shoulder at Zetros. "I thought the naga priestess resided with humans before the war. The stories say she never hosted guests."

Zetros meets his gaze straight on. "She didn't, but her humans were fond of prisoners."

My stomach twists at his admittance, at the implication that he'd once been imprisoned in the palace he's suggesting we should stay in. "We can find somewhere else," I offer.

Zetros' eyes turn to me as he studies my face, and his own haunted expression softens. "There are no ghosts left for me there, *measma*. Do no worry on my behalf." He reaches out and strokes along my jawline, making my stomach flip for a different reason. Bracken and Zetros seem to find excuses to touch me, and what I once thought would repulse me actually intrigues me.

"To the old palace then," Grimus murmurs, his eyes resting on Zetros for a long moment before he turns to lead the way.

I'm not sure what I expect, but what appears after ten minutes isn't it. The building is in ruins, just as most of the other ones are. It's been centuries since the war between humans and monsters, so anything still standing would be either a miracle in itself or just very sturdy craftsmanship. This one is neither. What's left of the building appears as if whoever built it favored beauty over eternalness.

While some parts of it are caved in and decrepit, the central section of the palace still stands, even if there are large cracks running along the stone and cutting through what was probably once gorgeous artwork. The architecture speaks of another realm, with tall, sweeping doorways leading into darkness, great swooping designs, and colorful artwork that's now chipped away. If I move just right, the light seems to catch on what looks like jewels embedded in the stone, but that can't be right. I've never seen jewels aside from those around the necks of gilded ladies.

Around the ruins of the palace, nature has risen up and reclaimed what was once hers. Trees and shrubs break through the stone walkways, replacing them with the cushion of a forest floor. The trees bow inwards as if reaching for the stone ruins. It's beautiful, but knowing about Zetros' ghosts almost makes me fear it.

"I don't see the natural springs," I comment, looking around.

"They are inside." Zetros points to the central part of the palace. "There is a courtyard in the center of that where many of them are. I do not know if they are still usable or safe, but if they are, we could utilize them."

"A bath?" I hum. "That sounds like heaven."

When was the last time I bathed? Right before I was thrown through the barrier for the hunt. I'm not even sure how many days that's been anymore.

Bracken glances over at me and wiggles his brow. "Perhaps I could join you."

Narrowing my eyes, I respond, "What will you give me for it?"

His eyes widen at my audacity, but then a sinister smile pulls at his lips, as if he's happy I'm now joining his game. He probably thinks he's corrupting me. If only he knew I was already corrupted. "What would you ask me for, Goldie?"

I don't get the chance to answer, because Grimus grunts at our conversation and points to a large, ornate door that's leaning as if something large once tried to break it down with its shoulder. "We worry about checking for threats first. The rest comes later."

The way he doesn't meet my eyes makes me think he's jealous that I'd been about to make a deal with Bracken, but I dismiss it from my mind. Grimus doesn't care. He may have softened toward me, but I doubt he sees me as anything more than a tempting burden.

It leaves me with the question in my own mind—what would I ask for from Bracken if given the opportunity? I'm reminded of our kiss, of the way I wanted to get closer and didn't actually want to stop, despite our situation. I want the fey just as much as he seems to want me. So what would I ask for? Pleasure? Another kiss? Or would I ask for something ridiculous, like for him to sing me a song and dance? Thankfully, I don't have to come up with the answer right away.

Grimus leads us toward the large door. All three of my monsters tower over me, so it makes sense that I'm in the middle of them. I still have the knife Grimus gave me strapped to my thigh, thanks to a strip of leather he offered, but I don't pretend to think I can hold my own against another monster.

"Stay close, *measma*," Zetros says, his large form next to mine as Grimus lifts the door from its hinges and pushes it open all the way. He doesn't close it yet, making sure we have a quick way out if we need it. "We don't know what calls this place home."

We step into what was once a beautiful entryway. The floor and ceiling are covered in mosaic murals, and though they are now covered with dirt and grime, all it would take to make them shine again is a bit of cleaning. I can make out some of the imagery—a depiction of a giant snake woman similar to Nero, her arms held wide with a sun over her.

"You mentioned the naga was a priestess," I comment, staring at the image, wanting to know as much as I can. "What does that mean?"

Zetros glances at the same image, and where I see beauty, he so clearly sees the opposite. "She thought herself a goddess who could speak to the sun and moon. The humans who once resided here with her believed she controlled them. That is why they worshiped her."

"But you didn't believe she held such power?" I ask as Grimus moves deeper inside. We follow, Bracken taking up the rear.

"*Measma*, rarely does a single being hold such power alone. Not even you, with all that magic in your veins, could move the mountains."

His eyes are bright in the broken darkness of the palace as we follow Grimus deeper inside. His hand hovers just beside mine, our skin almost touching. I'm tempted to close the distance, to take his fingers, and when I linger on the thought, I close the distance anyways. To hell with hesitation. He blinks in confusion at me as I curl my fingers with his, holding his hand.

"Whatever they did to you here," I whisper, "it's not who you are, nor will it happen again."

The shock on his face is almost comical. Has no one spoken to the kraken like this before?

"Would you protect me, *measma*?" he asks, leaning in close.

Smiling, I press my forehead against his when he leans down far enough for me to do so. "You saved me before. Of course I would protect you, even if I was not so good at it."

He sighs deeply, his warm breath fanning over my face. "I was wrong."

"About what?" I ask curiously.

"If anyone could move mountains, little human, it would be you."

Something inside me melts at his words, at his pained admission. Whatever he sees in me, I want to see it too. This monster of the sea, this fearsome creature, sees me as some bright spot of strength, and I don't know how to handle it, so I do the only thing I know how.

I get awkward.

"Yes, well," I say, giggling to distract myself from the sudden discomfort, "good thing we don't need to move the mountains and we can just go through them."

The smile that curls Zetros' lips makes something else melt, and I have to clear my throat at the sudden hoarseness there. Never in a million years did I think I would find myself attracted to the monsters meant to kill me, but here I am, lusting after a kraken, a fey, and a minotaur. Hell, I'm in danger if even a single one of them makes an advance. I don't even need a deal. I'd do it for the fun of it.

"Are you two done canoodling?" Bracken asks as he moves around the furniture across from us. "Because I found something interesting." We both turn to look as he holds up a large sheet of something. It's as wide as the length of one arm and longer than I can see. All I know is it drags over the floor on either side where he lifts it.

"What is that?" I ask, stepping closer, my brows furrowed in confusion.

"Naga skin," Zetros answers. "Not surprising, considering who used to reside here. When they shed, their skin doesn't break down. Many used to use them for decorations."

Grimus shakes his head and steps closer. "No, this is fresh. Look at the sheen." Sure enough, when he grabs a section of it and turns it in the light, there's a pearlescent sheen to it. "There was a naga in here recently."

"Or it's still in here," Zetros adds, immediately going on alert. "Stay close, *measma*."

I do as he says, keeping in step with him as we all scan the rooms around us, searching for the naga in case it's still here. All I can think about is the one I met at the beginning, Nero. Certainly this will be a different one. As we move, clearing first one room and then another, my eyes wander to the mosaics that decorate each wall. Some of them have tapestries long since decayed with barely any threads left, save for the top ones, while some of the mosaics sparkle like jewels. I'm staring at one, leaning in close to study the red jewel embedded in it that's the size of my fist. When I turn excitedly to Zetros and say, "It's a ruby!" I realize just how far away he is from me.

He turns at my exclamation, his eyes on me, but when his eyes widen and trail up, I know I've made a mistake. Swallowing my fear, I crane my neck back to look above me.

I see him almost immediately, his long white scales draped across the banister from the second floor and hanging around wherever there's room. He's massive, his coils glittering beneath the little light coming inside. His white scales are nothing compared to the body of the man on top of them, though, as he trails down and around me.

"Nero," I murmur, staring into his toxic green eyes that are slitted like a snake's.

"Did you miss me, *parum anguis*?" he asks, his mouth drawing out the S like a hiss.

I'm too scared to ask him what it means as his coils wrap around me, but he doesn't squeeze or attack, not yet.

The others rush around us, their weapons drawn, prepared to save me.

"Let her go, Nero," Grimus snarls, his morning star held aloft.

Zetros is tense, his shoulders tight as he stands. He has no weapon, but then again, he doesn't need one. He promised me that he's all the weapon he needs.

Bracken, on the other hand, doesn't seem worried in the slightest. He sighs deeply and takes a seat in one of the chairs, tipping his head back to watch. I furrow my brows at him, and he only winks at me as if we're in on some little secret.

"I mean her no harm," Nero offers, but when he looks at me, there's liquid heat there. "Not unless she's into such relations."

Hell, I might be if he keeps looking at me like that.

Wait, no, bad Cora. Stop thinking about monster dick, it's seriously becoming a problem.

"What do you want?" I rasp out, and I have to clear my throat the first time I try to say it.

"Isn't it obvious?" Nero asks, his white hair hanging around his shoulders. "I've been following you, watching you, and studying the way you've cowed these three to your every whim." He comes closer, his fingers brushing along my jaw. "Look how you've brought them together, *parum anguis*. Look at how they fight for you. The magic under your skin is fighting to come out. You only need to shed your flesh and release it."

I blink. "You've been following me?" My eyes trail over to Bracken. "You knew he was."

Grimus jerks his gaze over to Bracken, where he sits bored out of his mind.

"Of course I knew," Bracken admits, rolling his eyes. "I sense every creature around us at all times. How could I not know?"

"And you didn't think to inform us?" Grimus snarls, angry.

"He wasn't a danger." Bracken shrugs. "Not to anything but Goldie's nether bits."

My cheeks flush at his words, at the way Nero's coils move closer, hugging me, comforting me, or...is it a promise?

"You've made deals with these three," he says, his fingers touching my shoulders and then running down my arms in a caress that makes goose bumps rise in his wake. "Now I'd like to make a deal with you."

Zetros takes a step forward, as if prepared to rip me from Nero's arms, but Nero shoots him a look that freezes him while his coils tighten around me. I suspect Zetros doesn't pause because he's afraid so much as he realizes I'm in the line of fire. All it would take is Nero changing his mind and then I would be squeezed up human mush, and I quite like not being mush.

"What do you want?" I ask, my voice hesitant. How many deals can I make before I have nothing left to give? How many times can my magic be tasted before I'm an empty shell?

Nero smiles, and though there's a flash of fang, the smile is charming and soft, nonthreatening. "I ask only for your company, *parum anguis*, for as long as you desire to give it. In return, I give you my protection and my assistance."

"Oh, you noble bastard!" Bracken exclaims with a roll of his eyes. "You've always been more dependent on charm than brains."

Nero, instead of being insulted, grins at the fey, as if they are old friends.

My brows furrow. I'm sure this is a trick. "That's it?" I ask. "That's all you want?"

"Friendship, companionship, trust. Those aren't things we can barter with. I would much rather win your heart by normal means than have to make a deal for it." He shoots his gaze over to Grimus, who only snorts and looks away. "Do we have a deal?"

I study the snake who, when I first came to the Dead Lands, seemed like such a threat, but now I realize he'd only been playing. Standing here, between his coils, I feel no animosity, only comfort, and I wonder if, in my panic, I'd seen him as something far more dangerous than he is. That's not to say he isn't a monster and capable of great destruction, but he is no danger to me.

He never was. I know that with a certainty that scares me, as if something deep inside me already recognizes him.

Gently, I lay my hand on the coil closest to me, and he closes his eyes as if it's the best thing he's ever felt. "I can't promise you my heart, Nero, but I'll accept your deal."

His eyes pop open, and the smile that lights up his face makes my insides flip in a dangerous way. He leans down, his sharp jawline pressing against mine as he touches his lips to my cheek. "You won't regret it, Cora," he whispers, his breath warm against my skin, and the way he says my name makes me blush. "The things I'll make you feel..."

My face immediately flushes harder at his tone, at the cocksure way he's teasing me, and I have to clear my throat again to speak, much to his amusement.

Here I thought I would have to worry about my organs around all these monsters, but in fact, I think I might have to worry about my virtue.

"Care to let me out?" I ask, gesturing to his coils.

With a languid grin and a promise in his eyes, he slides away, leaving me free to step forward without fear of being wrapped up again.

Grimus grumbles, his eyes narrowing on Nero in annoyance. "This is becoming a habit." His gaze drops to my cheek, where Nero kissed me, as if it offends him, which shouldn't please me as much as it does.

"It seemed like an easy deal to make," I murmur.

"Yes, especially knowing how much the naga wants to fuck her," Bracken announces. "Then again, it's not such a secret that we all have the same thoughts."

I flush scarlet again and shoot him a look. "Shut up."

Bracken's grin widens. "Surprise, surprise. Goldie wants to fuck him too. You really have a thing for monsters, don't you, little human? Can't say I blame you. Monsters do it better." He drags his hand down his chest suggestively.

I press a hand to my cheek and look away, but I don't deny the accusation. It would be silly when the truth is written all across my face.

Zetros steps up then. "We should finish checking the palace."

"Don't bother," Nero declares. "I already ran off one rather nasty group of gnomes when I got here in preparation for you. There are no other monsters in the palace, and I've closed off any other openings where one might come in." He gestured through an open doorway. "I've even cleaned out one of the old bathing pools for Cora's use."

The fact that Nero is the only one of them to use my real name isn't lost on me. He took the time to learn it, and though he still uses a pet name for me, he shows respect with his address. I tilt my head toward him, showing him I recognize the effort.

Grimus' face scrunches up harder, clearly annoyed. "I'm going to double-check it all anyway. We take no risks."

"Suit yourself," Nero says, and then his eyes return to me. "If you desire to have new clothing, *parum anguis*, I've taken the liberty of making you new ones."

I stare at him in surprise. "You what?"

Nero moves around, his large body slithering through the furniture before he picks up a bundle of cloth and brings it over to me. "These heathens have left you in that dirty hunt cloth, and I can't bear to see you so. Therefore, while I waited for the four of you to arrive, I made you new ones."

Furrowing my brows, I look down at the clothing in my hands and stare at the fabric that shimmers in the light, just like—

"My scales," he says when I stroke my fingers over it. "When nagas shed, their skin is one of the toughest fabrics one can have. The greatest kings and queens have fought over the shedded skin of a naga."

I clear my throat. I don't know whether to be flattered or perturbed, but the quality of the clothing and the clear attention to detail has me looking up with a smile. Okay, I'm lying, it's kind but also strange to think I will be wearing Nero's skin. "Thank you."

"Anything for you, Cora," he murmurs and then backs off, giving me space to breathe.

"Great," Bracken says, scowling at the snake. "Now he's making us all look bad. I say we vote him out."

"Scared of a little competition, fey?" Nero teases, and though they glare at each other, there's a clear relationship there, as if they really are friends. It makes me curious, but I decide a bath is far superior to asking about it. I'll ask later.

"Grimus, can you show me where the spring is please?" I ask nicely. "I figure you'd like to check it before I use it."

Bracken and Nero continue to bicker, but Zetros watches Grimus and me closely.

"I've got other things to check that are more important first," Grimus rumbles, dismissing me.

"Can't you check the spring first?" I beg. I'm filthy, and I'm sure I'm starting to smell. "That way when I'm done, everyone else will be able to use it."

"No," he snarls, turning to go. I almost flinch at his harsh tone, deflating a bit.

Sighing, I say, "Fine. Nero, will you—"

"Fine," Grimus snaps, glaring at the naga. Nero simply grins at him. "We make it quick."

Relief fills me, and I nod my head enthusiastically. "Thank you."

A grunt is my only response as he turns to lead me deeper into the palace. He's cautious as we move, his eyes taking in every detail possible, but it seems as if Nero was telling the truth. All entry points appear to be blocked off already, and we encounter no obstacles.

When Zetros mentioned a courtyard, I expected that to mean it was outside, but instead, it's more like a great domed room. The roof looks like it's made of glass, like a greenhouse, but they are so dirty, light barely filters through now. It doesn't make a difference though. There are already candles lit around one of the large basins inside.

I gasp at the beauty of it, at the way the candles reflect on the steam curling up from the water. The ground here used to be covered in tiles, but Mother Nature has broken in here too, making it so grass and ferns and even a few trees pepper the once ornate floor. The candles that Nero set up flicker, and the steaming water is dark.

I move to the edge and peer inside, worrying my bottom lip. "We're sure it's safe?"

He glares at me as if my very presence annoys him. "It looks safe enough."

"The water is dark," I observe, looking down at it and then up to him.

"And?" He crosses his arms.

I raise my eyebrow. "What if there's something hiding in it and it tries to eat me?"

His eyes narrow. "There isn't."

"But what if there is?" I counter, knowing I should probably shut up, but it's too much fun to annoy him.

He sighs deeply and looks at the spring again. "Stay here," he orders, then sets his morning star to the side. I watch as Grimus steps down into the pool, armor and all, the water rushing around his hooves before he eases farther in. It's deeper than I expected, the water coming up to his chest, and he's far taller than I am. Once inside the pool, he stands there expectantly, as if waiting for something to jump out and attack. When nothing does, he spins and waits again. "Seems pretty safe."

I set the clothing Nero gave me off to the side and note as Grimus follows the movement, his eyes catching on the bundle. When I take a seat on the edge of the water and drop my legs in, his gaze flicks back to me.

"Thank you for checking," I say gratefully. I haven't been alone much since I crossed into the Dead Lands, and I have to say I'm starting to distrust any dark places.

He snorts. "Should I send Nero in to tend to your needs?" he asks, and while the words are a question, there's bitterness hiding beneath his tone.

Frowning, I slide into the water completely, still dressed in my gown. It comes up to my shoulders before my toes touch a roughly carved bottom, smooth enough to keep from hurting my feet. The water is warm, hot almost, and feels amazing on my aching muscles, but instead of lingering, I swim over to Grimus.

"Should I not have accepted his deal?" I ask seriously, looking up into his eyes.

His eyes soften. "You're doing what you must to survive."

"But we're a team now, aren't we? I should have asked."

Something shifts in his eyes. "We're not a team." The words hurt when he says them, but I try not to let that hurt show. "Nero took nothing from you but your company. I demanded your magic. We are not the same." That admission dances in the air between us.

"Grimus," I murmur, moving closer. "I do not judge you. I'm thankful you ever agreed to help in the first place. I'd be dead many times over if not for you."

He grunts, his form of deflection, and I place my hands on his biceps, where he keeps them crossed.

"I mean it. You've helped me far more than I expected. You've kept me fed. You've protected me. You made me slippers for my feet. None of that was part of the deal." When his eyes soften, I run my hands up his biceps to his shoulders, then circle his neck. I have to lift myself in the water to be closer to his face. "I'm not comparing you to Nero."

"You should be," he admits softly. "We're all monsters. You should fear us."

"And yet I don't." I twine my hand into the hair at the base of his skull, tempted to reach up and grab one of his horns, but that feels intimate and I'm not sure how he'd feel about that. I should back away and let him leave, but I can't. I won't. All my life, I have been denied everything I ever wanted or needed, and I refuse to back down now. I could die tomorrow, and I refuse to die a coward. "Ever since the first moment I laid eyes on you, I've wanted you, Grimus."

He blinks down at me in surprise, his nostrils flaring wide, his nose ring glinting in the candlelight. "Little human," he warns, but his large hands come to rest on my waist, helping me stay up in the water.

"I still owe you a taste of my magic," I point out, leaning in closer.

His eyes drop to my lips. "I'm not calling in the deal yet."

My body presses against him in the water, the thin slip barely any barrier at all between us. He sucks in a breath at the feeling of my breasts against him as my nipples pebble.

"Maybe I want a taste," I whisper, looking up at him through my lashes.

His breathing speeds up, his fingers clenching my sides. "You don't owe me this, Cora. I won't force you."

The sound of my name on his lips makes me throb beneath the water. Carefully, I wrap my legs around his waist, and his hands immediately go to my ass to hold me up. Despite his words, I feel his throbbing cock between us, pressing against me, begging for attention. He's massive, far bigger than anything I've ever had, and my mouth waters at the thought.

My whole body lights up, aching to taste the wildness, the unknown.

"I want you, Grimus," I murmur. "I want you so badly." I press my mouth against the corded muscles of his neck, tasting his skin, even as the heat of the spring rises around us.

It's the truth—I want him, and I refuse to be ashamed of that. I refuse to spend one more night denying myself because of what others think. There is no one here but us. Fuck the humans, fuck the other monsters.

Better yet, I'll fuck all the monsters, because why the hell not?

He groans in pleasure, his hands squeezing me tightly. "You're entering a point of no return, little human."

I grind against him and nip his neck. "Did it bother you to see Nero with me?" I ask.

His fingers squeeze my ass almost to the point of pain. "You speak his name while you're in my arms?"

"Were you jealous?" I ask, ignoring his question.

"This is a bad idea," he says and then leans down to breathe against my neck. "Yes, I was jealous. He made you blush so easily."

"How jealous?" He doesn't answer, so I grab his face, trusting him to hold me up. "Grimus, how jealous?"

His jaw clenches, his chest heaving with emotion. "Cora—"

"Tell me," I demand, getting in his face. "You can't hide your emotions and then get mad at me for still seeing them."

"Fine," he snarls, sliding his hand up my back and tangling it almost painfully in my hair. He grips my locks at my scalp and tightens his hold. "I was jealous enough to rip you away from him and fuck you right there," he says, and my body tightens. "I wanted to slide into your wet cunt and show him whom you belong to and claim you as they all watched."

"Yes," I murmur, grinding against him beneath the water.

"I wanted to fuck you until you creamed around me, until you begged me to stop, until you were covered in my seed, so all monsters would know they had to deal with me if they hurt you."

"Shadows, yes." I groan. "Grimus."

"Fuck!" he growls, and then his lips are on mine in a brutal, aggressive kiss.

I gasp, his tongue sweeping inside the moment I do. I kiss him back just as frantically, my pussy wet at the thought of what he'll feel like inside me. His fingers clench tightly in my hair, directing my head where he wants it to go, taking control.

Reaching between us, I slide my hands beneath the water and over his abdomen, tracing down until I find his hard length through the pants he wears. The leather is stiff from the water, but the ties are easy enough to tug loose. The moment I pull on them, his massive cock springs free, and I gasp against him at the sheer size.

Fuck, is that even going to fit?

Grimus moves us against the side of the spring and presses me back so he can release me. He tugs at his pants, pulling them off completely so he's only left in the leather harness stretching across his expansive chest.

Fuck, he's hot and so completely different with his bowed, hairy legs and horns.

I stroke his cock, my hand too small to wrap completely around him as I slide down to the base and continue until I feel his massive balls.

"Keep touching me that way, and you're going to be screaming," he warns against my lips.

"Isn't that the point?" I rasp out, not pausing in my exploration.

With a growl, he pulls back and drops me so I'm floating in the water again, but he doesn't back away. Instead, he reaches for the neckline of my slip. Before I know what he's doing, he rips it in two, the tiny material not standing a chance against his hands.

It's the hottest thing I've ever seen.

"You'll never need this again," he rumbles, throwing the uniform of the hunt somewhere else in the room. It makes a wet plop.

Grimus looks down at me, at my breasts floating in the water, and he groans. "Fuck, you're just as beautiful as I imagined." His hands span my rib cage, coming around to cup my breasts before pinching my nipples. "And the bite of magic on your skin threatens to make me finish alone."

His hand comes up to circle my neck like jewelry and squeezes just a little, revealing the strength he holds back. His other hand dips beneath the water, forces open my thighs, and strokes up my slit, the wetness there drawing a groan from his lips.

"Grimus," I beg, rubbing against his hand, desperate for him to touch me. "Please." I reach up and grab one of his horns, holding on, and he jerks against me, his cock begging for attention. "Please."

His fingers probe my entrance before one slips inside, then he adds two more too quickly so I feel a bite of pain, but I'm desperate for it. I just want him to be inside me, to fill me up and make good on his promise.

"You're so tight," he rumbles. "So perfect."

"Please," I murmur, needing him inside me more than I need my next breath. The electricity along his skin seems to zing into mine until I'm rocking on his fingers, riding them as he watches me. His mouth dips to the water, lapping the beads from my breasts. The sight is so erotic that my eyes slide closed and my head falls back. I trust him to keep me up, to give me what I need, as I relax. His tongue dances across my nipple before pulling it into his mouth and sucking. At the same time, his fingers pull from my channel and slam back in, pushing me back into the spring's wall.

"Oh, shadows." I groan, trying to move closer and take more.

With a snarl, he nips my nipple before pushing my breasts together and licking and nipping both of them. Pleasure arcs between my aching nipples and throbbing clit. "So soft, so pretty. You are so tiny, I don't think you will even fit me." He lifts his head, a wicked look in his eyes. "But you will, you will take every inch of my cock. I will make sure of it." With that, he adds another finger, stretching me so hard, it hurts. Yet that pain only makes me cry out, my pussy throbbing around his fingers.

"Please, please." I don't even know what I'm begging for anymore, but he does. His hand slips down my body, across my hips, to my pussy. Watching my face, he slides the blunt tip of his fingers across my pussy, stilling when he catches my slit and I cry out. Grinning, he drops his head and swallows my cries as he attacks my clit until that all-consuming feeling explodes through me.

My mouth falls from his with a scream that echoes around the chamber, my pussy clamping on his fingers as I move my hips. He watches me the entire time, smoke curling from his nose before he suddenly pulls his fingers free, making me whimper. He lifts them to his mouth and sucks them clean.

"Delicious," he snarls, grabbing me again. "I can't wait. I need you too badly, little human. I need to hear you scream like that again and feel your wet heat around me."

He grabs his cock in his hand and presses it against my opening as I crane my neck to watch. The sight of his monstrous cock pressed against my human pussy is more exciting than it should be. I hold my breath at the stretch as he pushes inside and the subsequent bite of pain that comes from something so large sliding inside me. I mewl in pleasure, trying to rock against him, but he moves slowly at first, gently easing inside me as if he's afraid to hurt me, so I do the only thing I can think of to make him hurry up.

"I bet Nero would already be fucking me," I say, a dangerous dig.

Grimus' nostrils flare, and his eyes narrow, and I know I've made trouble for myself. With his hand still around my throat and the other on my waist, Grimus pins me against the side of the spring and thrusts inside me, stretching until I cry out in pain. My cry is cut off by his lips, his teeth pulling at my bottom lip until I taste blood. He pulls out and thrusts into me again, splitting me in half, and I still ask for more.

"Grimus," I cry, holding onto his horn with one hand and clinging to his shoulder with the other as he starts to fuck me hard against the wall. The water sloshes around us and splashes out, glistening like little jewels on his body in a way that makes me want to lick them off.

His hand begins to squeeze my neck. "Say his name again," he threatens, his balls slapping against me with each thrust, adding to the feeling. Pleasure slams through me, and my body heats dangerously, even as I try to ride him harder, desperate for more. "I dare you."

Maybe I have a death wish.

"Nero," I rasp out, despite his hand on my throat. "Zetros. Bracken."

He bares his teeth at me and squeezes tighter, cutting off my air. "You're going to scream my name," he demands. "Or I'm going to fuck you until you can't scream at all."

I seal my lips shut, my pussy clenching tightly around his length, and at those words and the lack of air supply, my body tenses. He releases my neck just as the orgasm slams into me and I scream out in pleasure, clawing at his back.

But I don't scream his name.

"Stubborn. Little. Human," he snarls with each thrust, rocking me hard.

He grabs me waist and steps up on the stone step to the left, lifting me out of the water, but he doesn't pull out of me. He continues to fuck me as he lays me on the edge of the pool, my legs dangling in the water as he comes over me, fucking me into the ground.

"You're going to wear my cum on your skin," he promises, his thighs slapping against mine, the sound echoing in the large room.

"Yes," I cry, reaching for him. When I try to grab his horns again, he grabs my wrists and pins them over my head with one hand, holding me hostage as he fucks me harder.

"Release your magic," he orders.

The next orgasm begins to rise in my body, curling higher as he slides in and out of me, the chilly air pebbling my nipples as they beg for attention.

"I don't know how!"

"Let go!" he snarls. "Now come."

He plays my body like a fiddle, and I explode around him, my pussy milking his cock for the second time, but he still doesn't stop, driving me higher and taking everything.

"Once more," he says, leaning in to pull one of my nipples into his mouth. "Scream or I'm going to keep fucking you long into the night."

Exhaustion is already pulling at my body. I won't last much longer. The rising tide moves closer and threatens to finish me as he pumps harder inside me, faster, his nostrils flaring with each thrust as he looks down at me with desire and claims me like I've never been claimed.

My minotaur.

He reaches down and rubs my clit, stroking circles around it, and I begin to scream as he pulls the orgasm out.

"Grimus!" I cry, begging for release, begging for him. "Grimus!"

He grins down at me, pleased. "Good girl," he murmurs and flicks my clit one more time. I shatter, only this time, it's no normal release.

Something rises within me, and the flames of the candles around us grow larger and begin to spark as I shatter into a million pieces, Grimus' name on my lips as I let go. The air becomes electric, illuminating the room as light explodes out of me and slams into Grimus. He grunts in pleasure and roars as magic consumes both of us.

He jerks out of me, his hot cum spurting across my abdomen as he coats me just like he promised, shot after shot until I'm covered from my chest down.

The candles all go out at the same time.

I'm panting, my limbs growing heavy as I lie here and stare up at him. He stares down at me in return, his expression softening at the look of wonder on my face. "Beautiful," he whispers. "You're beautiful."

Someone whistles, and we both look up to find Nero sliding into another spring. Bracken and Zetros are standing against the wall. Every single one of their gazes is filled with heat.

"Don't look at me," Zetros says. "It was the fey's fault. He said he heard screams, and we thought you might be in trouble."

Bracken grins like he knew exactly what kind of screams he heard.

Grimus chuckles on a breath and scoops me up, pulling me back inside the water. "You're lucky I have a woman to attend to, or I'd get out of this spring and beat you," he teases.

"Oh, I'm so scared," Bracken responds with a grin. "Save me, Goldie, before the big bad minotaur gets me."

I giggle and nuzzle closer to Grimus, despite my cheeks flaming red. My body throbs from my releases, but mostly from the magic that sang in my blood and exploded out of me.

Now, I just have to figure out how to do it again.

CHAPTER SIXTEEN

I sleep so soundly, with no dreams or nightmares, that I wake up refreshed, and I wonder where I am for a moment. It takes me five long minutes to pull myself completely awake and realize why I'm so comfortable. I slept in Grimus' arms, nestled against his warm side, with Bracken and Zetros near, but at some point in the night, Nero had twined around all of us, his coils forming a sort of nest that we're all inside. He lies on top of his coils, hanging over the side nearest me, his arm just a hairsbreadth away from touching my own arm, as if he wanted to touch but didn't want to without permission.

Smiling at the scene, I begin to move, attempting to withdraw myself from the warm bodies, but Grimus pulls me in tighter and cracks his eye open.

"Settle down, little human," he grumbles.

I giggle and pull harder. "I have to relieve myself."

Grudgingly, he lets me go, and then I have to climb over Bracken's reaching arm, Zetros' large form, and Nero's piled coils. It's a task, especially with the soreness between my legs, each movement pulling on my pussy in a deliciously painful way that reminds me of just what —no, *whom* I did last night. Nero opens his eyes when I touch his body, a smile pulling at his lips as I straddle him and slide over. As I step away, I trail my hand across his scales in a teasing caress. When he hums low in his throat, I flush and go to relieve myself like I planned. When I return, everyone is getting ready, preparing for the trip to the mountains.

"We're almost there," Grimus says when I reappear dressed in Nero's clothing. His eyes drop down to the outfit, and I can see his admiration for the quality, despite his clear jealousy.

I tug at the shirt that hardly looks like it's made out of snakeskin and smile. Nero, it seems, knows my exact sizing. The pants hug my form, the scales creating a sheen as I walk. I wondered if they would be see through, but whatever magic Nero worked means they are not. They fit my legs all the way to my ankles and come up to my waist. The top is looser, flowing around my midsection, and though you can't see through the outfit, it's certainly breezy. Anytime I walk into the light, I'm reminded of Nero, because of the scales and their sparkle. It's beautiful, and yet the outfit looks like it's meant for a warrior.

I don't have proper shoes, but I slide on the leather slippers Grimus made me. They'll have to do for now, even though they are starting to get worn.

"Do you think we can make it there by tonight?" I ask.

"It depends on our pace," Grimus answers, and I know what he means by that—it depends on whether or not I'm able to keep up.

Nero perks up. "I can give you a ride, and we can make it there within hours."

I turn with furrowed brows. "A ride?"

His eyes meet mine, and he grins. "My body is plenty large enough. You simply sit on a length of my body and ride there. I move far faster than you do." He winks at Bracken. "It'll be a struggle for the others to keep up."

"I don't want to inconvenience you—"

"Nonsense," Nero argues. "You're so slight, it's no hindrance at all. We can make it to the mountain pass in a few hours if we do it my way."

Grimus seems to grunt in agreement. "You'll ride. It's better to arrive in the orc kingdom in what little light we have than in the dark." He glances at Bracken. "That way, the fey can handle his affairs."

Bracken shifts as if he's uncomfortable, but his grin completely counteracts the movement. "Daylight is better, yes."

And that's how I find myself riding on the back of a naga like he's a gilded horse. Honestly, Nero is far cooler than any horse in the Gilded Lands I've managed to see. We don't have them in the Shadow Lands, only other types of livestock. Horses are relegated to the rich and powerful, like the king, but I have a feeling if I returned to the Shadow Lands on the back of Nero, his scales shining for all to see, there would be a proper commotion.

I kind of want to see the king piss himself.

I thought riding on Nero's back would be uncomfortable, but it's the complete opposite. I've never put much thought into how Nero would move, but when I see him, his human body erect in front of me, the snake body twisting back and forth to propel him forward, it's almost majestic. He has me ride just behind his human torso, my hands on either side of his waist to keep myself steady, and as he moves, the muscles tensing, I find myself getting wet at the vibrations. When he looks over his shoulder at me with a knowing gaze, I flush and try desperately to mask my feelings.

It's difficult to do with monsters who have a heightened sense of smell.

Grimus, Bracken, and Zetros don't have as much trouble keeping up as Nero made it seem they would. Either Nero is purposely keeping pace for them, or they are faster than he thinks. I decide it's the former when the mountains rise high above us, casting their shadows until the world grows darker, though it's only been a few hours.

Nero slithers to a stop at the base of the mountains, at the entrance of the pass, and I slide off his back, my legs numb from so much riding. When I stumble and nearly fall, his arms are there to catch me, making sure I'm okay, his fingers lingering until he releases me.

"Thank you," I murmur, stomping some feeling back into my feet.

"Of course, *parum anguis*," he replies.

When he doesn't reach out for me again, I smile and thread my fingers with his. His hands are twice as large as mine, dwarfing them, but the cool warmth his provides makes me want to be wrapped in his coils again.

Bracken straightens, his eyes hard, and somehow, I notice the look first. Zetros is busy stretching and drinking some of the saltwater he collected in a canteen. Grimus is digging through his pack for something. Nero is so focused on me, he's not looking anywhere else, but Bracken? He's sniffing the air.

I see the moment his eyes widen. "Protect her," he hisses.

There are no questions, no demand to know what's wrong. One moment, they are all doing their own thing, and the next, I find myself in the center of them. Nero keeps hold of me, his eyes sharp, his coils circling our little group as an extra form of protection. I don't like that he'll be the first one in danger should something attack, but he seems intent on being there. Bracken, Zetros, and Grimus are around me a moment later, their bodies blocking me in like a wall.

The orcs appear seconds later...or what I am guessing are orcs, since Grim mentioned them.

At first, there's only one. He steps into the low light, his skin green, even in the shadows. He's wearing armor over impressive muscles. Large teeth sprout from his bottom lip and curl over his top. His hair is braided down his spine, and he's carrying a large club. The moment he steps out, more follow, until we're surrounded by orcs.

Grimus shoulders Bracken. "Do your thing, fey."

I see the panic on Bracken's face, and suddenly, I know he lied about having a deal with the orcs. I can't blame him, but I'm still annoyed that he got us into this position with no way out.

"About that..." He has a shit-eating grin on his face when he looks at Grimus.

Grimus' eyes flare in anger, but he doesn't speak of it right now. "You better have a plan."

We're surrounded by orcs, at least a dozen of them, and they are all large in nature. Though our group is growing, I don't think we can fight them all, but I don't underestimate my monsters. I understand, however, that if we kill them, the orc king will certainly never let us pass peacefully. Even if they are monsters, that seems obvious, especially after the stories Grim told me last night to help me fall asleep. He fears the orc warriors, but the king? Grimus spoke of him in hushed, respectful tones, and that is enough to make me afraid.

Bracken steps forward, his arms open in placation. "Ballow, friend, it's been a long time." The orc Bracken addresses is one of the bigger ones. He's wearing a necklace made of bones—they look human. "Think you could pull some strings and get us through?"

"The last time I saw you," Ballow responds, "you were running away after insulting my bride."

"I didn't know she was your bride," Bracken defends. "I thought she was your brother."

Ballow snarls and goes to step forward, but Grimus stomps his hoof, making the orc pause.

"Now's a good time to do something," Grimus rumbles at Bracken.

Bracken laughs, and without missing a beat, shoves Grimus forward, sending the orcs into defense mode. They swarm, and Grimus snarls at Bracken.

"This was your plan?" he snarls. "Throw me at them?"

Bracken narrowly avoids the club that nearly knocks him out. "I didn't think that far ahead, okay?"

"Don't hurt them!" I exclaim when Nero rises up, prepared to strike. "Lift me."

Nero does so without question. His strong arms circle my thighs, and he lifts me high so that all the orcs can see. Too many of them blink in confusion, as if they hadn't noticed me in the center. My monsters did a good job of protecting me.

"We request an audience with the orc king," I say, making sure they are all looking at me, even though I'm making this up as I go.

Ballow steps forward, his face twisted in a snarl. "And who are you to request such an audience?"

"I am the hunt." I don't know how much weight it will carry, but when their mouths go slack, I can only assume it carries something. I can imagine that no hunt has made it this far, and here I am with a group of monsters, seeking an audience with their king for safe passage. I thought Bracken would be the one to do it, but it looks like it'll be up to me.

"The hunts never make it this far," Ballow argues, his eyes narrowed.

"And yet here I am." My words are full of confidence, not because they need to be but because I'm putting on a show. If I appear strong, like I made it here because of that strength, perhaps it'll go a long way with the orcs. "Do you agree to an audience?"

Ballow glances at the others. "Fine. Let the king disembowel you." He glares at Bracken. "Perhaps he'll give me the pleasure of taking care of the fey myself."

Bracken only finger waves at him, as if it's all a joke.

The orcs gesture for us to move, circling us, and they all stay as close to me as possible once Nero lowers me. We walk slowly through the mountain pass, my eyes trailing over the stone walls around us. There's only one way in, which means if they betray us, we'll have to go out the same way we came in or through. I don't think we'll be able to scale these cliffs.

When the walls begin to trail away and then open up completely, I stare down in surprise at the city that appears in the valley of the mountains. I expected something rough and orc-like. Instead, the city looks to be in better shape than the Shadow Lands.

"The orcs are great builders," Zetros offers at my amazement. "They produce fast and take care of their own. Most monsters prefer solitude. Orcs form groups, and it appears they have been thriving."

In the center of the city is a large castle, where sharp spires curve up and around like the teeth the orcs have. It's dark and dangerous-looking, and yet somehow also inviting in a strange way. That is where the orcs lead us. People along the streets pause to watch our movements, their eyes lingering on my monsters but widening when they see me in their midst. Here, it isn't the monsters who are odd, it's me.

Once inside the castle, we're brought toward a large room, and my eyes go to the male who straightens on his throne. He's broad, and his shoulders are so wide, I doubt I could hold onto the muscle there. He wears no shirt, all his musculature on display. He's wearing a collar of some sort, decorated with bones and jewels, and there is a similar belt around his waist sitting above his pants. The teeth that poke from his lip are larger than most of the others, curling up and away. His skin is an olive green, beautiful even if it's riddled with pink scars. One of those scars cuts down over his eye and across his cheek. It's a wonder he didn't lose the eye.

"Why have you brought these beasts here?" the orc demands, standing up. He's tall, but Zetros is still taller.

I slip forward, drawing his eyes, and his gaze widens. "They have brought us at my request. We'd like an audience with you."

"A human," he rumbles. "I'd hoped you were all extinguished in the Dead Lands."

"I'm the hunt," I say instead, because that seems to make a difference. "We require passage through the mountains."

His eyes narrow and focus on the monsters around me. "A trick."

"No trick," I retort. "We'll leave in peace if you let us pass."

He straightens. "No human ever comes or leaves in peace." The words ring with the truth of this land, and I don't have words to argue, because I don't know what would make a difference.

"I give you my word," I vow.

"Your word means nothing," he spits out, but his eyes linger on my hips, on my breasts, and on the way Nero's clothing fits me. "And look at these fools helping you." His eyes linger on Grimus, as if he's confused why he's there. "The only proper fate for the group of you is death."

Panic fills me. "Wait—"

"Throw them in the dungeons! We'll make a show of it tomorrow!" he shouts, and the other orcs roar their approval.

"Grimus," I rasp out, looking toward him.

"It'll be okay, little human," he assures me, but I see the panic in his eyes. The orc numbers are too great for us to take on. There's no way.

Nero hisses at the orcs who step forward, and they take a step back, uncertain. They give a wide berth to Zetros, none of them daring to raise a weapon when he simply stares at them with black eyes.

"We'll go willingly," I say, "with the promise that you'll think of our offer."

The orc king watches me in contemplation, his fingers on his chin. "What have you to offer?"

"Can't you feel her magic?" Bracken asks, shaking his head. "If you can't, perhaps these years inside the mountains have made you blind to the obvious."

At Bracken's words, the orc king tilts his head and studies me closer. Whatever he sees must make him pause, because he freezes and glances at one of the other orcs. "I'll think on your offer," he says finally, and then waves his hand to dismiss us.

This time, we don't fight the orcs who lead us toward our cells, much to Grimus' annoyance.

"I don't like going into a prison without a fight," he grumbles.

"It's only temporary," I promise, hoping that I'm right.

"Until he kills us," Zetros grumbles. "Well, tries to."

"You'll split up," one of the orcs orders when we reach the prison cells. He holds a weapon out. I don't tell him that weapon wouldn't do any good against any of my monsters.

Zetros crosses his arms. "I will not be split from the hunt."

The orc grimaces. "The king said—"

Zetros tilts his head to the side. "Would you like to try and separate us and see what happens, orc pup?"

The orc's eyes widen, the color draining from his face. It seems even here, Zetros is feared. "Fine," he rasps out. "But the others are separate."

That's how I find myself in a prison cell with Zetros, his fingers tangled with mine. Nero is squished into the cell that isn't quite big enough for his form, his coils wrapped around in a pile that he lies on. Bracken immediately lies down in his cell and goes to sleep, but Grimus paces, anxiety in his movements.

"It'll be okay, Grimus," I say, trying to calm him down.

His eyes meet mine, and though he nods, I can see he doesn't believe my words.

That alone makes my heart skip a beat, and panic fills my own body.

Zetros pulls me closer, and I wrap myself around him, absorbing his warmth just in case everything isn't okay.

Just in case this is the end of the line.

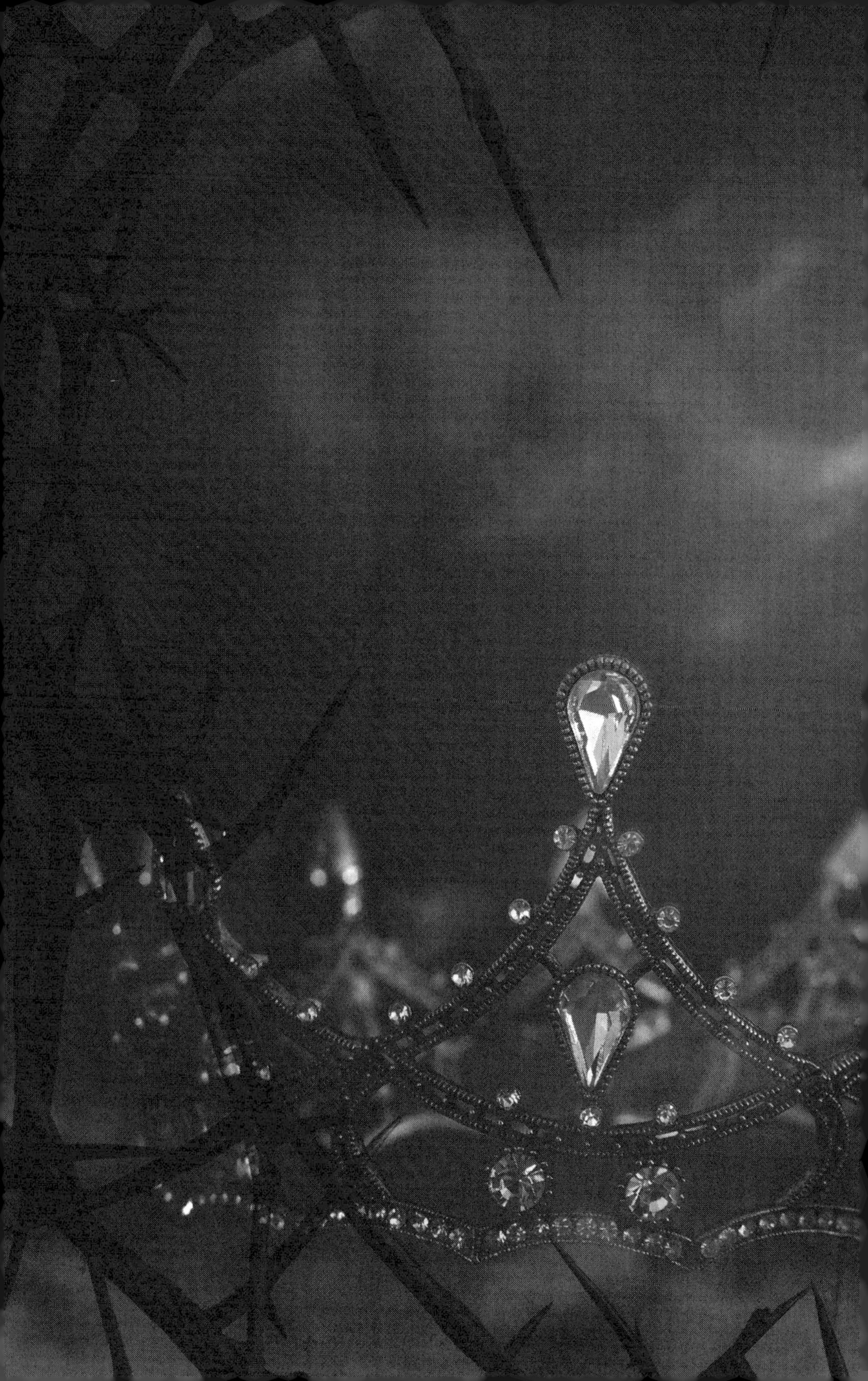

CHAPTER
SEVENTEEN

Being an orc prisoner is surprisingly boring. I can hear music, laughter, and chatter, and the ceilings of our cells seems to shake with their movements, but other than that, we are left alone. The gates are clearly made of bone, so I avoid them at all costs, sinking deeper into the small cell and into Zetros' side. He doesn't complain. In fact, when I move closer, he chuckles and just picks me up, settling me on his lap. His huge thighs are warm and comfy, so I lay my head against his chest, listening to his heartbeat.

I offered them magic, and the king didn't seem to care enough to let us live. It's clear they hate humans. Maybe I need to understand why so I can offer a good deal. Our lives depend on it.

"Zee?" I lift my head.

He grins widely at his shortened name. "Yes, *measma*?" he purrs as I sit up, straddling his legs.

"The orcs recognized you, right?" His face closes down, but I surge ahead, knowing the others are listening in their own cells nearby. "You recognized the king. I saw it."

"I did. I knew him a very long time ago," he responds, watching me carefully. "Why?"

"Where did you recognize him from? Do you know why he hates humans so much? What can I offer him?"

"We do not speak of another's past. That is his story and his story alone," he mutters, looking away from me.

"Please, Zee. I don't know how else we will make it out of here," I beg.

I see him debating his options, so I stay quiet. Finally, he slumps, glancing away for a moment. "I'm assuming you have figured out some things about my past already. Well, that is where I know him from. He was held captive at the same time I was, not in the naga lands but in a much worse place. His own leader at the time handed him over. He was just a boy, so young, but the king demanded one of their kind be given to the humans for their...entertainment." The way he sneers the word has me tensing, and a sick feeling starts to build in my stomach. "I was already numb at that time, having spent years of being passed around as a slave to my king's whims and the humans' desires. But he? He fought. He raged. He hated. He was so filled with emotion, and I had no choice but to watch as it destroyed him. The punishments he was given for disobeying..." He shakes his head. "His eye? That was because he killed a human when they chained him up and tried to mount him like an animal. That's all they thought of us as—animals bought for their amusement to fuck, kill, and eat. They did whatever they pleased, and the king allowed it. But that night, the orc who now holds the throne had enough. He refused to perform, he refused to be a plaything. Unlike most of us, who had given up, he never did. So yes, he killed that human, and he suffered for it greatly. I don't know what they did to him exactly. I only saw him once more, many years later, and he had changed so much. He had to be caged at all times, almost feral. As for the scars you see, who knows what they used him for. I can guess, but it was nothing good, *measma*."

I swallow, tears falling down my face at the true extent of what Zee, the orc king, and other monsters went through. Of course they hate us. How could they not? Zetros leans forward and licks the tears away, causing a shiver to run up my spine. It forces me out of my mind so I can focus on the present rather than a past I can't change, no matter how much I'd like to.

"So yes, he hates humans as much as I do."

It makes sense now, and I realize there is probably nothing I can offer the orc that he will want more than my death, but something else sticks with me—his confession.

What happened to Zetros makes me feel sick, angry, and furious. I want to kill all those who hurt him, but I have to know something first.

"Do you hate me?" I croak out, meeting this gaze.

"I should, but I do not. I cannot explain it. I was drawn to you, and despite everything your people have done to me, I couldn't hate you. Not ever, *measma*."

I hear the truth in his words. "I'm sorry for what my people did to you, to all of you." I shake my head, balling my hands into fists. "They are the monsters, not you, and if I could, I'd make them all pay. I cannot change what they did, but I can prove I'm not like them. I will never hurt you or take what is not given. I will protect you," I promise. I move to slide from his lap, not wanting to bring back any bad memories. I've been too forward and expected too much.

"Where are you going?" he demands, gripping my hips to keep me in his lap. The strength in his hands makes it impossible for me to move and has me shivering in a way I didn't expect. My kraken is hot, there's no doubt about it, and I had been debating just giving in to my wild desires like I did with Grim, but I won't. Not after he's been used so brutally by humans. I refuse to be another one who hurts him.

His eyes flash with a storm, like waves crashing against the shoreline, bursting above the rocks as he stares at me. He lowers his head when I don't answer, and when his voice comes again, it's like thunder, reminding me he's not a man. He's a monster. "I said, where are you going?"

"I didn't want to be like them—"

I gasp as he drags me down until our bodies are pressed together, one hand tilting my head back to look at him. Those stormy eyes lock on me as he leans in, his lips almost touching mine as he speaks. "You could never be like them. Yes, for a moment, when I saw you, all I saw was the people who had hurt me, but then you smiled at me. You spoke to me, and you became you. You became Cora. You became my *measma*. You could never be like them, and you're not. You are not human anymore, you are ours. You are part of the Dead Lands." He licks my lips, making my eyes widen. "Which makes you part monster in my eyes, and all mine right now."

"Zetros—"

"Say my name again," he murmurs, closing his eyes as he uses my hips to drag me back and forth across his hard cock, which I can feel pressing against my already awake and needy pussy. He has me throbbing and groaning as I press my hands to his chest, desperate for more but almost afraid to take it. Shaking my head, I try to push back the desire, not wanting to rush this with him. He needs time for him to be sure.

"Zetros," I say again, about to stop this, but it seems hearing his name on my lips is what unleashes the beast. One second, I'm astride him, and the next, I'm on my back in our cell with him hovering above me, his lips twisted in a snarl. He might look like a man right now, but when he presses his nose to my neck and inhales, he's just a beast. A groan vibrates through his body, and I feel it in my core, making me shiver below him.

"We made a deal to taste your magic, *measma*," he rumbles as I swallow. "And I plan to claim my price right now."

"But—"

I don't get time to finish. He cuts me off by slamming his lips to mine. I gasp in surprise, and he sweeps his tongue inside, tangling it with mine, tasting every inch of my surrender. That's what this is—I surrender to him. I stop trying to make his decision for him and just trust that this ancient kraken knows what he wants.

And it seems to be me.

He tastes like the wild, deep sea, like a storm brewing on the horizon as it moves closer, preparing to violently topple trees and flood whole cities. Zetros is all chaotic waves and violent riptides. Everything inside of me wants to be caught in his current and pulled beneath the waves of his consciousness, and if there's one thing I know, it's that I would happily let him pull me under.

Blood pumps through my body, awakening every inch of me. That same call I felt to the water pulls me now, forcing my heart into overdrive, every sensation tripled as I whimper. The ocean consumes me, swallows me whole.

When he pulls back, I have to force my eyes open, seeing a satisfied smirk pulling at his lips. "Thank the waves you've stopped trying to be good." Leaning back down, he licks my lips before dragging his lips to my ear. "I much prefer you bad. Now lie back and let me taste the magic like you promised."

"By all means, don't let me stop you," I mumble, reaching out to stroke his shoulders and down his back. He groans, his eyes sliding shut, and shivers under my touch. It's heady to watch such a powerful man be weak for me, so I lean up and nip his chin, making his eyes fly wide. "Better hurry, kraken. Who knows when the orcs will be back."

He wastes no more time. Spurred on by my teasing, he licks and nips down my neck, making me moan as I drag my nails up the corded muscle of his neck and through his hair, holding onto the wavy strands as he tastes every inch of me like he will die if he doesn't.

For a moment, I worry about the others watching, I worry about Grim's reaction, but when I turn my head and meet his eyes through the bars of the cell, he just smirks and doesn't look away. Even as Zetros pulls down my pants, licking down my legs and back up, Grim's desire continues to flicker in his eyes.

Zetros pulls my eyes back to him when he nips my thigh. "Eyes on me, *measma*, always on me."

I want to make a pun about him being used to wet environments, but all thoughts flee my mind when his mouth seals over my pussy and he starts to eat me like a starving man—er, beast. My back arches off the floor, and my eyes slam shut, especially when he drags his tongue from my clit to my ass and back, tasting every inch of me.

"Delicious, just like I knew you would be. Sweet. Soft and so pretty."

He groans, settling his big shoulders between my thighs and rolling his eyes up to mine. "I can almost taste the magic." He drops his mouth back to my pussy, licking and sucking me like it's his last meal. He flicks my clit before plunging his tongue inside me and fucking me with it, and I'm helpless.

I reach down and tangle my hands in his hair, pulling him closer as I throw my legs over his shoulders and grind into his tongue, needing more, needing everything. He doesn't go easy on me. He pulls his tongue free and thrusts two fingers inside me, curling them and stroking them inside me with expert movements. At the same time, his lips wrap around my clit and suck, and all the pleasure, all the need, explodes through me in an orgasm I didn't even feel coming. It rips through me, and he seals his mouth to my hole, sucking and drinking in my release and the magic that pulses from me like a physical wave.

He doesn't stop licking me until I push him away, oversensitive and breathing so heavily, it's embarrassing. Flopping to my back, I force my eyes open as he crawls up my body and kisses me softly, letting me taste myself on his lips.

Sweet and wild, just like he said.

He starts to pull away, and I frown, lifting my legs and wrapping them around his waist. "Where the hell do you think you're going, kraken?" I demand.

"I got my taste—that was our deal," he murmurs, glancing away.

I grab his face and jerk his gaze back to mine. "Then we make a new deal or no deal at all. I don't care, but fuck me already," I tell him and then hold my breath, wondering if I've pushed him too far, but the smile that blooms on his face is like the sun breaking through the darkness that exists for everyone in the Dead Lands.

"No deal. We don't need it anymore between us. Just desire." He leans down and kisses me hard, stealing all my words before lifting up. "You saw my cock, Cora," he purrs, licking my lips. "But did you know what my stilma are for?"

I'm having a really hard time following the conservation, but I shake my head.

"Stilma?" I reply raggedly.

"Tentacles, I believe you called them." He nips my lips as I rock my hips against his hard length, needing it inside me more than I need my next breath. "Well, they bring pleasure too. Shall I show you?"

"I—Fuck, yes," I mutter, eyes wide as he sits back on his knees and quickly strips so he's naked above me. He's so achingly beautiful, he looks like a god coming to steal my innocence. Even the small tentacles around his hard cock have me aching for him, because those differences just make him...him.

My kraken.

My Zetros.

I meet his eyes, and my chest warms as I see his need there, his pain, his hunger.

Wrenching my gaze from his stormy eyes, I look down at his cock and his...*stilma*. They wiggle like hands, and for a moment, I'm scared before I decide to lie back and embrace all of him. I refuse to look away as he lies between my legs. He kisses me softly, as if in thanks, and then I jerk at the first touch of his stilma. One tentacle strokes my pussy, almost petting me, and it should be weird and off-putting, but the soft yet sturdy feel of it has me moaning and grinding into that length.

"Oh, shit," I whisper, and then I scream into his mouth when that stilma moves higher. It has suckers like an actual tentacle, and it seals over my clit.

And sucks hard.

Chuckling, he breaks the kiss as the constant suction has me grinding into his cock, dripping all over him. Incomprehensible words roll off my tongue as my eyes almost cross at the pressure. "I thought you might like that," he purrs. "And it will stay there while I fuck this tight little pussy, sucking you the entire time until you come so many times you can't think, never mind sass me."

He's right—I can't think, let alone speak, and when I feel the blunt tip of his cock at my entrance, I let out a whine.

"*Measma*," he purrs as he leans down and kisses me. At the same time, he jerks his hips and slams into me. The sudden invasion of his huge length mixed with the suction has me seeing stars. I explode in another orgasm, and he kisses me through it, holding me tight. "Good girl," he praises, peppering my face with featherlight kisses, stilling inside of me as I pant and writhe beneath him. "Such a good girl, taking all of me. That's it, relax for me. Good girl."

"Fucking move!" I demand, kicking his ass as I wrap my legs and arms around him and try to take him deeper. That constant sucking on my oversensitive clit builds me back up again, making me crazed.

He pulls out and hammers back in, making me cry out, so I lean forward and bite his shoulder to muffle my sounds, groaning into his skin. He pulls me away gently and sits back, his teeth bared and neck strained as he hoists my legs up and starts to pound into me in rough, brutal strokes that push me harder onto his stilma.

His cock isn't solid like normal, no. When he slides it inside me, it's hard like steel, but then it seems to move of its own accord, growing, twisting, and seeking until I realize there's a sucker there too. It latches onto that spot inside me that has me screaming.

My knees are up in the air, my legs held in his grip, and then he starts to move again, smirking down at me as the sucker detaches before his cock slides out and back in.

"Oh god!" I try to cut off the scream, but it's no use, so instead, I lift my arm and bite into the skin there, not wanting the orcs to come investigate. Absolute bliss pounds through me from his talented stilma. It spirals higher and higher, never ebbing, even after I come three times. It leaves me boneless, just able to cry out as he pulls more and more pleasure from my body with each draw on my clit.

My eyes widen as another sucker slides down my ass and, before I can protest, the tentacle parts my cheeks and seals against my hole, sucking, throbbing, and pulsing.

I scream harder, fracturing around him.

Groaning, he fights my milking channel, watching me explode for him, and then, with a snarl, he flips me. He drags my ass into the air and pummels into me, his balls slapping against me as he takes me. I scratch at the floor, my back bowing as I push back to meet him. Both of his stilma still work me as his incredible cock fills me.

"*Measma.*" He grunts. "So beautiful, so perfect." He groans. "So close—Waves, you feel too good," he rumbles, and in the next second, his hips stutter and then he slams so hard inside me, it almost hurts. That internal sucker latches on, driving me higher as he comes with a hoarse yell, filling me with his release. At the same time, the stilma at my ass slides inside me, triggering another release that has my entire body giving out as I squirt around him.

I ride the waves of pleasure that never seem to stop until he gently pulls out of me and removes his stilma. He lets me collapse with a whimper before gathering me in his arms, kissing my shoulder and neck. He murmurs words of praise only for my ears, making me smile, even as I try to stay awake.

I struggle to breathe, my body limp and floating, but I start to come back when I hear clapping.

Furrowing my brow, I force my eyes open and turn my head to see the others at the doors of their cells, all watching, and Bracken...Bracken is clapping.

"Bravo, I mean it. I've never had a man, but you really do have me wondering with a talent like that."

I can't help but laugh and look back at Zetros. "Stilma fucking rock," I mutter, and they all laugh with me.

∼

I WISH I could say I sat and made a plan or tried to escape, but in actuality, I just lounge limply in Zee's arms, letting him hold me. My entire body throbs with exhaustion and satisfaction after our coupling.

If we are to die soon, I plan to make the most of it.

"I have a sister," I find myself sharing.

I hear them all moving and know they are listening, but I don't look. I watch the opposite wall. They have given so much of themselves to me, it's only fair I do the same. "She's older than me, but I always protected her, especially from my father." Zee's arms tighten around me, silently offering me comfort. "He's a cruel man." I laugh bitterly. "He loved to beat me. There, I had no life, no decision. I was just property, but my sister? She was happy. She was in love, and then the hunt came and she was selected. I couldn't let it be her. I had already lost hope, lost my way, but she hadn't. I knew I had to save her one last time, so I volunteered." I meet their eyes through the bars, seeing their shock. "I volunteered to come to the Dead Lands, to take her place, because I was already dead inside."

"Goldie," Bracken whispers.

I smile sadly at him. "How strange that in the one place in this land I shouldn't, a place literally called Dead, it's the only place I feel alive? Feel free? I could die at every single moment, yet I've never felt so at home, so at peace. How messed up is that? What I'm trying to say is, even if this is the end, even if I die here, it's okay, because I was supposed to die a long time ago, and at least here and now, it's my choice, and I go to death free and happy. For once, it would be my choice."

"You are not dying here," Grim snaps.

"You're not. We will think of something," Nero adds, but I just smile sadly and lean into a silent Zetros.

"Thank you all for saving me, for staying with me. I wish there were more I could give you back—" Zetros covers my lips.

"Do not say your goodbyes, *measma*, because I'm not. I have survived the unimaginable in this life. I haven't lived thousands of years to give up now, to finally find and lose you. We will survive this, I know it. Just have faith."

"Faith," I murmur. "I don't believe in anything."

"Then believe in yourself, like we all do," he says as we hear it.

"They are coming," Nero hisses.

I get to my feet, not wanting to die on my knees. Looking down, I hold out my hand to Zetros. He takes it, and we move to the bone gate. "Today is as good a day to die as any," I joke.

"Leave the jokes to me, Goldie," Bracken replies as orcs file before us. They open the gates and jerk us out. There are no words, no laughter, as we are marched before the orc king. His face is unreadable as he sits with his legs thrown over the throne's arms and watches us be pushed to our knees before him.

Our lives are held in his hands.

I refuse to die on my knees, that much is true, so I get to my feet. The orc behind me snarls and kicks my knees out, forcing me back down. Snarls ripple around me from my angry monsters, but they don't move, not right now. Gritting my teeth, I get back to my feet, despite knowing I'll probably be kicked again. The orc king watches it happen and holds his hand up when the orc behind me lifts his leg, prepared to kick me again. I don't flinch, but I brace myself.

"Leave her," he murmurs, watching me contemplatively. "You are a brave little thing, and you are right—I taste the magic on you. I felt it when you took one of your men." He licks his lips, and my cheeks flame. "We all did. The pure strength of it..." He shakes his head. "It's not something I have felt in a very long time. It gave me an idea. It gave me hope."

"Hope?" I ask, refusing to be silent when discussing our fates.

"Yes, human, hope—hope that the one who can finally bring back the magic has arrived. So, human, you and your people will be free to go through our pass with my escort if we make a deal. I heard you are good at those."

I blink. "A deal for what?"

His chin is high, but his eyes are hard, leaving no room for argument. "To bring back the magic, of course."

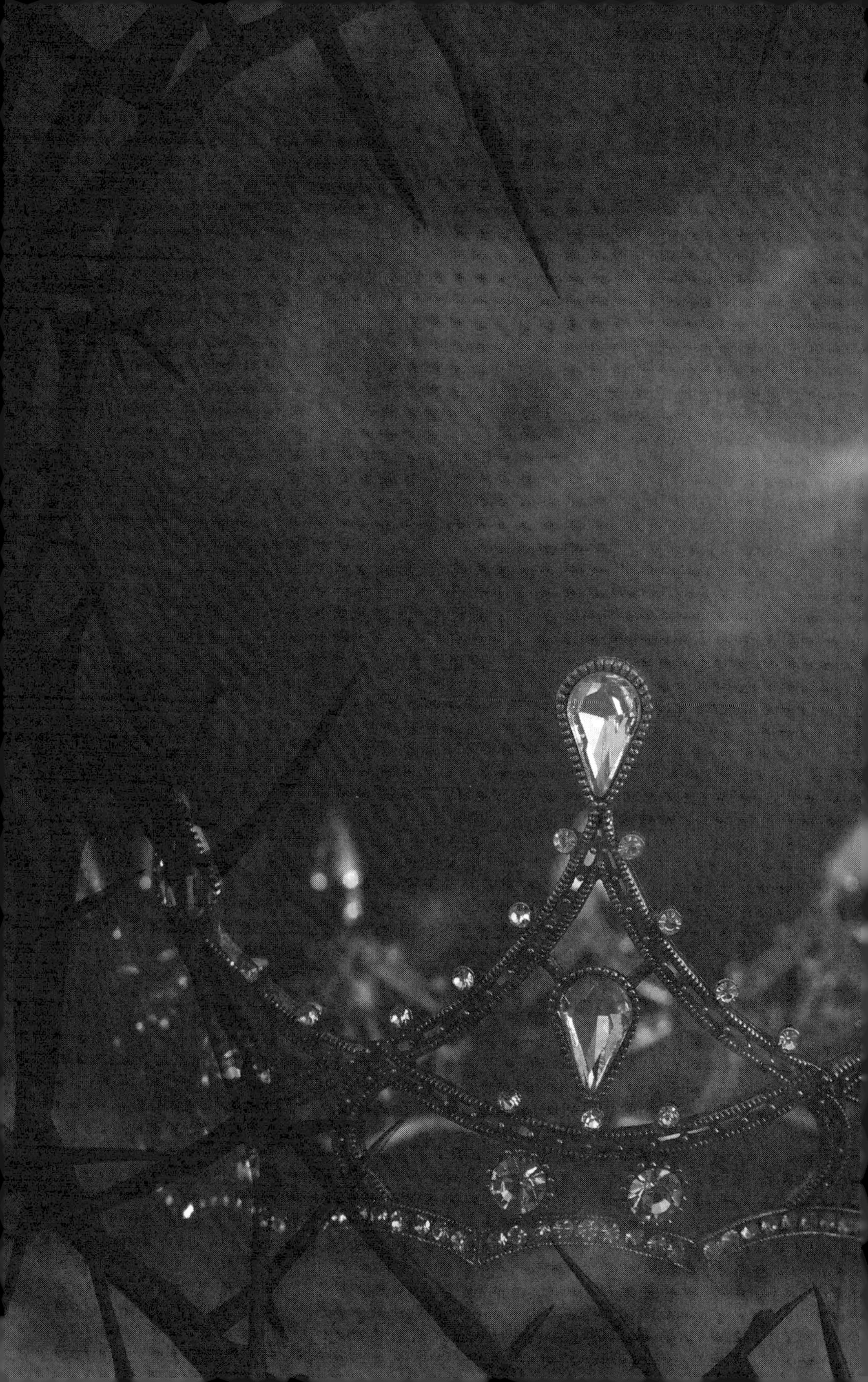

CHAPTER
EIGHTEEN

Honestly, when an orc king offers you your freedom and life in exchange for bringing back magic to the Dead Lands, what else can you do but agree?

I bluff my way through it and stare into his eyes, promising that I can and will. I don't know if he doesn't trust me or just wants to see it, but he climbs to his feet and stops before me. "I know you will because I will go with you, and if you cannot or you break our deal, I will kill you all myself." With that promise hanging in the air, he turns away. Two orcs instantly scurry forward, holding two massive axes. The king fastens them to his back, the leather straps bulging across his huge chest. He adds knives and a whip at his hip before turning to me.

"There is no time to waste. The longer we tarry, the more our world crumbles. So come, little human. Let us bring back the magic." He holds out his green hand, and I exchange looks with the others before putting my hand in his, letting him lead us through the city and mountain.

He doesn't say goodbye to anyone, just trusts in his people, which is strange for a king. The King of the Gilded Lands would never do such a thing, but then again, the orc is clearly a warrior, one I should fear, but I can only worry about one thing at a time.

I'll figure out the whole 'don't know how to bring back the magic' thing later. At least for now, we're alive.

The pass out of the mountain is simply that—a pass from the jagged black rock leading up and out. We break out into the constant darkness I've grown used to in the Dead Lands. It seems colder here, and I shiver, but I refuse to show weakness in front of the orc king, so I hasten my steps, trying to keep up with him, but it's no use. Eventually, he turns back to me, watching me curiously, even if he's slightly annoyed.

"Human legs," I mutter, having already dealt with the annoyance from my monsters before they understood.

He blinks before nodding and slowing down. The others stick close, really close, almost surrounding me and keeping me away from him. Grim hands me food, and Nero gets me water. Nero also offers to let me ride him again, but for some reason, I feel the need to walk, to be on my own two feet around the king, as if it's a weakness to accept the help.

The mountains on either side of us suddenly disappear, and I get my first good look at the land on the other side. We are still high up, the cracked black rock road before us leading down and into another forest. The forest itself stretches on as far as I can see, with some structures poking through the trees, but the one that has me gawking is the palace.

It stands on a shining, black mountain in the distance with a thin rock bridge leading to it, and its black spires actually pierce the dark sky. From here, it's intimidating and so beautiful. I see why the king built it. Amongst all this destruction, it almost seems whole from here, safe, and trapped in time—which can't be right.

It's also far away, definitely a few days' journey. My feet ache at the thought, but I don't moan or complain as we set out on the trail to the forest. Once at the edge, the orc looks down at me. Despite the fact that I know he hates me and why, he seems almost unsure.

"This will be a hard journey," he cautions, then he seems to harden before my eyes, throwing me a disgusted look. "Do not slow us down."

I flip him off when he turns his back and moves into the forest. Despite his size, he's silent on his feet, the bastard, whereas I make a lot of noise. I can't help it. Stupid human body.

The trek through the forest is tense. Zetros and the orc king don't speak to each other, despite knowing one another, and it's clear my monsters don't trust him. There's a divide, and I try to cross it. "So what's your name?" I ask casually. "We've never formally introduced ourselves."

The orc turns, snarling at me, and my eyes widen. Zetros slides before me, barking something back in a thick language before turning to me. "Names have power here, Cora," he murmurs. "He thought it was an insult."

"I'm sorry," I whisper, meeting the orc's hateful eyes. "I just didn't know what to call you. I meant no insult."

His nostrils flare as he watches me, and I shrink under that gaze. "You may call me Leefo, it means king in my language." With that haughty reply, he turns and stomps away, leaving me slumping and dragging my feet after him.

You may call me Leefo, I mock internally, not daring to speak it out loud.

I understand why he hates my kind, but the pure hatred rolling from him is hard to swallow and makes me reluctant to help, and this journey I was enjoying now feels like an ordeal.

"Ignore him, *parum anguis*," Nero purrs, sliding around me and squeezing me in a snake hug.

I smile softly at him and nod, and for the next few hours, Nero and Bracken tease and flirt with me, distracting me from the grumpy orc—until he roars and turns around, anger in his eyes.

"Will you three idiots shut up?" he yells, glaring at us.

That's when I start to get mad.

"Hey, orc asshole. You can hate me as much as you want, but they have done nothing to you, so don't you dare" —I storm toward him as I talk, going toe to toe with him— "speak to them like that!" I finish on my own yell, and silence stretches afterward.

"Wow, that's hot," Bracken mutters right before Grim snarls.

"Grab her!" I'm yanked back violently into Nero's coils as they surround me. I flinch, waiting for the orc's attack, but then I hear the sounds of swords clanging and whoops of a threat echo in the trees around us. Peering around Nero's body, I see it's not the orc as I suspected. It's other creatures.

Trolls, if I'm right, and they are swarming from the trees around us. Great.

Bracken grins, leaning back next to me in Nero's coils. "What are we betting orc boy gets his ass kicked?"

"Shh," I mutter, worriedly looking around. Nero has to turn to face an attack, sweeping down three eight-foot stone trolls, ripping one apart with his tail and leaving me standing next to Bracken for a moment. I'm not protected for only a second, but in that time, I feel a breath move my hair. Swallowing thickly, I turn and look up...

And up...

And up into a troll's face, where he hangs from the tree above.

"Nice troll," I squeak out just as Bracken yanks me out of the way. He flips us, bowing over me, and grunts as the troll hammers its fists down on him. When it stops, he lets me go. I stumble and catch my balance before turning.

"That. Wasn't. Nice," Bracken spits out before leaping at the troll. I stumble back near the trees, desperately trying to avoid the fists that would crush my body, when another grabs me.

"Help!" I scream, unable to reach my knife. Everyone else is engaged. Grim is fighting six, the orc is facing down almost ten, and Zetros is peeling them from Nero. Bracken rips the throat out of a troll's throat and then turns to me, muttering as he rushes after me. The troll that grabbed me runs through the trees so fast, I can't even see before we suddenly stop and I'm dropped to the ground hard enough to knock my breath free.

Bracken is there just as swiftly, standing over me with a frown.

"My human, stone bitch," he spits out.

With a mighty roar, the troll lunges at him for daring to take his prize. Bracken is quick and dodges some blows, but he begins to slow quickly, and the troll slams his fist into his side. He falls to his knees, breathing heavily as I scramble to mine, grabbing my knife.

The troll grips a tree trunk and hits Bracken with it, sending him flying before he's impaled on another broken one.

I realize I'm screaming, my eyes locked on Bracken, who looks shocked. He pulls himself from the trunk and falls to his knees, his hand coming up to cover the gaping hole spewing blood everywhere.

"Bracken!" I yell, terror racing through me.

His eyes flick up to mine in fear before he falls to his back. Something within me erupts, and the scream that rips from my throat is filled with agony, fear, fury, and pain. Just like when I had sex, it seems to carry the magic, exploding from me. The waves of my scream and magic slam the troll back into a tree, and it's out cold or dead—I don't bother to know which.

I stumble, sagging to the ground as if my strings were cut. Whatever magic was flowing through me is suddenly gone. My eyes go to Bracken in worry as I start to drag myself over.

"Help me, Goldie. I'm dying!" Bracken calls dramatically with a teasing lilt, but when I drop to his side, he's pale and losing blood. My eyes widen as panic takes hold. He may be joking, but he looks like he's in serious danger.

"Grim!" I scream, but Bracken takes my hand.

"Oh, shadows, tell me what to do!" I yell at him as he blinks dumbly.

Shock.

He's in shock.

"Grim, Zee, Nero, orc asshole!" I yell again.

"Will be too late," he rasps out. "I'm weak from not feeding for a few days. Help me, please?" he begs, his eyes wide as he falls back. I feel the tremor in his body and see him losing more and more blood.

He got hurt for me. He's dying for me.

"Tell me how," I demand.

"Feed me," he whispers, glancing at my throat before looking back at my face. "Give me your blood so I can heal."

I swallow my nerves, closing my eyes for a moment before opening them again and nodding. "Fine." Leaning in, I offer him my neck. His shaky, cold hand wraps around the back of my neck and pulls me closer until I'm lying on him, his blood coating me. Bracken's lips ghost across my thrumming pulse before closing around it and sucking hard, making me gasp and jerk against him. When he releases it, I feel his fangs scrape over my vein, making my pussy throb in time with it.

"Scream for me," he whispers against my skin, and then he strikes, sinking his fangs into my neck.

I do scream, just like he commands.

CHAPTER NINETEEN

The slide of Bracken's teeth in my skin is something I never thought would be sensual. I expected pain. Instead, pleasure courses through my body faster and higher than I thought possible. As his fangs slide into my skin and my scream slips out, I wonder how long it'll take for him to eat enough to heal. When he begins to draw my blood along those fangs, I stop caring about anything at all except for the feel of him, which should be horrifying but instead has me crying out.

Straddling him as I am, my hair falls around us like a curtain as his hand latches onto the back of my neck and holds me still. Despite being hurt, his grip is strong on my neck, and I know I can't pull away if he doesn't let me. My fingers curl into his chest, and I start to grind against him in the hopes of alleviating some of the pressure from the pleasure. I throb for him as his tongue caresses along the bite, encouraging more blood to well. I don't know how much is too much, or if I should stop him and let the others figure it out.

Fuck that. I'm not telling him to stop.

I can feel Bracken's cock pressing against me through his clothing, and I grind against him, drawing a groan from his lips. The sound reverberates through me, making my breath catch on a whine.

"Bracken," I rasp out, desperate for more.

His fangs retract from my skin, and he chuckles against the puncture wounds he leaves behind. "My, how prettily you shine, Goldie," he murmurs before licking my wounds, cleaning me up, but there's no healing or stinging sensation like I would have expected. I can still feel the holes, as if he wants me to scar. "Now you'll wear my mark for all to see."

My eyes are glassy when he leans back and meets my gaze. I'm still grinding against him, desperate for release, wanting to feel his cock inside me.

"Please," I mewl, digging my nails into his chest.

His eyes flash at my request, his sharp nails trailing along my back and hips as he helps me grind against him. "You sound so pretty when you beg," he rasps out. His claws dig in slightly on my hips. "Do it again."

"Please," I whisper.

He tilts his head, his sharp teeth speckled with my blood as he smiles. "Please what, Goldie?"

"Please fuck me," I tell him.

His cock is sizable in his pants, and when I reach between us to stroke him through the material, his hips jerk against me, grinding into my swollen flesh, and I gasp. Without waiting for another cue, I pull the leather strings keeping us apart and free his erection, staring at the solid length of him. While his size isn't the same as Grimus', Bracken's cock is different in other ways. His girth is wide enough that when I wrap my hand around it, my fingers don't touch. As I stroke up the length, I find a small bump on the underside, right beneath the mushroom head.

"Be careful," he advises with a groan, lifting his hips to thrust into my hand. "It's sharp."

Furrowing my brows, I press tighter against the bump and realize it's not a bump at all.

It's a barb.

There is a slight rough patch that feels strange at the base of his tip, and I gently flick at it, pulling it slightly away. The sharp point is a mechanism meant to keep him inside me once he finishes for however long. I won't be able to move away, and he won't be able to pull out.

Eyes widening at the realization, I can't help but be even more turned on by the thought of being locked together for a short amount of time after. With the fervor of his feeding still running through my veins, I desperately try to move to take him into me. Before I can do so much as loosen my own pants, Bracken flips us, and I find myself beneath him.

"So, so pretty," he sings before he pulls off my pants himself. He doesn't bother with my top, and I don't either. I'm desperate for him to touch me. My skin overheats everywhere he touches.

The pressure is too much.

I need him to make it stop.

Leaning down, he presses a kiss against my pelvic bone, and when he pulls away, he leaves the smallest flame dancing there. My eyes widen at the small inferno, despite it not burning my skin, and I watch, enraptured, as it begins to dance across my hips, leaving behind a trail of warmth and pleasure where it touches. Groaning, I lift my hips, but Bracken simply grins at me as the flame dances down, down, down...

Oh!

The tiny ball of warmth flickers near my clit, Bracken's magic adding to the pleasure as I twist and writhe beneath him.

"That's a good girl," he purrs, before he lines his cock up with my entrance and enters me in a single thrust, all while the flame continues to dance over my clit.

I cry out and reach up to claw at his shoulders, but his strong hands grip my wrists and slam them back to the ground, pinning me as he begins to pump inside me. I moan and try to push my hips against his. I can feel the slight bump of his barb inside me, not catching but preparing to.

"Bracken!" I cry out, and he flashes his teeth at me.

"That's right, Goldie," he rumbles. "Tell them who's fucking you. Tell them all."

He leans down and strikes, sinking his teeth into the tender flesh of my areola before he takes a long pull of blood. I shatter, the feeling only heightened by the flame and his cock pumping in and out of me. His tongue traces his mark, stroking my nipple, and I jerk beneath him, riding out the orgasm. When he leans back, there's a drop of my blood on his lip, and he leans in to kiss me. I can taste my blood, a metallic zing mixed with something else that feels equally as wild. The magic? The moment I kiss him back, he groans into my mouth, clearly enjoying himself as much as I am.

"You belong here, Goldie," he murmurs against my lips, drawing out my pleasure. "You belong with us."

"Yes," I cry, my body convulsing with more waves of pleasure as his thrusts sweep me into another orgasm.

He grunts, his hips jerking against mine, and as I roll into another finish, I feel his barb lock inside of me, digging in, securing his cock in me as his scalding cum splashes and fills me. It's hot, as hot as the fire he controls, and it overflows around him as he convulses above me, his lips pressing reverent kisses along my skin as he claims me. The barb locking us together is so tight, so hot, another release slams through me, wringing a whimper from my pained, hoarse throat. We're both panting hard, and after a few moments, the barb releases and he's able to slide out. I'm aching in the best way as I reach for him. He obliges, helping me get dressed before adjusting himself.

"We leave you two alone for five minutes while we fight, and you go and fuck each other," Grimus grumbles, shaking his head, but he's clearly amused. I turn to find him leaning against a tree cleaning his weapon, blood covering every inch of him.

Flushing bright, I gesture toward Bracken. "He was going to die. I fed him so he wouldn't."

Nero tilts his head toward me where he winds around the tree Grim is leaning against. "The dark fey can't die, not from something so simple as being stabbed. I believe it takes much more effort to kill someone as old as Bracken."

I scowl. "He can't die?" I look over at Bracken to see his shit-eating grin and know they are right. That sneaky fey bastard. I smack at him. "You asshole! I was actually worried!"

He just laughs at me as if it's all a game. "Are you complaining, Goldie?" He leans closer. "I think you liked it."

Huffing, I look away, feeling embarrassed, and finally notice the others spread around, watching the show. The orc king stands there, observing us, before shaking his head. "We should keep going before more threats show up."

What else is there to say? I throw Bracken a mock glare, but my pussy is still quivering with aftershocks, so I can't be too mad. Grim pulls me to his side with a small smile, and Nero chuckles as he checks out my neck.

Men, monsters or not, are all the same.

With that declaration, we set off again, trying to cover as much distance between us and the castle as possible before night sets in and the worst of the creatures come out to play.

WE'VE WALKED FOR MILES, and though the castle is drawing closer, we're still at least a couple days from reaching it, according to Grimus. I've never done quite so much walking in my life as I have since being given as the hunt in the Dead Lands. Still, I don't complain. This adventure is by far one of the highlights of my life, and to think, I never would have experienced it if I hadn't volunteered. I can't help thinking about home, about how I hope Kai married her love and is living happily, about how I hope my father rots away to give my mother some relief from his fist. I hope the king still thinks of the way I stared him down as I stepped into the Dead Lands.

I doubt he even remembers me.

I'm not sure what we hope to accomplish while in the king's castle, if I'm to be bound to the walls of some long-dead king's castle for the rest of my days in order to stay safe, or if it's some sort of next step we must take, but I know I hope for one thing.

I hope my monsters stay with me.

Somehow, on this trip I never planned to survive, I've started to fall for each of them. Their personalities are as different from each other as their bodies are. What a sight we would make if I were able to return to the Shadow Lands, my monsters around me.

I squint my eyes at what appears to be stone springing from the forest. At first, I'm barely able to differentiate between the forest and what it is, but as we draw closer, I see the pillars and walls and assume it's some sort of building.

"What is that?" I ask Nero, whose back I'm riding on. "Another house?"

"If my memory serves me correctly, this area was once riddled with temples." The slide of Nero's scales between my thighs nearly drives me mad as he twists and looks at me over his shoulder. "If I had to guess by the pillars, I'd say it's one of those."

Sure enough, as we near, I can see what were once intricate carvings in the sides of the pillars and walls, as well as small indents showing where jewels or mosaics might have once been nestled. Nature has long since taken the temple back, as it does to all things abandoned. There isn't even much evidence left to indicate which deity it might have been dedicated to. We could have just gone past, but something tells me to step inside, so I tap Nero on the side and he pauses.

"Hold on a second," I tell everyone, sliding from his back.

The orc king growls in frustration. "We don't have time for petty explorations."

Grimus glares at the king, boldly stepping in front of me as if to protect me from his words. "Keep in mind what she's agreed to do for our world. If she wants to see the temple, then she can."

I ignore their bickering and walk alongside Nero into the crumbling temple, looking around at the vines covering the walls. There's no longer any ceiling, the pieces having long since collapsed, but within the temple, there still seems to be some evidence of the past—a statue broken off at the neck in the corner, a few stone stages, some mosaic tiles that barely sparkle in the low light.

"I bet this was once beautiful," I muse, trailing my fingers over the small tiles left behind. The dust brushes away, revealing a sparkling red underneath the dirt.

"The temples of the olden days were often spoken of as the jewels of this world," Nero agrees. "I never saw them myself but—"

"They were beautiful," Zetros interrupts, trailing in behind us as he looks around. "I never visited this one, but the ones I did were works of art." He touches his fingers to the same tile I did. "It saddens me that we can no longer bask in its beauty."

Watching him sadly, I tilt my head back. "Perhaps, one day, we can build temples again, and the jewels of this world will shine just as brightly."

Zetros glances at me. "Ah, but you are the jewel now, *measma*, shining brightly for all to see. What need do we have of temples in comparison to that?"

I flush at the compliment, standing on tiptoes to press a quick kiss to his cheek. He blinks down at me in surprise and then strokes his fingers along my jaw, a caress that makes me want for more, but we're not in the right place for that.

Turning, I intend to lead us out of the temple, but instead, my eyes catch on a design on the opposite wall. The tiles there aren't as decayed as the others, and in the very center, there's a large jewel that hasn't been taken by nature. Despite the dirt and vines covering much of the other parts, this jewel shines as if dust has never touched it, the bright red drawing me closer. Around the sparkling red jewel, the tiles and other small jewels form a strange circular design, something other that I've never seen. It speaks of magic in a way I can't explain, and I'm drawn closer and closer until I'm right before it.

"I'm surprised this hasn't crumbled," Nero comments, staring at the large jewel. "That's a rather large diamond."

I jerk my gaze to his. "It's the size of my fist."

"And?" he asks, staring at me quizzically.

The amount of money something like that could bring in the Shadow Lands...

I reach out, something drawing me to touch it. Whether it's because I don't believe it's actually a diamond, the types of jewels only reserved for those in the Gilded Lands, or because I want to see if it's loose, I don't really know. Still, my hand is reaching for it before I'm conscious of it.

"*Parum anguis,*" Nero warns, hesitation in his voice, but he couldn't stop me from touching the red diamond if he tried.

My fingers touch the surface a moment later, and the reaction is instantaneous. I'm not sure what I expect, but what happens certainly isn't it. The moment my flesh touches the stone, my fingers almost feel as if they lock in place and a burst of wind blasts me, forcing my head back.

"Cora!"

I can no longer see the world around me. Nero is no longer there. Zetros isn't beside me. I'm looking up at bright stars, and then I'm whisked away on...a memory? A vision? I don't really know.

I'm looking at the king's old castle, but the gray world that I know is now bright with magic and color. There's intrigue and beauty. Just as quickly, I'm led to a divide, witnessing the monsters standing on one side and the humans on the other, as if someone drew a line between them—war. Each is standing on the side they'd fight on. The monsters come in peace, standing tall and pushing a treaty. The humans are armed and declare war, denouncing the treaty brought forth by the monsters, wanting the magic they claim for themselves. They rush forward, two sides of the same coin, their weapons raised high. I gasp as the two worlds collide, preparing to watch the bloodshed, but I'm turned away from that vision and instead shown a scene I know all too well.

The wall between the Shadow Lands and the Dead Lands is growing, brought by magic. Reaching into the sky, it twists and slithers together. Cutting off all hope, all friendship, all connections. Dividing us.

The next scene is of the wall crumbling, decaying, and two worlds collide again. The wall I've known and seen my entire life disappears, and the monsters that the humans fear are revealed. My monsters. Many others. The humans' faces are stricken with fear and fury. There's no more wall. There's nothing separating the Shadow Lands from the Dead Lands. There will be no more hunts.

Standing before the monsters, I see a single glowing woman in a crown leading the charge.

Just as quickly as the visions came, I blink and find myself back in the temple, staring at a panicked Nero and Zetros. The others are around me with worry on their faces, but the orc king is staring at me in wonder.

"What the fuck was that?" Grimus demands as I'm pulled away from the stone.

"I...don't know," I murmur, blinking to clear the confusion. "One minute, I was here, and the next, I was being shown... I think I saw a vision of the war."

"The war?" Bracken repeats, staring intently at me. "What do you mean you saw the war?"

"That's what I mean," I say. "I saw the war between the monsters and humans. I saw them put up the wall, like a memory."

"The temple was showing you the past," Zetros murmurs softly, glancing at the red diamond again. "But for it to react so..."

"Your magic must be strong," the orc king finishes. "Every creature within this world will have felt that pulse. I suggest we move before they hunt us down here."

Nero is studying me, his eyes on my face. "Is that all you saw, *parum anguis*?"

I meet his eyes and consider my options. Biting my lip, I say, "No, but I'm not ready to talk about the rest yet."

He nods and helps me out of the temple. The others grumble at my silence, but they respect it, which is good, because I don't know how to explain that I saw a vision of me, dressed in pale lilac, walking at the head of the monsters.

I don't know how to tell them about the crown upon my head.

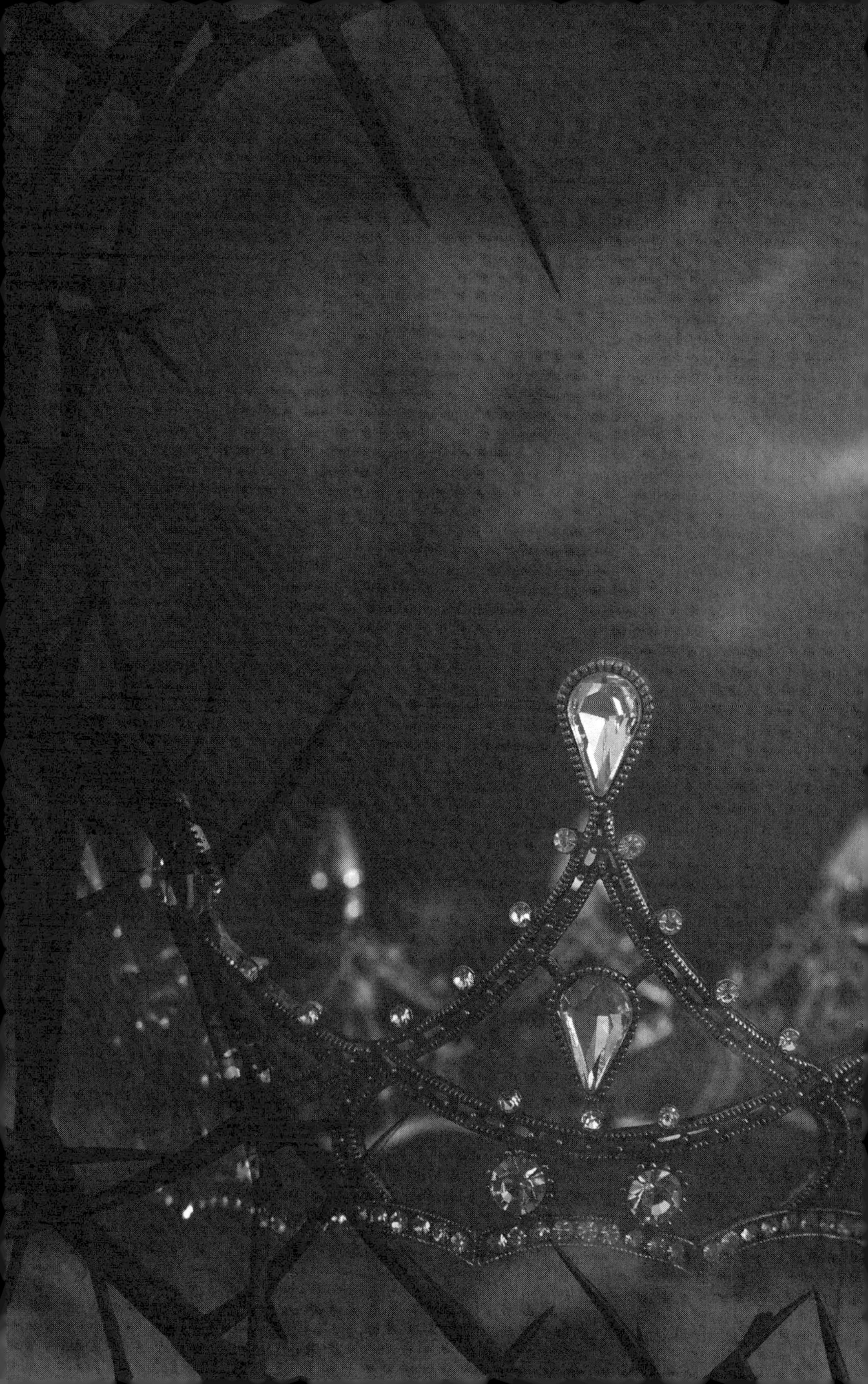

CHAPTER
TWENTY

We encounter more creatures through the rest of our travels, everything from strange reptile beings to things I have no names for. My monsters easily take care of them, and we quickly cross more of the distance, but eventually, we have to camp for the night, all exhausted and needing to rest.

Grimus builds a fire large enough to keep the smaller creatures away, and they all decide on their schedule for who will keep watch. After the temple, they are no longer taking any chances, especially since I seem to have blown magic far and wide, summoning all the monsters like a beacon.

I don't even know how I did it, but my mind keeps drifting back to the red diamond and the visions it gave me.

The past and the possible future.

I take a seat near the fire, warming up, even as Nero curls around me, offering his coils for both warmth and rest. He's always near, always conscious of my comfort and making sure I'm okay. Of all my monsters, he's the most caring, and to think I thought he was going to eat me in the beginning. What would have happened had Grimus not rescued me from him when he did? Would he have even realized who I am? Or what I am?

Do I even know what I am?

"If I have so much magic at my fingertips, does that mean I'm not human?" I ask as I stare into the fire.

The others all pause at my question, turning to look at me.

"I think we can all agree you're achingly human," Zetros offers. "But you carry magic within you unlike any human in my memory. When the war happened, the humans wanted the magic we're born with because any they possessed was muted." His eyes soften. "But you, you carry magic like a monster."

My eyes crinkle. "Maybe I'm a monster then," I joke, thinking it'll be funny, but too many serious eyes study me. "I'm just teasing."

"It's a good question," Nero muses. "Even more so because none of us know the answer."

We fall into silence except for the crackle of the fire. While we all think about those words, and the vision of myself in a crown filters through my mind again. Grimus grabs a large stick and begins preparing some sort of creature we encountered earlier in the day for cooking. I hadn't even realized he'd picked up a few of them. My stomach turns at the sight of the three-legged tree creature and Grimus skinning it, but I know I'll eat it. Growing up in the Shadow Lands, I didn't know where my next meal would come from. It was best to eat whatever crossed my path.

As time moves on, the conversation picks up again. Zetros and Bracken are laughing about something. Grimus says something to Nero that makes him snort and shake his head. Grimus grins at him and bumps him with his elbow, as if they are friends.

"Look at them," the orc king murmurs.

I jump, not realizing how close he's sitting to me. He doesn't join in the joking and conversation. Instead, he sits beside me and watches them.

"What do you mean?" I ask.

He gestured to them, at the way Zetros suddenly throws back his head and laughs at something Bracken says. "You did this—you brought them together like this."

"I don't know about that…"

The orc king leans closer. "They have spent years killing each other, fighting, and holding their territories like beasts, and now one little human has stopped that." He meets my eyes, and I realize, for the first time, just how beautiful his are. They are the color of beaten steel, shining brightly beneath the flames. "You are more powerful than you know, Cora. All humans are, but you are something different. That's what scares the monsters so much and why they kill them like they should have killed the king."

"Why are you telling me this?" I ask, staring into his eyes. "You don't even like me."

He tilts his head. "Now what exactly gave you that impression, little human?"

I open my mouth to respond, but nothing comes out. I'm surprised, certainly, but I don't know how to interact with this monster. He'd been so aloof, so angry before, and now here he is, looking at me like that.

"I'm sorry about how you were treated by humans in the past, Your Majesty," I whisper, and he freezes. I realize my mistake a moment later. I shouldn't really know any of his past, but he surprises me yet again.

He reaches forward to slide a strand of hair behind my ear and smiles, just barely. "You can call me Krug, Amata. Just Krug."

Blinking, I offer my hand. "It's a pleasure to finally meet you officially."

He looks at my hand before gently taking my fingers in his and pressing a kiss to the back of them. "I hope to continue to get to know you better," he purrs before releasing me and moving over to help Grimus.

"Well, what do you know," Bracken comments suddenly from behind me. I nearly jump out of my skin. "The orc is just as smitten now that he's seen your magic." He leans in close to the shell of my ear. "Think I can watch when you let him taste it?"

"Who says I'm going to let him taste it?" I ask, narrowing my eyes.

Bracken laughs, delight in his eyes. "Oh, I don't know," he sings. "Call it a feeling."

He prances off into the forest alone, as if we're not being hunted by every monster in the Dead Lands.

Snorting at the dark fay's antics, I focus back on the group before me and realize Krug was right—they are getting along because of me. I did this, even if it was unintentional. It started out as a means to survive, but now, I not only need them to survive, I also crave them. I want them with me for as long as possible. I don't want them to go. I don't want to lose them.

After we eat the meal Grimus cooks, I settle down close enough to the dying fire in the hopes the heat will warm me. Instead, it fades too quickly to do so, but I need not have worried. Nero's coils move around me, touching one side. Grimus settles on another side, his head pressed against me. Zetros takes up the remaining spot, and Bracken drapes himself over Nero's coils and falls asleep on top as if he won't topple off with any movement. Krug takes first watch, his eyes on the forest, but every now and then, before I can fall asleep completely, I see his eyes drift over to me and the monsters around me.

In his gaze, I see his longing, his urge to be a part of something, and I curse Bracken for speaking of the future so soon.

CHAPTER
TWENTY-ONE

The slicking sound is familiar. I huddle deeper into my bed, freezing when I feel his shadow fall over me. "You can't hide from me, girl. I know you're awake." His voice is angry, furious even. I hear a whimper escape my choked throat, and when he rips my blanket back, turning me over, my eyes land on the empty bed across the room. I'm glad Kai isn't here to see this. Raising my eyes, I meet the vicious, gleeful gaze of my father as he slides his belt from his trousers and wraps it around his fist.

"On your knees," he orders. "Now, or it will be much worse."

Tears fill my eyes as I slowly get to my knees, turning to give him my back.

I knew this would happen, knew this was coming—

A scream rips from my throat as I jerk upwards, almost sliding from Nero's back with the force of it. The hazy nightmares based on my memory cling to me so tightly, I slip from him and stumble to the trees, gagging before sucking in deep breaths. There are tears in my eyes as I struggle to breathe.

Panic claws at my throat until I'm digging my nails into the skin there, trying to let air in.

It's not real. He's not here. I'm safe from him.

He can't hurt me anymore.

I repeat it over and over until the panic recedes and I can breathe again, then I slide down the tree with my hand pressed to my racing heart. I look over to the dying fire to see the others all asleep. A frown tugs at my lips as I watch them. They are silent, unmoving.

No one is on watch.

Why?

That has me staggering to my feet and moving closer. "Nero?" I whisper, since he's the closest, and shouldn't he have noticed me moving? But he doesn't react.

"Bracken, Zee, Grim?" I call.

No response. I circle our little camp, seeing Grim with his weapon in hand, sitting by the fire, his head slumped like he fell asleep before he could even move.

What the...

A noise has me jerking around. I reach for a weapon, but it fades through my hand, and when I lift it up, I see it's almost see through. My eyes drift from my hand to the trees beyond. Now that I'm looking, I see it.

The fog wraps around everything, and the lack of color makes it seem as if everything has been leaked from the land or it hasn't formed correctly. Some things are even hard to make out, but the one thing that isn't is the castle.

It beckons me like a whisper on the wind, pulling me forward.

I don't even realize I'm moving until the trees part for me, welcoming me into their darkened midst, allowing me to pass without issue.

It's a dream, it has to be.

But why, and what is happening? I have no answers, but something tells me I should follow it and let it guide me. It could be important, so I bolster myself and allow myself to be pulled. I walk and walk, and then suddenly, I find myself before the castle, as if the distance was shortened or I missed time.

Either is a terrifying prospect, and almost as scary as what I might find inside those black walls.

Why would I dream of a place I've never been to?

The large iron doors stand open as if waiting for me, and I head inside, my footsteps silent on the polished black stone floors glistening with an inner light. I can only see directly before me. The outskirts of my vision are hazy and not fully formed, and when I turn my head, it mists, so I focus on each step.

The chamber I'm in is long, but I'm suddenly before a throne sitting on a raised platform. It's made of jagged, shiny black rock with white spiraling through it like lightning, and there, sitting on the huge throne, is a king. I can't make out his face, but there's a crown sitting between his horns, and his back is bowed as he shakes in agony, clutching a black silhouette spread across his lap.

It's a person, I realize as I step closer, the shadows clinging to her—a human.

His head drops back, and an anguished roar splits the air, sending me stumbling back in fear. Only then do I comprehend that the human in his arms is dead.

He roars harder, clutching her to his chest and rocking her, and my heart breaks for him. His pain becomes mine before he, too, fades into shadows, and then they both disappear as the castle around me turns to smoke.

Wait, what?

"Why did you bring me here? What was I supposed to see?" I shout, but it's no use. It's like clutching onto air. It slips through my fingers, flinging me back to my body.

And to wakefulness.

My eyes fly wide with a gasp, and the world around me explodes in color...and pleasure.

I lift my head, my eyes locking on Bracken, who has my thighs thrown over his shoulders and his head buried between my thighs. My nipples are hard and begging for attention, and desire spirals through me as his fang filled mouth wraps around my clit and sucks.

I fall back with a gasp, sliding my hands down my body to tangle my fingers in his hair and tug him closer. His touch, his tongue, chase away the rest of that dream and bring me back to him.

To them.

"Glad you could join me, Goldie," he purrs, lifting his mouth from my pussy, his lips and chin glistening with my need. "Now scream for me again, won't you?" he whispers before his tongue darts out and drags down my folds from my clit to asshole and back up, thrusting inside me.

"Bracken!" I pant, pushing him away, even as I tighten my thighs over his shoulders, pulling him closer. "What—"

"You were having bad dreams, so I figured I would wake you," he purrs, placing a gentle kiss on my clit. Chuckling softly, he drags his tongue down my pussy again before he groans and closes his eyes as if to savor my taste, his fingers gripping my thighs to keep me spread for him. "I had a bet with myself that you would taste good, too good."

"Brack—" My voice cuts off on a choked moan as his lips wrap around my clit once more and suck. Smirking, he releases it and ignores any protests I have as he licks and sucks every inch of my pussy. One hand strokes across my thigh, and then a finger presses against my entrance. I whimper as I watch him, trying to slide it inside myself. My need is great. With his dark, hungry eyes locked on me, he slides that finger inside me before adding another and curling them, stroking a spot inside me that has my legs jerking. My head falls back to the earth, and my heart slams as pleasure spears through me.

"Good girl, Goldie. Lie back and let me feast," he murmurs against my pussy, the vibrations making me cry out. "So pretty, such a pretty little pussy. So pink and wet for me. Before I'd even touched you, you were wet. Did you know that? Wet and begging for my mouth, even in your sleep."

I grip his face, rolling my hips and grinding into his touch as he pulls his fingers from my channel and thrusts them back in before adding another. He stretches me deliciously, his tongue lashing my clit in flirty touches.

I need more, I need—

My thighs stiffen and my back arches as a scream rips from my throat. He nips and sucks my clit while he rubs his fingers inside of me.

I hear the others, but I can't stop, the pressure spiraling through me as he sucks my clit. His fangs only make pleasure explode through me again, flooding my channel and soaking his hand as his fingers thrust into me.

When he finally releases my clit with a greedy lick, I slump back, my gaze locking on him as he sits up. He watches me as he sucks his fingers clean with a groan. "I won the bet. Like I said, you taste amazing, Goldie, and now you're awake."

"Fuck me, I thought we were under attack," Grim mutters, and I blush hard as I sit up, pushing my skirt down as I glance around to see all of them on their feet with their weapons in their hands as if ready to fight.

Brilliant.

I grin sheepishly as Bracken chuckles. "Well, now that we are all awake, shall we start breakfast? I don't know about you, but I'm ravenous." He winks, making me shake my head, and the others grumble but reluctantly relax.

My eyes flick to the lone figure at the other side of the fire, his eyes on me and filled with...

Heat.

Hunger.

The orc king looks ravenous too.

I gulp.

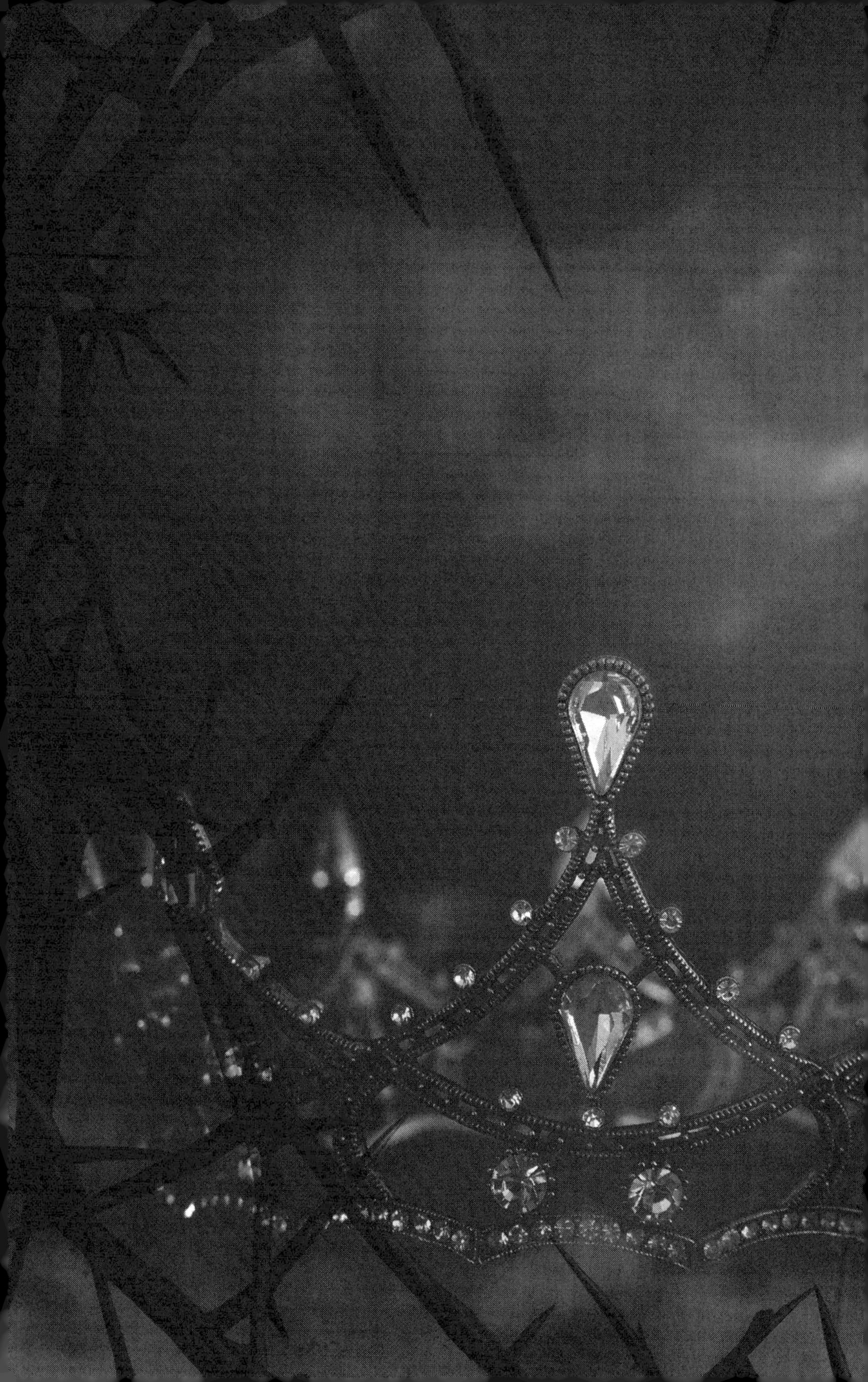

CHAPTER TWENTY-TWO

Zee and Bracken tease me about my morning screams, but I just roll my eyes as a grin tugs at my lips. My mind wanders back to my dream, wondering what it meant and why I was shown it. I mean, I had to have been, right?

The magic here is so unpredictable, and I can't tell if it's friend or foe.

All I know is that we have to get to that castle, so after covering our fire and tracks, we set off back into the forest with renewed speed. They all seem on alert after the recent attacks, so I keep quiet and watch my feet as I try to think about what the dream meant.

"Still thinking about my tongue, Goldie?" Bracken comments sometime later.

"Or tips to improve it," Zee retorts, slapping Bracken's shoulder as he passes before catching up to me and grinning. Grim is at the back, and Bracken is before him. Nero is in the trees, keeping watch, and our orc king is setting the pace. Unlike when we first met, he slows his strides and looks back to check on me a lot.

I can't tell if he plans on killing and eating me or just plain, well, eating me.

Either way, the contemplative looks he shoots at me when he thinks

I'm not watching has me on edge all day as I wait for something to happen. I know the others are picking up on my tension because they become extra attentive. Even Bracken quits his jokes and peers into the forest for threats.

It shouldn't come as a surprise when we stumble onto one—or into one, I should say.

Krug freezes in front of me, a twig snapping under his foot as his head shoots around. "Run!" he roars just as a cage descends from the top of the trees and crashes down around him. Nero grabs me and hoists me up into a tree as Grim and Bracken circle the orc, protecting him and waiting for the threats. I don't see Zee anywhere. "Where's Zee?" I hiss at Nero.

"I don't know. Hold on, love," Nero whispers, sliding higher, but no one comes, and Grim releases a whistling noise, looking at the orc and then Bracken, telling him something with his eyes.

"Leave him. This way, we won't have to kill him later," Grim says. With that statement, he and Bracken fade into the trees.

I go to scream, but Nero covers my mouth and wraps me tighter in his arms, holding me immobile. I can't see the others, only Krug.

He's crouched in the tiny cage with his hands fisted on the bars. He snarls, gnashing his teeth, and his eyes are wild and unfocused. He's not with us. Gone is the king, and in his place is a wild animal.

Moments pass, and then there's movement below us as two hooded figures slink from the trees. "Looks like they left him. Lucky us." One giggles, the sound slightly mad. "He'll make the mistress very happy."

The words make me sick to my stomach, and they must pierce whatever haze is in Krug's mind, because he roars and attacks the cage with renewed anger and panic. I see his fear and remember what Zee said about his past.

Turning in Nero's arms, I drag his head down to me and kiss him hard. It shocks him enough to cause him to loosen his grip, and I slide from his hold, tumbling to the forest floor below. Before he can grab me again, I jump to my feet and run out of the trees, sliding to a stop before the two figures.

"That's my orc. Get your own," I snarl, my hand coming up on instinct, and magic explodes from me, drawn by my anger. The two figures go flying back into the trees, and I hurry to Krug's side. His chest is heaving, and his eyes are wild. I don't think he even sees me as I search for a way to free him.

"Hurry, please." His voice cracks. "Please, human, please." His begging rips open my heart as I cut my hand on the bars, tugging and pulling as I try to free him, all while those panic-stricken eyes watch me hopelessly.

"Grab her too!" that mad voice calls, and I know they are coming back.

I hear thumps, and when I look, Nero is sliding toward them. I spot Zee coming from the trees behind them with blood on his face, holding two additional dead hooded figures in his arms. Grim throws two more on the ground as he bursts from the trees, and Bracken dances out with a grin.

"Looks like you're alone and your mistress is going to be very angry. See, that's our human." Bracken strikes.

I trust them to protect us, so I examine the bars hurriedly before I step back. "Look away," I demand, and with a snarl, my magic explodes out of me again, smashing the cage open. Krug immediately crawls free, collapsing on the ground, panting and shaking.

There's a noise, and his head snaps up before a roar leaves his lips. Gone is the broken orc, and in his place is a feral one. He leaps to his feet with his claws out, his tusks shining as he roars again. Nero is the closest, and he freezes.

I watch as Krug leaps at him. Nero barely manages to get out of the way, and then the others are there, trying to pull Krug away, but all it does is make it worse, sending him deeper into a feral rage that makes him see all as foe rather than friend.

I cover my mouth in horror as blood flies. He's thrown toward me and lands on his hands and knees, skidding to a stop as he pants with rage and fear. His head snaps up again, then his eyes lock on me and he freezes.

"Goldie, no!" Bracken calls, but I ignore him. I step before Krug, showing no fear.

I don't fear him. Not the broken man I saw in the cage who has given into years of hurt and anger to escape those memories. "Come back," I demand.

He snarls again, his body vibrating with the force of it, so I drop to my knees before him and cup his face, staring into his eyes.

"I need you. We need you. Come back. You're safe. I would never let anyone hurt you."

Something akin to humanity bleeds into his eyes for a moment before one of the guys moves and he snarls at them.

"Stay fucking still!" I yell, my eyes on Krug as I grip his face harder and force him to look at me once more. "Come back," I whisper as I lean in and brush my lips softly across his. "Come back to me." When I pull back, he lets out a shuddering breath, his eyes filling with emotions.

"Little human," he rasps out, and then collapses to his side, groaning and shaking as his memories overwhelm him again.

I place my hand on his shoulder, offering him comfort. "It's okay," I tell him, and his head turns, pressing against my arm, and I swallow.

Pulling him into my arms, I move his head to my lap, stroking his hair and face as he shivers. "Shh, hey, everything is okay. You're safe. No more cage. No mistress. You are free. You are safe." I keep repeating it as the others circle us, protecting us silently as they allow the orc to break and rebuild himself.

"Sing to him," Zee says, and when I lift my head and meet his eyes, I notice they are stricken. "It always helped me to sing."

Licking my lips, I look down into Krug's eyes and start to sing a song I used to sing while working in the fields. We used to sing it as a group, my voice joining dozens of others until it was a choir of agony, exhaustion, and conformity. Now, singing it here with Krug, it's a different sort of song, one of hope. All the while, I stroke his face, and when he starts to relax and close his eyes, I don't stop. I sing one song and then the next until they flutter back open again, alive and soft.

"Hey," I murmur, cutting off the song.

"You have a beautiful voice," he croaks out and rubs his face, his cheeks tinting a darker green. Is he blushing? "Fuck, I don't know what happened."

"The same thing that happens to me when I see chains," Zee remarks and shoots Krug a friendly, knowing look. "It is nothing to be ashamed of, brother."

Krug nods but won't look at me. I refuse to stop stroking him though, and he doesn't move away. Eventually, he sighs again. "I feel so weak, so helpless, but when there's a cage..." He looks up at me. "I'm sorry I wasn't much help back there."

"We all have our weaknesses. That's why we work together." I shrug, hating the self-hatred I see in his eyes. "Your past is your own, but it is nothing to be ashamed of. For me, it's not a cage, it's belts."

"Belts?" He frowns.

"My father would whip me with them while I was asleep...while I was eating. He would force me onto my knees and berate me as he ripped open my skin time and time again," I explain, laying my pain bare for him. "It still haunts me, even here, where I know he could never touch me again."

I feel the other guys shift restlessly, but I watch Krug as he nods in understanding. "The people who hurt me are long gone. I hunted them all down and killed them."

"Good." I grin, and he chuckles at the look on my face.

"I will never be able to talk about...everything they did," he begins, and I still before continuing to stroke him. "But you need to know why I hated you so much at first. I was given to the humans as a gift. The first night, one tried to rape me, and I killed her. I was punished for that over and over again. I was tortured, then made to kill and fight for them. When I won, I was given to a human for the night, and if I tried to kill them... Well, it was worse than death. My choices were taken away, apart from being raped or forced to kill. I was kept in a cage smaller than that." He points to the cage behind him. "Sometimes for days, until I would go mad." He looks up at me. "I blamed the humans, but it wasn't just them. It was some of my people too, and I'm starting to realize that."

"Krug." I shake my head. "I'm so sorry."

"My past is that—my past. I cannot change it, so instead, I did everything to move on from it, but one look at you and it all came back." I wince and try to move away, but his hand comes up and stops my movement. "I needed that. I needed to face it instead of running. If you cannot hate our kind for what we have done to you since you arrived, then I cannot hate you for something your people did to me. I am so tired of being angry and filled with hate...of being afraid."

"Me too," I admit.

"Then let us not be." He nods like it's decided, then squeezes my hand. "Together."

His words stay with me as we clean up the area, giving him time to recoup, and then we begin our journey again, getting away from the creatures that Grim called pixies. But something has changed now. The others keep a watchful eye on Krug, protecting him like they protect me, and that's when I realize exactly what's happened.

He's one of us now.

With a smile, I look up at the orc king at my side, and another puzzle piece locks into place.

CHAPTER
TWENTY-THREE

The castle looms in the distance, coming closer, and yet it still seems so far away. I'm not sure how long the actual distance is, but it must be miles upon miles. Even the thought of covering that distance makes me tired. Sometimes, I walk alongside the others, but when I see my slow pace wearing on them, I climb onto Nero's back and enjoy the ride. If someone would have told me I'd regularly be riding on the back of a snake man before I was thrown into the Dead Lands, I would have laughed at them, and then I would have dreamed what it would be like. It wouldn't have even come close to the feeling of his scales between my legs, or the way I can feel his coils pulse beneath me, or how the muscles along his abdomen and back flex as I wrap my arms around them.

Then again, nothing much can come close to Nero.

The men in the Shadow Lands were adequate, I suppose. There were a few nicer ones, but nicer didn't mean they were prime pickings. They were only the lesser evils in a society meant to force the women to comply. Here, in the Dead Lands, my monsters are more than any human I might have had dalliances with in the Shadow Lands. If for some reason I had to go back, I know nothing would compare to the monsters around me.

Nor did any of the Shadow Land men ever...excite me the way my men do. Just looking at them makes it hard to breathe, and I find myself in a constant state of arousal.

Along the way, we're attacked by various small creatures. The others make quick work of them, slaughtering any monster that dares to come after us, but I can't help but notice a pattern as the time goes on. Zetros says that they are drawn to my magic, hungry for it, but as we draw closer to the castle, it doesn't seem like the monsters are here to take me.

They are here to kill me.

The suspicion solidifies when a cluster of creatures attacks. One moment, we're moving through the forest, my feet moving to keep up the pace, and the next, an awful screech has me ducking and covering my ears. At first, I thought it might be some creature passing by, but the moment Grimus raises his nose to the wind and stares at the sky he can glimpse through the trees, his face twists.

"Harpy," he grunts, raising his morning star.

Zetros tenses and moves closer to me. "They rarely travel alone."

Grim nods. "That's what I'm afraid of."

Another screech has me moving closer to Zetros and Nero. Krug watches the sky along with Grim. Bracken seems unconcerned, but even he moves a little bit closer to me.

"Don't run away," Zetros instructs. "They are faster than you will ever be."

"What are they?" I ask, because although the word *harpy* sounds familiar, I don't know what it is, only that it's a monster.

"Half bird, half woman," Nero murmurs. "Don't let their singing get to you."

"Why would it get to me?" I ask, staring up at the sky for the creatures.

Zetros looks down at me. "Their powers only affect humans. We are immune."

I grimace. "Fantastic." Another screech hurts my ears, making me flinch and cling to my kraken. "We're going to be okay though, right?" No one answers. "Right?"

Nero's eyes meet mine. "Just stay close, *parum anguis*."

Worry fills me at his tone, at the way they all move closer to me, as if I'm the weakness here. I suppose I am, even if I have some sort of magic that I can't yet control. Sure, when my emotions are high, the magic comes easier, but I can't control it outside of those emotions.

I am the weakness.

When the first one drops from the sky and lands before us, I nearly stumble back in surprise. When Nero said half bird, half woman, I don't know what I expected. The terrifying creature in front of me isn't anything I could have imagined. It has the face and body of a woman, but past that, she's clearly avian. In the place of her arms are great, brown feathered wings that she curls against herself as she rises to stand before us. Her skin matches the color of her feathers, the soft striations in the pattern continuing across her entire body. Her thighs run into a knee that turns birdlike until you find dagger-tipped claws. Feathers run down her back and fall from her tailbone like a tail. Her hair is made up of feathers rather than the strands I know, and when she smiles, her teeth are as sharp as any sword.

But that isn't what unnerves me the most.

It's her eyes.

Her features are sharp, as if they have to be in order to mimic a bird, but her eyes are black pools of darkness. I've always been a bit afraid of the ravens in the Shadow Lands, but looking at the harpy before me, I now understand why the birds unnerve me. This woman, this monster, is not going to be like my monsters.

Her head tilts to the side as she studies our group, even as more of the monsters drop from the sky, surrounding us. My fingers clutch at those closest to me, tempted to both hide in their midst and get a better look at the leader.

"What do we have here?" she asks in a voice pitched a bit too high to be human. "A group of males just walking through my forest?"

I duck lower, deciding it's best to not reveal my presence if it hasn't been made known yet.

"Let us pass, and we'll let you live," Grim declares, his chin tilted up.

The harpy laughs. "You think you have power here just because of your lineage, minotaur? This land is our land, gifted to us by the old king—"

"The old king is dead," Krug states. "You have no claim."

"We have *every* claim," the harpy snarls. "Just because he's dead does not mean our treaties are not upheld. You are trespassing on our territory."

I peek over Grim's shoulder, taking in the harpies around us, who are clearly getting more riled up by the moment. Nero squeezes my thigh in warning, but I can't help but look at the creatures.

"We mean no harm," Zetros soothes. "We're only passing through."

The harpy's eyes focus on my kraken, her head twisting in a birdlike movement that makes my skin crawl. "And what is a creature of the sea like you doing so far from your home?" She takes a step forward. "Are you the source of the magic that drew us here?"

Zetros tenses. "It matters not. We ask for safe passage. Nothing more."

I'm looking at the harpy, barely peeking over their shoulders, when my eyes land on one of the other creatures. This one is painted in shades of deep blues and whites, and it would be beautiful if not for the harshness of her expression. Our eyes meet, and I realize my mistake the moment she screeches an alarm.

"There's a human!"

The others join in, and even though I duck back into hiding, it's too late.

"A human!"

"There's a human!"

"Nolia, there's a human in their midst!"

I close my eyes and cling to my monsters, wishing I could take back my curiosity.

"A human?" the leader, Nolia I presume, repeats. "You dare bring one of those pests into our territory? You bring the very thing that trapped us here?" She inhales. "She's the source of the power you harbor."

"I suggest you get her scent out of your mind," Bracken warns, and although he's usually carefree and happy, there's a seriousness in his tone now, a threat. "She is not for you."

"A female human," Nolia says, and when I peek out again, her eyes move to me. "The hunt this far inland?" Her gaze focuses on Grim. "What have you done, minotaur?"

There is no other warning. One second, we're standing around, speaking to each other, and the next, Grim springs forward with his morning star, swinging it toward Nolia. One would think a being with wings and claws for feet would be slow on the ground, but the harpies are anything but. Nolia is gone before Grim can get near her, and her movements are so fast, I can barely track them.

"Stay close," Nero commands, his coils forming a barrier around me, but that does nothing for beings with wings.

I crouch down between his coils as the others raise their weapons and attack. They made quick work of the other creatures, but the harpies are something else entirely. They are brutal and strong enough to fight, and it quickly becomes a gruesome dance of monsters. Zetros slams into one of the nearest harpies, pinning her against a tree. He doesn't kill her —either because he doesn't want to or because he physically can't—and instead, he rips a branch from the tree and slams it into her stomach, embedding it into the tree and leaving her to flap and screech like a pinned butterfly. His eyes meet mine briefly as he turns before he's rushing forward to help Grim with Nolia.

Bracken is nearly as fast as the harpies, if not faster. I watch as he and the blue and white harpy dance, clawing at each other. Her talons get far too close to Bracken's stomach, but my fey is clever. He ducks out of the way, rolls beneath her as she flaps her wings, and jams a sword into her spine. The screech nearly makes my ears bleed.

Panic fills me as I watch my monsters fight the brutal creatures that seem to be greater foes than any of the others before. Krug swings a sword toward them, spilling blood and splattering it on the trees. Nero hisses at a harpy that dares to get too close, his expression fierce.

And then I hear it.

"Come, little human, an adventure awaits. Give in to temptation and agony. Step free of your chains and move into the light, only then will you be wild and free."

Such a beautiful voice. A feeling of weightlessness overcomes me until I find myself climbing over Nero's coils in an attempt to follow it.

"Cora, no!" Nero shouts, but a harpy attacks him, distracting him and keeping him from following. "Bracken!"

The fey turns and sees me moving as if in a trance, my eyes on the orange and brown harpy who's currently singing. Her teeth flash as she drags me in.

In the distance, through the fog, I hear Grimus roar, Zetros shout for the others, and Krug spout off orders, but all I can do is watch the harpy.

"Come, little creature, we'll break you free. This cage was not meant to hold such power. Follow my voice, and you will know who you'll be. It's time for you to cower."

I blink in confusion but still step forward. The magic under my skin buzzes in warning, and it clears some of the fog, but no matter how hard I try, that magic doesn't wake up. I can't fight it, the trance is too strong.

"Come, little creature," she coos.

Once I'm close enough, the singing abruptly stops and the trance breaks. I blink and realize just how far I've walked from the others.

The harpy grins. "Good girl." With a screech, she leaps toward me. I'm nowhere near as fast as Nero. I have no hopes of avoiding her before her talons are closing around my shoulders and lifting me into the air.

"Kill the abomination!" Nolia commands, and it takes me a moment to understand she means me. "Kill her before she can imbalance the realm!"

"You don't understand!" Grim roars, his eyes on me as I'm slowly lifted.

Nero shoves his harpy away and rushes after me, his coils moving far faster than I've ever seen them as he scrambles up a tree to get to me, panic clearly written on his features.

"Cora, your magic! Use it!" he shouts.

But the magic doesn't come. It's as if it's decided not to listen to me, as if it's a petulant child that doesn't want to come out. I push harder, trying to make it listen, but it stubbornly stays put while I'm lifted into the air.

Nero leaps from tree to tree, and just when I think he's going to be too slow to capture me, he leaps into the air, and he manages to grab onto the legs of the harpy, putting him chest to chest with me. The harpy shrieks as the naga's weight drags her down, drags us both down. I scream as we plummet, my hands going to Nero's sides as we land roughly on the ground and his coils immediately twist around us. The harpy flaps and screeches, trying to get away, but Nero doesn't release her. He pulls back his fist and punches the harpy right in the face.

"Let. Her. Go!" he snarls, each word punctuated with a slam of his fist.

The screech goes right to my head and makes it ache as Nero hits her again and again, spraying blood, until I feel her talons begin to loosen. I reach up and pull at the claws, desperate to get away with only small puncture wounds. If she clamps down...

The coils around us tighten as Nero continues to mutilate the harpy until she stops moving and her screeches die. The talons come away, and I'm free, but Nero doesn't stop. His eyes are wild with rage as he continues to swing.

"Nero," I croak out, but he doesn't hear me, so I reach for his shoulders. "Nero!"

He turns his wild eyes on me, and when he realizes I'm standing in front of him, his shoulders sag and he drags me to him. I don't even flinch at the blood on his skin. I hold him back, uncaring of anything else.

"I thought we were going to lose you," he whispers against my neck as he holds me tightly.

"I'm okay," I promise, stroking my hand down his back.

Nolia shrieks, and we both turn as her eyes pierce mine. "You will bring about the destruction of everything!" she declares. "I hope you're prepared for the graves you'll stand upon."

The few remaining harpies lift into the air, leaving those trapped or dead behind, and they disappear into the dark sky.

~

"They didn't want to take me. They wanted to kill me," I point out after we've regrouped and gotten away from harpy territory. "I don't understand."

Grim is sitting on the far side of the fire, carefully cleaning a wound on his shoulder. "You're a threat to them. The last human in the king's castle caused a war."

"It was not her fault," I argue.

"No," Grim agrees. "But she still caused it nevertheless. Even if by her death."

"The real problem," Krug begins as he wipes down his blade, "is why you didn't use your magic on the harpy." He looks up, and those bright eyes focus on me, pinning me to the spot.

I shrivel under that look, under the expectation there.

"It isn't always something I can control," I mumble, looking away. I feel ashamed, as if I should somehow know anything about this new power in my veins. "I tried..."

Zetros shoots a glare at Krug. "She's just barely learning to wield it, orc. Don't dare shame her for it."

"I don't mean to shame," Krug responds, putting his sword away. "What I mean is that if this is going to work, shouldn't she know how to use the power in every way?" His eyes meet mine. "Cora, if you're going to stand in that castle and declare anything, you must be at full strength to do so."

"Don't chastise her like that." Nero scowls.

I place my hand on Nero's coil and study Krug. "He's right," I agree.

Nero jerks and glances at me. "It's not a matter of shame. It's a matter of us knowing our strengths and weaknesses. And right now, not being able to fully wield my magic as needed is a weakness."

No one says anything. I know they don't want to admit that I'm the weak spot in our group, but they don't have to. I already know it. I saw it. And now that I'm being hunted to be killed rather than to be taken, that weakness is glaringly obvious. I don't know what I'll be able to do once we get to the castle, but how can I expect to do anything at all when the magic is so unstable?

"But I don't know how to go about learning how to wield it," I admit with a grumble. "So if you have any ideas, now would be a good time to hear them."

Silence. At first, I think they aren't going to offer any plans or thoughts on the matter, but in the end, it's Krug who speaks up.

"I say we camp here for a few days, focus on Cora learning how to control her magic, then continue on our journey," he suggests, his eyes meeting mine.

Relief fills me. "I like that plan."

Realistically, I would have been okay with any plan at all. I certainly don't know what to do.

"Then it's settled," Grim says. "We make the area safe, and we spend time working with Cora."

I stand with a smile. "I'm excited to—"

"Don't get too excited," Krug interrupts, his eyes glittering. "You're going to be cursing our names after only a few hours of training, little human." He gets to his feet and comes around the fire to stand right in front of me. When he leans down, I nearly shiver at the feeling of his breath against my ear. "I, for one, can't wait to see you sweating, your hair wild as you curse my name, both as a threat and in arousal."

With a smug look on his face, he heads off into the trees to prepare the perimeter while I just gawk after him.

"We rest for the night," Zetros orders. "Then we begin training in the morning."

Something tells me I'm going to hate the training, but I nod and find a good place on Nero's coils to fall into sleep, dreams of singing following me under.

CHAPTER
TWENTY-FOUR

"Come on, *parum anguis*. You did it only seconds ago," Nero coos, his coils moving around me like a tease, sliding across my skin until I gasp at the sensation like he knew I would.

Gritting my teeth, I hold my hand out in front of me, trying to make the sparks appear again. "That's because I was pissed at Grim," I grumble, sweat beading on my forehead.

The minotaur's lips quirk up into a smile. "You're only mad because you couldn't catch me."

"No," I snarl. "I'm mad because you nicked my ass with your horn."

A soft chuckle is my response. "Learn to be faster then."

"Bastard," I growl, and a spark appears on my fingers and fades away. "Ugh!"

"Anger makes your magic come out," Zetros says. "Fear is less stable. When someone you care about is in danger, it comes easily. We need to find a way for you to use that at any time."

"So what?" I ask, sweat beginning to roll down my temples the longer I stand here concentrating. "I should just be angry all the time?"

"No," Nero answers. "You should remember the feeling of anger, of what makes that pulse come alive. Remember it, feel it in your bones, in your fingers, and then use it until it becomes second nature."

Frowning, I furrow my brows and close my eyes in concentration. I think of the anger I feel when it comes to the King of the Gilded Lands, of the way he dismissed me, sitting on his horse dripping in gold and jewels, as those of us in the Shadow Lands starve and kill ourselves with exhaustion. I think of the way my father beat us and commanded submission no matter how little I would submit. I barely feel the magic swirling beneath my skin and immediately decide that anger isn't strong enough for what I need.

The feeling of seeing my monsters or my sister in danger, however... I think about how I felt when Krug had been in that cage and when Zetros told me his story. I remember how I felt watching them fight the harpies and the other monsters we've come across.

"That's it," Nero coos. "Keep going, *parum anguis*."

I think about the way Bracken looks at me and his teasing, lewd comments. I think about how Grim grunts and remains coarse, but still always makes sure I get the best part of the meat each time he cooks it. I think of the way Nero always surrounds me, his coils offering a safe space, a bed, a ride, anything I may need. I think about the way Zetros runs his hand along my hip and how he trusts me, despite the way my kind has treated him. I think about the way Krug has started to warm up to me, and the way his eyes linger on my skin for too long.

The magic comes alive beneath my skin like a beacon of change. It goes from a tingle to a raging fire, and when I open my eyes, I'm practically glowing with it. As Nero dances in front of me, his eyes lit with excitement, I flick my finger toward him, and his coils lift into the air, dragging him up. His laughter is like a drug, and I smile as I twirl my finger and he begins to lift higher.

Krug shoots to his feet, staring up at Nero, his mouth slack.

Bracken whistles. "It took you a couple of days, Goldie, but once you find your stride, it's something else." His eyes linger on my skin. "Now your flesh matches your hair. I wonder if it tastes the same when you're glowing with magic."

Arousal slams through me, but instead of acting on it, I gently bring Nero back down and grin at him. "That wasn't so bad."

"Now that you've figured out the feeling," Grim says, coming forward, "I guess it's time to try again."

Planting my feet, I focus on my monsters, on the way I feel about them, and funnel those thoughts into the sensation beneath my skin. The glow brightens, and Grim's eyes widen.

"Bring it, minotaur," I goad.

Grim tips his head down in challenge, desire flooding his eyes, and charges.

He's been trying to teach me hand-to-hand combat, and while it will work against another human, I don't have the strength to take on another monster. Still, I play by his rules, using my size and quickness to my advantage. I dodge his charge and dive to the side, rolling before I spring to my feet and face off against him again. Like I'm in a bullfight, I hold my hand out at my side and wave my fingers.

"Is that all you've got, Grim?" I purr.

With a roar, Grim charges again, his horns aimed right for me. I dance out of the way, moving quickly, and the magic in my veins waits for it.

Bracken appears beside me so suddenly, I nearly jump when his voice sounds right in my ear. "Play dirty, Goldie," he murmurs. "You can't hope to win with strength, but use the magic in your veins. This isn't about fairness. It's about winning."

When I go to glance at him, he's already moving away with a wink. Focusing back on Grim, I take Bracken's advice and plant my feet, determined not to move. Grim digs his hoof into the ground and kicks dirt back. I swear steam comes out of his nose and curls around his nose ring before he charges.

This time, I don't move or dodge as he comes closer. Instead, I hold up my hand and let the magic flow out of me. My entire body comes alive with the feeling of it, and the area we cleared for training lights up with the magic that pulses from my palm. Grim runs right into that pulse, and it flips him on his ass, shoving him down on the ground and holding him there. With a grin, I straddle his hips and release the magic, letting his hands come to my waist.

"I win," I declare, and pride flares in his eyes before he jerks me down for a kiss that makes me grind against him.

"You win," he repeats when we break apart, and he grins up at me, as if I'm the most beautiful thing in the world.

As my monsters gather around me, their excitement palpable, I can't help but feel as if everything is as it's meant to be, except for one thing.

Something's missing. I don't know what, but it's coming. I can feel it like a warning on the wind.

I just don't know if it is friend or foe.

CHAPTER
TWENTY-FIVE

Usually, I wake with the sun, but there isn't much here, yet I know it's morning. After spending our night talking, laughing, and eating, I fell into an exhausted sleep. I know we need to leave soon, but we are staying for a few days to help me get a better grasp on my magic. It feels like a countdown. This time here, with just us, before we have to get back to what we need to do, makes me anxious.

Stretching, I slide from Bracken's arms. He groans and reaches for me in his sleep, making me grin. The fey might be a flirt and a deadly monster, but he sure is a cuddler. Sneaking past Nero, I hurry to the trees to pee. I've just finished when I look up and almost scream. Grim is leaning back against another tree, watching me as he cuts into some form of fruit with a blade.

"Fucking hell, dude," I mutter. "Warn a girl before you spy on her peeing."

He quirks a brow at me, continuing to eat as I march up to him and poke him in the chest. "You scared me. Unless you're into the whole pee kink..." When he just stares, a slow grin crawls up my face. "Is that it? Big, bad Grim wants to watch me relieve myself? Gets him off—"

He moves faster than I can blink, wrapping his huge hand around my throat like a necklace as the blade and fruit drop to the ground. "I was protecting you, but you don't know when to stop, do you?" He slams me to my knees. "You want to taunt me and be a brat? Then I'll fill that teasing mouth until you can't anymore."

The change has desire roaring through me. Wiggling, I flutter my lashes up at him. "Gods, yes."

"Open your mouth," he orders, his eyes hard as he watches me. His nostrils flare as he stands straighter, looking down at me with those dark eyes as the scent of my arousal fills the air. "Do not make me ask again," he warns, sliding his hand up to grip my chin and digging his thumb in until I open my mouth for him.

"Wider," he commands.

Breathing heavily, I widen my mouth as he looks down at me. "Good girl. Now, you're going to be quiet as you suck my cock, aren't you? We don't want the others finding you here. You're all mine now. So be a good girl and make me come, and I'll bend you over that tree stump and fuck you raw until you can't walk."

Fucking hell.

I actually shiver at his words. I don't know what made Grim decide to play, but I'm not going to ask since I'm already wet and imagining him doing just that. My clit throbs in time with my heart as I stare up at my minotaur, beyond turned on and wanting exactly that. I need to taste him just as much as I want to fuck him.

Tilting his head down, he spits into my mouth. "Swallow," he orders, and I do. It shouldn't be a turn on, but it is when he strokes my neck in praise. "Good girl. Feel that magic moving through you, claiming you."

His other hand releases his cock before stroking the huge, hard length. He drags me closer and runs the tip of his cock over my mouth, coating it in his magic pre-cum. My lips tingle, and my tongue darts out, licking it as he watches. Snarling, he thrusts into my mouth without warning, his other hand gripping my hair and controlling my movements as he watches me. I gag at the sudden intrusion, my throat not prepared.

"Good girl. Take me all the way back." My hands come out, gripping his thighs, my nails digging into the hairy muscles to hold myself still as I suck. "I wanted to do this all day yesterday while you were teasing me with that incredible body, rubbing against me and flirting. I told myself I would be good, but then you wandered here, looking all sleepy and beautiful, and I couldn't resist."

I moan around his cock, loving the fact that he wants me so much.

Growling, he slowly pulls his cock from my mouth before slamming back in, fucking my mouth hard. He watches me the entire time. When he pulls out again, I lap at the tip, sucking and flicking until he gives up all semblance of control. His claws tighten in my hair to the point of pain as he hammers into my mouth, forcing me to take his massive length as he stares down at me.

Praise falls from his lips, his words making me desperate to come as he uses me. "Such a good girl," he rumbles. "Fuck, you should see how perfect you look right now."

I slide my hand under my skirt and slip my fingers through my messy, wet cunt.

He snarls as he watches me, gripping my hair hard. "Don't you dare make yourself come. Your releases are mine and mine alone right now." He reaches down and pulls my hand away, dragging it back to his leg. "Suck me harder," he demands, setting a brutal pace.

I slide my hands up and around to his ass, gripping his flexing cheeks and pulling him closer until he slams down my throat. He roars, hammering into my mouth.

"You'll swallow every drop of my cum or I will feed it to you," he snarls, feral now. He's close, I can tell, so I pull back slightly and suck harder. He yells and his hips flex, his cock swelling in my mouth as he explodes. His cum splashes inside my mouth, and I swallow reflexively, trying to keep up with the amount filling my mouth as he watches me. I can taste his musk and the wildness of his magic as it seems to warm me on the way down. Only then does he release my hair, but I lap and lave his cock until it's clean before sitting back with a smug grin.

My lips are swollen, and I'm sure my hair is a mess, yet he watches me in awe.

Dropping to his knees, he stares into my eyes. I might be on my knees for him, but I have all the power, and he knows it.

"Hurry up, you two," Bracken shouts, "before we come in there! Some of us are starving."

"Fuck."

We both say the word at the same time and laugh. My desire hasn't abated, and I practically groan in need.

He lifts his hand and sucks his fingers before sliding them up my skirt and slamming them into my channel. He works me hard and fast, his thumb finding my clit and rubbing hard as he fucks me with his fingers.

I come so hard and quickly, it's embarrassing. Moaning as my legs lock, I throw my head back. He strokes me through my release before pulling his fingers out and licking them clean.

Damn if I don't want his cock. Feeling empty and needy, I'm tempted to throw caution to the wind and have my way with him, but just then, we hear the others start to look for us.

"Time to go, little one." He smirks, reading my annoyance as he pulls me to my feet and pats my ass. "If you're good, I'll fuck you later."

"I'm always good," I mutter.

My words make him laugh as he follows me out to meet the others.

AFTER BREAKFAST, we continue to practice my magic, but after a while of just trying to catch them with it, I get bored. "How about we play a game instead?" I offer.

"A game?" Zee replies, grinning at me, panting from running so I could try and stop him.

"Hide-and-seek?" I suggest, and I meet five sets of equally puzzled eyes. "Basically, someone is 'it,' the others all hide, and the one who is 'it' has to find them. When they do, they change to being 'it.'"

Nero grins at me, while Bracken winks. "But I'd just let you find me and have your wicked way with me."

I huff, crossing my arms. "Go hide, and I'll use my magic to find you."

I turn my back and start to count. I don't hear them move for a moment before Bracken takes off past me with a laugh. Eventually, I hear the others go as well, and when I get to a hundred, I can't help but grin.

"Ready or not, here I come!" I call, giggling as I hurry into the woods. Joy fills me as I leap around trees and search broken remains for them. For a while, I forget to use my magic, just having a good time, before I focus and bring it forward. It's getting easier and easier every time, and this time it's so fast, it shocks me. It flows out of me, reaching for them. I realized earlier that I can feel them when they are close. It's as if my magic recognizes them and lays out a map in my head of their location.

I use that now.

"I'm going to find you!" I call. Hearing the sound of scales on wood, I glance up to see Nero sliding through tree branches above me. Before I can catch him, he's gone again, making me laugh. "Cheater!"

I can hear his echoing laugh.

Not surprisingly, Grim and Zee take it super seriously. I almost find Bracken at least five times before he manages to slip away. Grinning, I sneak up on the massive, hollowed out tree in front of me. I can feel one of them hiding in it. I expect Zee or Bracken again, but when I leap through with an "Aha! You're it!" I see Krug there.

"Oh, hi," I squeal. He's crouched in the rotten log, looking at me with a blank expression.

"You found me, so now I am it?" he concludes, standing and moving closer. He towers above me as he watches me.

"Now you're it," I reply, my voice unsure. "And you can find us..."

"But I've already found you." He grins, looking down at me, his smile so uncensored and soft, it shocks me for a moment before it fades. "Unless you want to run so I can chase you?" His voice comes out in a growl.

The desire Grim stoked this morning roars back to life as I lick my lips. He tracks the movement, eyes narrowing.

"Human," he warns.

"Do you want me to run?" I flirt and flutter my lashes at him.

"You are playing with fire."

"My favorite type of game," I tease, stepping closer.

Krug snarls, grabs me, and lifts me into the air so our heads are level, then his eyes search mine. "What do you want, human?"

"Right now?" I ask softly.

He nods, and I swallow.

"For you to kiss me."

As if my answer gives him permission, he slams his lips onto mine, swallowing my gasp. I wrap my arms and legs around him, climbing him in a way I've been dreaming about. As he grips my chin, tilting my head the way he wants, he decimates my lips. His tusks press to my face in a way that should be unpleasant, but instead, I'm shivering and imagining them between my thighs as his tongue sweeps into my mouth.

The kiss is over way too fast and leaves me panting and staring at him wide-eyed. He has the same look on his face as he watches me.

His scarred, deadly hands grip my ass, holding me against him. "Run, little human," he orders, sliding me down his body. "And when I find you, you are mine."

Laughing, I turn and start to run, knowing he's watching and counting down the time.

I infuse magic in my movements, not wanting to make it easy for him. I'm unsure if I want him to catch me or not. After all, we are still almost strangers, but that kiss...it stained my lips and soul. I seem to move faster, hopping through the trees in a way I couldn't before. The magic almost gives me wings, and I can't hear him anymore. I look around, spotting a hole in the base of a tree that's just the right size for me. Hesitating for a moment, I check to make sure there's nothing hiding inside before I slip into the darkness, curling up to fit and wait.

And wait...

And wait...

I'm just about to give up and climb out when I hear a sound as familiar as my own breathing—the sliding of scales. I cover my grinning lips, curling up tighter. "*Parum anguis*, I can smell you," Nero calls softly. "Your little orc found me, and now it's my turn to find you."

I bite my lip, shivering at his purring voice.

"And when I find you..." He trails off as I almost stop breathing. "You're close. I can smell your desire. Is that for me, little one, or for your orc?"

Panting, I stare out at the forest, watching him slide through the trees as he moves closer. My heart hammers, knowing he will find me.

And when he does...

I'll be his.

I know it, and I can't wait.

Clenching my thighs together to hold back my desire, I wait.

"Cora," he hisses. "Come out and play."

He slides into the clearing before the tree I'm hiding in, standing on his tail as he searches for me. "I can smell your need. Do you really want to hide anymore?"

He slides around the clearing, disappearing out of sight. Letting out the breath I'd been holding, I lean out of the tree and look for him. I nearly jump out of my skin when his face suddenly appears in front of me, upside down and grinning. "Got you!" His forked tongue slithers out as I squeak and jump back.

Laughing, he reaches in and pulls me out as he slides down the tree. Putting me on my feet, he curls his coils around me. "You didn't answer me, *parum anguis*. Who is your desire for?"

"All off you," I admit unashamedly, craning my neck to watch him wrap me up in his coils. Boldness fills me. "Do you plan to do something about it?"

When he speaks, he is behind me and so close, I can smell him.

"I plan to do everything about it, *parum anguis*."

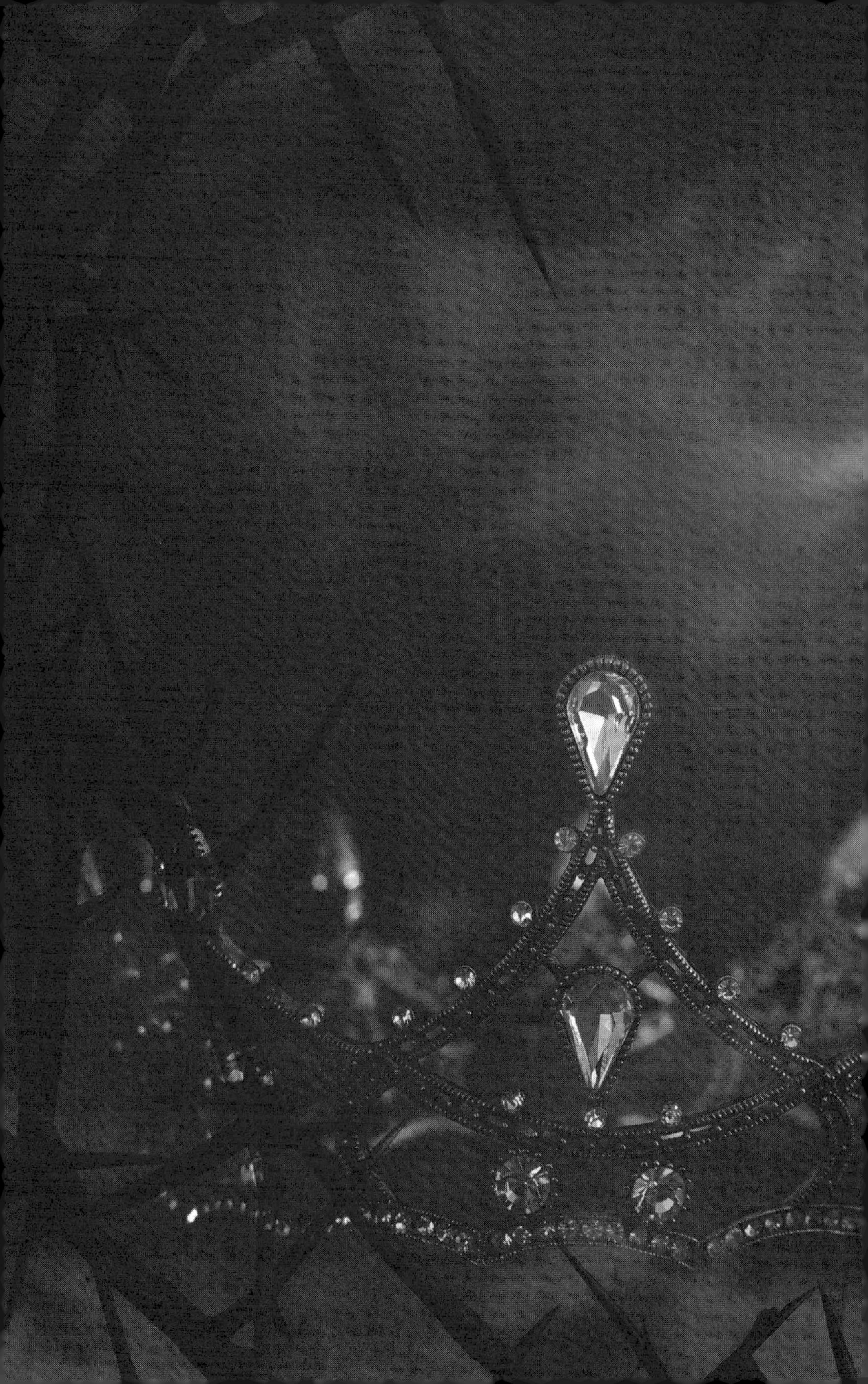

CHAPTER
TWENTY-SIX

His tail wraps around me, pinning me into the nest of his coils as he looms above me. "Nero," I whimper, and in one move, he rips away my clothes, leaving me bare for him. His huge hands cup my breasts, tweaking my nipples as my head falls back with a moan.

Grinning wickedly, he leans down and delicately wraps that sharp, vicious mouth around one tip and sucks, his fangs pressing to either side. I jerk and cry out. "Please," I beg, gripping his shoulders as he releases my nipple before abusing my other bud.

When he lifts his head again, his eyes are beastly. "Beautiful," he purrs, his hand sliding down my belly and cupping my slick cunt. "Fuck, *parum anguis*. Feel how wet you are for me, how desperate you are to be claimed."

"Fuck," I groan, watching him as he teases my pussy, his fingers dancing across every inch. I cry out when his fingers twirl around my clit. Eyes narrowing, he does it again, and I groan, wiggling in his grasp. He flicks my clit, and I swear I almost come undone. Moving his fingers away from the throbbing bundle, he slides two digits inside me with no warning, and I almost scream.

"You are tight, so very tight," he rumbles, pumping his fingers inside me. His tail comes up and flicks my clit, and I come so suddenly, I start to slide from his coils. He catches me, pumping his fingers inside me, the aftershocks leaving my legs weak. Nero keeps me standing before pulling his fingers out and running them across my lips. I taste myself before he leans down and kisses me.

His forked tongue flicks against mine as I whimper and pull him closer. His tail slides down my pussy, the scales smooth and soft and so foreign, it makes me moan into his mouth. As he dominates my mouth, the tip of his tail slides into me, and my eyes fly wide.

It's wide and so thick, it leaves me choking on air.

Pulling back, he flicks my clit with it before sliding the tip inside me again. He does this over and over as I stare into his eyes, panting heavily.

He encourages me to ride the tip of his tail. "You need to be so wet, it drips down you, my love, otherwise you will not take my length."

"Nero," I rasp out, my head falling back.

"I've got you. I've always got you, *parum anguis*," he promises as he pushes his tail deeper, making my mouth open on a wordless scream as he fills me. His fingers dance over my clit until I come again, clenching around the tip of his tail. He lets me rock and fuck against him, petting me the entire time until I slump, and then he pulls free of my clenching cunt.

"Look at me," he orders, and I force my heavy head up. My entire body is slick with sweat and filled with a need so great, it still doesn't abate, even after two orgasms.

I watch in both awe and confusion as his scales seem to part, and then his cock, hard and glistening, slides from inside. It's huge and thick, with a thinner pointed tip, but at the bottom is a huge bundle. "Erm, Nero?" I gulp. "What is the bulge?"

He strokes himself as I stare. "It's my knot. You will take every inch of me, and it will stretch you so wide, you will not be able to move."

"That won't fit." I shake my head, trying to back away, but he hisses and pulls me back to him, his tail coming up to hold me in place.

"It will. You will take it."

His scales glisten with my arousal as he slides the tip of his tail up to my mouth. I suck it automatically, and he snarls, biting at the air.

Turning me quickly, he bends me over his tail with my legs spread for him. My pink, swollen cunt drips with my own cum as he strokes me again, working two fingers inside me, then three, getting me all worked up before pulling away. His front presses against my back as his mouth brushes my ear.

"You are so magnificent, *parum anguis*," he hisses, nipping my neck. "I can't wait to fill you with my length and watch my cum drip from you."

Fuck.

I stiffen slightly when I feel the tip of his cock pressing against my entrance, but he nips and lips at my neck until I relax. He thrusts inside me, just the tip at first, before working it into me. It's not enough, though, and when I start to push back, he slides in deeper, all the way to that massive bulge, until I'm practically sitting on him.

Panting and moaning, I push back and grind against him, cum dripping down him from my embarrassingly slick cunt. The wet sounds of us coming together are loud as he pulls out and slams back in, stretching me for him. His slimmer tip seems to find that place inside me that has me groaning.

Just as suddenly as he fills me, though, he pulls back, leaving me gasping, cold, and empty.

He grips my hips and hauls me up as he turns me so I can see him again. "Straddle me, *parum anguis*, I want to see you ride me."

My hands fall to his chest as I spread my legs to either side of his coils, my thighs stretching wide because of his girth. His cock waves before me, wet with my juices and still hard. He lifts me and drops me until I'm taking most of him, and then I stiffen as he grips my hips and starts to work that bulge into me.

I start to panic, digging my nails into his scales as he hisses. "Relax, *parum anguis*," he purrs, his other hand finding my clit and flicking it until I relax, my pussy stretching farther. I take more of him in until that bulge is half filling my pussy. My head drops back with a muted scream. It feels too big and too hard.

Too much.

I need to move, to get off, but at the same time, I couldn't even if I wanted to. I stay pinned in place and filled to the brim, while his other hand rubs my clit. With a brutal thrust, he fills me, that knot slipping inside me.

I come so hard, I fall forward, spots of darkness dancing in my eyes, and when I come to, he starts to move. He pumps with soft little thrusts before his hands grip my ass, spreading my cheeks and digging in as he takes me deeper, harder. The knot stretches me each time until I'm a whimpering, desperate mess spread over his coils.

"Good, *parum anguis*," he murmurs, his eyes wild and feral. "Look at you taking me."

I groan and lean forward, nipping at his scales. He snarls and stills, and then I feel his release filling me, the warmth coating me from the inside.

He doesn't soften, but his bulge seems to grow a little smaller as he continues to pound into me.

"Nero!" I groan.

Pulling free of my body, he spins me once more, laying me across his tail, and then he drags me back by my hips and impales me on his cock.

That bulge stretches me every time he thrusts, filling me so much, I can't even speak.

His snarls fill the air as he works me on him like a rag doll, fucking me roughly as I cry out and claiming me just like he said. He comes twice more, never relenting, just fucking me harder each time, and his bulge grows smaller until it's almost normal-sized and feels incredible inside me.

He pulls out and spins me again so I'm facing him. With my feet pressed to his coil, he lifts me and impales me once more. I grip his face and kiss him. It's sloppy and dirty, but that's what this fucking is, and fuck if it doesn't feel good.

He takes me in every way, his cum dripping from me and around his cock as he hammers into me. His fangs are on display, and his eyes are slitted as he watches me.

My eyes fly wide with a scream as something brushes across my ass, tickling before pressing slightly.

He grins at me, still rocking me on his cock. "I have two cocks, *parum anguis*, and you'll ride them both." He yanks me down until I'm spread across him, filled with his cock in my slick pussy. His other one seems to have a mind of its own, sliding across my ass and seeking entrance. I tense, but he thrusts up, fucking me until I relax, and when I do, his other cock finds my ass and presses inside.

I scream as it slips past my defenses.

It fills my ass until I'm too full. I'm just writhing on him, both my pussy and ass filled to the brim. "Fuck, *parum anguis*," he rumbles, lifting me like I weigh nothing before dropping me down onto his cocks again. "You feel so good, too good. Look at you riding me like a goddess, letting this poor snake worship her. You glow with magic," he hisses, flashing his fangs as he slams me down on him over and over.

"Nero!" I scream, my body completely his.

With a roar, he slams me down so hard, it almost hurts. He strikes at the same moment, slamming his fangs into my neck as my scream grows shrill.

An orgasm overtakes me, and it's so strong, it bowls me over like a wave, gushing from me as I feel both of his cocks jerking inside me, filling me with his releases as my own squirts out of me. I fade into the blackness before I finish coming.

When I come to, I'm panting and boneless. He lifts me from his cocks, laying me across him as I whine, unable to do anything else.

He slides his hands all over me as I purr in contentment. His cum drips from me, covering my thighs and legs, mixing with my own. I'm covered in sweat, and I swear I couldn't walk even if I tried.

I'm broken and ruined, and he purrs happily.

"Well, shit. We have all been hiding forever while you two have been fucking," Bracken complains as he emerges from the trees. "And we weren't even invited. I'm wounded, Nero. I thought we were friends. Hell, if I had known that was going to happen when she caught us, I would have let her."

I can't help but laugh, my body giving a sore pulse as I do.

This is what happiness feels like.

CHAPTER TWENTY-SEVEN

The night is calmer than normal. The wind barely blows through the trees, making it a motionless darkness that doesn't exactly feel threatening, despite the sounds of the creatures stalking through them. I know we'll have to keep fighting off creatures. It seems the stronger my control over my magic becomes, the more monsters are drawn to our location. This magic in my veins, this feeling, pulses through my bloodstream now like a steady beacon. Using it is far easier than it used to be. Even as I lie down to nestle between my monsters, I hold up my hand and tiny sparks dance at my command. Bracken watches the little lights in awe, but when his eyes meet mine, there's a far softer look on his face than I've ever seen.

"Look how you shine, Goldie," he whispers before closing his eyes. "Look how you shine."

With those words running through my head, I fall asleep to the gentle rise and fall of Nero's coils, trapped within the warmth of the monsters who protect me. Throughout the night, I know they'll take turns keeping guard, making sure that nothing gets past our defenses, but for now, I simply enjoy being surrounded by the men who care about me.

I drift off to sleep quickly. I'm not surprised by the speed of it, not after a day of hide-and-seek and earth-shattering sex with Nero. I know I need rest if we're going to reach the castle within the next couple of days.

Dreams plague me almost immediately, but just when I think they don't make any sense, I see him again—the old king.

I don't know how I recognize him, but I do. I take the time to really study him this time and take in all the details. Even though everyone refers to him as the old king, he's anything but elderly. Now that I can focus, I see similarities between this king and Grim. The same horns. The same gait. The same features that suggest they could be related. A crown sits on the old king's head, perched between his horns in a way that almost doesn't make sense. The gold it's forged from glitters in the low light as he stands proudly before his throne, his eyes fierce.

That fierce expression changes into one of horror, and I furrow my brows as I stand like a silent sentinel at his side. Confused, I turn to face the direction of his gaze, only to see a live image from what looks like the Gilded Lands. The magic it takes to speak like this between distances astounds me, and I've never seen anything like it.

Could I do that?

My focus shifts as I comprehend the scene in front of me. The human king stands with his head tipped back, his crown far heavier than the old king's. The human king's crown is studded with jewels for every life he's taken, so it makes sense that he nearly bends beneath the weight of that burden. He holds a woman in his arms, her eyes bright with grief as the king holds a knife to her throat.

"What do you want, Haveron?" the old king asks. I can hear the panic in his voice as he takes another unsteady step toward the screen. He's too far away to do anything.

"What I've always wanted," Haveron, the human king, sneers. "Your magic, Kulmak. I thought giving Emelyn to you would seal some sort of deal and any child resulting from the match would be an easily manipulated monster, but Emelyn has let it slip that you do not intend to procreate—"

"Any procreation between us could result in Emelyn's death," King Kulmak snarls. "To subject her to that means she'll perish."

"That's a risk I'm willing to take," Haveron spits. "You will birth a child with Emelyn or—"

"I will not risk her death!" King Kulmak shouts, storming closer. "Release her, or I'll storm into your lands and destroy everything! No shadow will be safe for you."

Haveron smiles, and I already know he's going to refuse. Although I'm a silent spectator, I can feel the charge in the air—this is the monumental moment that changes everything. Emelyn, in her father's arms, begins to cry. She understands what is about to happen.

She's ready, her eyes heartbroken but resolved. An inner steel runs through her that leaves me in awe.

"Kulmak," she says, and the minotaur king's eyes go to her, softening instantly. Tears rush down her face, leaving wet trails behind as they reach her chin and fall off. "I love you."

Kulmak becomes feral. "Release her! Release her!"

Haveron only tilts his head. "Look at you. Even if you're wearing a crown, it doesn't hide the beast you are." He looks down at Emelyn, and I see the calculation in his gaze. "I suppose I have no use for this tainted daughter of mine then, do I?"

With a sweep across her neck, Haveron slits his daughter's throat.

I gasp at the gruesomeness of it, at the way her bright red blood sprays and then leaks from her flesh. Her hands go to her throat as if it'll help, but her life leaves her body far too quickly. Her eyes stay locked on the monster she loves, and tiny sparkles of magic appear around her blood, as if it had resided there... as if she was like me.

Haveron dumps her body on the ground like trash, and Kulmak loses everything within him that resembles humanity. He goes completely still, steam curling from his nose, as he looks at Haveron with a hatred the likes of which I've never seen.

"I'm going to rip your head from your shoulders, human, and then I'll bring Emelyn home."

Haveron laughs. "Good luck, beast." He turns to depart, leaving the body of his daughter on the cobblestones. "You'll never be able to find her."

I move around the room, stepping closer to the screen. A roar rips out of the king behind me, so loud and full of anguish, it shakes the walls. I turn toward him, and our eyes lock. He dips his head, his horns pointed right at me.

"You'll be the death of every last one of them," he spits out, the words warped into a monstrous threat. "Be ready for battle."

He launches himself toward me, his horns aimed straight for my heart.

~

I WAKE UP SCREAMING, my voice shrill, even to my own ears. My arms are swinging wildly around me, and my body convulses as if it can't get the proper functions to run and get away from the horns. There was anguish and pure hatred in his voice, but not for me.

Not for me.

The human king, Haveron, murdered his own daughter in cold blood when his plans failed. Clearly, he hadn't expected Kulmak to fall in love with Emelyn, causing him to keep her alive rather than risk her body. For whatever reason, Emelyn had been in the Gilded Lands, and that's where she remains.

You'll never find her.

As I'm screaming, too many arms to count come around me, offering comfort and trying to calm me down. I see Nero first, his bright eyes and brighter hair appearing in my vision. My eyes shift from blurry to clear as he whispers soft nothings to me before slipping into a gentle lullaby that I've never heard before. It soothes me in a way I've never been calmed, and I'm finally able to take a deep breath and look him in the eyes.

"What happened, *parum anguis*?" he asks gently as he studies my face.

I'm covered in a cold sweat, and when I wipe my arm across my forehead, it comes away with a sparkle, as if my magic is leaking from me. The others all watch me expectantly, waiting for an answer.

"Just a nightmare," I whisper. "Nothing more."

"Something like that is not just a nightmare," Grim points out. "Magic was flinging from your fingertips as if you were in a fight."

Biting my lip, I shift nervously where I sit cradled in Nero's coils. "I saw them," I admit.

"Who?" Krug asks, leaning in.

"The old king. Kulmak, and Emelyn. I saw them both in my dream."

Silence. All of my monsters stare at me with wide eyes.

"Is this the first time you have dreamed of him?" Zetros inquires, worry in his gaze.

I hesitate. I haven't brought up the dreams before now because they didn't seem important, but considering the way they are looking at me now, I might have made the wrong call.

With a grimace, I shake my head.

"Why didn't you tell us?" Grim rumbles. He straightens and crosses his arms over his expansive chest, and he looks even more like Kulmak. I wonder again if they are related, or if that slant of the eyes and shape of the nose is common in minotaurs.

"I didn't want to worry you," I murmur, looking down to avoid their eyes.

Strong fingers grip my chin and force my gaze up again, making it clash with my kraken's. "Here, in the Dead Lands, dreams are not just dreams, *measma*."

"Then what are they?" I ask, desperate to understand.

"They show the truth," Bracken replies, and for once, there's no joking mirth in his tone. His voice resonates with seriousness. "They show the past, future, and sometimes even the present."

My fingers start to clench and unclench on their own.

You'll be the death of every last one of them.

"What does it mean?" I rasp out, terrified to think that those words could have been for the future.

"Your magic must be calling it forth," Krug says, but even with that explanation in the air, I don't feel any better.

In fact, the worry on their faces only makes me edgier.

The small bites of magic on my fingertips begin to move.

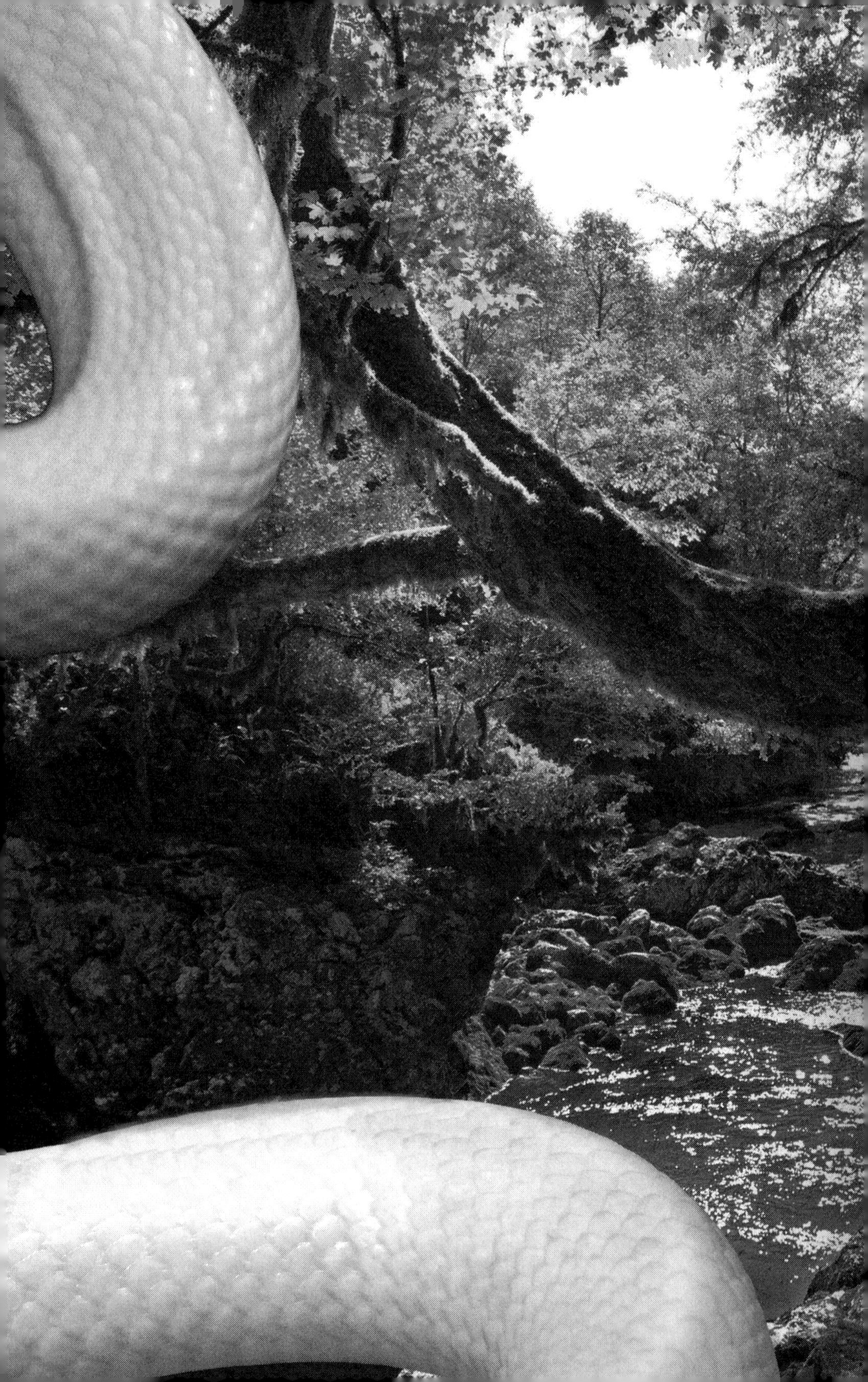

CHAPTER TWENTY-EIGHT
NERO

"We need to get to the castle as fast as possible," Krug states, his head tilted back into the wind. "I can feel Cora's magic in the air, and if I can, then every other monster in the vicinity can too."

"Looks like you'll be riding me," I tell Cora, and I am rewarded with the sight of her blushing. I lean in closer, letting my lips touch the shell of her ear. "Later, maybe I'll let you ride me another way."

The flush brightens, and I lean back in amusement, addicted to the effect I have on her.

"Cruel, wicked snake," she says, but her eyes are bright, unlike how they'd been when she awoke screaming.

Earlier, her eyes had been bright with fear and dread, and she'd been so desperate to get away from whatever was in her mind that it had taken her far too long to understand she was safe. We still haven't asked exactly what the dream was about, what scene she saw, but it couldn't have been pretty. That scream was shrill and terrified. I hadn't had the heart to ask what part of history she saw.

"We keep moving," Grim commands, taking the lead as he always does. "We don't stop again unless we have to."

As Cora climbs onto my coils and wraps her slight hands around my torso, I can't help but feel cherished with the touch. She does so gently, carefully, as if she worries she'll hurt my scales. Reaching back, I squeeze her thigh gently and turn. Our eyes meet, and I see everything reflected there, all the worry, before she quickly pushes it away.

"*Parum anguis*," I murmur, soothing her. "We're all here with you. You're safe."

Pain flickers in her eyes again before she can hide it. "I know," she says, but there isn't a ring of truth to her words, and that has my own tension rising.

What exactly did she see in her dreams?

I twist until I can meet her eyes, briefly forcing her back on my coils. I cup her face between my hands and make her look at me. "Cora, *parum anguis*, I love you." She sucks in a heavy breath at the words that I haven't said before. "I will not let anything happen to you or those you care about."

Her hands come up to cover mine, holding my fingers to her flesh. "You promise?"

I lean down and press my forehead against hers. "I promise with every fiber of my being."

Something inside her seems to relax, even if it's just a little. "I love you too, Nero," she whispers, and something within me breaks and soars high, until I nearly grab her and wind through the trees in excitement. I hadn't expected anything back when I said the words, but here she is, speaking them as if they are common knowledge.

She is giving me such a gift. I am a monster. I do not deserve such a bright, shining being, yet I cannot...

I will not let her go.

"We need to go," Bracken says, and there's a lack of mirth in his voice that has me pausing.

When I turn to look at the fey, his eyes are on the trees behind us. "What is it?" I ask.

"Arachne fey."

Cora's eyes widen. "What are arachne fey?"

Bracken meets her gaze. "Let us hope you don't have to find out, Goldie. They are not the most pleasant of my kind."

"Time to move," Zetros says, reaching up to adjust Cora on my back, making sure she's seated properly. "I'll take up the rear."

Despite the situation, I can't help but joke, "Only because you want to stare at my ass."

Zetros quirks a smile and pats Cora on the ass. "He's discovered my secrets."

Cora laughs nervously, and it makes us both relax. We don't want her to worry or fear whatever is coming, but the truth is there. With her magic growing every day, there's no longer a way to hide her. Monsters from far and wide will be drawn to us, and we'll have no choice but to fight those brave enough to tackle our group, especially if they get a hold of Cora…

I can't even think of that possibility.

We begin to move, pushing through the trees at a rate far faster than we've traveled before. Cora hangs onto me, making sure she doesn't slide off as we push through. My coils dig through the undergrowth, pushing it aside as I wind around and between trees. The others keep up easily, making short work of the distance.

While we could reach the castle within a day at this pace, we're held back.

The first creatures who dare to attack are a horde of screamers. They are grotesque creatures twisted by dark magic, and there's nothing about them even remotely human. They crawl on all fours, their bodies misshapen and sporting wounds that are caused by dark magic that oozes out. There's nothing pleasant about them, but at least their smell is the first warning. They are relatively weak as far as monsters go, their strength in their numbers more than anything, but we make quick work of them before we continue on.

With each attack, we're slowed down, until I know we won't reach the castle within the day. Cora's power is too strong, too tempting, and every creature is coming for us. There's no way to hide her magic other than to get her to the castle, but it seems the closer we get, the more we must face.

"Flesh beetles on the right," Grim calls just before the things attack.

I've never been a fan of the creatures. Though their shells shine with morphing colors, their faces and bodies are as twisted and ugly as the screamers. They are stronger than the monsters before, but still no match for our group. Cora seems especially squeamish about the insect-like creatures.

"Oh, ew," she grumbles, tucking her legs up so they don't drag too closely to the ground.

"Don't fret, *parum anguis*," I purr as my coils crush the beetles who dare to get too close. "As long as they don't touch you, they are harmless."

"What happens if they touch you?" she asks hesitantly, as if she's afraid to know.

"They feast on your flesh while you're still alive," I answer matter-of-factly. I won't lie to her, even if it makes her face turn a frightening shade of green.

Like the screamers, the flesh beetles are easily dispatched, and we're able to continue forward again.

"This is going to take forever," Krug grumbles, and I have to second his sentiment. Now more than ever, we need to make quick work of the distance, and we're being held back by the monsters.

Bracken is standing in front of me, his head tilted to the side as he listens. Out of all of us, his senses are the strongest. Although I can hear and smell creatures coming in, something about Bracken's old magic and his powers enables him to sense far more. It's the reason he knew I was following them and still chose not to say anything.

"We must move," he states, his eyes hard. "We keep moving, and we do our best not to stop."

"What is it?" Cora asks, reaching for him.

It speaks volumes that Bracken offers her his hand without complaint, that he allows her to comfort him. "The arachne are gaining ground each time we stop."

"What happens if they catch us?" I ask, studying the fey.

His eyes meet mine. "Then we hope they haven't brought the queen with them."

Cora's hand tightens on my body. "And if they did?"

Bracken's eyes rove around the forest, as if he's feeling for them, searching. "We hide and hope they can't follow."

Zetros straightens. "If they come within a mile of us, sound the alarm," he orders Bracken. "We will take cover quickly and do our best to mask our trail."

We begin to move again, a sense of urgency in our movements. I've never ran into the arachne before, but if Bracken fears them, then we should all fear them.

In all my years, I've never once seen the dark fey afraid, but now, he looks over his shoulder as if the greatest monster he's ever seen follows us.

It takes everything to swallow the pit in my chest. For the first time, I wonder if Cora is really safer with us, or if we're taking her deeper into danger.

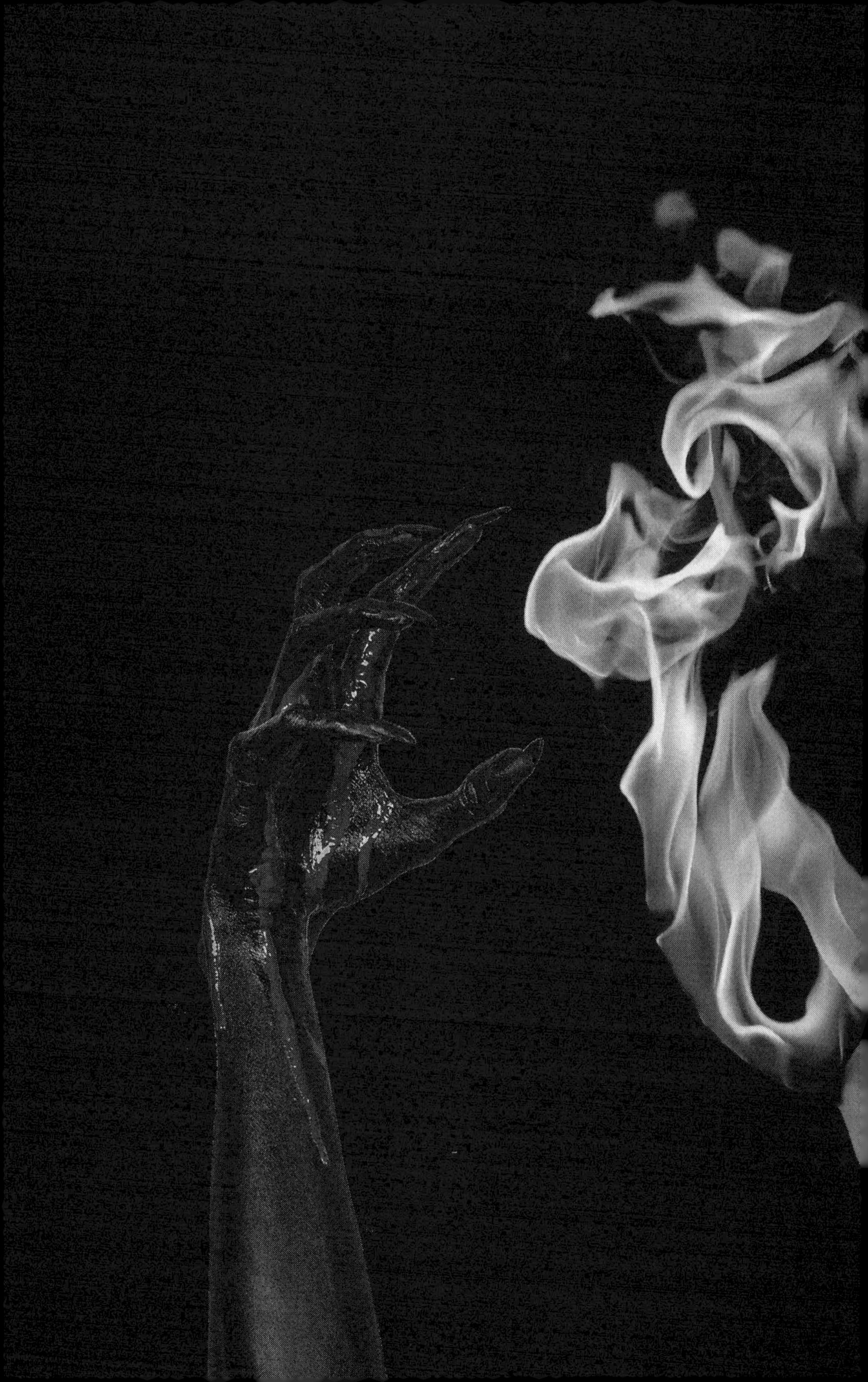

CHAPTER TWENTY-NINE

BRACKEN

They are drawing closer. I can feel it. An instinctual alarm is going off in the back of my mind, their magic brushing over me, searching for her.

My goldie.

Mine.

Not theirs.

I speed up, and the others do the same, following my lead. We need to get far away from them, because the idea of them getting their hands on my little human is unthinkable, and for the first time ever, I'm not so sure we would win, and that cannot happen.

We have to keep her safe.

When I first saw Goldie, I was transfixed by the way one is when they see a pretty gem. I needed to hoard it, clutch it, and destroy it, but then she happened. She aimed those stunning eyes at me, leaving me weak and wordless. She showed me the true depth of a human's strength and capability, and I was lost—not in the way that I wanted to possess her, although I do, but in a way that I now can't live without her.

For so long, I existed in the shadows, in the fog, feeling nothing and doing the same thing day in and day out. The only time I ever even felt a hint of happiness—no, happiness isn't the right word, a hint of excitement, was when I was killing and other monsters' blood spilled across my hands, but even that pales in comparison to how I feel when she simply looks at me.

If she knew the power she held over me or how deeply I feel about her, she would run, because I'm never letting her go. She makes me feel alive, but more than that, she makes me want to be a better monster, a better man. She never asks for it, though, and she accepts all of me, even the parts my own people found ugly and hated. She accepts my bloodlust, my lack of seriousness...

Yet around her, I've never been more serious.

I tease and flirt, but under all the pretty words is the truth.

I am hopelessly, irrevocably in love with the human.

I am one of the strongest fey to ever live, but Goldie holds my heart in her tiny little hands, and I can't be mad about that. Not when she reaches for me, letting me comfort her. Her eyes seek mine, filled with fear, so I force cockiness into my expression, my lips tilting in my usual smirk, but for once, it falls flat. She sees through it.

She always does.

My clever, tricky little human.

"They are close, aren't they?" she whispers.

I nod, unable to lie to her or deny her anything. She thinks Grim is protective and obsessive, but she doesn't know the true depths of my feelings for her or what I would be willing to do just to put a smile on her face.

I would face a thousand arachne fey. I would throw myself into a war. I would stand between her and all the monsters if that's what it took.

All this time, monsters were hunting humans, and now I'm beginning to understand why—they are dangerous, more so than any monster. We crave that spark of life and need to consume it, yet I'm finding I don't want to consume her anymore. No, I want to be consumed *by* her.

Grim snarls, the others speeding up, spreading out behind her to protect her.

Her skin starts to glow slightly with her magic, so faintly I don't think she even realizes it. She's magnificent and so beautiful, it hurts to look at her. She shines so brightly and glitters.

She's like gold—beautifully unique, shines through the darkness, addictive, and hard to obtain.

That's why I call her Goldie, not just because of her hair.

"We aren't going to make it," I realize, saying it out loud. "We need to hide."

Even as I say that, I know it won't work. For once, I feel hopeless, and I hate that feeling.

Her eyes close and, as always, I track her every movement, stumbling over a root because I'm so intently focused on her. Luckily, she doesn't notice, and when her eyes snap open, they glow like trapped jewels.

Like the sun used to.

They focus on something we cannot see in the distance before she turns those glowing eyes to us. "There. We must go there."

Even her voice is filled with magic.

I share a look with Grim. "What's there?" he demands.

"Safety." She frowns, as if she's unsure what else is there.

"Good enough for me." I shrug before grabbing her. I throw her over my shoulder and start to sprint, truly sprint, not the slow pace I use when I run alongside them.

I show them exactly how fast a fey can move, almost too fast for them to keep up. If I wanted to, I could lose them all, but she cares for them, so I make sure they can stay on my heels, even as a dark part of me tells me to leave them behind and keep her for myself, but she would be upset, and I hate her tears more than I hate sharing.

She mumbles directions to me, her voice still thick with magic, and we run for so long, even I start to tire. Finally, we break through the trees and I skid to a stop, letting her slide down my body. She doesn't spare me a look, even as I steady her with my hands on her hips.

No, her eyes are locked on the seemingly solid rock of the black mountains that lead to the castle. "Goldie," I start, but she pulls away.

She doesn't look at any of us as she heads straight for the rock. I glance at the others, shrugging at their silent questions, and follow after her. She stops before a piece of solid glowing stone. Her hand dances above it as if she feels something none of us can, then she throws me a grin over her shoulder. "Safety." She nods, turns, and steps into the rock.

My mouth drops open when she disappears. One second, she was before me, and the next, she's gone.

"Cora!" Grim roars, his madness taking over, but suddenly her delicate, tan arm slides from the rock, her hand outstretched.

Unwilling to leave her alone, I place my hand in hers, trusting her, and I'm pulled through with her. She reaches for the others, pulling them through. Magic explodes across my skin, like a barrier popping and reforming around us, granting us access, but as it does, it explores what and who we are, and I feel Cora sheltering us from it.

Once everyone is huddled in the darkness, she turns and walks again. There's a black archway of rock before us, and she stands there as we watch from behind.

"I felt it pulling me here, whispering of safety," she explains, and then she steps through the archway with a gasp. Once on the other side, she turns to us with round eyes. "Now I know why."

I follow after her quickly, almost groaning at the pain that washes over me as I move through the entryway, the others grunting when they feel it too, but once on the other side, I understand her shock. The space expands into a huge cavern, with light in a seemingly endless fire brightening and warming the space. Paintings cover the walls and ceiling, a tale of love and loss.

A tale of the old king and his human.

There are treasures, jewels, statues, books, a bed, and a fire. It's like a haven, a forgotten place of safety, and when I look back to find Goldie and ask her how she knew about it, I see her standing in the middle of the room. Her hand hovers above a plain, black leather book as she skims it, then her gaze meets ours.

"This was her place, Emelyn. She and the king created this as a place to keep her safe, to be alone. It is a shrine to their love story. She brought me here. She granted me access, only ever me and those I trust. I know because I saw her in my dreams. I thought it was the magic, that the king showed me, but it wasn't, it was her. I feel her now—her sadness, her hopelessness, her anger, and her determination. She was so strong and so in love with the king and this world." She swallows, then glances back at the book before looking back at us.

"Did her death start the war?"

CHAPTER
THIRTY

It's all so clear now.

I feel the shroud of the shadows releasing and showing me the truth it obscures—her, her power, her magic.

She and the king shared it, allowed it to flow between them like a lifeforce, and when she was taken from him, when she was killed, it was ripped away from her and thrown back into him. He couldn't save her, and that enhanced magic drove him mad.

She whispered to me when I needed it, as if we were finally close enough to hear her. I'm just glad this place is safe. No one can get in unless she allows them to. I know that with certainty, but I'm not sure how.

You are safe here.

It's a whisper only I can hear, settling my nerves as I stop before the book. I feel the others glancing around, but my entire focus is engrossed by the simple black writings on a page of the book.

It is time you saw. It is time to see.

See what? I almost ask out loud.

To truly see past your mortality, past your humanity, to the heart of this land and the magic it possesses. After all, it belongs to it. We are simply borrowing it, the whisper responds, and without meaning to, I reach out and touch the book.

Memories crowd my brain—hers, the king's, and all the people who came before. It's all the memories of this land.

Of magic.

Of its corruption, misuse, and stolen strength.

It crowds my brain until I scream, but I also know I'm not. I'm standing before the book. It all happens in mere seconds, yet inside, I'm screaming and writhing in agony as my brain fills and overflows with too much knowledge.

Too many memories.

Too much pain.

Heartache.

Horror.

Hope.

All of it crashes over me like a wave until I'm drowning.

Breathe, chosen one, just breathe, and it will pass. This was the only way. I injected my magic into these words with my last breath. When my love found this book, he brought it here, which was my last request, for you. You are the one this world and I have been waiting for—the one who can stabilize the balance and save magic.

The soft, almost motherly whisper is like a balm on an open wound, and I slowly start to breathe again. When I open my eyes, I look over the words in the book, but I don't need to read them to understand them.

I turn to the others, words spewing from my mouth before the truth of the matter escapes my lips.

"Did her death start the war?" Horror fills me as I stare at them in shock. "It did. The humans killed her. Her own father, the king, killed the princess in their own land to start the war. But why?"

I search the memories, but there are too many.

"Power," Grim replies as I come to the same conclusion.

The others watch me carefully, and I realize I'm glowing again. Magic runs through me, and I follow it like a living, breathing vein pumping around my body and into the ground. "It was power that was not theirs to steal. That's why magic has deserted the Gilded Lands and the Shadow Lands and only sparks remain like echoes of what it once was. It was never the king's to capture. It is this world's, and we simply borrow it. He tried to corrupt it. He killed an innocent being whom this world chose to bridge the gap between its creatures."

"The humans wanted the power of the monsters and were tired of sharing it with her beasts. Her father thought her death was needed to overthrow the lands, and he was right. Our king was a broken, ruined man after his love's death. He declared war, but even in death, the human king was haunted by his daughter, so with the last of the stolen power, he built the wall to keep out the monsters and the memories," Bracken explains.

Nodding, I look back at the book. "He was right. Her memory is locked in here with magic—magic that is becoming corrupted and rotten with no outlet. She brought me here so I could see and know the truth... so I could change it." I meet every one of their eyes. "She chose me, the land chose me, it had been trying to find the one each cycle. Every hunt, it tests the human to make sure they are strong enough for what it needs."

"What it needs?" Zee repeats, confused.

"*Parum anguis...*" Nero frowns, but my eyes lock on Krug.

"I can save magic, but it's much bigger than that now. To save magic, we must save the lands, and to do that, we must heal them. We must free their memories."

My eyes close as I feel a comforting hand stroke my arm.

Her ghost.

"We must reunite the king and his lost love."

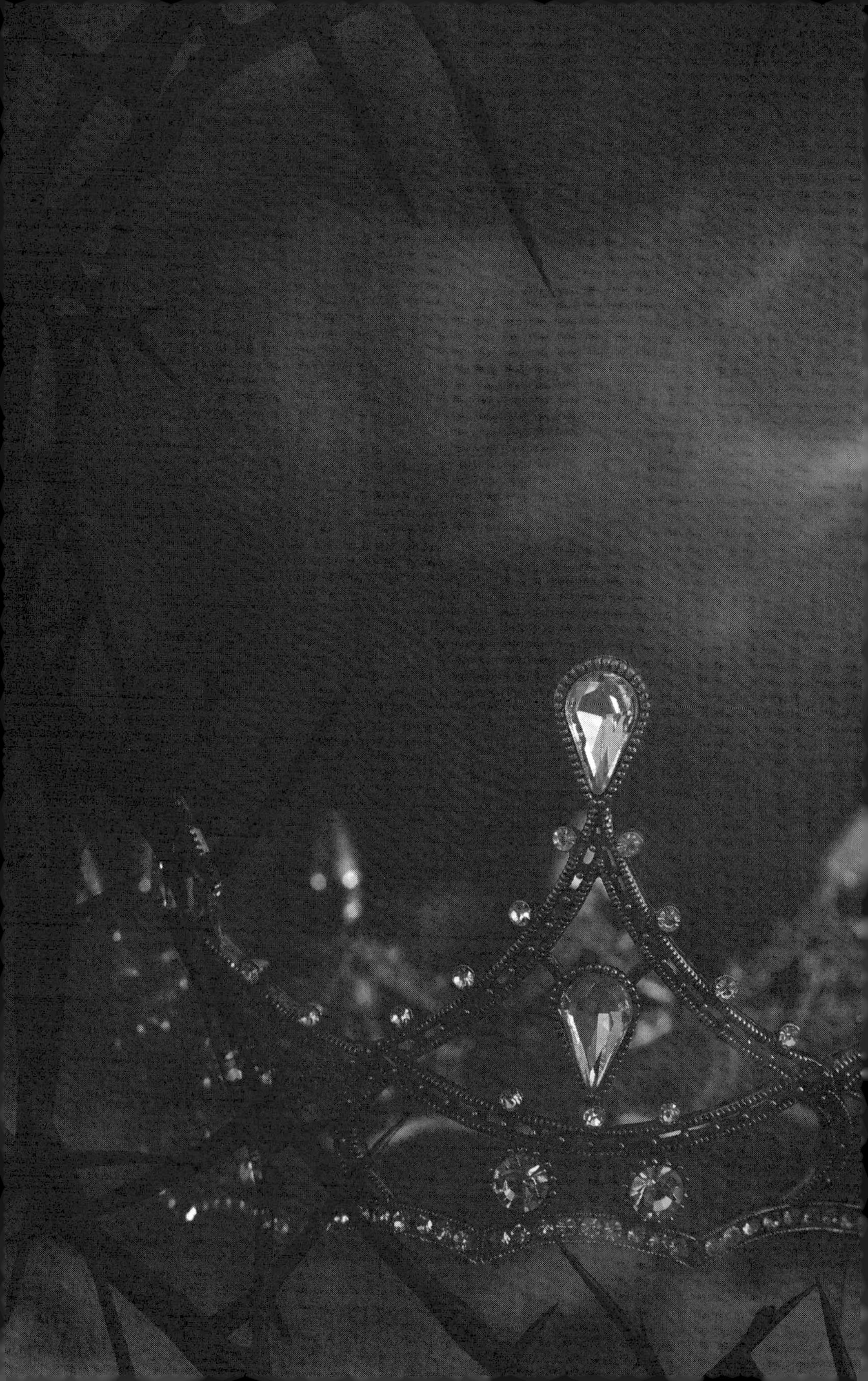

CHAPTER
THIRTY-ONE

"What do you mean?" Grim rumbles, standing against the wall with his arms crossed as if he's afraid to touch anything. "Reunite them? They are dead."

"I understand that, but—" I begin, picking up the small black journal.

"Saving magic is one thing," Krug adds, "but saving the lands? The humans will never allow it."

I glance at him. "Look, I know—"

"And besides all that, didn't you say the king is an asshole?" Grim asks. "He won't agree to such a thing, and that's if the older kings were thoughtful enough to leave things where they need to be for this to work—"

"Stop!" Nero snarls, cutting everyone off. "Let her speak."

I shoot a grateful glance at the naga and take a deep breath. "I know it sounds crazy, and I can't explain how I know anything at all, but...she told me."

Zetros tilts his head. "Who told you?"

"Emelyn. The old king's human love." I hold up the journal. "I told you she allowed us in, but it's more than that. This place is infused with her memory, with her spirit, and her magic is brushing against me, telling me what must be done. I'm the only hunt to ever make it this far, and now I know what has to be done."

"We reunite them," Bracken repeats. "I remember a time before the war, when there were talks of King Kulmak and his bride. There wasn't much time between the announcement and the declaration of war."

"Because the King of the Humans, Haveron, murdered his own daughter," I explain. "He took Emelyn and killed her because Kulmak refused to produce offspring with Emelyn. It was too risky for a minotaur and a human, even with magic, to reproduce."

"Wait," Zetros says, taking a step closer and eyeing the journal. "You're saying that the human king planned to steal the baby for himself for its magic?"

"That's exactly what I'm saying," I reply with a nod. "He'd always planned a power grab, but poor Emelyn paid the price."

Grim has been silent the whole time, watching me carefully. "When you say reunite them, you mean..."

"Reunite their bodies so they can rest in peace," I murmur.

"But it's been centuries," Bracken points out. "Surely there's nothing but dust and ash left."

I don't know how I know it, but when I feel that phantom touch on my arm again, I shake my head. "No. We'll be able to unite them."

"How do you know?" Krug asks, studying me.

I shrug, having no real answer. "I just do."

Everyone falls into silence, my words no doubt repeating in their minds as they mull them over. I don't know what they are thinking or if they believe I am insane, but when Nero slides forward and takes my hand, I smile gratefully at him.

"If you say we must reunite them, then that is what we shall do," he says gently, the soft curl of his lips revealing just the barest flash of his teeth.

One by one, they all move forward and place their hands on my skin, offering their support, until only Krug stands apart from us. I meet his eyes, waiting.

"What do you say, Your Majesty? Will you help us bring back magic?" I whisper.

Krug hesitates. "When you first appeared in my home, I had my reservations. No hunt had made it so far, so that was already impressive, but when you stood before me and didn't cower, that's when you earned my respect." He steps forward and lays his hand on my shoulder. "I will follow you wherever you lead, Cora the Fearless, for in following you, I know you will succeed in anything you do."

My throat grows thick with emotion at the name he'd given me, a tradition among orcs. Krug the Destroyer. Cora the Fearless. He's recognizing me as an equal, and it means more to me than I could ever explain.

"It'll be dangerous," I warn. "Kulmak withheld magic and locked it up so the humans could never get ahold of it. Unless he and Emelyn are at peace, it'll never return."

Krug grins. "Little human, we've been in danger since the moment you stepped into the Dead Lands. Why would I be afraid, when Cora the Fearless leads our cause?"

I guess he's right.

～

For the rest of the night, we settle into the safety of the cave. I'm surrounded by limbs, and there are so many strokes along my flesh, I don't know whom they belong to. I don't know where I end or begin, or where anyone does. I've started to realize it's not only about me and surviving the Dead Lands, like I first thought when I'd been thrown to the monsters. This isn't about my revenge or any petty vendettas I might carry against the Gilded Lands. All the lands need to change, each must be returned to its former glory, and the monsters deserve to live without fear.

This isn't about me.

It never was.

This is about everyone, about the balance between lands, the future, and monsters and humans alike.

When dawn arrives, muted in the Dead Lands in a way it shouldn't be, the last dredges of Emelyn's magic fades with it. I feel her spirit urge me forward, and with her final phantom caress, I tuck the tiny journal into Grim's satchel and straighten. I know the arachne fey have already long since passed, Bracken's own powers lending to that knowledge.

"Everyone ready?" I ask, facing the rock.

I'm met by a chorus of, "Ready," and I smile at the many voices of my monsters.

With a satisfied sigh, we leave the safety of the cave and make our way toward the castle.

CHAPTER
THIRTY-TWO

The castle is closer than I expected.

When Bracken picked me up and I directed him to the cave, we covered some of the last distance between us and the old castle that still stands. Even with magic dying and the time that's passed, it stands like a silent sentinel in the realm, both a warning and a beacon. Its architecture is stunning and unlike anything I've seen before. Built with spires and points that serve as a threat to any enemies, it's meant to intimidate, but I do not fear it. How could I when I know the love story that once unfolded here? A young princess was sent on a peace delegation, only for her to fall in love with a minotaur king, the king of all monsters.

My eyes trail over to Grim, who walks beside me, and I understand. I never knew Kulmak, but I know Grimus, and I would give up everything for him, for each of my monsters. Without them, I wouldn't be the Cora I want to be.

I never really found myself until I was thrown to the monsters.

"Should we go inside?" Krug asks, staring up at the castle. We passed over the rock bridge without issue, and now we stand before the sprawling black palace. "No one has set foot inside the castle since the war. No one dares to."

I study the front door and the iron pieces molded with the wood, none of them decaying. There's an overwhelming feeling of animosity in the structure, but it's not directed at us.

"We should," I answer. "We'll be safe inside."

I take a step forward and press my fingers to the door. I don't push or try to pry it open, but I let some of my magic trickle out, let it touch the iron and wood. Without any effort at all, the door pops open with an ominous click, allowing us passage.

"He wants us to be here," I say, staring into the castle as flames erupt on the lanterns along the walls.

I step inside and take in the opulent yet coarse decor, the beautiful paintings of monsters lining the walls, the tapestries depicting scenes of older times, and the items that look human, which have been displayed with care, as if they were gifts from a particular woman, a special human.

"We should split up," Bracken suggests.

"Splitting up is a terrible idea," Grim rumbles.

Nero sighs. "Regardless, this castle is large, and we have a lot of ground to cover. We need to find where the final resting places are for King Kulmak and Emelyn and then reunite them. If there will be clues, then they'll be here."

Grim sniffs. "We go in groups of two."

"I'll go with Cora," Krug offers, pulling a club from his back.

Bracken rolls his eyes. "Of course you will." Even though he rolls his eyes at Krug, he winks at me to tell me he's not mad. "Try to actually look around."

Sniffing in indignation and trying my hardest to stifle my giggle, I look up at Krug. "Let's go this way." I lead him to the right, down a long corridor, while the others spread in other directions.

The old castle is not what I expected. If anything, it's in pristine condition. Nothing has crumbled after all these centuries, and nothing is out of place. There isn't even any dust coating the items on display along the walls—some things I recognize, others I don't. I wonder at the kind of magic that holds this castle out of time and keeps it from aging and crumbling, despite there being no king.

"Have you ever been here before?" I inquire, glancing up at Krug.

He shakes his head. "I remember seeing King Kulmak from afar once, but I was young and he was high up. Kings didn't concern themselves with young orcs."

Biting my lip, I push open a large door, but it only seems to be storage, the room piled high with chairs and tables. "Was he a good king?"

Krug pauses and glances down at me. "Kulmak reigned over monsters, Cora. He was a strong king, a fair one, but was he a good one?" He shrugs. "We prospered under his rule, but he was cruel, and ultimately, it was his decisions that brought us to war."

"But he fell in love," I point out.

"Love does not diminish his duties, and he should have suspected what the human king was planning when he gave his daughter over as a gift. Falling in love is one thing, but pretending there isn't trouble brewing in your kingdom is another."

Frowning, I push another door open and peek inside, only then realizing that Krug is leaning over me to check for danger first. "I guess that makes sense, but love is a strong motivator."

Inside the room, there's furniture set up as if to accept company, but otherwise, there's nothing important.

When I close the door and turn, Krug is looking down at me. "No matter what happens, Cora, I have a duty in this world. We all do. Just because I've been enchanted by you does not take away from those duties, and they must come first." His words are coarse, harsh, and though they make me cringe internally, outwardly, I don't react.

"I've never asked to be put first, nor, as far as I'm concerned, have I asked you to be enchanted by me," I retort, looking up into his handsome scarred face.

Bright blue eyes focus on me and study my face. "You may not have asked, little human, but here I am, enchanted nonetheless." He leans in and presses my back against the door, and the air rushes from my lungs at the sheer size of him. "You may not ask it of me, but I'd still consider giving it all up for you, just so you'd look at me just like this." His finger comes up and strokes down my jawline.

"Like what?" I murmur.

"Like you'd love me just as fiercely as any warrior loves battle if I'd let you."

I blink up at him, taking in everything from the honesty in his gaze to the small tusks protruding from his bottom lip. "I would never ask you to give up your duties."

The corner of his lips curls up. "Which is why these feelings persist, despite my resistance," he admits. "Because you, Cora the Fearless, are far more than simply the hunt." He leans closer, his breath fanning across my cheek as he presses his lips there, his tusk scraping across my sensitive skin. "You are a queen."

My heart seizes, and the vision I'd seen before of a crown on my head flashes in my mind as he leans back and offers me his hand. "Come. Let's keep searching."

I slide my hand into his and allow him to pull me along, searching room after room, hoping to find anything that could help. After we travel deeper into the castle, I remember I can follow my magic and see if it leads us anywhere. Focusing on the feeling in my veins, I close my eyes for a second before I feel a tug.

"This way," I say, and Krug turns without any further prompting.

We follow the tug until we reach two large double doors, the wood carved in intricate patterns that I don't recognize. Words roll across the top, but not in any language I understand.

"Knowledge is power," Krug translates. "It's the old language."

The doors are taller than the orc and heavy. When he reaches forward and pushes one of them open, even he struggles with it, his muscles bulging as he opens the door just enough for us both to fit through. My jaw drops when he releases it, and the door closes behind us.

It's a library larger than anything I've ever witnessed, and the shelves are completely filled with books from floor to ceiling, calling my name.

The things I could learn in here that I wouldn't need a man's permission to learn...

"Wow," I whisper. The room is far larger than I suspected, and it just keeps going. As we venture farther inside, more lanterns light up, leading the way. "I've never seen so many books."

"We have a good library in my castle, but nothing like this," Krug comments, looking around.

"The orcs have a library too?" I look at him eagerly.

Upon seeing my excitement, Krug steps forward and cups my chin. "When we return, I can show you, and you can read any book you'd like."

"Are women allowed to learn in your kingdom?" I ask, staring up at him.

He freezes, his eyes going from soft to hard. "What sort of question is that, Cora the Fearless?"

I swallow, carefully reaching up to lay my hand on his forearm. "In the Shadow Lands, women are forbidden to learn. We're possessions to be traded by our fathers to our husbands. They prefer we remain dumb and silent, mere tools for them to fuck and command, nothing more."

His eyes flash with anger so fierce, I nearly take a step back. "Were you traded?"

I shake my head. "I volunteered as the hunt to save my sister before I could be traded, not for my father's lack of trying." I study his face. "I did not fit their mold, Krug, and it made sense for me to step through the wall when it was time."

He leans down, his face level with mine, and sternly states, "In my kingdom, women and men learn equally. Women can be warriors, scholars, homemakers, or anything they choose, but the important thing is that it's their choice. No one commands them to be silent, and if you ever find yourself silenced, I'll cut the one who dares to cause you harm into tiny pieces until they are nothing but a pile of meat, and then I'll present their beating heart to you."

Somehow, that's one of the most romantic things anyone has ever said to me. The imagery is strong and gruesome, but I find myself leaning in to kiss the orc king who would dare to defend my voice and allow me to rise to my greatest potential. Despite his earlier words that he would still have duties, he's gifting me with a greater gift than anything else—knowledge and protection of my autonomy.

His lips are softer than I expected and plush against mine as I linger, wondering for a moment how things would work with his tusks, but before I can ponder things too deeply, his arms wrap around my waist and pull me in. His hands are large against my body, completely spanning my waist, but when he takes control of the kiss, I melt. His tusks press against me as his tongue darts out and tangles with mine. I circle his neck with my arms and tangle my fingers in his long hair. He backs me against the nearest bookshelf and pins me there before he releases my lips to trail kisses down my neck, his tusks scraping my skin, even while his tongue follows their path.

"I've imagined this moment since I first saw you," he murmurs. "I've imagined throwing you over the nearest object and fucking you there a million times. Once, I imagined bending you over Nero's coils and fucking you until you screamed, only for the snake to slide between your lips and fuck you from that side."

Wetness pools between my thighs at the imagery, and I grind against him, desperate for some release. "Why didn't you?"

"Because I was not ready for you to hold so much control over me." He nips my neck, and I gasp. "Now I know you've always held some sway over me, and I do not fear that control."

He steps back so suddenly, I sway and reach for him to steady myself. "What are—"

"Undress," he commands, his eyes on the clothing Nero made for me. "If I do it, I'm going to rip it to shreds in desperation."

My eyes widen at his admission and at the care with which he speaks. He knows the clothing means something to me, so I slowly pull the top over my head. I feel his eyes on me, tracing my skin as it's revealed, and he groans in desire when my breasts appear. I drop the shirt to the side and reach for the trousers, carefully sliding them down my legs until I stand naked before him.

With a grunt of agony, Krug reaches down and adjusts himself beneath his leathers, and when my eyes drop to the sizable erection there, he grins.

"Shall I show you, *rainha*?"

I don't even question what the word means before I'm nodding, my mouth salivating at the thought of seeing him in all his glory.

He slowly pulls the ties of the leathers loose, revealing slight green skin riddled with scars and badges of his battles. I see the base of his cock, but above it, there's a large nodule, like an extra bone. He completely strips himself of his leathers, freeing his cock, and I marvel at the sheer size of it. Without waiting for his instructions, I kneel before him and wrap my hand around the base of his cock, feeling the ridges, as if it has been textured for pleasure. Piercings travel up the bottom of his dick like a ladder.

His fingers thread into my hair as he watches me study him and the metal that runs along his length. "You were not made to be on your knees, *rainha*. You are meant to have men on their knees before you."

I glance up at him as I squeeze his cock, making it jump in my hand. "What does that word mean?"

He groans as I stroke my hand along his shaft, my fingers not even touching around his large girth. "Queen," he rasps out. "It means queen."

I stroke him again. "Then a queen can choose to kneel before whomever she chooses," I retort, looking up at him. "She can tease whomever she wishes." I lean forward and swipe my tongue along the tip, drawing a guttural groan from his lips. He clearly likes it, so I spread my lips around the mushroom head and suck. He's far too big to fit entirely in my mouth, and I can only work about half of him into my throat before I'm forced to move back and take him again. His fingers tangle in my hair, and he's careful not to push too hard, but I can tell he's holding back, desperately trying not to hurt me. I moan as I run my tongue along the piercings, tracing and flicking them while my hand strokes his base.

"Enough," he rumbles, jerking his hips back and removing himself from my mouth. "It's my turn."

I find myself hauled off my feet and thrown into the air. I lose my equilibrium and cling to him as he lifts me until my legs wrap around his shoulders and I'm well off the ground. I'm pressed back against the shelves as he dives into the slit between my thighs, his tusks pressing against my skin as his tongue swipes. My eyes widen when I realize his tusks are perfectly placed to keep my lips parted for his attack. I cry out at the initial contact and then moan when he repeats the action, his hands holding me up easily, even as I squeeze his head between my thighs. I lose all sense of anything but pleasure as he swirls his tongue around my clit and drives me high so quickly, I nearly panic.

"I need you," I rasp out, spearing my hands into his hair and pulling him closer. "I want you inside of me. I *need* you inside of me."

He groans against my skin, sending bolts of pleasure through me as he continues to tongue fuck me. I can't fight it, can't move, so I use the only weapon I have in my arsenal. Magic dances from my fingertips and touches his scalp, moving down to wrap around his waist and cock, adding my own pleasure. He jerks against me before pressing me harder into the spines of the books and the shelf at my back. A growl is my answer as he remains buried between my thighs. He moves one hand, holding me aloft with the other, before I feel his fingers press against my core. He spears one inside of me, his thick digit stretching me, before he brutally fucks me with it. I cry out in pleasure and gush around his hand, dripping down his arm, his shoulders, and his chest.

He adds another finger, and one orgasm turns into another, until I scream with release, digging my nails into his scalp, even as my magic wraps around him and squeezes.

His fingers disappear, and he roars against my clit, his tusks nicking me as he drags my legs from around his shoulders. I drop, but he captures me before I have a chance to panic as he pins me against the shelves again, his cock nudging at my entrance.

"Cora the Fearless," he rumbles, his chin and lips still coated with my slickness, "do you fear me?"

"No," I answer, pressing my magic into his skin and sending bites of pleasure along his body. "I don't fear you."

"Correct answer," he snarls, sounding more feral than tame, and then he spears me with his cock.

There are bites of pain at the stretch, but I loosen quickly after my releases, and I'm slick for the movement as his ridges and piercings stroke inside me and drive me insane. I scream at the connection and throw my head back, hitting the shelf behind me. Wrapping my legs around his hips, I hold on for the ride as he fucks me against the knowledge I was never allowed to harness before.

And yet he has promised to gift me all the knowledge I can get.

"Yes!" I cry out, my magic leaking from me as I begin to glow. "Krug!"

"I will vanquish every foe who dares to face you," he promises. "I'll fight at your side and keep you safe. I will protect you, encourage you, and love you." His words filter in past the pleasure, but I can't keep my eyes open, can't respond, so instead, I let my magic stroke him and give him my answer as I claim him completely.

With a roar, he fucks me harder, the piercings digging in as the bone above his cock hits my clit when he bottoms out in me, driving me insane. I shout as release after release rolls through me and those piercings stroke the sensitive spot inside me, and I gush around him, coating him. He presses his lips against mine, swallowing my scream. His tusks dent my flesh, threatening to pierce it, and I can taste myself on his lips. His kiss drives me wild and drags me through a valley of pleasure so large, I don't know if I'm having one large orgasm or a succession of many.

"I claim you in return," he snarls against my lips.

He slams into me, that bone hitting my clit, and grinds against me, shattering me completely before he tumbles after me. His cock jumps inside me, his hot seed coating my insides before running out and mingling with my own release.

I'm panting. Shadows, I might be hyperventilating. I can hardly breathe with the pleasure rolling through me in waves. I'm pretty sure I can't stand, but I need not worry. As Krug pulls from me, releasing more seed down my leg, he gently lifts me into his arms.

"It seems I made it so we cannot search." He chuckles, carefully sitting me on the nearest table.

A raspy chuckle slips from my lips as I push my hair back and point to a large golden tome I'm sitting by. "There's no need to search," I say. "The answer we seek is right here."

Krug blinks in surprise. "What?"

"When I released my magic on you, I sensed it," I admit, smiling mischievously at him.

"Why didn't you say something?" He steps forward and strokes his hand over the gilded cover.

"I was enjoying myself," I reply, biting my lip.

His eyes follow the motion, and he grins. "Next time, *rainha*, I'm going to fuck you while the others watch, and they join in. We'll lay you in the middle of us, like a nest, and descend upon you until you're writhing with so much pleasure, you can't breathe."

I suck in air. "Is that a promise?"

His eyes darken, and he caresses my jaw with his fingers. "Yes, Cora the Fearless," he answers. "And I always keep my promises."

CHAPTER
THIRTY-THREE

K rug delicately opens the book, and I lean into him, watching as he does, but the words are in a strange language I don't understand. When I look at him, he grunts in displeasure.

"It is an ancient language, one I doubt any of us know."

"Fuck, then we need to find someone who does," I grumble and leap to my feet, stumbling over my unsteady legs. He quickly catches me, grinning as he sweeps my sweaty hair back over my shoulder. Blowing out a breath, I go to tease him for ruining me when I stiffen.

I feel a call.

"*Rainha?*" Krug questions worriedly as I blink to bring him back into focus.

"I think the magic was pulling me to someone who can read the book," I murmur. Turning, I start to walk from the room, following the tug on my bones deeper into the castle. Krug follows, book in hand, with a guiding palm on my back as I stumble on shaky legs.

A mixture of magic and weakness from the pleasure he brought makes me careless.

We move down corridor after corridor, spotting Nero and Bracken down one of them, but I pay them no mind, focused on the magic we are following.

"I knew it! You owe me a new blade," Bracken teases Nero when he sees my state.

Nero simply grins, but it fades when he looks at me. "Cora?" he murmurs.

"She's following magic," Krug tells him and holds the book up for them to see, "to someone who can read this. It has the answers we seek."

They fall into step behind us as we maneuver through the castle, past stone chambers and out the other side of the throne room, until we break into an outside courtyard. The black stone forms incredible pillars along corridors that surround the square courtyard. The stone under foot is polished and perfect, inlaid with golden designs that swirl through them. The castle's arch seems to come together overhead, letting in what light there is but reflecting down the swirling patterns from the castle. All point to the middle of the courtyard, where vines crawl to and where the magic beckons me forward.

A huge stone fountain sits in the center, with a stone figure bent on one knee, his wings partially covering him.

I send my magic out, and a pulse returns from the statue.

"It's alive!" I gasp, hurrying over to the stone and stopping before him.

I hear more footsteps and glance over to see the others joining us. Zee whistles when he spots the statue. "I thought he was dead."

Turning to him, I frown. "He?"

"The king's protector, a gargoyle." When I look confused, he continues, "He can turn to stone like a statue. He was an incredible fighter. He was also the king's best friend, but a good man. When the king died, we thought he did too. I guess we were wrong. I suppose he turned to stone, heartbroken and lost, and has just been here all this time."

"I heard gargoyles become the statues they inhabit if they are in stone form too long," Grim muses as he stares at the statue before us.

Turning back, I consider the stone figure. "I hope not. We need him to read the book and tell us what happened and where they are." I glance up at the statue's face. Even like this, I can tell the man was beautiful. With round eyes, a long, elegant nose, plump lips, and high cheekbones surrounded by wavy hair, he's a work of art, and not just because he's carved from stone. At the top of his forehead are two small horns, curving back slightly. His chest is bare and built with muscles, and his wings look almost leathery, like a bat's, with horns at each tip. The one foot I can see peeking from behind it has three toes tipped with the same sharp claws as the ones on his fingers.

A gargoyle.

"Any ideas on how we should wake him?" Bracken asks, and there's silence. "Anybody? Nobody? Well shit."

"Maybe try your magic, Cora?" Zee suggests. "It's what called us all, and it led you to him, therefore you must be able to wake him."

"Smart." Bracken nods. "And pretty. Leave something for the rest of us."

Ignoring their bickering, I climb onto the base of the hexagonal fountain to get close. Pushing up on my toes, my front to the podium of the fountain he is frozen to, I carefully stretch my hand out. Before my hand touches him, however, I blow out an unsure breath. "Please work." I send up the plea to whoever is watching over us and then lay my hand on his stone wing.

I feel the moment my magic crawls inside the stone, circling the remaining magic inside.

Within seconds, it flows through the statue and the stone cracks as the gargoyle explodes from inside. I'm thrown back, but arms catch me and pull me away as wings arch high into the sky and the man leaps up from the shattered remains before landing on two feet. His wings spread on either side of him, almost filling the courtyard with their dark black flesh. Veins of gold and white move through his wings, nearly making them shine. His hair is a matching black, falling to his shoulders in glossy waves, mixed with stars throughout as if he's the night sky incarnate, and his eyes are as black as night as they lock on me.

He stumbles away from me before falling to his knees. He bends his head and folds his wings back before his hands dangle before him.

"I'm sorry, my queen. I did not mean to frighten you…" He trails off and lifts his head, his eyes narrowing as they focus on me. "You are not my queen. Who are you, human?"

I blink in surprise at the way he still kneels before me, but he asked me a question, and now isn't the time to gawk at the beautiful gargoyle.

"My name is Cora, and I woke you because we need your help."

CHAPTER
THIRTY-FOUR

We all sit in the courtyard, gathering on a set of benches I didn't see behind the fountain. They form a meeting space with a fire in the middle that Grim lights before shuffling to my side. He stretches his arm behind me, so I lean back into it. Zee sits on my other side with his hand on my thigh. Nero's coils wrap around my legs, even though he sits on the bench to the left, lounging like the serpent he is. Bracken and Krug are both squished on the one to my right, while the gargoyle sits before me on the opposite bench.

His wings are carefully placed behind him over the bench, and his hair partially covers one side of his face as he tilts his head and watches me. "Cora, human, tell me why you have woken me," he demands. His voice is rough, like crumbling stone, and it sends shivers through me with how deep it is.

My magic reacts, wanting to stretch toward him, but I ignore it.

"I need—we need your help. I'm sorry, I don't know your name," I reply as he glances at the monsters bracketing me possessively.

"I apologize for my manners. It can be confusing when turning back from stone. It takes a little while for my mind to thaw, but this time, it is taking longer than normal." He stands and bows, his wings flaring out to the sides in a display that would put any lady from the Gilded Lands to shame. "I am Sir Razcorr, protector of the realm and the rightful king, flier of the great wars and winner of the Rubel Cup."

Okay. I don't know what most of that means, but I incline my head in acknowledgement, and he sits again. "Nice to meet you, Sir Razcorr." I hesitate, biting my lip before continuing. "What do you remember?"

He frowns then, his eyes going blank as he seems to search his mind. "It is hazy," he admits, and he seems to hate that weakness, judging by the scowl on his lips, which reveals the sharp points of his teeth.

"The king..." I hedge, unsure how to tell him.

"Is dead," Grim states bluntly without care for sensitivity. "As is the queen. It has been many, many years since their deaths and the war."

Razcorr jerks like he's been struck, and his expression crumbles as he stares at us. "Truly...I, yes, I remember now." I watch emotions flit across his face and eyes—pain, heartache, agony, and grief—before they turn to stone, and he clears his throat. "I see. I have been stone for a long time. So why wake me now? I had resigned myself to die like that to join my friend and my queen. I withdrew when there was nothing to protect. It is our way, to turn to stone and be lost in oblivion."

"I'm sorry," I offer truthfully as I lean forward. "I wish I could have left you to your grief and peace, but we need your help."

"You have said that," he murmurs. "Why?"

"We are trying to reunite the king and queen to bring them peace and end this curse once and for all."

"While you have been gone, much has changed," Krug offers. "Our lands have fallen into great darkness, and the magic inside rots until we are just beasts. Cora the Fearless is trying to stop that and unite the kingdoms once more, to bring peace back to our lands. She is trying to save us and magic. Can't you feel the wrongness here?"

Razcorr nods and glances back at me. "You believe you can do this?"

"I do. She chose me. Your queen," I tell him.

He eyes me. "Lady Emelyn always said a woman could do many things a man could not, and that none of us understood magic like she did. She knew best. She was a good woman. A true leader. Kind, honest, and refreshing. She loved the king like no other, and her father hated that." He frowns as if more memories are coming back. "Oh, but she loved him and he her, so much they thought they could conquer anything. She is dead now, though, Cora the Fearless, and long gone."

"And so were you," Bracken reasons. "Yet here you are."

"Here we all are," Nero adds.

"Because of Cora." Zee nods.

"I felt her. She called to me. She showed me her safe place in the cave." He jerks at my words, and his eyes widen. "She showed me some of the past and some of the future. The magic kept part of her alive for as long as it could, until she could help someone bring it back. She's gone now, and I don't know what to do. All I know is I have this book and none of us can read it...but you."

He frowns as Krug hands him the book, and then his eyes clear as he strokes the cover. "It is the story of our lands, the story of the king and queen and their deaths. An old friend of theirs wrote this, the keeper of our history, before he was lost into the shadow's reach." His gaze comes back to me. "You need me to read this?"

"Please, and then you can return to stone. We will leave you in peace, I promise," I assure him, and he watches me.

"It has been a very long time since anyone needed me." He seems to sit up straighter. "I will help you, Cora the Fearless."

He opens the cover, but his eyes close and his fingers dance over the words on the page. I share a confused look with the others, but just as I'm about to question his tactics, smoke seems to flow from him. My eyes widen as I watch it swirl and form a ball before him, then it suddenly clears, and his mouth moves, telling the story without words.

It appears before us in the smoke, like a memory.

I see the palace and the human king presenting his human daughter, Emelyn. King Kulmak is instantly taken by her beauty, and the image speeds through their courtship and their marriage. The love in the king's eyes makes me grip my chest. The same sentiment is reflected back in the queen's gaze, and for a while, they are happy. I see the land as it was before, with vast, green forests and hills, bright rolling seas filled with ships, and marshes occupied with families and laughing children.

They are all monsters, but they are happy, and magic is everywhere—in the sky, the ground, and in the people.

It's beautiful, but suddenly, a dark cloud rolls in, and the king and queen argue in fear. Razcorr's mouth moves faster, even as his face seems to stiffen in fury and sadness. We are forced to watch as the human king learns that his plan will not work.

That his daughter betrayed him by falling in love with the king.

Scenes of bloodshed and death split the story before it focuses on a still frame of the queen. She is clearly dead, her body on a stone slab before a gilded throne.

"The Gilded Castle," I whisper as the image zooms out to show the lands beyond the Shadow Lands. "She was killed in the Gilded Castle."

The image changes to King Kulmak, on his knees, roaring. He holds smoke in his arms, where his love once was, as he drags himself to his throne and cries. When his head lifts, there is nothing but hatred and evil in his eyes.

After that, we see scenes of the war as the land bleeds and magic suffers.

And then the king...the king dies in battle, heartbroken and ready to join his lost love.

Only he never does.

His body is entombed, as is tradition, in the crypts below the castle with a stone effigy of him above it. There is a matching sarcophagus for the queen, which lies empty, next to his, waiting. Razcorr is there, with a hand on each of the crypts, as he cries and then flies to the podium and turns to stone.

The smoke evaporates, and I look to Razcorr as his face loosens and his dark eyes focus on me. "She was killed in the human world and buried there. He was buried here. They have been reaching for each other for years. All that death, all that bloodshed..." I murmur.

"It was war," Razcorr whispers. "And for a while, we were winning, but hate can never trump love, and our people did not have that anymore. The humans did, and greed," he offers sadly, looking at the book and then back to me. "I will help you, Cora. I will help you reunite my king and his love, my queen. I will do my duty like I should have done all those years ago, and then I will lay to rest with them."

"You...You'll help me?" I ask softly.

"I owe my king and queen my life. I couldn't save them then, but I can offer them peace now." Standing, he holds the book to his chest as he drops to his knees before me. "I offer you my loyalty, Cora, the bringer of truth and magic. Until our quest is successful, I will be your blade, your protector."

I stare, my heart thumping hard, as he rises to his feet once more.

Something like hope fills me—hope that we can truly do this.

"Not another one," Bracken grumbles, making us all laugh, and I share a smile with Razcorr, silently thanking him for his offer.

It's time to reunite the lost lovers and save our lands.

It's time to fracture the shadows that have surrounded us into a million tiny pieces...

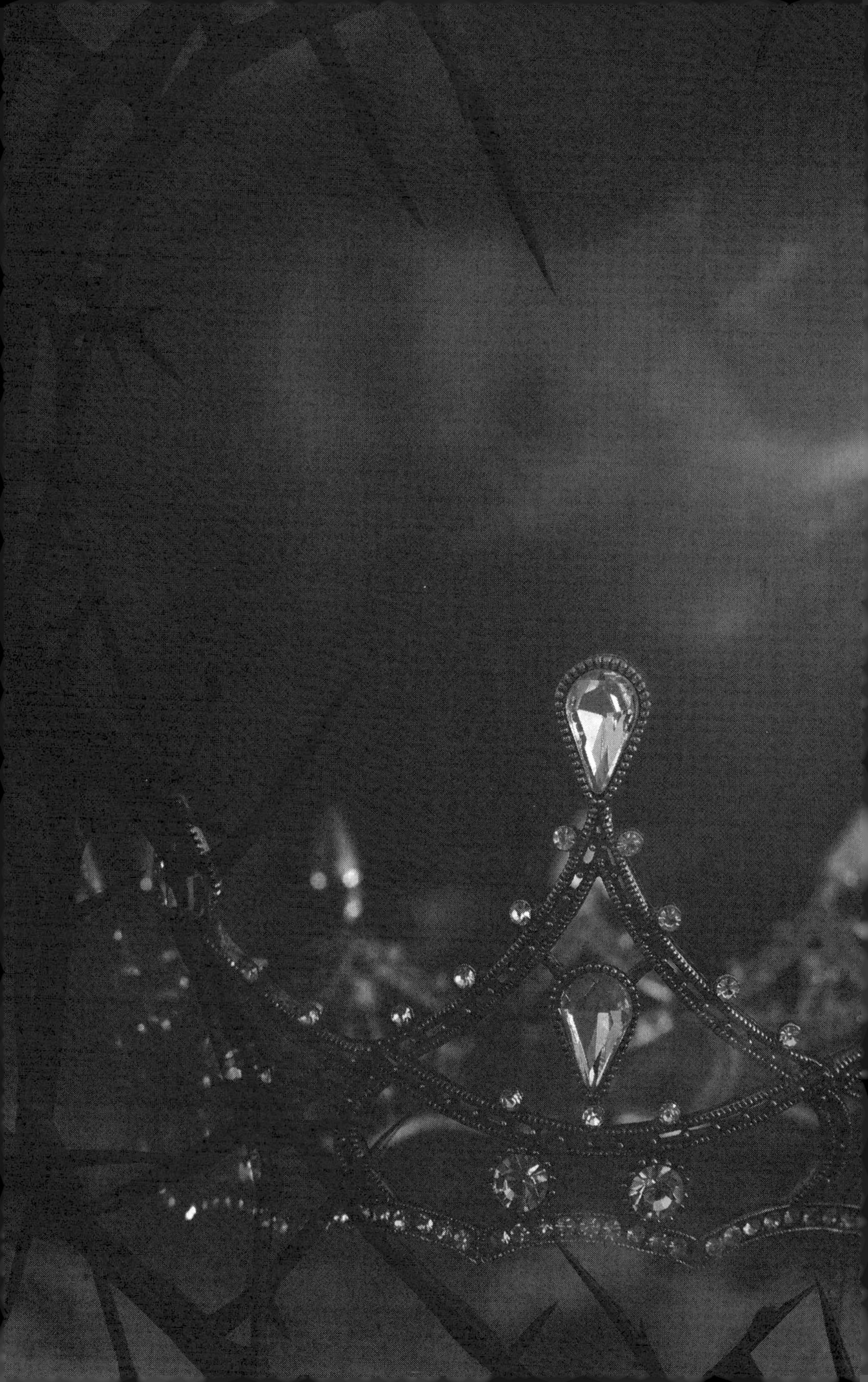

CHAPTER
THIRTY-FIVE

"The only solution is to travel to the human realm and find the queen's resting place," I argue, standing in the courtyard with my hands on my hips as I survey my men.

"It's too dangerous," Grim rumbles, shaking his head. "We don't exactly blend in."

"Good," Zetros retorts, his expression stern. "Let them run from us as we storm their castle."

Krug sniffs. "The human king will never allow us to get near the castle, let alone close enough to find the queen's resting place, steal her body, and get out unscathed."

Nero is closest to me, his coils wrapped around me in comfort. His eyes trail over to Razcorr every now and then, as if he's studying the gargoyle. I can't blame him. Past his initial words, Razcorr has mostly been silent as he watches us, but his eyes continuously trail back to me. At first, I thought it was simply because I woke him up, but now, I'm starting to think there's something else. It doesn't help that when he looks at me, my magic wakes up and dances under my skin as if calling to him.

From the queen...or something else?

"Do you think he learned the skill of being so still or he was born with it?" Nero whispers, studying the gargoyle. Razcorr is so still, I'd almost think he turned to stone again, if not for seeing the stone break away, leaving a sensual, gray-skinned monster in its wake.

"Born with it," Bracken answers on my other side. "All gargoyles have the skill, but this one is a master at it. Think if I throw something at him, he'll move?"

In answer, Razcorr blinks but remains still. "I can hear you."

"Oh, good!" Bracken continues. "Will you move if I throw something at you?"

Razcorr's dark eyes focus on the fey, locked and unwavering. "Attempt it, and learn why gargoyles are not to be trifled with, feyling."

Bracken puffs up. "I'm no feyling."

"To me, you are," Razcorr murmurs, his gaze trailing back to me, making me straighten. "I have lived many of your lifetimes."

The others continue to argue about the best way to slip into the human realm without incident. I'm starting to think there is no sure way to achieve our goal. This will end in another war, whether after or before we complete our task. The human king will never allow us to slip into the Gilded Lands and steal the body unscathed, and if we succeed, he'll never allow the monsters to live in peace, not when they have their magic back—magic he will want for himself. Some twisted part of me relishes the idea of seeing the look that will undoubtedly be on his face as I storm into the castle, front and center of my monsters, but another part understands that moving in the silence of the night would be the better option. If we can reunite Emelyn and Kulmak without anyone being the wiser, then we'll bring magic back to the land before we descend into battle. Something tells me that's our better option, but another part understands it might not be possible. While I can blend into the Shadow Lands and even the Gilded Lands, none of my monsters can pass for human. Most are entirely too big to even wear a cloak, and then there is Nero and his coils. There's no way he can step foot inside the Shadow Lands without an alarm sounding. Of the group, only Zetros could pass for some semblance of a human, but even he, with his height, would stand out.

"Do we even know where Kulmak is buried?" I ask suddenly, and everyone grows silent. "We know we have to find Emelyn in the Gilded Lands, but shouldn't the king be here?"

Razcorr nods his head slowly. "He's buried beneath the castle, Cora the Fearless, in the underbelly of the mausoleum."

Biting my lip, I offer my hand to him. "Can we see it?" At first, he looks at my fingers and at me in confusion. "It might offer more clues," I add when he hesitates.

Eventually, he reaches his clawed hand forward and takes my fingers in his to lead us inside the castle. His hand is warm in mine, engulfing my fingers in his clasp without even trying. Everything about Razcorr is sensual, from the way he moves to the way his wings shuffle delicately on his back. The urge to stroke those leathery membranes is strong, but I'm sure that would be improper.

Still, I'm tempted to ask if I can touch them.

His fingers tighten on mine when we reach a staircase that leads down into the belly of the castle, just like he said. This is where I'd imagine dungeons to be located, but when we reach the bottom of the stairs, there are no cells, so I assume they are in a different part of the castle. This section is reserved for the past kings and their families.

At first, the wall is the only thing I note. Plaque after plaque is affixed to the black stone, declaring another notable person long since dead. I don't recognize any of the names, but Razcorr strokes his fingers over many of them.

"I have served the kings of this castle for many eons, Cora the Fearless. I have buried many friends." His gaze is sad as he studies them. "But Kulmak, my dearest friend, is not behind one of these plaques. He's farther inside."

We continue deeper, past an insurmountable number of graves, until we reach a large back room.

"Why does he get his own room while the others only get plaques?" Nero asks curiously.

"It is customary for the last reigning king to be placed in the large chamber, so that monsters can pay their respects. When another king dies, Kulmak can be reinterred in the walls, but..."

"I don't think that's what will be done," I hedge, my eyes going to the large sarcophagus in front of us—one of two. The large stone coffin on the left draws my gaze first. It takes up a huge part of the room, but I suppose it would need to be a large coffin to fit a minotaur. On top of the sarcophagus, the stone is carved into a perfectly detailed sculpture of the king from my visions. He's strong and stoic, his face stern, but even in that sternness, I see grief. He holds a sword in one hand and sports a crown on his head, but his other hand is carved in a way to show him reaching for the other sarcophagus.

The one reserved for Emelyn.

The lid isn't fastened onto the second, smaller coffin, as if alerting everyone who visits that she's not resting there. The stone depicts her in a serene manner, just like from my visions, but it doesn't depict her fierceness or her love. She was a great woman, a brave one, but the stone almost lacks—

"Her spirit," Razcorr whispers. "Her spirit is not inside the stone the way Kulmak's is."

"Will it change when we bring her back?" I inquire, staring sadly at the way their hands are separated as they reach for each other in stone, but never close the distance.

"Perhaps." Razcorr strolls forward. "It has been many centuries since Kulmak and Emelyn's passing. If the magic still lives, then I believe we can reunite them."

Grimus moves throughout the room, studying the twin coffins as if they are a puzzle he has to piece together. As he moves, the air charges, and for a moment, I'm not sure where it's coming from.

On the king's sarcophagus, a golden crown glimmers in the light of the lanterns, drawing my eyes in a way that makes me think there's a bit of magic to it. There's hardly enough light to sparkle in such a way, but when I take a step closer, the shine brightens and flashes, as if beckoning someone.

"Grim," I whisper, watching the crown brighten the closer Grim moves to it. "Grim, stop." The minotaur freezes immediately, and the shine stays steady. "Take a step forward." He does as I ask, and the crown flashes, drawing everyone else's eyes to the phenomenon. "Take a step back." It fades as he moves away. "What..."

Razcorr reaches forward and lifts the crown in his claws. "The king's crown is very special," he begins, looking between it and Grim. "It's enchanted so that those of royal blood will be declared upon receipt. Many a bastard has been claimed by this crown and declared royalty because of the blood flowing in their veins."

I take a step forward, staring at Grim intently. "What does that mean?"

Razcorr looks between us, realization dawning in his eyes. "It means, Cora the Fearless," he says, strolling closer to Grim, the glow brightening, "that your minotaur is a direct descendant of King Kulmak the Mighty."

I blink in shock at Grim as he stands with his arms crossed over his chest, looking as unsurprised as ever.

"You're shitting me," Bracken mutters. "This whole time, we've been walking around with the rightful king, and he has the audacity to act offended at the declaration?"

"I'm no king," Grim grumbles, his face twisted in a snarl.

Razcorr shakes his head. "The crown says otherwise." He hands the crown to Grim, who barely takes it. Light explodes out of the gold and dances around the room before it settles into a more tolerable glow.

"The throne belongs to you."

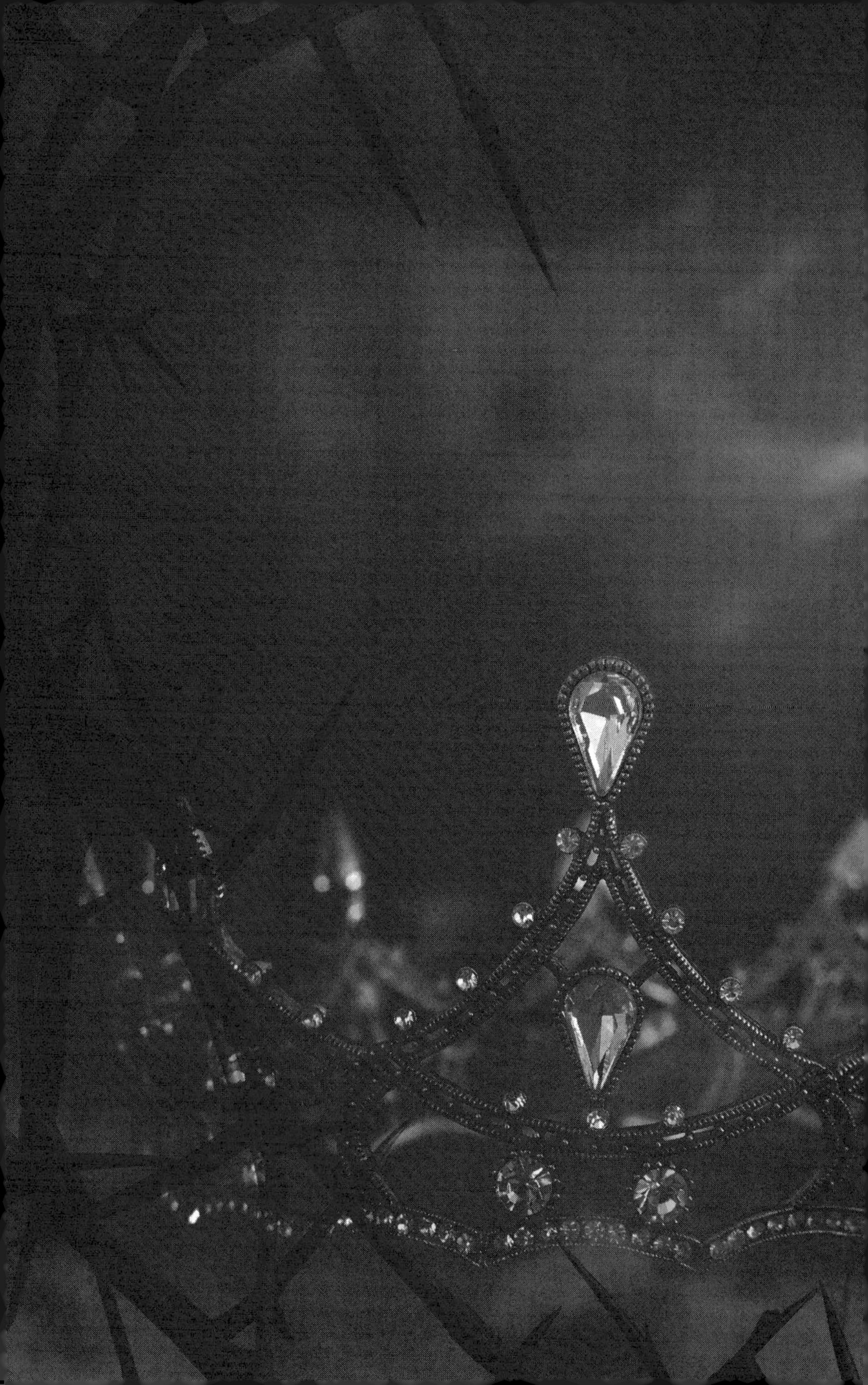

CHAPTER
THIRTY-SIX

"If you are going to march into the Gilded Lands and steal the queen's body from those traitorous leeches, you must be trained properly," Razcorr begins the moment we're back in the main part of the castle.

"We've already trained her with her magic," Zetros points out. "She can handle herself."

Razcorr studies me. "While her magic is strong, there are secrets to such magic that not even a group of monsters such as yourselves can hope to train her in. Magic is not easy, and while you did the best with what you knew, there are things Cora still needs to learn."

"Are you suggesting that we're not capable of helping her?" Grim snarls, more on edge since the crown chose him. He refused to discuss it and placed the crown back on the stone coffin before storming upstairs.

Razcorr, without hesitation, looks the supposedly rightful king in the eye and says, "Yes."

The very air freezes, as if Razcorr just spoke the worst possible thing he could have said. I see Grim begin to wind up, steam billowing from his nostrils.

"He's been the royal protector for eons," Bracken points out. "It would make sense that he knows things we do not."

I blink in surprise. Of all my monsters, he's not usually the voice of reason, but at his words, the air seems to shift and calmness descends again.

"He's right," Krug agrees. "Even if I don't like it."

Razcorr, to his credit, doesn't seem worried that he was seconds away from tussling with my group of monsters. If anything, he doesn't show much emotion at all. The only time I see a flicker of feeling is when he looks at me, and then something in his dark eyes shift, and I find temptation crashing into me, but Razcorr hasn't made any indication that he's interested in joining me in such a way. He's agreed to help us, sure, but that doesn't mean he's interested, and shadows, I have my hands full as it is. What business do I have wanting to ride the gargoyle in front of me to find out if his cock is as hard as stone?

Razcorr offers his hand to me, and for a moment, I forget he's just being nice and not asking me to try out his cock after all. "Come with me, Cora the Fearless, and I shall show you all you need to know."

"Now, hold on," Nero begins, moving in front of me.

"This is something Cora must do alone," Razcorr states so matter-of-factly, it leaves no room for argument.

"Cora doesn't go without protection," Zetros snarls.

Razcorr raises his brow. "She will have the greatest protection available in the Dead Lands." By the way his wings shift, it's clear he means himself, and there's something inherently sexy about that confidence.

Fuck. How am I supposed to focus on learning when I keep thinking about how much I'd like to stroke his wings?

Grim steps forward. "Promise you'll keep her safe," he demands.

Razcorr stares into his eyes, two monsters facing off with each other. "I will protect her with my life."

A few seconds pass before Grim offers his arm, and Razcorr reaches forward and clasps his like warriors. There's an understanding that passes between them, a bond that seems to form, and I wonder again at the way we just glossed over the fact that Grimus is the next king. No one is talking about it, despite the crown and the declaration. Grim doesn't seem to want to focus on it, but it sits in my mind, along with the vision I had of an unknown minotaur wearing a crown and me wearing a crown next to him. Now, I realize that minotaur had to be Grimus, but not a single one of my monsters has asked any more about it. Why?

Razcorr offers his hand to me again. "Cora."

That one word goes straight through my body and into my core. Shadows, that voice.

"Have fun training," Bracken purrs, adding in a wiggle of his eyebrows for good measure.

I roll my eyes at him but slide my fingers into Razcorr's claws, allowing his warmth to once again engulf me as he leads me through the corridors and passages inside the castle. The sounds of my monsters fade behind me, leaving a silence unlike any other echoing around us. My footsteps are light, but I can still hear them. Razcorr, despite his size, moves so silently, I can't even pick up the tick of his claws on the marble floors.

"Where are we going?" I ask as we continue deeper. This section of the castle was clearly used less. The floor is still rough, as if less foot traffic comes this way.

"When Emelyn came to the castle and Kulmak declared his love, he had space set up for Emelyn to practice her magic. He believed that Emelyn was capable of great things, and she was, but before she could harness her full power, her father killed her."

The sadness in his voice has me squeezing his hand in comfort. "I'm sorry for your loss."

"They were my friends," he admits, glancing at me. "The queen was what a queen should be—strong and spirited. I sense that same spirit in you." He stops us at a door. "It is in this room that we will train, though I suspect it will not take long for you to learn what is left."

He pushes the door open, revealing a dark room that bursts to life at our entrance, the flaming lanterns igniting on the walls. As light spills forth, I take in the sparse room with only a table in the center. On the table, stones are spread out, as well as some parchments. When I step farther into the room, a phantom breeze seems to sweep around the space, bringing a sense of comfort, like a friend welcoming me home.

Razcorr lifts his face into the wind, feeling it too, and for the first time, I see the barest hint of a smile on his face. "Her spirit still lingers in this room."

When the wind passes, I step up to the table, studying it. "What are all the stones for?" There is every stone imaginable—pale stones, bright stones, and some I recognize as precious gems. A single large ruby grabs my attention and reminds me of the temple we passed on the way to the castle.

"Your magic comes from inside you," Razcorr begins as he picks up a large citrine. "But that magic can be stored inside stones. You can place a spell on them, leave behind a remnant of your memory, or simply use them as backup in case you begin to tire. Each stone has its own strengths and weaknesses, but it has been described as a feeling. You should be able to feel the stone and utilize it. Your magic will tell you what you need to know."

He passes the citrine to me, and I take it gently in my hand. The moment my skin touches it, it comes alive, and the glow immediately makes me brighten, as if my own confidence has grown.

"Positivity and abundance," I murmur, staring down at the stone.

Razcorr nods. "Your own personal power is tied to your positivity. Encouraging that makes you stronger."

In awe, I set the citrine down and reach for a black stone. "Protection," I rasp out. At his encouraging nod, I reach for another, and another, until I've gone through them all and named their uses. My magic recognizes each stone I lift, but it isn't until I reach the rose quartz that something else happens.

The moment my fingers touch the stone, I'm thrown into a memory that isn't mine. Gasping at the vividness of it, I stare in open-mouthed awe as the same room I'm in appears, but brighter. Emelyn is standing at the same table I am, touching her hands to stones, searching for something.

"*If you keep focusing so hard, you are going to harm your brain.*" *The voice comes from the right, and when I turn, I'm not surprised to see King Kulmak standing there with a tender expression on his face as he watches Emelyn.*

"I have to learn," *she says, clearly frustrated.* "There's too much to absorb and too little time before I have to return to my father and declare our realms united."

"Why the hurry?" *Kulmak asks, strolling forward to wrap his arms around her from behind. She sinks into the touch, absorbing his warmth.*

"Something tells me I need to know this, that something is coming."

"We'll face whatever comes," *Kulmak promises as he nuzzles her.* "I promise you, my love."

She turns in his arms, and her eyes are bright with so much love, it makes me feel as if I'm intruding. "I love you," *she murmurs.*

"And I love you, more than all the magic in the realms," *he answers, and leans down for a kiss.*

The vision disappears before their lips touch, and I blink back into reality, unsurprised to find tears in my eyes.

"They loved each other so much," I whisper. "They didn't deserve the fate they got."

"No," Razcorr agrees. "No, they did not." He studies me for a moment before reaching forward and taking the rose quartz from my hand. The slide of his claws on my palms does strange things to me, despite it being such a simple touch. "Come with me, Cora. I'd like to show you something."

∼

RAZCORR LEADS me through the castle again. It seems he's always leading me somewhere and showing me new things, so I'm not surprised when we climb a bunch of stairs and end up on top of the castle, overlooking the Dead Lands. From this angle, I can see far and wide. In the distance, too far for my human eyes to see, I know the wall sits, waiting for us to dismantle it and bring balance back to the realm, but something about seeing it all laid out before me draws moisture to my eyes. I made it across all that land. I fought my way through it and survived, and now here I am, finding love and preparing to take on the evil that plagues us.

If you'd asked me what I thought about this so long ago, I would have laughed.

No one survives the hunt.

No one returns.

Yet here I am.

"It's hauntingly beautiful," I murmur, staring at the scene before me. "I can't imagine what it will be like when magic returns."

Razcorr looks out with me, his eyes sad. "There will be so much green, you won't know where to look. The trees will be lush with leaves. The marshes will be teeming with life. And the monsters? They'll have control over their senses again, those who have already succumbed to the darkness."

"What was it like? Before?"

He glances at me. "Just as dangerous, but there was peace. Kulmak thought he could keep that peace, not understanding humanity's penchant for greed. He thought he could fix that, but instead, he found himself deep in the worst of that treachery."

Carefully, I thread my fingers through his. "Thank you for showing me this."

"Oh, this is not what I want to show you, Cora," he says, and a hint of a smile tugs at his lips. "For this, I must ask you to trust me."

Frowning, I stare between him and the scenery. "Trust you?"

He nods and moves over to the edge of the castle, his heels just kissing the ledge. "Trust is an important part of any protector's duty. You trust your monsters explicitly, and you brought them together, and they trust you in return. You must trust me if we are going to be successful."

I study his face and see the determination there. "I trust you."

He gives me a real smile this time before he holds out his hand for me, giving me a choice. "Then come, Cora the Fearless, and take my hand."

I hesitate, only because mischief dances in his eyes, but I want to know more about Razcorr and this world I'm trying to save. This gargoyle is a fount of knowledge, but also, I just want to spend time with him. Like the others, there's a connection here I didn't plan on feeling and don't know how to handle, but instead of fighting it, I'll allow it to develop on its own time. That's what will form a bond. I meant it when I said I trust him. The magic inside me tells me that it's okay to trust him, despite us not knowing each other very well.

The magic inside me also wants him.

Desperately.

I take a shaky step forward, not liking getting so close to the edge but trusting the gargoyle with whatever plans he has. When I'm just in front of him, I slide my fingers into his claws and clasp tightly before looking up at him expectantly.

"Now what?" I ask.

The corners of his eyes crinkle. "Now, we fly."

I don't have time to panic or insist that I shouldn't be flying anywhere as a human. My feet belong solidly on the ground, but Razcorr seems to have other ideas. He pulls me against his chest and envelops me in his arms, tight enough that I know I won't fall. Without another word, he tips backward off the edge of the castle.

I scream.

Of course I scream.

I meant it when I said my feet belong on the ground, but as my hair whips around my face while we plummet, my scream is stolen from my lips as my heart beats wildly in my chest. The ground grows closer, but just when true panic begins to set in, his wings snap out and we're soaring again. I nearly swallow my tongue at the shift in direction, at the way my stomach drops and rearranges itself inside my abdomen.

I wrap myself around the gargoyle, both terrified and excited. It's exhilarating, but I'm also achingly aware I don't have my own wings to catch me.

"How are you faring, Cora the Fearless?" he asks, and there's laughter in his voice that I like way too much.

"Just great," I grumble, clinging tighter. "A little warning would have been nice."

"Where would be the fun in that?" he responds as he swoops to the right and sails through the air around the castle. He aims for a section behind the castle, past where we were always meant to go, to a large stone outcropping covered with trees. The trees around it still have a green tinge to them, as if they are not quite as dead as the rest of the Dead Lands.

Razcorr lands on steady legs, and that's when I notice the cave. He gently puts me on my feet, keeping a hold of me until I don't wobble, before giving me space to gather my bearings.

The cave wouldn't be exciting if not for the very purposeful markings around the entrance—the same sort of language that was in the history book.

"What is this place?" I ask, glancing between him and the opening.

"A holy place. Long ago, before the first monster king was crowned, the gargoyles protected this land. This is where the first gargoyle was born, or so the story goes." He smiles at me. "It is also a place where gargoyles bring the people most important to them."

I try not to let that go to my head. "Why?"

"Sometimes, it's to simply show their history. Other times, it's to receive a blessing." He gestures toward the entrance. "Come, I'll show you inside."

The moment we get closer to the entrance, I feel a deep pulse of magic far more ancient than what I've experienced before. It beckons me inside and promises a message of some sort. Frowning, I follow Razcorr inside, wondering at the strange call. The markings continue along the walls inside, artfully carved into the stone with sharp tools. Some of the pictures are decorated with paint that is far from peeling, though I can feel the ancient work of their swirls. There are vases in recessed parts of the walls, and I don't know what they are for, but they feel important. The cave opens up into a larger chamber, and I gasp at the sight.

"Are they all alive?" I ask, my eyes wide.

Around the chamber are dozens of stone gargoyles, each as different as the next, perched in their frozen state. Each stand on their pedestal, waiting for whatever they may need.

"They have returned to the eternal sleep," Razcorr replies, staring at his brethren. "Gargoyles do not die naturally. It is our duty to decide when our place in this realm is finished."

I look at him sharply. "So, one day, you'll just turn to stone and never wake up?" He inclines his head. "How incredibly sad."

"It is our way," he reasons. "However, as long as I have a purpose and a reason to remain in this realm, I will do so, which brings me to why we are here." He gestures to the pool in the center of the cave, as if a fountain has been left dormant.

Carefully, I move up to the edge and look in, seeing nothing but clear water. "What am I looking for?"

He takes my hand in his, and together, we dip our fingers into the water. At first, nothing happens, and I frown at the letdown. Perhaps we did it wrong? But then the ripples that move out from our touch come sailing back to our edge, and they explode in a rainbow of color.

Except, there's nothing there at all.

"What—"

The colors explode outward again, like a sheen on the water, dancing around before coming back to our side. Razcorr dips our fingers again, and the color stains my fingers, leaving behind a strange, rippling mark.

He holds our hands up together, studying the matching marks, and delight fills his eyes in a way that takes my breath away. Beautiful. The gargoyle is absolutely beautiful when he smiles.

My core tightens when he looks at me. His expression turns to heat so fast, I nearly stumble beneath his gaze. I was wrong—Razcorr was just good at hiding it.

"I never believed I would find you," Razcorr murmurs, staring at me. He tugs me close and holds me tenderly, and I'm as confused as I've ever been.

"What?" I say, because what else is there to say?

He pulls back and meets my gaze. "Gargoyles mate for life," he murmurs, reaching up to tuck a strand of hair behind my ear. My lower abdomen flutters at the gesture. It's tender, familiar.

"I never found my mate. I always believed I would never find one."

"That's very romantic," I rasp out, "but what does that have to do with me?"

He cups my face and stares lovingly at me, making sure I'm listening. "Your magic woke me up, but it did more than that. It freed me. It released me from years of despair and eons of agony. I wasn't sure, I could barely believe it, and I had to know..." He leans in close, his breath tickling my face. "Cora the Fearless, *you* are my mate."

He presses his lips to mine, and those same rainbow colors explode behind my eyelids. I wrap my arms around his shoulders before I know what I'm doing. His lips press against mine in a kiss that rocks my world, and it solidifies what I knew from the moment he woke up.

A new bond is formed.

I don't have five monsters, I have six.

Razcorr is mine, and I am his.

CHAPTER THIRTY-SEVEN

After the earth-shattering kiss, I'm left breathless and unsure. How can he go from being reserved to acting so tender? He must see the question in my eyes, because he cups my cheeks. "I will give you time. I know this is a lot. I had been hoping for so many years, so when I felt your call, it did not seem real. I kept my distance. I apologize, mate. I had to come here to know, but you are human, and I know it does not work the same way. I am patient, and I can wait forever if need be. Just knowing you are alive is enough." With that, he takes my hand and leads me from the cave.

Once outside, he silently wraps his arms around me and lifts into the air once more. I lose myself in the passing scenery and wind, unsure what to say or do.

With the others, our family grew from friendship, but this is a declared bond I had no choice over.

However, I cannot deny the pull I feel to him, the attraction and familiarity, that puts me at ease.

Maybe he's right—I need time.

The flight is almost gentle this time, and when we land, his fingers stroke my cheek longingly before he releases me and takes my hand, smiling as he leads me back downstairs to the others. "Your other mates will be getting antsy," he comments softly.

I don't respond, uncertain what to say.

Are they also mates?

All this time, I hadn't been labeling us. They are just mine, and I am theirs.

Mates makes sense.

But six mates? Is that normal? Do I even care?

The questions crowd my head as we find them lounging around a formal sitting room. When we enter, Bracken's eyes narrow, and when Razcorr turns to me and presses his forehead to mine, I feel them all shift in agitation. "Thank you for trusting me, Cora. Thank you for being real, mate."

"Mate?" Grim demands, his eyes locking on me. "You're his mate?"

"It has been proven," Razcorr replies, shooting me a gentle grin. "She is mine, and I am hers. She is the soul I have spent hundreds of years searching for."

"Oh, fuck no." Bracken leaps to his feet, standing side by side with Grim, copying his crossed arms and snarl. "You don't get to just show up and claim our Cora."

"What he said," Grim grumbles, and I'm shocked they are in agreement for once.

"Cora," Zee murmurs, and his voice is pained. "Is it true? You are his?"

"But..." Nero trails off, looking at me with a similarly agonized expression.

Krug moves closer, frowning at the gargoyle, who seems oblivious. Scrubbing my face, I try to push away the headache I feel coming on. "Guys..." I stop because I don't have a clue what to say.

Bracken looks at Grim seriously. "I say we kill him."

Grim meets his eyes and inclines his head, making my mouth drop open. The jealousy pouring from them shows me the reason for their behavior, but I'm speechless.

"You can't—" I start, but Bracken flies through the air, heading for Razcorr, who easily sidesteps him and rolls his eyes as Grim charges.

Helplessness explodes through me as Razcorr fights them both off. Bracken leaps at his back, his fangs bared. Anger, shame, and pain flow through me, the heightened emotions only bringing my magic out until my mouth opens in a scream.

"Stop it!" The magic infused howl is followed by a flurry of pure, unfiltered magic from my hands.

It explodes through the room, the force throwing them all back into the walls, where it pins them midair. They try to fight it before stilling as I walk slowly through the room, studying each of them in turn. I see myself for a moment in the glass above the mantel before turning away. My eyes are basically white with magic, my hair floats in an invisible breeze, and my skin glows like moonlight.

I look powerful, and that's when it truly hits me.

I *am* powerful.

They are fighting over me, but they are going to have to learn to share, because this is my life and no one makes decisions for me, not anymore.

Never again.

"You are acting like animals!" I roar, my voice like a lash of magic, tightening my hold on them as they watch me. "I can mate whomever I want, wherever I want. Just because a gargoyle suddenly says I'm his mate doesn't mean I'm not still with you. That I'm not still yours!" I narrow my eyes on all of them, feeling my magic filling the room, almost suffocating them. "You will learn to share, or you will leave. I will not spend the rest of my life like I did in the beginning—afraid, sad, and torn. We will work together, all of us, or not at all. You do not have to like each other, but you do have to accept it. My heart is big enough to love all of you." My voice cracks a little when I ask, "Is yours big enough to accept that?" When there is nothing but silence, I let the magic flow through them, making them groan. "You need to decide. I am not some weak human you can fight over and expect to get your way. I am Cora the

Fearless, and this is my life, my future, and my fucking body!" I yell, and I turn and storm out, only letting my magic drop once I'm out the door.

I hear them fall to the floor with matching groans before Bracken's lovesick voice reaches me.

"I love her so much."

"You would," Grim mutters.

"No, he's right—she's incredible," Krug adds.

Huffing, I ignore them as I storm farther into the castle, needing to get away from all that testosterone.

I have to make some decisions about my future and what I want, and for the first time in my life, I realize I can.

Now if only the idea of losing them didn't hurt so much...

CHAPTER
THIRTY-EIGHT

I'm standing—okay, hiding in an old ballroom. The windows here are beautiful mosaics casting rainbows across the empty, echoing chamber. I stand outside the open double doors on a stone balcony that overlooks the kingdom.

My mind is a mess.

My magic curls through me protectively, drawn by the hurt inside and the idea that I might lose them.

I never realized just how deeply integrated my monsters were inside me until that moment, until I saw them descend into feral beasts as they fought over me. I have been alone my entire life, bar my sister, but she had her own life. I was always off somewhere, lost in my thoughts, and my monsters brought me back. They share my life with me. I don't even think I could sleep alone anymore. Could I truly give them all up for Razcorr, simply because fate says we are mates? And what about the pull I feel toward the others?

It's confusing, and I'm lost and alone...until I feel it.

I can't help the small smile that curls my lips, my shoulders sagging in relief.

"I know you are there," I say without turning. My magic alerted me the moment Zee snuck inside the ballroom, followed by Bracken.

"I wanted to give you your space, *measma*," Zee tells me before stepping up to my left. He watches me as I watch the land.

"And you, Bracken?" I call without looking.

"Fuck, that's hot," he mutters as he comes to my right.

Neither touches me nor reaches for me, and that hurts.

A lot.

Are we too broken now?

Do they fear or hate me?

I don't know, and part of me doesn't want to, so I keep my eyes on the land, as if hoping it will stop the inevitable—the part where they leave me.

"I want to apologize, Cora," Zee murmurs. "We shouldn't have behaved like that."

"What Tentacles said," Bracken adds. "We took a vote on who should come and apologize without overwhelming you. I truly am sorry, Goldie." There's sincerity in his voice. "I was…jealous." I look at him, seeing how hard this is for him. "I've never been jealous before, but the idea he could take you from me…from us?" The smile he gives me is so sad, it hurts my heart. "I couldn't bear it. I can't lose you, Goldie, not even if you are destined to be his and never mine…ours."

I turn to Zee to see his guarded gaze. I hate that. I hate the distance. "And you?"

"I want you to be happy, that is all. You are right—it is your body, your future, and your choice. Yes, it hurt when he called you his mate, and the idea that he could take you from us made us crazy. I apologize, they all do. They only did it because they care for you so much and the idea of losing you forever made them a little…"

"Insane?" I offer. "Petulant? Childlike?" I keep going, making him smile.

"Desperate," he adds.

Nodding, I turn back to the view, unsure how to bridge this gap that seems to have grown between us.

"Goldie," Bracken whispers, making me close my eyes in pain.

"Please don't give up on us. Please don't walk away from us. You're the only person who has ever cared for any of us, the only person we want to. I know I joke a lot, and I play and tease, but I've never had a family, and now I do because of you. We are all terrified of losing that. We've all been alone for so very long, wandering in the darkness, and then you came. You brought the light back, along with laughter and love, and none of us could live without you. They will all tell you to do what you need to, to follow what your heart desires, but I'll beg for them, for you, on my knees if I have to."

"Then do it." I turn to him, keeping my voice even as an idea comes to mind.

All of us need to reconnect, and right now, I need them.

I need to feel like I am still theirs.

Bracken swallows but drops to his knees, his eyes pained as they meet mine. "I'm yours, Goldie. We all are. Choose us."

"I already did," I retort as I step forward and grip his hair. I bend down and kiss him before nipping his lip. "So why don't you thank me?" I purr, and when I pull back, his eyes are closed with ecstasy, his lips slack. He blinks his eyes open again as my meaning sinks in, and they quickly heat.

Desire glimmers in his gaze as he watches me.

"You're already on your knees, so why don't you make yourself useful?" I grin.

"Dirty little human." He smirks wickedly, flashing fang. Relief pours through me at the return of the teasing, happy fey I'm used to.

Parting my legs, I magic away my clothes, watching them strip from my body and flutter to the ground, leaving me bare before him. I place one foot on his shoulder and drag him closer with his hair. Turning my head, I beckon Zee closer, and he comes quickly, happy to oblige. Arms wrap around me from behind as I kiss him and absorb my mates.

I let him taste the truth on my lips. "I have always been yours and always will be, no matter what happens, so prove you are still mine," I murmur into his mouth.

His hands slide upwards, cupping my bare breasts and tweaking my nipples, reminding me what his stilma can do. "With great pleasure," he promises.

Bracken's hands slide up my thighs possessively as Zee decimates my mouth, and when fangs scrape across my pussy, I moan against his tongue, making Bracken chuckle smugly. "Hold on, Goldie," he warns, and then his mouth attacks my pussy, his lips and tongue tracing over every inch. Tasting every part of me, Bracken makes me his again.

Both males imprint on my soul so deeply, they can never doubt this again. All the while, Zee rolls, twists, and pinches my nipples, arching an agonizing heat and pain straight to my clit, and when Bracken sucks it into his mouth, his fangs nipping at each side, I come. Zee swallows my cries as Bracken laps up my cum. Slumping into them, I pull myself from Zee's mouth, panting as I look down at a grinning Bracken, his face coated in my cream.

"You taste like mine, Goldie," he purrs.

My hand is still in his hair, so I use my grip to tug him up. He crawls up my body, stopping to kiss and lick every inch before he grips my hips and lifts me, letting me wrap my legs around his waist.

His eyes flick to Zee for a moment before he grins smugly. They flip me, and my legs wrap back around Zee when I find him naked. Those molten, stormy eyes watch me possessively as he grips my throat and pushes me backwards, leaning me back against Bracken's chest. His hands grip my ass and hold me up. "You are ours, *measma*, and sometimes, we will fight. We will clash heads, but we will always come after you, always apologize, and always fight for you," Zee promises, his face stern before his eyes skim down my body. "Now let me remind you that I'm yours too."

I feel his cock dragging along my pussy, wetting his length, and when one of his stilma locks on my clit with that maddening suck, my eyes slam closed and my back arches into Bracken, who turns my head and claims my mouth.

Zee thrusts into me, stretching me around his length, and I scream into Bracken's wicked mouth. Zee doesn't hold back, his head dipping to my breasts, where he licks and sucks my sensitive nipples as he pulls out and slams back in. The force smashes me into Bracken so hard, his fang nips my tongue and the slight taste of blood fills my mouth. He freezes before an inhuman growl erupts from his lips, and then he's sucking on my bleeding tongue. Hands massage my ass, parting me wider as Zee fucks me with hard, quick thrusts as Bracken tastes a different part of me.

It's all too much, with too many hands, stilma, and fangs. I'm unable to do anything but whimper between them and trust them to hold me up.

When Bracken pulls back, he's snarling. "That's it, Zee, get her nice and wet. Stretch her cunt for me."

Fuck!

My head falls back to his shoulder as I tighten my legs around Zee, holding on for dear life as my kraken powers inside of me, pummeling into my cunt with wet sucking sounds as Bracken's mouth drops to my ear, whispering dirty promises.

"You're going to come for him. You're going to let him feel you explode around his cock, and then I'm going to slide inside of you alongside him, and you'll take it, Goldie. You'll take every inch we have, and then we are going to fuck you so you never forget that you are ours. Not just his, ours." His fang nips my ear, drawing blood, and he sucks it away again.

The pressure, the stilma, Zee's cock...

My body can't take it.

I must say it out loud.

"No, you were made for this, *measma*. You were made for us," Zee snarls, speeding up and tilting my hips so he drags along my engorged nerves.

My breath hitches, and my legs begin to shake. I feel my orgasm clawing at my insides, wanting out. Suddenly, just like my magic, it explodes through me.

I scream and jerk between them as I come all over Zee's length just like Bracken promised. Zee fights my clamping cunt as he thrusts into me, fucking me through the aftershocks, and when I relax, I feel Bracken.

His cock presses against my ass, sliding over my cheeks and wetting them with my juices, and then Zee stills, letting Bracken control the situation.

"I told you what was going to happen, Goldie," Bracken purrs in my ear as his cock slides to my already full entrance.

"You...You won't fit," I rasp out.

"Oh, I will. You were made for us. Let me prove it." That dark voice in my ear makes me shiver in need, even after coming twice, and then the blunt tip of him pushes into me, stretching me to the point of pain as his cock slides along Zee's. The slow stretch, the burn, makes me whimper like a hurt animal, but Zee licks my breasts, his stilma sucking at my clit until I relax.

"That's it, Goldie. Take every inch," Bracken rumbles. "Fuck, you're so tight, so fucking wet. Shit, I didn't know it would feel this good with him inside you as well."

Oh, shadows!

Several slow, tortuous seconds later, he's fully seated in me, and then we are all panting and holding still. The fullness is indescribable, but when they start to move, my eyes close as I fade into nothing but theirs, just like they promised.

"That's it, *measma*. Let go. Let us take care of you," Zee rumbles, nipping my breast, no doubt leaving red marks behind.

Bracken's fangs drag along my shoulder, both a threat and a promise, as he pulls out and thrusts back in, until they find a rhythm and move together.

Claiming me.

Their hands are possessive, their mouths are promising, and their fangs are all mine.

"Please!" I cry out when it gets to be too much. I'm shaking and overwhelmed by the sensations, and then there are claws in my hair, tugging my head around viciously.

My eyes snap open, clashing with Grim's heated gaze. "You can and you will. Eyes on us. Let us see them claim you."

"Grim!" I shout.

"Ours," he snarls, his face in mine. "You are ours. I won't apologize for trying to kill anyone who tries to take you away. They might to appease you, but I never will. I'll rip anyone who gets in my way to shreds—that's a promise." He slams his lips to mine, his kiss brutal and perfect.

Coils slide along my legs, stroking me, and when my eyes open once more, they clash with Krug's, who's standing next to Grim.

All of them watch and touch me in some way, proving I am theirs.

The orgasm that slams through me is so strong, magic pours from me and into all of them, like a rope tethering us together. Zee howls, his head dropping back, and just hammers into it. Bracken sinks his fangs into me as he thrusts before stilling. The barb follows a moment later, hooking inside me.

Zee's hips stutter, and he jerks at the feeling of the barb, and then I feel their release splashing inside me.

My name is scrawled across their souls so brightly, it sings to my soul.

I feel it across all of them.

It's something you can't see with the naked eye, but with my magic moving through them, I can.

Mates.

They are mine. I am theirs.

Echoing groans sound around us, and when my eyes open, I see Nero, Grim, and Krug have fallen to their knees with ecstasy on their faces, their eyes closed as they come from the force of my magic alone.

Eventually, the magic pulls back, releasing us all, and I slump.

Zee and Bracken carefully pull from my clinging body. I wince when I feel the slight pain, but I don't protest as I feel their combined cum sliding down my thighs. I'm gathered in warm arms and led back inside, where whoever is holding me slides to their back on the floor. He holds me tight, and then there are more arms, legs, and hands thrown over me.

All of my mates are gathered on the floor, just embracing me.

"We aren't giving you up, ever, *parum angius*," Nero whispers. "I'm sorry it came out like that though."

"He's right," Grim rumbles, tugging me closer. "You're ours. I'm sorry for being pig-headed." Just like he promised, he doesn't apologize for trying to kill Razcorr.

"And I'm yours, all of yours. We have to be in this together," I murmur.

"We are," they say in unison. "We are yours. Even if you are his mate, you are still ours."

We all feel the moment Razcorr enters, lingering hesitantly near where we are piled on the floor.

He looks down at us all sprawled together, their hands clutching me. "I never expected her to give you up," he says suddenly. "My people mate for life, that is true, but times have changed. I see what you mean to Cora. I would never hurt her, and losing you would hurt her. I simply ask this—give me the chance to love her the way you all do."

They don't reply, but I feel them relaxing around me. Their eyes go to me, letting me decide.

If I say no, they would make him leave. If I say yes, they will accept him.

I am in control.

It is my choice, my fate, my life.

I lift my hand and offer it to him.

I decide to give him a chance, not because of magic or destiny, but because I like Razcorr, and something about that lonely man who turned to stone to escape the years calls to the girl who lay in bed at night wishing for a happy life.

The relief that pours across his face lets me know I chose right, and he drops to his knees before us, then slides into a spot we didn't even know we had, filling it.

Uniting us.

My magic pulses in happiness and settles in a way I didn't know it could.

We are complete.

CHAPTER THIRTY-NINE

"It took us weeks to reach the castle," I point out, running a hand through my hair. "Are we doomed to trek all the way back the way we came?"

"It's too risky," Grim argues. "You're more powerful now, and the magic calls to every monster in the area. We would be overrun just by stepping outside of the castle, never mind traipsing through the Dead Lands."

"Regardless, we still must travel it," Zee retorts. "We have the plan. We need to reach the Gilded Lands in order to enact it."

"Which brings up another problem," Nero interjects. "We don't exactly blend in." As if to prove his point, he gestures to his coils twining around the room. I have to agree. Nero might be one of the more difficult ones to hide, but Razcorr has a sizable pair of wings as well, not to mention Krug and Grim. Shadows, even Zee is tall enough to draw attention. Bracken, if left in shadow, could blend in, but the moment he opened his mouth, we'd be made.

Razcorr stands slightly off to the side, listening to our conversation, and he only speaks up after we start trying to figure out the best route through the Dead Lands in order to reach the wall.

"I may have another way," he says suddenly, his eyes darting to me and then away, as if still a little shy. It's endearing. When I raise my brows at him, encouraging him to continue, he clears his throat. "Kulmak wanted a way to visit Emelyn when she had duties in the Gilded Lands, but he didn't want his travels known, nor did he want it to take the same length of time, and Emelyn, her power called to many of the monsters, so he didn't want to risk her life."

"Okay." I nod. "That makes sense and is the same issue we face."

"Precisely." His wings shift on his back, making a soft sound I'll only ever liken to wings. Nothing else could sound like that. "In answer to the problem, Kulmak commissioned a tunnel."

Krug perks up. "He dug a tunnel all the way to the Gilded Lands?"

Razcorr hesitates. "Yes…and no."

"What does that mean?" Grim rumbles. "Spit it out."

"The construction started, but the tunnel is incomplete. It stops and exits in the Shadow Lands."

Silence falls. "Which means we'll have to travel through the Shadow Lands and the Gilded Lands on foot and somehow remain undetected," I murmur softly, glancing around at my monsters. "It's risky."

"It would make more sense for some of us to remain behind," Razcorr begins, but five other monsters protest.

"Absolutely not."

"Where she goes, we all go."

"She's not going in alone."

"Fuck that idea!"

"Okay," I snap, cutting off their objections. "We get it—no one gets left behind." I run a hand through my hair again. "So we all go in, sneak through the Shadow Lands and Gilded Lands undetected, find Emelyn's resting place, rob her grave, then bring her back." Sighing, I start to rub my eyes. "Four things. It's only four things." I look at the six of them. "Tell me this is going to work."

At first, no one answers, and surprisingly, it's Bracken who steps forward and takes my hand. "This is going to work, Goldie."

It has to. There's no other choice. To free magic and help the monsters stabilize, this is the only choice, and I didn't survive as the hunt to fail now.

Besides, some small part of me wants to see the look on the human king's face when he realizes I'm still alive, even if we're planning to be in and out undetected.

At some point, he'll know, and that brings me a wicked sense of joy and determination.

It only takes us a few hours to prepare. We're all armed with our weapons of choice. Razcorr strapped a sword down my spine that he thinks I'll need. Honestly, I won't even remember it's there. My magic is second nature now. It flows to my fingertips easily. Despite that, I filled my pockets with gems and crystals that Emelyn had once touched, each one filled with a bit of my magic in the hopes they'll help. The rose quartz is tucked over my heart, hanging from a string Razcorr fashioned for me when I expressed what I wanted.

Now it hangs heavily between my breasts, a reminder of the love I'm surrounded by and the power that love holds.

The seven of us stand before the large stone doorway Razcorr swears is the passage we need. On the stone is a scene of a lush forest—a depiction of the Dead Lands before it started to die. At the top of the scene, a minotaur and a human woman hold hands, staring at each other with love. Even in the construction of the tunnel, Kulmak was declaring his love. How humbling it must have felt to love something so fragile. My eyes trail over to my monsters, wondering if they feel the same and worry about my humanity.

The tunnel appears to be sealed up, likely a product of Emelyn's death, but when Razcorr pushes it and Zee joins in, the door swings open easily, revealing the darkened tunnel beyond. The air smells stale after centuries of being closed up, but just like the castle, everything else is well preserved.

"Touch your magic here," Razcorr instructs me, and I do as he says, pressing my fingers to a part on the wall and coaxing my magic to life.

Something sparks, and then light flares in a small lantern before it speeds down the line and illuminates the way. With each lantern that lights, we can see farther.

"How long will it take to travel?" I ask, because the longer it takes us to reach our goal, the longer it takes for the plan to fall into place.

"A day," Razcorr answers, "if traveled at a monster's pace."

Which means I'll be riding Nero again. There's something comforting about that thought, because even after all we've been through and all the new revelations, some things don't change. Nero, in answer, meets my eyes and wiggles his eyebrows, clearly happy to provide the transportation. Giggling at him, I thread my fingers through his and nod.

"Are we ready?" I ask, meeting all of their eyes. This is it. The real risk begins at the end of this tunnel. Some of us could be injured. It hurts to think that worse things can happen than that. Either way, we know what must be done, and there's no other monsters I'd rather do this with.

I'm met by a chorus of, "Ready," and so I climb onto Nero's back and settle in. The tunnel is narrow enough that we can only walk two abreast, but the journey will pass quickly at our pace. Grim takes up the lead, as he always does, and looks back at me once.

"You're sure about this?" he asks, and I know if I say I'd rather stay here and live out my life without any other cares, he'll agree to it. They all would.

"Yes," I reply, and then because I'm an asshole, I add, "Your Majesty."

He scowls and leans around Nero to glare at me. "Keep it up, little human, and I'll make you kneel before your king."

I suck in a breath, both at the sensuality of his comment and the fact he admitted to the crown. It's the first time he's acknowledged it, and because my heart is full, I reach up and stroke his jaw.

"I will gladly kneel before you," I murmur. "If only you return the favor."

FRACTURED SHADOWS

His eyes heat, and a smile pulls at his lips as he presses his forehead to mine. It's such a tender gesture for the minotaur that it almost brings moisture to the corners of my eyes.

He moves back and takes up his place again.

Razcorr is staring at me, his eyes glancing between me and Grim.

"Is everything okay?" I ask, watching him carefully.

He nods. "It is all just so...familiar, and yet not."

Smiling, I pat his chest. "You get used to it."

In answer, he tucks his wing around me gently in a hug that warms me from the inside out before he moves into position beside Grim.

My monsters.

Each has stolen a piece of me and brought me joy I never knew I could feel. When I left the Shadow Lands, I assumed it would be to die, but instead, I've found the greatest life.

In a dark fey who teases first but will draw blood for me.

In a royal minotaur, gruff in nature but more tender than I ever imagined.

In a kraken who gives me the sea and takes me deep.

In a naga who wraps me up so tightly, I could never feel unloved.

In an orc king who sees me as a fearless warrior he'll happily follow.

In a gargoyle destiny chose, and who I continue to choose after.

My heart is full, and for the first time in my life, I feel complete.

Because of them.

"Let's go," I announce, holding onto Nero, hugging him so he knows how much I love him.

Love. Because that's what it is. I gave them my heart before I even knew I had one to give.

∼

RAZCORR IS RIGHT—IT only takes a day to move through the tunnels, and at the end of it, as we wait for nightfall, we come together in a nest of limbs. In a huge cavern with leftover mining tools, deep underground under my old home, we meld together. There's no way to know where each begins and ends, but that doesn't matter. We're no longer seven separate beings.

We're a family, and I wouldn't have it any other way.

CHAPTER
FORTY

I feel the night ease in like a silent lover slipping through the window for a secret coupling, despite being in the tunnel. The ease with which I can tell the exact hour should worry me. Instead, it feels like another strength. With that thought in mind, I stretch and coax my magic to my fingertips in an unconscious action that more or less reassures me it's still there. My monsters watch the tiny sparks with wonder, as if I'm a magician.

The magicians on the streets of the Shadow Lands used to enthrall me. Now, I understand that real magic lives inside us.

We ease out of the tunnel, and I'm shocked to realize the tunnel opens up just on the edge of the wall. Part of the rock face I played on as a child gives way to reveal the world I grew up in. It's both familiar and yet somehow foreign to my senses. It looks grimmer than I remember, as if the conditions have gotten worse since I left, but it's only been a matter of weeks. It couldn't have gotten so much worse. The only thing I can think of is that my perceptions of it all have changed.

The yellow paint on the butcher's home used to look so bright, but now I see the chipped and peeling paint, and I notice how faded the color is. The lampposts used to seem like a beacon in the night, and now they are barely bright enough to lead the way. In the distance, the Gilded Lands glitter just as they always have, as if that's where the brightness in the Shadow Lands went and the Gilded Ladies steal whatever brightness the Shadow Lands can muster and tuck it into their bosoms.

A thought has never angered me more.

No one is around as we emerge. I glance toward Nero for a moment, worried about how his white body shines in the low light, but it's dark. He appears more like a ghost than anything else.

For once, there doesn't seem to be any last-minute field tenders rushing home after being forced to work longer in the fields with no extra pay. Everyone is settled in for the night. I can't decide if it's a blessing or if it's a warning of how badly things have gotten since I left.

"Stay close," Grim whispers, his voice barely loud enough to carry to our ears.

We move silently through the Shadow Lands, sticking to the shadows that are in abundance. It has always bothered me that the Gilded Lands call us the Shadow Lands, as if we're too dim to deserve any light. Almost as if done purposely, the sparse lanterns cast more shadows, proving their point, when really, all it would take is better lanterns to make a difference.

I don't have any plans on stopping. We have our agenda—get in and get out with none the wiser—but as the house I grew up in comes into view, I stumble to a stop, my heart beating hard in my chest.

It looks sadder now. Before, it had been the only option, but now I see the leaking roof, the way the front wall pitches forward as if it will fall any day now, and the grime coating the wood panels. It's never looked as pathetic as it does right now, but still, it was once my home.

"What's wrong?" Grim asks, his eyes following the direction of my gaze. "Is there something wrong with that building?"

"That's it," I whisper, my voice rough. "That's where I grew up."

Six sets of eyes focus on the house and take in the dismal appearance, and I can feel their shock and anger, but none more so than Zee.

"This was your prison?" he asks, his eyes hard with anger. "This is where your father sleeps?"

Razcorr shifts. "Father? Is he a good man?"

I realize some of them don't know my story, don't know what the Shadow Lands are like, but I can't find the words to describe it, not right now, not when faced with that reality.

Luckily for me, I don't have to explain it.

"No," Bracken snarls. "He beat and starved her."

"He kept her from learning," Krug added. "Tried to snuff out her flame."

"She sacrificed herself to the hunt to save her sister, and her father laughed," Nero adds.

With each word, Razcorr's eyes harden, and I see hatred in his gaze that reflects my feelings. My father is all of that and more. He's terrible, hateful, selfish, and childish. I want him to suffer, but it isn't part of the plan.

"This man tried to hurt my mate before she ever found her way to us," Razcorr rumbles, his voice low enough for us to hear but not carry. "I say we make him suffer."

Grim straightens. "For once, I agree with you, gargoyle."

I watch as five monsters move toward the small house, and I don't stop them. When fingers thread into mine, I turn to look at Bracken, who stands beside me.

"You're not joining in?" I rasp out. There's pain in my throat, and past that, deep in my soul, there's fear too, and I hate that. I hate that I can still fear the man. I hate that I have all this magic in my veins, and I still flinch at the thought of his belt.

"If I go in there, Goldie, there will be no mercy," he murmurs. "If I go in there, I will leave only death."

Despite all my pain, Bracken understands I don't want them to kill my father. I want him to suffer. Death would be too quick, but I cannot dish out that punishment myself. My trauma is too deep.

But my monsters? They will do it for me.

Bracken leads me toward the run-down shack, and I stop in the entryway, staring into the dimly lit room, where Krug holds up my father by the back of his neck. Despite there being no noise outside of the house, it's clear they have already roughed him up. Blood drips from his mouth, his lip is split, and there's a nice cut above his eyebrow that will turn into a black eye. I can only imagine what the rest of his body feels like and how many ribs he might have broken.

Tomorrow, I hope the field manager comes and forces him to work despite his pain, the same way he forced Kai and me back into the fields after he beat us.

"Should we kill him?" Razcorr asks, drawing a large blade. My father stares at the sword, and relief flashes in his eyes, but he won't escape his fate so easily.

I shake my head. "No," I say, and he jerks, his eyes trailing up to me. He hadn't even realized I was there before I spoke, but when he sees me standing before him, healthier than I've ever been, his eyes widen. "Let him suffer."

He spits a wad of blood on the floor at my feet. "Leave it to you to whore your way back," he snarls. His voice is pained, but the words still come out with that same venom as always. "How long did it take you to open your legs for these beasts?"

My monsters shift with fury, but as I stare at the man I once feared more than anything, all I feel is...pity. He's weak, so weak, and rotting from the inside. The fear dissipates as soon as I realize the only hold he had over me was terror.

I stroll forward, looking into his eyes, and though the child in me is afraid, the woman I've become doesn't back down. "Seven days," I tell him, my eyes hard. "I fucked them the first chance I got. Does that make you feel superior?" I lift up my hand, and a single spark appears on the tip of my finger. His eyes widen in fear. "Would you like to know how I screamed in pleasure?" The spark dances around. "Would you like me to tell you how I moaned their names?"

"Whore," he spits. "You belong over there with them."

"You're right," I agree. "I do."

The single spark travels from my finger and into his eye, burning. Grim clamps a hand over his mouth before the scream comes out, keeping it muffled. Only then do I realize no one else has come out to check on the sounds.

Furrowing my brow, I recall my magic as panic winds through me.

"Where's Kai?" I ask, looking toward the door where we slept. The door is open, and I can see the empty room beyond. When I lean over to the other small room, I see my mother staring up at the ceiling with glazed eyes, as if she doesn't realize there are monsters in her house. I doubt she even knows she's alive. She's an empty vessel, nothing more.

My father spits blood and starts to laugh, despite the fact he'll be blind in one eye now.

"The king took her." He laughs, and there's pure glee on his face, despite his pain. "You didn't save her after all."

Fury floods through me until I feel my magic glowing under my skin. I snarl and grab his face in my fingers, forcing him to look at me. "Where did he take her?"

His laughter twists my soul, but I've long since accepted that this man is no father of mine, despite his sperm donation. "She's his now," he rasps out, and it's like a nail in the coffin. "Your sacrifice meant nothing."

I bare my teeth at him, and sparks fly from my fingers, giving him burn after burn after burn.

His muffled screams only make it worse…

Where the fuck is my sister?

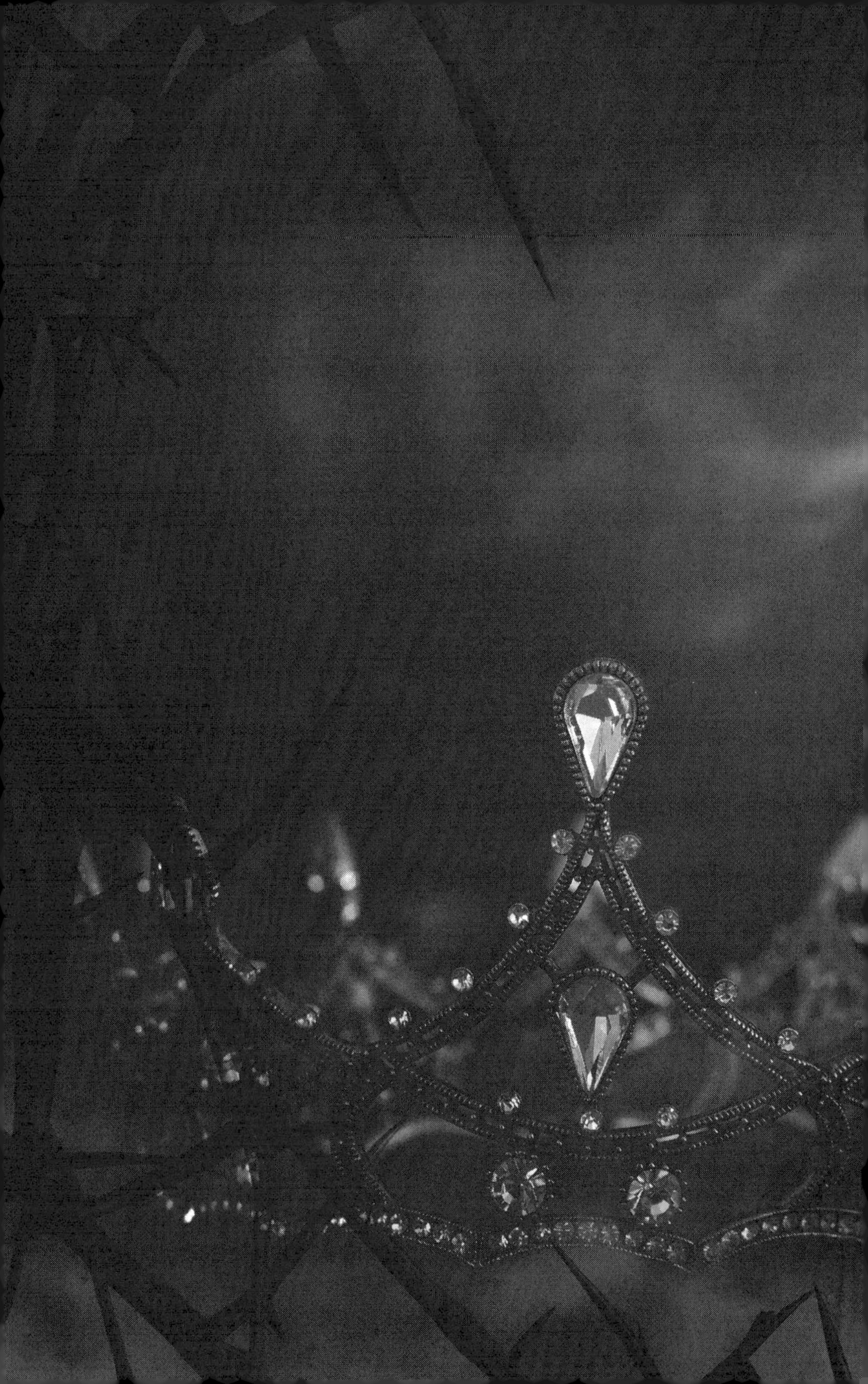

CHAPTER FORTY-ONE

I can't contain my magic. It explodes out of me with a ragged, agonized scream.

Falling to my knees, I watch my men fling through the walls of the shack I used to live in, the walls splintering as they disappear into the shadows beyond. My father writhes and then stills, and yet I can't stop.

My heart breaks and cracks.

Everything I did was to protect her, to give her a better life, and she's gone.

She's with him, the king, the man who descends from a long line of men willing to kill their daughters for power.

There's a grunt, and then a hand wraps around my neck from behind. When I glance down, I see my magic burning Grim's skin, but he still holds on. "Cora, calm down," he orders, "or you'll kill us all."

That makes me gasp and pull my magic back. I slump into him with a cry, turning and burying my face into his expansive chest.

"Shh, I have you, little one," he promises, his big hand stroking up and down my back as sobs rack my body.

Fear, something I never wanted to feel again, roars through me.

"He has my sister, Grim," I whisper as I lift my head. My tear-stained face makes him growl, and his mesmerizing eyes flash with anger and understanding.

"I know." He wipes under my eyes, his lips ghosting over the same path. "Tell us what you want to do."

I search his eyes, and I see the truth there—he will follow me anywhere, no matter what I decide to do.

That has me sitting up straighter, feeling determined.

After all, I'm not Cora the weak human anymore.

I have magic, and it's time I used it.

It's time for me to live up to Krug's name for me.

"I want to get my sister," I murmur, and when I glance back, I see my other men climbing through the holes in the shack. I wince with guilt. "We are going to get my sister back."

"Then I suggest we move. I sense humans heading this way," Bracken drawls as he brushes wood from his shoulder with a frown.

Grim helps me to my feet, and I nod, hesitating as I look down at my father. He's out cold but not dead.

I could kill him so easily, but he's not worth it. Turning away, I follow my monsters into the night, determination filling every step.

The king will regret the day he touched my family.

I'll ensure it.

∼

WE HIDE BEHIND AN OLD BARN, watching the guards sweep the destroyed shack where I used to live and pull my father from the wreckage. Leaning back with a sigh, I meet everyone's unsure gazes.

"The castle, the magic..." Zee starts with a wince.

I know he's worried about me right now, they all are, but I need to do this, and I need them with me.

"Don't you think if Emelyn was anywhere, it would be there? In the one place her love, the king, could never get to?"

Razcorr nods. "She's right—he would have kept his daughter's body close."

"Then that's where we go," Grim states, throwing them all a narrow-eyed look. "We go to the castle, we rescue your sister, and we free the queen's body."

"You forget we have to make it through the Shadow Lands and the Gilded Lands," Nero adds but winks at me.

"These puny humans will not stand in the way of what my Cora wants," Krug says, making me smile.

"Ah, fuck it, I'm in. I love a bit of chaos anyway." Bracken grins.

"So we are doing this?" I confirm.

"Together," Zee murmurs. "Now let's move before we get trapped here. I think the humans inside this barn might scream if they come out and see us, especially him." He jerks his head at Nero.

"What did I do?" Nero scoffs, making us all laugh, and when he grins at me, I know he did it on purpose.

"Let's get moving." I get to my knees and glance around the barn. "We move through the fields and then to the road that leads into the Gilded Lands. I've never been, so from there, we are on our own, but I know the night patrols here."

"And why is that, Goldie?" Bracken smirks.

Rolling my eyes, I get to my feet. "Because I used to sneak out for secret night orgies, obviously."

"And you didn't invite me?" He grabs his chest. "Guys, we have time for a secret night orgy, right?"

"Next time." Zee grins when he tugs Bracken after me as we run toward the field. Luckily, at this time of year, the crops are high. They cover me and more, but my men have to crouch behind me as we move.

Between each field is a dirt track, and we linger in the darkness of the crops for the guards to pass, shying away from the light. If they looked too close, though, they would see a glowing half human, a fey, a minotaur, a kraken, an orc, a naga, and a gargoyle.

That would be fun to explain.

It's slow going as we make our way through the fields, and by the time we reach the last one, I'm sweating with nerves. Now there are only homes and the open road between us and the Gilded Lands.

No shade, no shadows, just openness.

Stepping out, I gaze around for the best plan when I freeze. I shift to cover my men behind me as a young man stops before me, his brows furrowed. He had been coming around a tree, no doubt after taking a leak, and now he's looking right at me.

He stumbles closer, and his mouth drops open when he sees me. "Cora? Cora Black?"

Fuck.

I recognize him. I worked alongside him in the field a few times. He was one of the nice ones.

"Erm, nope?" I say, stepping backward.

"It is, it's you!" he gushes, stepping closer.

I hear the others behind me gearing up to kill him, so I grab him, yank him to me, and press my lips to his. I infuse magic into my touch and push it into his body before he can exclaim in surprise. When I pull back, his eyes are closed, his lips parted. With my magic moving through him, I wipe him of his memories, though I'm not sure how I know the process.

"You saw nothing. I am not the woman you think I am." When I step back, he's blinking and confused.

Suddenly, Krug appears behind him from the dark like a demon and smashes him across the back of the head, knocking him out. The poor guy slumps to the ground. He's not dead, but he'll definitely have a terrible goose egg tomorrow.

Meeting my eyes, Krug snarls, "He touched you. He's lucky he's not dead."

"I agree," Bracken drawls as he grabs the human man and none too gently throws him into the field behind us. "Next time, don't kiss someone else," he mutters, and I roll my eyes.

"Jealous much? I panicked."

"And your first thought was to kiss him?" Grim grumbles.

"It worked, didn't it?" I throw my hands in the air. "Now let's get moving."

"I can't believe she kissed him," Nero mumbles. "He looked like the offspring of a donkey who had sex with a pig."

"Humans," Zee agrees.

Men, I think to myself.

Nero scoops me up, and I ride him as we travel over the darkened road. We need to get near the castle before day breaks. There will be no hiding then, not when the sunlight of the Gilded Lands touches the horizon. As we move, the dirt changes to paved gold, hard and glittering.

The barely living land around us changes to natural growth and thriving life. Beautiful trees stretch over us, and plants shimmer with whatever magic is left in our lands. All of it is calling to me.

Then we crest the hill, a hill I didn't even know was here since I'd never really crossed the barrier, and there, laid out before us, is an entirely different world.

"Welcome to the Gilded Lands," I mutter bitterly, remembering all the times I starved while no one here even knows what it's like to be hungry. Disgust fills me, but still, even I can't deny the beauty of the realm.

It's like a crown studded with corpses, or a heaven filled with devils.

CHAPTER
FORTY-TWO

We stare longer than we should, me included.

I knew their lands would be opulent, but I wasn't prepared for...this.

The road winds down the hill to a huge gate below, the only visible opening in a low wall that runs as far as I can see, splitting us from them. Guards patrol the gate, but not the wall, or so it seems. I guess they aren't too worried about the Shadow Landers sneaking in. After all, we're all just trying to survive and not starve.

But the Gilded Lands? It's perfect and beautiful. Behind the wall are shops and homes, all made from bright white brick and paint, some as tall as three stories. Their roads are paved with gold, and they glitter under the moon. The whole city is bright and shiny, with perfect rows upon perfect rows of houses and markets.

There's a circle in the middle, which I'm guessing is their town center.

In the distance, almost mirroring the black castle of the monsters, is a glittering gold palace. Shining in the moonlight like a jewel, it reaches up into the sky, lording above everyone.

My sister is in there, and in those golden walls is also my destiny.

That's what gets me moving again.

"Let's go. Dawn will be here before we know it, and we don't want to get caught. I suggest we move farther down, get over that wall, and find someplace to hide near the castle."

"Good plan, *parum anguis*," Nero purrs.

It's definitely going to be harder to hide in the Gilded Lands, but we have a job to do and my sister to save. Nothing will stop us now.

As one, my monsters and I use the darkness to our advantage, moving far away from the gate until we can't see it anymore, and then we climb over the wall, which is effortless for most of them. Nero lifts me until I straddle the top, and then on the other side, Zee waits with open arms. I don't hesitate to throw myself down, and he catches me, stealing a quick kiss before setting me down as we turn to figure out a path and where to go.

The houses here stretch into the dark, with small, paved roads between them. Some have streetlights chasing away the shadows, so we quickly avoid them. Instead, we slip between the three-story buildings, crawling between them when we see light inside.

Everything here is different, even the air is sweeter.

Unnaturally so.

Flowers bloom, and life moves on. It's nothing like the Shadow Lands or the Dead Lands.

It's pretty, bright, and unpredictable, just like gold, but under the surface? I feel the dishonor, the lies, and the pain it tries to mask. It might be pretty, but pretty isn't enough.

Pretty isn't real.

When we reach the circle in the middle, we hide deep in the shadows, pressed against the side of a darkened bakery as we try to determine our next move. Guards wander through the circle, making us duck even lower.

It's clear every inch of this place is surveyed, and I can see the orange glow of dawn starting to streak through the sky as it lightens.

We're running out of time.

"What now?" Bracken murmurs.

"I don't know," I whisper, and it's true—I don't.

I'm lost.

I was sure we would get to the castle and could lie low somewhere close, so the next night we could attack…

"We need to find food and shelter, and fast. When the sun breaks through, we'll be found and killed," Grim points out, voicing what all of us are thinking. "Shelter is our priority. Everyone, search the streets around us for somewhere to hide."

Nodding, they slip into the clinging shadows the light hasn't stolen yet. I scan the area around us. There has to be something.

Anything.

Grim is still at my back, unwilling to leave me alone, and I turn into the dark, letting it wrap around me like a lover. Taking a deep breath, I close my eyes and call my magic, letting it fill me. The comforting warmth chases away my doubts, so I decide to try something.

I'm not sure if it will work, but I'm desperate.

I brought my monsters here, and I will protect them.

We need shelter, we need safety.

I whisper to it, hoping, pleading.

It surges through me and wraps me in its warmth before it flows from me, shooting across the city, and then I feel a tug, like my magic has tied a rope to me and is pulling me.

My eyes open, and I meet Grim's gaze. "I know where to go. Follow me."

"The others," Grim reminds me.

Nodding, I close my eyes again. Reaching out with my magic, I brush each and every one of them individually, pulling them back to me, and when I open my eyes, it takes mere seconds for them to reappear.

"We have somewhere," Grim tells them, and without another word, they follow me through the city.

We have to stop to avoid patrols and work our way around brightly lit areas. Grim's hand remains on me the entire time, anchoring me as I focus on the magic. It pulls us closer and closer to the castle, until we feel the sun beginning to rise.

Until we are outrunning it.

"Cora," Grim grits out.

"Almost there," I assure him, panting as we run.

I can feel their panic, even as we draw closer to our destination.

"There!" I call, pointing my finger at a grate in the ground in a back alley. They don't question me. Krug rips it up and drops inside, followed by Bracken. We wait, and then there is a soft confirmation from below, so Zee lifts me into his arms and drops into the hole.

Darkness swallows us just as the sun rises, flooding the Gilded Lands with light.

~

It must be a water tunnel system, I realize. It's just like the king to hide something like this underground. After all, it's not pleasing to the eye.

The tunnel is round and big enough that we can all stand without bending our heads or wings. Water runs in a shallow river down the middle, with two walkways on either side. The brick down here is dark, stained, and old.

It smells like earth, though, and we begin to follow the water with nothing else to do, hoping it might lead us to a room or an outcropping where we can rest for the day.

At least we are closer to the castle.

When we round the tunnel's corner, we all slide to a stop in shock.

Before us, in a massive cavern with light streaming in from grates above, are people.

Not just people...monsters.

"What?" I whisper as they all turn to look at us.

Fear contorts their faces. Some hurry to hide in nearby tunnels, while others throw themselves into constructed tents.

They are hiding from us.

"We aren't here to hurt you," I murmur slowly, stepping into the light.

There must be hundreds of them in a cavern big enough to be a castle, but they are odd—not quite human, and not quite monster.

One to my left, a short female, has stubby wings and small horns, but the rest of her is human. A man before me has a clawed hand on one arm. Another has the face of an animal but the body of a man.

"What are you?" Grim asks as he stops next to me. They seem to settle when they see him.

They fear humans, I realize, not monsters.

"Halflings," the man with one arm answers proudly, his head tilted back. "We are the king's creations."

~

Seated in the middle of the cavern on some blankets, we accept food and water graciously as we are surrounded by the halflings. "So the king created you?" I ask, addressing no one in particular.

An older woman winds through the crowd, checking on others as she goes, before she sits gracefully before me. I cannot see what the king has done to her, but there is knowledge in her eyes derived from years of pain and experience.

"Experiments gone wrong," she clarifies. Her voice is soft and musical, almost alluring. "He was trying to bring magic back. Apparently, some humans have monster blood in them." She winks at my men behind me. "Breeding, I would guess. He tried to bring that forth, but...it changed us. Our bodies are not meant for that, and so here we are. We escaped from the castle and his reach."

"You escaped?" I gasp, leaning back into Bracken, who wraps himself around me like a teddy. She watches with amusement.

"We did." She nods proudly. "It took years, but we managed to get out. We tried to free all of us, but I know he hasn't stopped. The king is a cruel bastard who delights in pain."

It's my turn to nod. "I know that all too well."

"Girl, who are you?" she asks.

"My name's Cora. I was the hunt," I say smugly, my grin widening. "Only I didn't die like he wanted."

"No, I can see that." She laughs, and the sound makes me sigh in happiness. "Well, Cora, any enemy of the king is a friend of ours."

"Thank you. We just need somewhere to hide during the day. My mates won't blend in up there." I grin.

"No, they definitely won't." She eyes them and looks back at me. "I can offer you refuge. It isn't much, but it's what we have."

I take her hand, almost compelled to as I squeeze it. "It is more than enough," I assure her.

"Then welcome, Cora, survivor of the hunt," she calls, and various greetings are called as more come over to us. "I'm afraid that is the last of our food, but we have beds and warmth."

I nod as I look down at the food I was eating and pass it over to a child nearby, who looks to be starving. It's then I truly look around.

The king did this. He created these people with his perverted nature. He corrupts everything he touches.

This is about more than us now, more than me. This is about everyone.

This is about the future of all the lands.

We have to help them. They are trapped here and starving.

They never asked to be made into this. All they have known is pain and rejection. They need to be safe, they need a home, and the rest of our world needs to know the truth.

Humans need to see behind the gilded mask to the true monster who sits on the throne.

"I think we can help each other," I state.

The old woman watches me before giving me a blinding smile. "I think we can too. I'm Marne, and I've been waiting a long time for you, Cora."

CHAPTER
FORTY-THREE

"We need food," I murmur, sitting in the middle of my monsters. Glancing around at the starving halflings, I correct, "They need food."

"We should stay here," Grim argues. "None of us can blend in."

I meet his eyes. "I can."

"Cora," he warns, his fingers tightening on the sword he'd been cleaning.

"I know it's dangerous, but I could go up top, find some food, and be back down with no one the wiser."

"And what if someone recognizes you again?" Krug asks, his eyes telling me I don't need to be kissing any more men, even to stop them from recognizing me.

I sigh. "No one but the king would know me in the Gilded Lands, and even he probably wouldn't recognize me now. I was scrawny and starving the last he saw me."

Grim's eyes trace over my body, acknowledging the muscle and weight I've put on since I was first thrown into the Dead Lands as the hunt. "I doubt the king will be walking the streets."

"Exactly," I agree. "The only time I've even come close to the Gilded

Lands was when I was being prepared as the hunt, and even then, I was barely taken to the edge of it. I'll be fine walking, and I'll be back before you even miss me."

"Impossible," Bracken declares. "I miss you the moment you're gone."

Melting at his words, I stroke my hand along his jaw and meet Grim's eyes. "I'll be careful. I promise. Besides, I'm not as helpless as I was when you first found me."

He's silent for a minute before he sighs, and a bit of smoke curls from his nostrils. "Fine, but you have an hour. If you're not back, I'm coming after you, plans be damned."

I nod. "I shouldn't need long. I'll find the closest food and bring it down. It's the least I can do."

When I talk to Marne about my plan, she shows me a grate that leads up into the Gilded Lands through an alley. I brush myself off and climb through the grate, and I'm grateful to see it's protected by a large dumpster sitting near the wall, making it more shielded.

I dust off the bits of dirt on my clothing and step out into the sunshine, and I nearly lose my breath.

In the Shadow Lands, the sunshine is muted by the air pollution and the shadows that coat every surface. In the Dead Lands, it's hidden behind whatever dreariness fills the sky. In the Gilded Lands, however, the sun shines down unhindered, touching every clean surface and making it sparkle. Bitterness makes me want to wipe some dirt on the walls to make them feel what I've felt my whole life, but instead, I adjust everything on me and hope I can blend in.

When I step into the sunshine, the sunlight catches on my outfit, and Nero's scales shimmer with iridescence, drawing eyes to me. A woman dressed in a flowy dress and jewels immediately comes over, and I tense.

"Where did you get that beautiful fabric? You must tell me."

"Oh, um, a friend gifted it to me," I reply. "I don't think you can find it in any shop."

She pouts. "Pity. It would make a lovely dress."

She disappears back into the crowd. A few more people stare at me as

I walk, but most continue about their business, and I relax. The market is thriving in a way I've never seen before. At the market in the Shadow Lands, you can get stale bread and old fruit that's almost or already rotten. Here, the fruit is fresh and whole, and the bread looks like it just came out of the oven.

Then I realize I have no money.

How am I supposed to purchase food with nothing to my name?

Curious, I wander up to the nearest baker sitting with his fresh bread. "Excuse me, sir. I'm afraid I've forgotten how things work. Do you accept—"

"Oh, you're from the king's castle, aren't you? The girls who come down never know what they are doing," he says. "If you're wanting to purchase something, just tell the vendors to add it to the king's account, and it'll be settled at a later date."

I blink. "That's it?"

He nods. "The king's girls can't be expected to carry coins. Too dainty."

"Oh, uh, can I get everything then?" I say hesitantly.

He pauses where he'd been opening a brown paper bag. "I beg your pardon?"

"I'm putting a feast together," I murmur. "It's a surprise, so I need this kept between us. I even want to hide the food so I can slowly take it in and set it up. There's an alley just around the corner..."

"You want everything?" he clarifies. "And then you want me to put it in an alley?"

"Yes, sir." I nod. "If you don't mind. It would all go on the king's account of course."

His eyes widen. "Oh, of course. Of course. I'll get it packed up for you right away. Which alley would you like me to hide it in?"

The smile that pulls at my lips makes him flounder as I direct him toward the alley. I continue my way through the market, doing the same at the fruit stand and the butcher, buying as much as they will allow me to purchase, putting it all on the king's credit. A sense of sick satisfaction fills me as the alley is filled with food, and then when I know it's getting close to an hour, I return and open the grate. I'm met with Nero's yellow eyes.

"Make way," I declare, and I start passing food down to him, his eyes widening.

"*Parum anguis*," he says in surprise as we fill the underground cavern with packages. "How?"

"Apparently, the king has credit, and he allows some of his girls to come down to the markets to purchase whatever they want." Marne grins as she passes out food. "So feast in the name of the king's pocketbook."

There's a small cheer as the fresh food is passed between everyone. Marne comes over and hands me a large loaf of bread. "You are something else, Cora."

I take the bread gratefully and touch her shoulder. "I'm just trying to help."

She nods. "It's far more than anyone has done. We thank you."

That day, we all eat like kings and queens.

Somewhere, I hope the king blinks at his line of credit and wonders how his girls were able to purchase so much. I hope he hates it. I hope he pays without a second thought, not realizing he's feeding his creations and the monsters he fears.

With a grin, I bite into the loaf of bread, and the flavor explodes on my tongue.

CHAPTER
FORTY-FOUR

As sunset approaches, I decide to go up again to see if there is anything else useful at the end of the market. There isn't much left, since I purchased most of what the vendors had earlier, but there are still some who are selling trinkets, jewelry, and clothing that sparkles in the light. I'm studying a particularly pretty dress when movement catches my eyes behind me.

I turn, expecting it to be more market goers, but instead, I spy a guard leading a single woman through the market, her eyes dull and lifeless, and I startle. Shock reverberates through me, and I swear I must be seeing a ghost.

It can't be... It can't be her...

Kai.

I follow her, even though I know my monsters are waiting for me below. I move as if I'm only perusing the wares, but instead, I shadow her as the guard gestures to a table filled with jewels and tells my sister to pick one, but she looks down in disinterest. I'm not even sure she sees the table, considering how glazed her eyes are. It's as if she can't bear to be here, as if she can't even bear to be alive.

Guilt and agony fill me, pulling on my magic, even as I try to mute it.

"Just pick something," the guard snarls. "The king wants you to liven up."

Kai looks at the guard with haunted eyes. "Dressing his toys will not make them happy," she says, and the guard scowls.

"Ungrateful brat." He shakes his head. "Suit yourself. When he finds you tonight without a new trinket, he'll have my ass." He picks up a pink necklace, the color Kai hates most, and holds it up to the light, inspecting it. "We'll take this one."

Scowling, I move up the street and hover in a darkening alley, waiting. I shouldn't, but it's my sister. How could I not? I have to save her. I watch as the jewels are wrapped, and all the while, my sister stands there like a wraith. They move my way, finished with their business, and the moment they appear, I grab their hands and pull them both into the alley. Surprisingly, the guard comes without complaint until he sees me, but my magic spears into him before he can pull his sword, silencing him effortlessly. Kai looks down at the guard and then looks up with relief, not because she knows who I am immediately, but because she clearly thinks she's about to be killed. When her eyes finally find mine, the glaze clears and she blinks, as if coming out of a stupor.

We need to hurry, I know that, but I find myself grasping both of her hands, begging her to come back to me.

"Cora?" she rasps out. I watch as she pinches herself to see if she's imagining me or not, and that makes me just as sad as the look of relief does. "Is that you?"

I nod, tears welling in my eyes. "Kai..." Reaching forward, I wrap my arms around her, but she just stands there, her arms loose at her sides, as if she doesn't quite know what to do.

"But...I watched you walk through the wall..." Her voice is small, scared, and so alone, it makes me ache. My magic roars within me, ready to do my bidding.

"I survived," I tell her. "Kai, the Dead Lands and the monsters aren't what they want us to think." I cup her face. "What happened? How are you here?"

She blinks and averts her eyes, the haunted look coming back.

"When you left, I was so sad, but the king sent guards the next day. I was lying in my bed, crying, when Father came barreling in, telling me to get up. I was dragged from our home and brought to the king's castle, chosen as one of the king's concubines." Her eyes focus on me once more, and for a moment, fire ignites in them, the same fire I always wish I had, before it's doused. "He said I should be proud."

"I'm so sorry, Kai. I'm going to get you out of here," I promise, looking around to figure out what to do. She's wearing a dress that clearly designates her as the king's property, his emblem stamped into the metal clasp holding it together below her throat. The golden material she wears barely covers her skin as it falls in sheer waterfalls to the ground. I won't be able to walk her through the streets without unwanted attention, and my monsters will be waiting for me as the sun starts to set and the market begins to close.

Maybe we can go through the shadows. After all, we are old friends.

"Cora," she says, and I look back at her. The pain I see in her eyes hits me hard. "He let me go."

"Who?"

"Merryl, we were engaged...but he watched the guards drag me away and didn't speak up."

I grimace. "He would have been killed, Kai."

"But he didn't fight for me." She meets my eyes once more, looking so broken and lost, it steals my breath. "You would have fought for me."

I don't argue because it's true. I would have grabbed Kai and fought for her freedom. I would have done everything in my power to stop her from being taken, regardless of the threat to my own life.

"I'm here now," I tell her, silently promising to save her and fight for her now. "Let's get you out of here."

I turn, holding her hand, and run right into an armored chest. My breath rushes from my body as I bounce back, and my instincts scream at me to use my magic, but I tamp it down. Three guards stand before us, scowling and watching us. All of their pretty gold armor is emblazoned with the king's crown, their eyes hard and empty. They are huge and unmovable, and weapons cover every inch of them.

They are meant to inspire fear and submission.

I've never been very good at tolerating either.

"Unhand the king's concubine," the one I ran into orders, withdrawing a blade.

I could take him on, but a sudden realization has me releasing Kai and furrowing my brows. It might not have been the plan, but plans change, and this is exactly what I need. "Fuck you," I spit at him.

I don't fight as they grab me and secure my wrists. I don't do anything but look at Kai. "I'm going to get you out," I repeat. "I promise, Kai."

Her expression saddens as the guards grab her gently, careful not to bruise her, and pull her toward the castle, the same place they drag me toward. The guard I knocked out with my magic is left there, the necklace he held fastened around Kai like a collar that weighs on her soul. She doesn't even resist as we are marched through the streets, across the glittering bridge, and into the castle.

I am taken farther and farther away from my monsters until my magic cries for them.

My men are going to be so pissed at me, but I'm in the belly of the castle, exactly where I need to be. I'll do what I have to do and get Kai out. Fury makes me want to face the king and make him pay for what he's done to my sister. Her spirit, her soul, is muted, and the liveliness and happiness in her eyes is gone.

For that, he's going to pay.

~

THE GILDED CASTLE is large and imposing, both a statement and a declaration. The vastness of the space inside could fit the whole of our lands and more. Bitterness makes me want to spit on it as I'm dragged inside and led through the opulent castle. Paintings fill the walls, and golden trinkets stand on every shelf and table. Everything is gold and marble and bejeweled with a richness that could have been passed onto the people who farm the lands they profit from. We don't even get to eat anything we grow and collect. We get nothing but scraps, while these disgusting people get fat on our food.

The closer we get to the throne room, the angrier I get, until I'm almost panting with fury. When the double doors open, and Kai and I are led inside, my eyes go right to the king, who's sitting on his gaudy throne with another blank-eyed girl beside him. This one is young, far younger than either me or Kai, and she's much too young to be sitting on an old man's lap as he pets her like an animal. His eyes are bored, his face is fat, and his body is draped in a ridiculous number of jewels and silks, as if anyone could ever doubt who he was.

I never saw the monster king dressed like that. He didn't need to gild himself to inspire. This one does.

He's like a peacock I saw once.

The king's eyes go to Kai first, and a frown mars his ugly face. "What is this? Has someone hurt my trophy?"

"No, Your Majesty," one of the guards answers and bows his head. "She's safe. We apprehended this one before she could harm her."

The king's eyes go to me.

I tense, waiting for the moment he comprehends who I am, but his eyes move away quickly, and he waves his hand.

"Take her back to her room," he says, speaking of Kai. His eyes focus on the necklace. "I'm glad to see you picked out a trinket."

Kai doesn't answer. Her eyes remain unfocused, empty, hopeless, and dead. The guard leads her away, and I watch the direction she's taken, remembering it for later.

"And the rule breaker?" the guard asks.

The king rolls his eyes and waves his hand again, already dismissing us and focusing back on his current pet. "Take her to the cells. I can't be bothered with some simpleton today."

There is no recognition. I was such a passing fancy, he didn't even recall who I am. He didn't even think twice.

The hunt is just a fleeting inconvenience.

Nothing more.

With a scowl, I go willingly with the guards, trying my hardest to control my magic. Still, one small spark seeps out and hits the closest guard with a jolt. He jumps and furrows his brow. "What the..." He doesn't ask any more questions as he leads me deeper into the castle—precisely where I want to be.

My monsters are going to be angry, but I can't wait to see their expressions when they find me in the depths of the dragon's lair. I can't wait to lead them out, rescue Kai from this hell, and send my sparks into the king's room.

Not only is he going to pay for upholding the repression of the monsters, and for creating the halflings without their consent and torturing them, but he's going to pay for the look in my sister's eyes as she was led back into the castle.

For the look of fear, of dread.

Of defeat.

Oh, yes.

He's going to suffer for a very long time at the very hands of the girl he sent to die.

CHAPTER FORTY-FIVE

I'm led down to the cells and tossed inside like forgotten garbage. The metal door slams into place, and then the guards are gone, leaving me alone in the cold, empty cell. I'm surprised it's not gold, but I guess a pretty, shiny dungeon wouldn't fit with the goal of terrifying those who stand against him.

Instead, the space is shadowed and dark, meant to disorient and bring fear.

I don't fear it though. I fade into it, welcoming the shadows and their warm embrace as I inspect my cell and the area outside. As I do, my fury continues to grow.

At the king, at fate, at everything.

My cell is barely big enough to pace in, with three walls and no windows. A sack of hay is on the floor to sleep on, and there's a hole running into the ground to piss in. Nothing more. The brick is cold and wet, and the metal gate is sturdy and strong. Beyond is a corridor with more cells as far as I can see. I made note of the directions we took as we came down, storing the information for later. We had to pass two locked metal doors before descending a hundred and fifty stone steps I stumbled upon while being jerked around by the guards, and then we reached the dungeon. The proud metal door had a torch on either side, and the guards declared our location as if there were idiots who needed the reminder. The cell I currently reside in is just beyond those torches.

I debate my options as I linger in the darkness.

No doubt hours have passed since I was taken by the guards, so my monsters have to know something is wrong, even if they can't feel it.

I know they will come for me.

But first, I need to free my sister, which means getting out of the cell. Moving toward the door, I test the metal. It barely moves, even under my enchanted strength. My magic rolls through me then, a reminder. I could use it and easily free myself, but others would feel it.

The king would feel it.

No, I need to be sneaky about this, which means leaning on an old skill.

Hurrying around the cell, I search for something to use and find a nail in the sack of hay, either left by another prisoner or simply a lost trinket before it had been stuffed into the sack. Moving back to the gate, I slip to my knees on the filthy stone and reach my skinny arms through the bars, straining. My eyes close as I focus on the feel of the lock, locating the edges before slipping the nail inside.

I learned this trick for fun when I was younger, a way to play tricks on adults, but I'm glad it's coming in handy now.

My ear presses to the cool metal as I listen for the tumbler, moving the nail inch by inch until...

Click.

Grinning, I carefully tug the nail free and swing the gate outwards, stepping into the corridor.

I'm about to head to the door when an explosion rocks the earth, sending me flying into the other wall. I'm lucky my magic protects me, cushioning me before I can slam against the stone so I just drop to my feet. I whirl, trying to figure out what just happened. Waving my hand through the dirt in the air, I cough as I peer through it, trying to find the source of the explosion.

As the dust begins to settle, I can only gawk when I realize there's a huge, gaping hole at the very end of the hallway next to my cell. Stones litter the ground, marking the once smooth structure. Now, it's torn to bits, a beautiful bit of destruction in a picture-perfect castle. It gives me great satisfaction.

My monsters step out from the dark.

Grim reaches me first, gripping my face and searching my body. When he finds no injuries, he sighs. "Little one," is all he says, but in those two words, I sense his panic, his fear.

"I'm okay," I promise as I'm passed through loving arms. First to Bracken, then Zee, Nero, Krug, and finally, Razcorr. The hallway is suddenly too small to fit us all while clustered together. They speak at once until I chuckle and hold up my hands.

"I'm fine, I promise. I saw my sister and followed. I allowed them to take me so I could get close." I spot their narrowing eyes and roll my own at their looks of displeasure. "You can punish me later," I tease, "For now, what happened?"

I spot some familiar halflings lingering at the entrance, but it's Grim who speaks. "The halflings know of the tunnel that led here. Apparently, some were kept here before being disposed of. It was sealed after they escaped, on the king's orders, but it was no match for us."

"I see that." I grin as I nod and thank the halflings with them. More seem to be behind them in the tunnel, waiting, but I don't know what they are waiting for exactly. They have more than helped us.

"I saw some more of your kind deeper in the cells," I admit. "Free them?" I ask and watch as some hurry to do just that. I'm turning away to relay my plan when a new one forms.

"Actually, free everyone," I call with a wicked grin. "Cause a distraction. Kill the guards if you want."

It's Marne who climbs from the tunnel and meets my gaze head-on, speaking the question on everyone's lips. "And what will you do?"

I don't flinch as I look her in the eye and declare my plan for all to hear.

I bare my teeth. "Kill the king, of course."

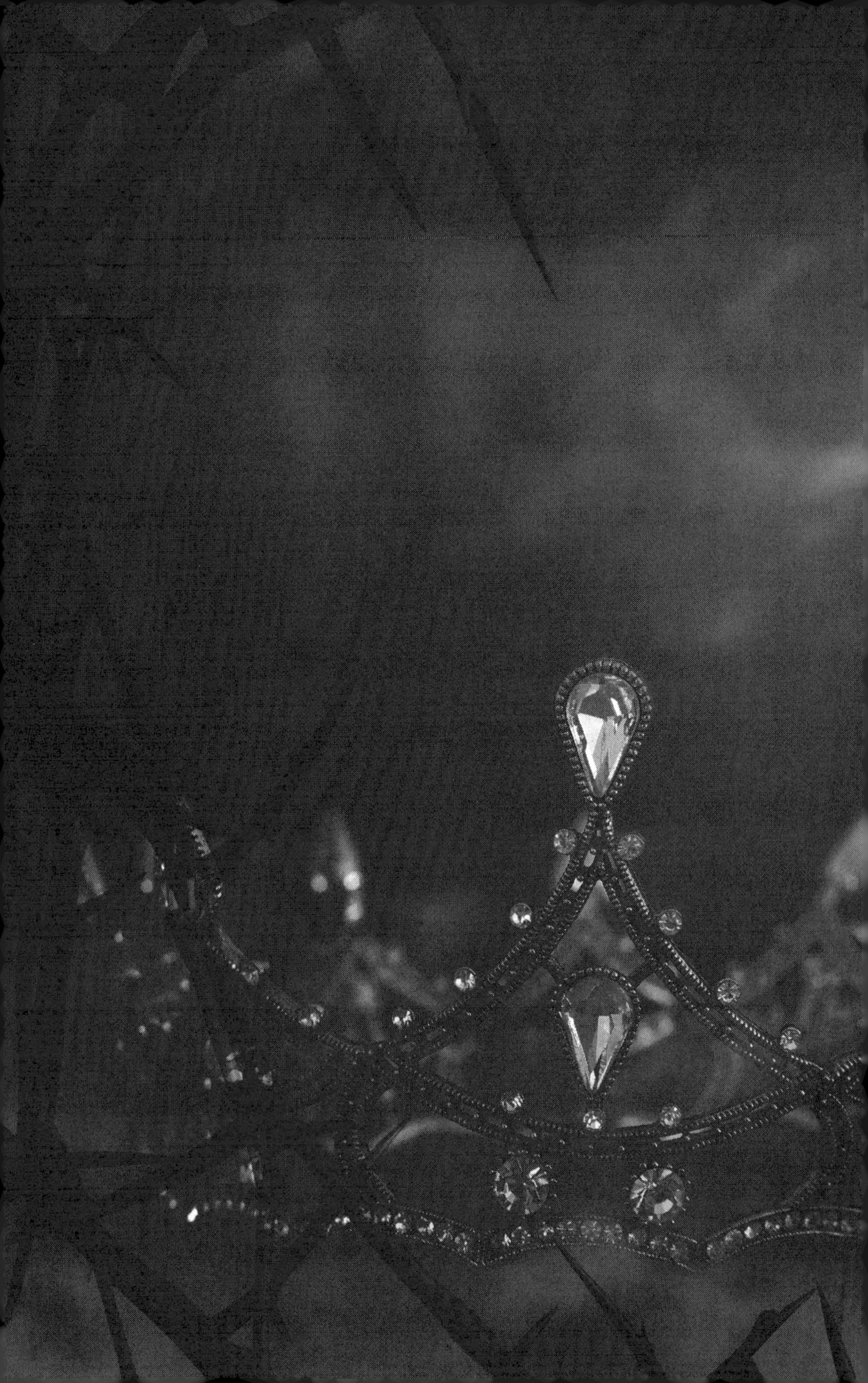

CHAPTER FORTY-SIX

More halflings come after the call, and I watch with great pleasure as they rush from cell to cell, causing chaos as they open each one.

The halflings who had been imprisoned, those the king continued to work on, swarm outward to join their brethren and reap their revenge.

They surge through the outer door the moment alarms begin to sound, barely letting the guards get a word out before they are cut down by the halflings. Their monstrous abilities the king deemed monstrosities make them excellent soldiers in this war—angry soldiers who aren't afraid of death.

After all, this is what it is—a war against the gilded king.

I spare my men one more look before turning and hardening my heart, knowing that before the night is through, I will be a killer.

The king's blood will stain my hands and soul forever, but it's a price I'm willing to pay to free my sister and save our lands.

After all, the hero always pays the price, and I suppose, in this case, I'm the hero, even if it makes me a monster as well.

I hurry past the dead guards, follow the flow of halflings up the many stairs, and burst out into the gilded castle above, where madness reigns.

Soldiers rush the halflings as servants hide and run, screaming at the sight of their monstrous appearance. Blood splatters the gilded floors, and yells and shouts sound from the soldiers who haven't been cut down yet. They are horrified by the halflings, but they run when I appear with my monsters surrounding me.

It's just the distraction I need, but for a moment, I hesitate, unsure where to go.

Until I feel the magic.

It pulls me, like a vice around my heart, telling me where to go, and in it, I feel its purpose and determination. I feel how long the magic has been waiting for this moment, waiting for me, the one to free it.

In turn, that determination fills me as I let magic flow through my body, lifting me up above the stairs, even as my monsters thunder up them. Razcorr flies by my side as I land on the golden banister and tilt my head, my eyes closed as I let the magic fuel me.

My eyes snap open when I find what I'm looking for. I turn my head and leap off the railing as if I've always been so acrobatic. I land on soft, silent feet and follow the pull.

My destiny.

I know it will lead me where I need to go.

I'm here, use me, I tell it. *Let us end this. Let us bring peace back to the land.*

The resounding warmth that spreads through me lets me know it hears me, it sees me, and it's with me. The magic gathered from all four corners of our world surges through me. I am merely a weapon, one meant to carve the rot from our lands.

After all, there must always be a price paid, and magic requires sacrifice—death.

Just as I was sacrificed to the monsters, so shall the king be.

The magic was reborn with me, but with him, it will be free.

Our tale was told before our birth. I feel it in the air and the collapsing of time, as if every moment has come together to create this single event. Along the way, I made choices that led me here. I could have given in.

I could have stopped fighting to survive.

I could have let my sister be sacrificed.

I chose to fight though. I chose this path, and now I must see it through to the end.

Ignoring the paintings and decorations littering the castle, the soldiers rush toward us, determined to stop our progress, but my monsters easily deal with them. I hurry along the corridor on silent feet, following the magic that pulls me, knowing I have a duty to the realms. When the soldiers spot me, I have no doubt I glow with the power in my veins. Despite the fear in their eyes, a few try to get in my way and stop me.

With a simple flick of my fingers, they are out of my path, nothing more than a temporary hindrance.

With each step, I hasten more, feeling this all-powerful knowing that if I miss this chance, it will be the end for all of us—monsters and humans alike.

I turn to the right sharply, taking some curving steps higher into the castle, into the tower and turret beyond, until I end before a simple golden door. Despite the humble design, I feel him hiding behind it.

The glow of his evil reaches out for the pure magic inside me, as if whatever is left in him is corrupted and wishes to do the same to every other ounce of power. I won't let it.

I will blot out his golden rule and swallow it into the shadows where, I will feast.

I simply think of the door opening, and it swings inwards, its locks falling to the ground as I step over them and across the threshold.

Lanterns light the room in a warm glow, the wind from my power making the flames flicker, and some die out. The stone room is a circular space, with open doors at the back thrashing from the power I'm oozing, revealing hints of outside. My power leaks through the room, searching for its target.

The ceiling is high, no doubt the highest point of the entire palace, and the room is sparsely decorated, as if it's meant for something else other than the king. It's a chamber meant for hiding, always prepared in case he needed to get out. Too bad for him, there's no escaping me, there's no escaping the monsters he harmed, and there's no escaping the sins he committed on the halflings. There will be no mercy for what he's done to my sister.

I look around the room, searching, and when I see the tips of his crown peeking out from behind the curtains of his bed, I snarl like an animal.

There he is, hiding like a scared little child on an ornate bed, his harem of stolen women before him like a shield. Fear dances in their eyes, and tears flow down their perfectly made-up faces, their skin displaying bruises and marks from his cruelty.

Golden collars tighten around their necks with his hold on their leashes.

For a moment, I hesitate, my eyes running over them and falling to her.

Kai.

She sits toward the back, her wide eyes on me. For a moment, I see the true her—the laughing, proud, incredible sister I sacrificed everything for. She looks to be so full of life before it's doused like water on flames with the reminder of what and whom she belongs to.

With my eyes, I promise her freedom. Tonight, she will be rid of him. She will have a chance at a life again.

I cannot erase the scars of the king's cruelty and ownership, but I can give her freedom and a chance at a better life.

A new life.

A chance at happiness, where she will blossom once more.

"Leave!" the king demands, his deep voice booming through the room.

But it's just a voice, and he is just a man.

I am so much more. I represent the countless souls of those he has killed and stolen from, and when my voice comes, it lashes him like a whip. In it, he sees his destiny, his future.

His final reckoning.

"Not without your head." I tilt my own, eyeing him. "You are weak without your fortress walls and willing soldiers. You are just a man, a weak, horrible man. Your power?" I lick my lips. "It's nothing. I could eat it for breakfast. You feel it. I see it in your eyes. You feel the pure magic flowing through me—me, the poor peasant girl you tossed to the monsters, did what you were never able to do." I grin. "I've harnessed magic. You failed, and I did not."

"You are nothing," he spits out. He brings a knife up and holds the glittering blade to a girl's neck, her throat riddled with bruises in the shape of fingers. I don't spare her a glance, and she doesn't flinch. "I will kill you like I did all the others, like my father before me, and his father before him."

"Because your lineage is built on the death of powerful women!" I snarl. "Oh yes, the old king, the one who started all this." I lift my hand and let the magic bounce over my fingertips, shadows curling around them lovingly. "The man who killed his daughter and cursed our lands to wither and die. He started this war, this curse, but it ends with you and me."

"You have no weapon," he points out, fear winding through his tone, even as he tries to remain strong.

"I *am* the weapon," I declare, a wicked grin splitting my lips. My monsters surround me, their own power fueling mine. Their hard eyes remain on the king who dares to hide behind powerless women. He uses them as a shield, but they will no longer be abused by this man. Not if I have a say in it.

I stare, and he stares back, but there's a whimper, and my eyes dart to my sister for a moment. It's just a moment, but he must see something in my gaze, because he throws the other girl away and drags Kai across his chest, pressing his blade into her neck.

An inhuman growl escapes my lips, and with it, all the flames, all the light in the room, blows out. The darkness comes to do my bidding as I step closer.

"Ah, ah, ah. Stop," he orders, glancing over his shoulder as he clambers off the bed and starts to drag her toward the open door. "Or she dies."

"Sister," Kai gasps as blood beads on the blade, her eyes on me, even as her head is wrenched back. In her gaze, I see hopelessness and bitterness. She's given into this land and the hold it has on everyone.

"Sister?" the king repeats, and he freezes, his cruel eyes locking on me and truly seeing me for the first time.

He looks beyond the power, beyond the magic, and beyond the threat to me, the once human girl.

"You...you were the hunt," he recalls correctly. It took him far too long.

My men spread out around the room, but they know this is my fight, not theirs.

"It was the best thing to ever happen to me," I purr. "My name's Cora. I bet you've forgotten."

"Your name never mattered. You never mattered. You will be forgotten quicker than this whore here," he spits out, dragging Kai closer. Her whimper boils my blood.

"I don't need to be remembered to have lived, to have loved. That's your legacy, not mine. I don't need greatness, fame, castles, or crowns. I never did. All I ever wanted was happiness and a choice. You took that from me and from her, and you're going to pay for it."

"Not if I kill you first," he sneers as he drags Kai outside.

I rush after him, stepping out into the darkness beyond.

The moon welcomes me, a storm brewing in the sky brought by my fury so the sky can rage with me.

I can't throw my magic at him, not without hurting Kai, and I will not risk her, not for anything.

He drags her across the stone platform we are on, the tower's edge a rounded thing, and I can see the drop into the abyss below. Nerves fill me as I meet Kai's eyes, but she just nods slowly, trusting me.

She trusts me to do this, to do what needs to be done

I glance back at the king, and I see his fear.

He knows what my presence means, especially since I have returned with monsters at my back.

He knows this is his end, and when his eyes harden, I see the truth.

He knows he will die, but he's going to take my sister with him.

"Me or her?" he calls.

"Let her go now," I order, "and I'll make it quick."

"Wrong answer." With a cunning grin, he lifts my sister by the throat and dangles her over the edge of the tower, his meaty fist cutting off her air. I didn't expect him to have that amount of strength, and when his arm begins to shake, I know I don't have much time. He meets my eyes, unflinching, hard, and evil.

My heart stops as she kicks and struggles, her face going pale as she struggles for breath.

The magic inside me swirls, looking for an outlet, but I hold it back with gritted teeth. After all, I'm still human, and to be human is to love.

I love my sister more than anything, more than my own life.

I died for her once, but she will not die for me.

"Don't," I beg.

He tosses the knife to me. "Kill yourself, and I'll let her live."

It's a lie, I know it, and the magic knows it.

My eyes meet Kai's as I search for a way out, knowing I can't kill myself, that it wouldn't change anything. Her familiar eyes close for a moment before they flutter open, and then she nods once more, despite the hand around her throat.

She knows it too.

"Kai, I love you," I tell her, magic building in my hands and flowing through every fiber of my being. "It's going to be okay."

Another lie.

Her toes catch on the ledge, giving her just enough leverage to pull air into her lungs. "Do what you need to do. I am already lost," she croaks out, and then with more strength than I thought my sister possessed, she uses her feet on the stone to wrench her body from the king's arms and throws herself into the darkness.

"Razcorr!" I shout, and he takes off, but I know not even he's fast enough to save her. He won't be able to stop her from falling into the rocky river below.

The scream of pure agony that spills from me echoes in the night as I drop to my knees. The sound shatters through the lands, my magic spilling from my flesh with the fury and grief that overtakes me.

It rips through everything and tears it apart as magic explodes from me in a burst of power the realms have never seen.

It hits the king, but it doesn't stop.

Not as my grief overwhelms me.

Not as I stare at the spot my sister hung while sobs rack my body and tears flow from my eyes.

In my pain, I find a darkness I didn't know I had, a depth I didn't know I possessed, and I turn it on him—the gilded king.

I strip him of every gilded edge.

CHAPTER
FORTY-SEVEN

Getting to my feet, I storm toward him.

Everything I have done, I did it for her, my sister.

He took her from me, just like his ancestor took love from the monsters.

He's once again stolen the heart of our side and taken something precious.

This time, though, I let the pain flow through me, learning from the past, guided by the king and queen from so long ago. I do not let it consume me. I do not let it kill me.

Not yet.

I harness it, just as I have utilized every ounce of suffering in my life.

All the times I was beaten and abused. All the times I was spoken down to for simply being a female. All the times I was denied and dismissed. All the times I was teased and questioned.

My entire life, I have been seen as less than, until them.

My loves fight the storm swirling around us to get to me, to be with me, but I hold them back. I know that when I end this, when my purpose is over, I will crumble and fall just like she did.

It seems the monsters are always doomed to love and lose, but it will end here with him and me.

No more death, no more suffering.

Our fractured lands will be whole once more, and the shadows and the sun will be united.

Even in agony, even in fury, I know that what I'm doing is important, that it matters.

That I matter.

Despite the fact that my heart is tearing from my chest, my eyes sting with my tears, and my body heats with the pain, I stop before the king and give him mercy.

I vow to free him from this mortal suffering and the rot in his soul.

He raises his arm to shield himself from the tornado of agony lashing him, his eyes wide, lost, and terrified.

He is just a man.

"Please," he begs, getting to his knees, his hair blowing back from his face. "Please, don't kill me."

"How many others begged you to spare them? How many girls begged you not to hurt them?" He swallows as I tilt his chin up with a finger like I saw him do to so many others.

I let him see the justice and reckoning in my eyes.

"How many others have you killed to line your golden throne?" I whisper as he breaks. "You are the source of so much death, so much greed, all in the name of a crown you do not deserve."

The magic speaks through me now.

"You could have been the greatest king of all. You had choices, ones that would have led you back to our greatness, our magic, and you didn't take them. Instead, you chose the easy way. You chose to let others suffer for you. You chose money and gold, while others withered away and died. But the magic saw it all, every crime and every death, and it judges you, King Tinos, and finds you guilty. You will die here as a sacrifice to the future, to the past, and to the present. With your death, and the death of your line, our people will be free." Kneeling before him, I meet his eyes. "Know this. After you are gone, the wall will fall and monsters will be free, magic too. We will prosper, we will live, and your golden throne will be forgotten, along with your name. The darkness will steal it and keep it for its own." I pull back then, power still in my voice. "And I, the female you discarded and sent to her death for your own power, will be the wielder of the sword that kills you."

Without torturing him further, I send my magic into his body, obliterating him.

I stand back and watch as the magic rips him to pieces, his scream hollow and silenced as light fills him and escapes his throat. He explodes in a cloud of golden dust before it's swallowed into the darkness, the sacrifice accepted.

His crown falls where he begged for his life.

The magic comes back to me, wrapping around me as I stumble and fall forward onto my hands and knees before collapsing completely. My face presses to the stone as I howl my agony.

My sister!

"Cora!" one of my men yells, his voice breaking through as the storm dissipates. "Look!"

Lifting my tear-stained face as the magic settles, I look where he points and see the fingers gripping the edge of the tower.

Kai!

CHAPTER
FORTY-EIGHT

Without waiting for anyone else, I rush to the edge, desperate to make sure...to see.

It's her.

It's really her. Her heart-shaped face strains as she stares up at me, dangling from the edge.

I reach over and try my best to help her up, despite the way she hangs there. I grip her dainty wrists and pull, and although she barely helps me, Grim leans over and helps her up the rest of the way. I could cry when she appears and stares at me with bloodshot eyes, but she doesn't look distressed in the way someone who's been saved would.

She looks upset that she's alive.

"Kai," I croak out as I cup her face with my hands. "I thought I lost you."

Her eyes, that used to be so full of laughter and happiness, are filled with nothing but phantoms and pain now. When she meets my gaze, I nearly stumble back at what I see.

"You lost me the moment you stepped through the wall, Cora," she whispers.

Horror fills me. "No, don't say that. Kai—"

"Cora," she interrupts, and her hands come up to hold my face. Her forearms are covered with bruises.

Bruises she didn't have before I'd been taken to the cells.

White-hot fury fills me again, but I can't do anything about it. I've already disposed of the king.

So why then does it still feel like he's here causing pain?

"Kai, it's going to be okay. Everything will change now," I assure her, but the phantoms in her eyes grow thicker.

"Do you know what he did to me?" More tears start to roll down her face. "Do you know what he made me do?"

"I'm so sorry, Kai," I rasp out, my own tears spilling over my lashes. "I didn't know—"

"No. How could you have? You were supposed to die." She takes a stuttering breath. "I mourned you the moment you walked through the wall. No hunt survives."

"But I did," I say, not knowing what else to do. I see her pain, her hurt, and none of it is directed at me. I might as well be another phantom in her eyes. I died, but then I didn't. I appeared, but I'm not the same.

Nothing is and nothing ever will be again.

"Kai, we can get through this. I can help you," I plead.

When we were children, Kai was always the beautiful, vibrant older sister. I was the one who was troublesome, the one filled with anger and always getting beat for some foolish trick or another. Now, here we stand on opposite sides. The magic in my veins makes me glow, and my monsters bring me happiness, but Kai stands before me as a shell of her former self. I don't know how to reach her, but I know I have to try. Everything I've done, everything that led me to this point, was for her. It's always been my job to protect her.

I failed once, and I won't do so again.

"The wall is going to fall, Kai. Things will change. I can help you heal..."

She's not listening to me though. Her eyes are unfocused, fixated on some memory that haunts her. "He would force us to watch him slaughter. I saw one of the concubines, an older one, get brutalized for daring to flinch when he raised his hand." Her eyes meet mine. "I was her replacement, so I had to take the jewels from her body while she breathed her last breath on the floor. I had to collar myself."

"Kai—"

"No, Cora," she spits out. "You were thrown to the monsters and came back leading them." Her eyes soften. "You were always so great at changing the status quo, but I'm not you. I was given to a monster, but I did not come out the victor. I came out this...this...hollow shell. I'm no longer the sister you left behind."

"Don't say that!"

"It's true," she chokes out. "You were always meant to be great, Cora." She releases my face and takes a step back, and I stare at her, aghast. "You sacrificed yourself for me and gave me a chance at happiness, but I was never going to be happy. I wasn't meant for that." Another step.

"Kai, what are you saying?" I stumble after her, my hand outstretched, but she recoils from my touch, as if I'm only another monster.

Something inside of me breaks at that, at the way she can't seem to see through the anguish in her eyes. I thought she was dead before, but now I see it wasn't like I thought. She hadn't fallen, the king didn't slit her throat, but there's death in her eyes.

"You sacrificed yourself for me," she repeats, pressing her hand against her chest as she backs up a final step, the backs of her thighs hitting the edge of the wall. "I won't let you sacrifice your happiness for me again. I'm not me any longer. The king killed who I was. You were too late. I'm just another ghost to haunt these walls."

"Kai—"

"You were too late," she rasps out again. "I love you, baby sister. I always will."

Then, before I can understand what she's doing, before it makes sense in my mind, before I can stop her, Kai tips backwards. Everything slows as I watch her close her eyes and lean back, as her strands of hair go wild in the wind. I'm screaming, but there's no sound as I reach forward too slowly. Desperation fills me as I reach the edge and nearly throw myself over to catch her, but strong arms circle me, knowing that I can't leap off the edge to the rocky river below. Still, the shriek that leaves my throat shreds my vocal cords until I go hoarse with agony. I watch Razcorr leap off the edge again, in slow motion this time, and I know there will be no soft surprise, no fingers gripping the ledge.

She didn't want to live. She grasped the only choice she'd ever been able to make.

Death.

I collapse when Razcorr reappears, his face solemn and arms empty. Six sets of arms come around me, holding me together so I don't shatter into a million pieces. I can't breathe for the utter devastation in my mind.

The world is silent, too silent, for what just happened.

My magic leaks from me in waves as I mourn the death of the sister I tried so very hard to save.

But death comes for us all.

Sometimes, it comes sooner than we'd like.

Sometimes, it comes when we beckon it.

And sometimes, it comes as an escape.

CHAPTER FORTY-NINE

My eyes see, but they don't focus as I'm led through the castle. My feet catch on cobblestones, threatening to send me tumbling across them, so eventually, Bracken lifts me into his arms and cradles me close. Tears flow freely down my face, taking what little pain I have left and spilling them over the castle where she'd been killed, waiting for someone to save her.

I failed Kai. She's dead because of me.

"Don't do that," Bracken chastises softly. When my gaze focuses and I can see his angular face, his eyes soften even further. "It's not your fault, Goldie."

"Of course it is," I croak out. "If I hadn't left—"

"Then Kai would have been the hunt," Nero reminds me, and though he doesn't say the words, I can feel them. Kai would not have survived the Dead Lands, not because she was weak, but because she is—*was* softer. She would have happily taken a monster's hand and let them pleasure her into a stupor before she succumbed to death. She would have welcomed it, just like she welcomed her fate at the end.

"I should have gotten here faster."

Razcorr steps forward, his arms outstretched. Without hesitation,

Bracken passes me into his arms. "I was there when Kulmak was killed," he says. "I stood a little too far away, allowed too much space between us. Kulmak was a mighty king, a fierce warrior, but even he was cut down, Cora." His eyes meet mine, and I get lost in the darkness of the night sky there. "Even the fiercest warriors die. Kai suffered, but it was not your fault, just as it was not my fault that I was two seconds too slow to save my best friend. You tried to reach her, but she was unreachable."

"I'll never forgive myself."

"I understand," he whispers. "We relive these moments in our nightmares, over and over again, wishing one detail would change, wishing we had been a split second quicker." Razcorr's wings come around us, cocooning me in his warmth. "And when those nightmares plague you, we will all be here to remind you of who you are, of the power in your veins. Kai chose to die for you, just as you tried to die for her. Now, you must live for her."

I choke on the words in my throat, unable to get anything out, so I wrap my arms around the gargoyle and let him hold me while I cry. I don't know when this agony will ease, or if it will ever ease, but despite this struggle, I know we still have a job to do.

I have a duty. I must live.

Still, I'm in a daze as we walk through the castle and I let my magic lead me through gilded excess. I hate this place. I hate what it represents, and as more and more jewels and wealth appear, I grow physically sick with how much the king has kept from the Shadow Lands. The people could have survived, could have gone without hunger, but instead, he allowed them to starve, beg, and die.

No more.

My magic pulls us to the deepest part of the castle, into a chapel that I've never seen before. The Shadow Lands has no religion except for the power of food, but here, the king clearly still worshiped something. The sun shines through the stained glass windows, highlighting a minotaur being slayed by the king. As I stare at the image depicting the downfall of our realms, anger fills me until my magic expands and whips out.

The glass shatters, the image ground to dust as it rains down on us.

FRACTURED SHADOWS

The sun streams in brighter now, falling on a simple stone sarcophagus in the middle of the room. There are no inscriptions on the stone coffin, nothing signifying it's what we need, but I know without a doubt it's what we've searched for.

Emelyn.

"There," I croak out, pointing to the coffin. "She's in there."

Razcorr is the one who steps forward and grips the edge of the coffin. He shoves it off with a flex of his muscles and stares down at what's inside. He knew her, was her friend, and when I see the grief on his face, I step up beside him and take his hand.

There, nestled in silk, is Emelyn's perfectly preserved body. Where I expected bones, there is flesh sparkling with magic, keeping her whole. The magic inside her made sure she can be returned to her love. The thought makes tears spring to my eyes. She's waited all this time, hoping to be reunited, and now it's going to happen.

I'm going to make sure it happens.

"We're going to return her to her rightful place," I tell Razcorr, and he nods his head, lost for words. I glance back at Grim, imagining him wearing a crown, and smile gently. "We're going to reunite the lands." Without hesitation, Grim, the rightful monster king, takes my hand and bows his head to me.

A human.

~

THERE'S NO LONGER any use in hiding. The king is dead, and the guards have scattered in chaos, not wanting to die for a deceased king who treated them like pawns. The halflings run through the streets, causing the gilded ladies to scream, but not as much as they scream when we leave the castle and start walking along the sparkling streets—a minotaur, a naga, a dark fey, a gargoyle, a kraken, an orc, and a tear-stained human.

We make a strange sight as we walk as a group, with Emelyn's body held on a platform between us. We escort her through the Gilded Lands, surrounded by jeweled women and pompous men who don't know hunger or poverty or powerlessness, but when we reach the Shadow Lands, the tone changes.

They come from their houses with fear on their faces and hope in their eyes. They recognize me as I walk with my chin tilted high, my hair flowing around my shoulders in waves.

"Cora," someone whispers, but I don't turn. More and more people repeat my name, not because they are uncertain, but because they are reassuring themselves I am real.

"The king is dead," I declare as we pass through the center of town, the shadows stretching longer here. "You are free."

No one moves, their eyes on me. "And the monsters?" someone asks.

"They are as much of a part of this land as you are," I say, looking up at Grim, where he stands beside me. Sparks dance around my body, a show of power that makes them gasp. "There will no longer only be shadows and death. The Gilded Lands is fracturing, and it's time for the wall to fall."

Sounds of panic and excitement fill the air, but my eyes aren't on the townspeople who have known me my whole life—some of them having a hand in my punishments and pain. No, my eyes are fixated on a woman who pushes through the crowd with bruises on her cheekbone. She has a soft sparkle in her eyes I've rarely seen. I stop, and my monsters stop with me, Emelyn's sparkling body suspended between us.

Tension fills the air as I look at the woman who birthed me, who became a shell. I wonder if I should tell her that her oldest daughter became just like her. I wonder if I should speak on her failures now that no power can hold me.

Pride sparkles in her eyes, but I see pain when she looks among our group and doesn't find Kai. She knows. I don't have to tell her. A mother always knows.

I wonder if it will break her once more.

The crowd becomes silent with tension as she takes two limping steps forward. I don't move to help her. There were too many times when I begged for her help and she simply stared at me blankly as my father beat me until I couldn't walk. There were too many times when I asked for her to love me, only to be met with a husk of a woman.

I see that knowledge flicker in her eyes, and she doesn't step any closer, so she speaks from her position. "I always knew the Shadow Lands wasn't big enough for you, Cora," she says, and the crowd shifts. "You were always meant for more."

I glance back at my men, at the monsters who woke me in more ways than one. Each of them gives me something I never expected to find—love. My mother may be able to express those words, but that doesn't make her deserving of my forgiveness. It doesn't make up for the years of abuse she allowed to happen.

"Yes," I reply, "I was."

I meet her eyes one last time before we continue through the Shadow Lands, leaving the woman incapable of being a good mother behind.

CHAPTER FIFTY

Eyes watch our journey along the streets as if we're a royal parade. I suppose we are, as the next would-be king as well as the past queen are among us. Most are too afraid to approach for fear of my monsters retaliating, but they are also too curious to run. Children come out to watch the procession, seeing it for what it is. Their dirty faces are aimed at me, on the human who walks in front of the monsters. I hold Grim's and Zee's hands, needing that connection so I don't collapse in agony in front of all these people.

Hold it together just a little while longer, I tell myself.

The wall appears before us, the crisscrossing thorns just as I remember them. A hush falls over the crowd as we step toward it. I'm both numb and feel too much all at once as I stand in the same place where it all began. I've come full circle, and in the end, this will change everything.

Some of the humans behind me don't deserve to live, but many of them deserve a chance they'd never had before. There were chains around our necks when the king was alive, but now those chains lie at our feet.

Because of me.

I gave them freedom, but they'll have to earn it.

When the wall falls—and it will fall—they'll have to learn to survive in a world filled with monsters, both creature and human. There will be no separation. There will only be one world, one realm.

I lift my hand, and my magic fills the courtyard around us, making those of the Shadow Lands "ooh" and "ahh" as if I'm some jester show. The temptation to send it into the crowd and have it chase after those who were like my father is strong, but we have a task to complete first. I'm reminded of that when I glance back at Emelyn, who appears so pristine in her death, so perfect.

She should have had the chance to unite the realms. She'd been so close, but greed had taken that away.

As my magic fills the air, it touches on the thorns before us, causing them to shift and move with the magic. I press it deeper until the thorns begin to slither back like snakes, pulling away until an opening wide enough for our procession is created. I glance back at the world I know one last time, at the shadows that used to coat my skin. Once I step through this wall for the second time, everything will change. No longer will I just be Cora Black, the hunt. I will be Cora the Fearless, Cora...the queen.

I saw the vision, so I know what this world has planned for me.

My mother's eyes meet mine, and I look on, unflinching. I never wanted to be her, and I wasn't, but because of her, Kai is dead. If only she'd been stronger, Kai might never have been taken by the king.

It's an unfair notion, I know that. My mother couldn't do anything, but I'm bitter and angry and filled with agony over losing the one person outside of my men I cared about.

Still, forgiveness is not in the cards. It will never be in the cards.

"Let's go," I say, my voice raspy from the pain in my heart.

Together, we step across the wall, over the thorns, and they begin to close up behind us. It'll be the last time they do so.

We travel silently through the Dead Lands, Emelyn's remaining magic reaching out and touching what it can. The trees somehow look more vibrant, and the monsters watch as we pass, not attacking. Even they know things are about to change and that the world will no longer be dead and rotting. Soon, each part of the realm will return to what it once was—beautiful, magical, and alive.

After some time, my legs refuse to carry me. Though the king's castle looms in the distance, a beacon calling Emelyn home, I collapse with grief, but I never hit the ground.

Strong arms catch me and hold me tight, while hands caress my body, offering comfort where they can. I also hear whispered words that mean so much and yet nothing at all. They are here for me, and in their love, I feel a little piece of myself glue back together. I may have fractured when Kai died, but I will not remain that way. The shadows I carry won't overtake the cracks in my soul. Instead, I'll fill them with the gilded edges, sealing myself back together and becoming a work of art in my brokenness.

In that brokenness, I'll love my monsters just as fiercely as they dare to love me.

One life. One journey. One family.

Just as it was always meant to be.

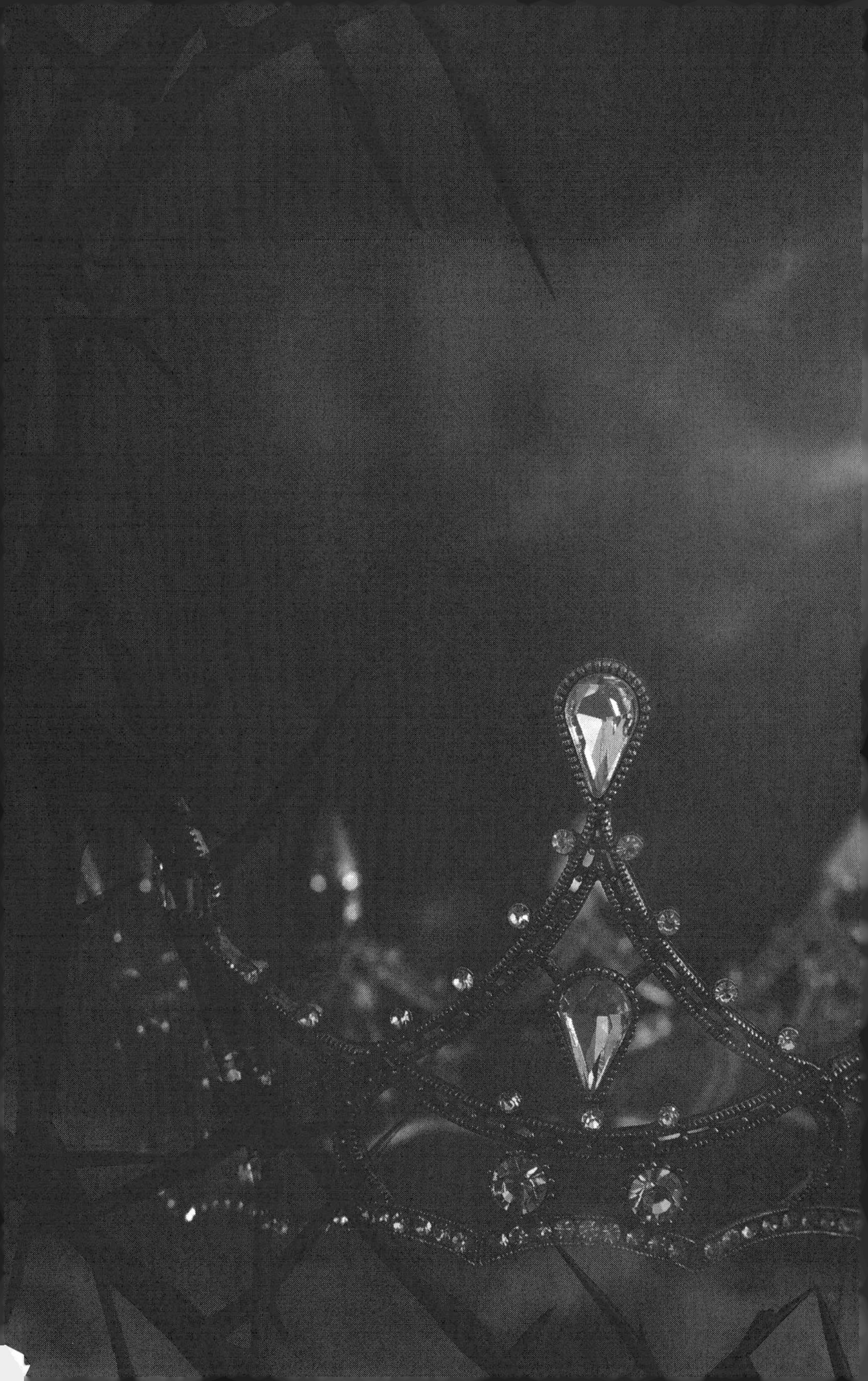

CHAPTER
FIFTY-ONE

The journey back to the castle is a blur.

I allow my monsters to shield me as I suffer in my agony. I try to rest, but my dreams are filled with Kai's face as she plummets to her death, my hand reaching for her.

Too late, always too late.

When we reach the shining black castle, I'm exhausted, mentally and emotionally.

I can't appreciate the glossy black stone or the feel of warmth that fills me as we enter the castle. Instead, we follow behind Emelyn as her body seems to float of its own accord. She leads us now once more, her spirit recognizing that she's home.

Down we go, into the castle, until we stand before the king's resting place.

Without a word, we lift the empty stone lid of the matching sarcophagus and watch as her body moves over and settles inside as if she were always there, as if she is where she belonged all along. Her perfectly preserved body nestles inside the stone the king once lovingly sculpted, awaiting this very point in time.

We hold our breaths, and for a moment, nothing happens.

Then, so suddenly it nearly blinds me, she glows brightly before it fades, the power snapping between her and her love.

The circle is complete.

When they connect, the power is so strong, it sends us all to our knees as it explodes through the room, going through and around us.

I feel it stretch out into the lands, touching phantom fingers to every surface, every creature, and every human. I close my eyes and piggyback on the magic, letting it be my eyes as I ride it through the lands. I can see the magic bringing the trees back to life and unshrouding the sun, giving the animals shelter and sunlight for the first time ever. It wakes the forgotten gargoyles and fixes the temples. The magic fills the monsters and chases off the rot and mist, until they, too, fall to their knees.

When the magic comes to the barrier, I watch with awe as the thorns slowly part before being sucked back into the ground and absorbed.

All the shadows and all the death is replaced with hope.

Magic even flows through the humans.

It touches every living creature and being before settling to rest where it belongs.

When my eyes open, I feel tears dripping down my cheeks.

We did it.

We saved the lands, and we reunited the lost lovers.

Magic is back in our world, and with it, so is the chance to rewrite our past and do better, but all I feel is agony.

Even as I turn to my men, I feel like a shell.

Just like my mother before me.

Just like my sister.

I have completed my quest, but at what cost?

CHAPTER FIFTY-TWO

The celebrations last for days.
Feasts are held, and monsters flock to the castle to pay their respects, displaying their restored health and magic.
Even those who attacked us come with forgiveness on their lips, something they don't have to ask for.
The Shadow Lands are gone, blending with the Gilded and the Dead until we are one, and monsters and humans live side by side. I see some fearless humans trekking into the Dead Lands to greet their fate, while some monsters are settling into different homes within our realm.
A question floats through all though, whispers brought to me on magic.
What now?
Who leads us?
They are questions I cannot answer.
I cannot celebrate, and I cannot rest.
I can't even eat.
I see the worry in my monsters' gazes. I am simply a wraith, floating through the dark castle without purpose or hope.
I have done everything I was asked to, and I have sacrificed so much.

Even though I have the love of many good men, it almost doesn't feel right.

It's almost as if I should plunge from this tower and join my sister.

Slipping from their arms in the middle of the night, I find myself in the highest point of the black castle, my gaze trained east to the golden one.

My feet dangle on the edge, my eyes closing with the breeze.

Lights flicker all over the realm, and laughter and music reach me even here, but my heart is broken, and I do not know how to fix it.

"You cannot. Only time can heal it, but it will never be the same. Not fully."

I whirl at the voice, my heart thumping as Emelyn stops before me.

She is as ghost-like as I feel, her magic keeping her alive, despite being the phantom who healed the lands.

Her memory, or soul at least, floats before me, watching me carefully where I perch on the edge. A crown sits upon her head, and a soft smile curls her lips.

"To love is to suffer. To live is to be in pain, Cora, our savior. You know that more than most. In pain, we find darkness, and in darkness, we find truth. I wish your journey had been easier, but I'd be lying if I said I was sorry."

"At least you are at peace," I whisper as a large, black shadow forms behind her.

Her smile softens as she looks over her shoulder and back to me. The shadow morphs and solidifies until I see King Kulmak standing behind her, his strong hand cupping her shoulder.

His crown is on his head, and his once grief-stricken, mad gaze is at peace as they watch me, his arms coming around to embrace his wife.

"I know how you felt now," I find myself admitting. "Why you would burn the world, start a war...do anything. This feeling..." I slam my fist to my chest as more tears fall. I didn't think it was possible to find more tears to cry. Succumbing to it, I drop to my knees and weep. "I can't live with it."

"You can and you will," the king rumbles, and in his voice, I hear my own minotaur's ancestor. "You must. The realms need a leader now. They need a queen, and queens do not live on their knees."

"It is okay to grieve, Cora, but remember she is still with you in memory, in your heart. Destiny has a plan for us all," she offers mysteriously as they crouch before me, their hands outstretched. "As it does for you. Your purpose is not yet over. My king is right—these lands need a leader, one who is sure, strong, steadfast, and dedicated. One who knows the pains of life, one who came from a humble beginning but has a drive for equality and happiness. They need you, Cora, as it was always supposed to be. I saw you so many years ago. You were so brilliant and bright that even in death, I had hope, and I give that to you now. Save them, Cora, and they might just save you back."

I place my hand in theirs, and although it's just a ghostly touch, their strength fills me, even as my tears fall.

"Do not give into the pain. Use it as you always have, my queen." The king bows with his words—a sign of respect I don't expect.

"And know we will always be here, and that we are eternally grateful," Emelyn adds.

Their touch slowly disappears, and once more, I am alone with only the moonlight, but something in their words gives me comfort.

They are right—I can't give into this pain.

Kai is gone, my suffering will not change that, but to honor her memory, I must live on.

To tell the stories about her.

To breathe life back into her and into our lands.

There will always be a place inside me that aches with longing and grief for the sister I lost, but there is also so much more room now.

For love, passion, and hope.

Hope is such a simple concept, but a world-shattering one.

With hope, anything can be accomplished.

When my monsters appear and pull me into their embraces under the moon, I give into their love and find my hope once more.

For our future.

For what is to come.

Together, I know we will have a brilliant life and that Kai will live on in all of us.

She will be remembered forever in the fractured pieces of our memories.

As the magic that once guided me here wraps around us all, I realize something else.

I am whole.

I am loved.

I am strong.

And together, we are capable of anything.

CHAPTER
FIFTY-THREE

"I'm nervous," I admit, staring at the effigies of the king and queen that grace the tops of their sarcophagi. I've come here often to speak to them in the weeks that have passed since the wall came down.

Everyone seems to look to us for answers, and I happily oblige.

I lose myself in mundane daily tasks to forget, and every night, my monsters blind me with pleasure until I fall into a dreamless sleep.

But today?

Today is different.

"I wonder if you were," I murmur.

"He was terrified," Razcorr calls out. I smile, feeling him behind me. "If I remember correctly, he asked me to run away with him."

Chuckling, I turn as his arms wrap around me, his smile softening as he meets my eyes. "You will be incredible, mate, and we will all be there with you."

"Promise?" I ask.

"Always, my love, now and forever." Taking my hand, he steps back. "But it is time. Your people await their new queen."

Swallowing, I take one last look back at the king and queen, pressing my fingers to my lips in a sign of respect before following him up the stairs. My coronation gown flows behind me. The train holds our story, stitched by a kind fey who turned up at the castle the day after the wall fell and proclaimed herself as my new modiste, even though Nero fights with her sometimes.

The bodice hugs my breasts and then flares out, infused with magic to make it shine and move with our story. The fur cape that sits on my shoulders stops at my hips, my hair is coiled back for the crown, and my makeup is artfully done.

When we reach the throne room, I spy Grim already waiting there. He looks uncomfortable in front of all of our people.

Humans and monsters gather in the black castle to watch the coronation, and there are so many, they stretch into what was once the Dead Lands.

No one protested when Grim declared his lineage, and as for me, well, it was obvious, apparently, that we would become the next king and queen. Even the humans didn't seem to have issues with the declaration.

Though I'm not saying that will last.

Taking Razcorr's arm, I hold my head high and paste a serene smile on my lips as he leads me through the people. Cheers and calls go up, a celebration for the coronation before we've even completed it. Once before the podium, I curtsy to my king before slowly turning to stand by his side, my hand in his.

Behind us, my other loves spread out.

Nothing but love and pride shine in their eyes when I wink at them.

"Today, we are gathered to crown the new king and queen of our lands," Razcorr calls, his voice echoing. "Grimus, last of the line of Asterion, the rightful king of our lands, stands before you as a humble servant, accepting his duty." A crown is brought out on a cushion held by a grinning wolf shifter.

It's the same crown the previous minotaur king wore.

"Cora Black, also known as Cora the Fearless and Cora the Liberator, the woman from humble beginnings who once again brought magic and freed us from tyranny willingly accepts the crown of her people. Once more, the humans and the monsters will be united by marriage and love. With our king and queen, we are whole again!"

Thunderous applause goes up as a lovely human woman brings my crown forward.

Unlike the twisting metal of Grim's, mine is almost dainty.

Thorns of both black and gold weave together to embrace a jewel filled with magic at the front.

I look at Grim, and he squeezes my hand as we both kneel.

"I, Razcorr, representative of our realm and people, hereby crown you, Grimus, the new king." His crown settles on his head, the weight substantial not in reality, but metaphorically. "I, Razcorr, representative of our realms, crown you, Cora, our new queen." My own crown is placed on my head.

It's secured there like it was always meant to be, and as we rise as one, both humans and monsters celebrate our new beginnings.

Together.

As it was always supposed to be.

~

WE STAY for the celebrations as long as I can.

There are so many congratulations and so many new clans of people seeking our attention, but it can all wait.

Fueled by fey wine and dancing, I lead my monsters back to our rooms at the top of the tower. Once inside, I flick my fingers, and magic peels my dress and robe from me as I turn to them.

The moonlight in which they all found me bathes my body.

"Well, my king? Shall we celebrate?"

I grin as Grimus huffs, his eyes locked on my body.

"Keep the crown on." Bracken smirks as he prowls toward me. "That way, I can proudly tell everyone how I fucked my queen."

Grim steps toward me as he sheds his clothes with efficient fingers. Eyes burning with lust, he prowls around me, trailing his fingers along my flesh and leaving fire and shivers in his wake. I watch as he gracefully mounts the bed and sits with his back to the wall, his cock is hard and pointing upwards. He watches me as he strokes his length, the tip glistening.

"Come claim your king," he orders, his voice husky with need.

Smirking, I crawl onto the bed, swaying my ass, and I hear echoing groans behind me. I stop to lick his hooves before I straddle his waist, and then I press the tip of his cock to my pussy and wiggle my hips, dragging him through my wetness.

Dampness gathered as I watched them drink, dance, and celebrate, stealing teasing touches and kisses.

Dragging my hands across his muscular chest, I grip Grim's shoulders, digging my nails in as I lean forward and kiss him.

He doesn't help me, but he kisses me back as I slowly sink onto his length.

I am forced to stretch around his massive girth, and a gasp leaves my lips, breaking us apart. Holding his gaze, I let him watch every emotion flicker over my face as I lift and work my way down each solid inch until I finally settle at his base.

His cock twitches inside me, and I feel so full, it's almost too much, almost too painful.

I start to move, using him as leverage to lift and drop, letting my body adjust to him.

Riding him, I take my king like he demanded.

His eyes trail over my body as I do, my nipples hardening under his gaze.

"Come for your king. Let me feel it. Let me feel your need like I have all night."

My head falls back, and I moan as I roll my hips and grind. I tilt my hips to hit my clit with each thrust, until, just like he demanded, I splinter.

I fracture into thousands of tiny pieces, but they collect each one and put me back together again.

I'm flipped, forced face down as Grim slams into me from behind, too impatient to let me have complete control.

My fingers dig into the coarse fur on his thighs, holding on as he powers into me with a roar. The sound is primal and loud, and it reverberates into me and heads straight to my clit.

My king is claiming me before my mates.

"Mine, my queen," he snarls.

"Yes," I whimper, lifting my head when he wraps his thick fist around my hair.

"Watch them. Watch what you do to them. Watch how we love you. Watch how we need you."

My eyes flutter open to see my other mates.

Bracken paces like a caged beast, his fangs down and his eyes bright red. He's naked and hard.

Zee's stilma search for me, his eyes hard as he watches me be fucked.

Nero coils around the bed with a hiss, his cocks hard and free.

Krug is pressed against the wall as if to stop himself, stroking his length.

Razcorr... He lingers in the darkness.

All I can see are his eyes, and like he knows I seek him, he steps into the moonlight, letting me see the stark need and hunger etched into his body.

It sends me over the edge once more, and with an echoing roar, Grim powers into me, his balls slapping against me until he stills and begins to fill me with his release.

I cry out, his release prolonging my own.

When he finishes, I slump forward before I'm gathered into his arms and lifted off his dripping cock. He trails kisses along my shoulder. "Now, my queen, take your other mates. Claim every single one of them, and prove to them they are yours."

"Yes," I murmur, and when my eyes open, they land on Bracken, and I crook my finger.

He comes willingly, my teasing fey, only he's not teasing right now.

He's needy, lustful.

Demanding.

When he's in reach, I grip his long braid decorated in golden beads and yank his head back as my other hand slides down his body and grips his cock, stroking it as his hips stutter and jut.

"Do you want me, my fey?" I demand, my voice strong and sure, despite the fact that I'm naked and sitting between a massive minotaur's legs who could easily overpower me.

They all could if not for my magic, but they don't because they love me.

"Always," he groans. "Forever."

For once, he isn't playing.

Dragging his head down, I kiss him deeply, cutting myself on his fangs and making him groan into my mouth when a bead of my blood drips onto his tongue. When I pull back, he licks the blood from his lips with a needy grunt.

Using his hair as a handle, I drag him down to my breasts and feed them to him. "Suck and feed, my fey, while I fuck you."

Using Grim as leverage, I wrap my legs around Bracken and sink onto his cock as he does as he's told. He sucks and licks my nipples, the pleasure arcing straight to my clit.

My head drops back to Grim's chest as I watch Bracken fuck me.

"Feed," I order, and he moves his head back before striking.

His fangs close around one nipple and sink deep. The pain makes me cry out before it fades to immense pleasure, and when he drinks my blood, he goes wild. He hammers into me, claiming my cunt with loud, wet slaps, while his hand drags down my body and cups my pussy, grinding into my clit.

I scream another release, clenching around him, and with a final thrust, he follows me into oblivion.

He moans as he pulls his fangs free. Both of us watch the blood trail down my stomach, and with a wicked smirk, he licks it up before sliding from my clenching cunt and falling to the bed with a contented, sleepy smile.

Zee is already there, replacing him, his mouth going to my cunt.

His talented tongue thrusts inside of me, uncaring about the other men's cum running from me. He laps me up, fucking me with his tongue before sliding up my body and kissing me.

When he slides home, his stilma sucking at my clit, I'm lost.

He doesn't fuck me hard and fast though. He moves with slow, leisurely thrusts, making love to me as he gives me time to catch my breath.

The pleasure grows lazily but desperately as we kiss, sharing promises between us until we both find completion once more. With a final kiss, he slides from my body.

Nero hesitates, coiled around the bed. Grim instantly senses the problem and lifts me, moving me where I need to go.

"Go to him," he orders.

Grabbing the sheets, I pull myself over to the edge of the bed. Once there, he lifts me onto his coils and I sink onto his main cock with a cry. His head lowers to suck my nipples, my neck.

Everything.

The pleasure only seems to grow like the magic within me.

"Please," I groan.

I feel his other cock pressing against my ass, and without warning, I impale myself on it, writhing on his coils. My and my men's cum stain his scales as my magic flares while I ride him.

"*Parum anguis*," he murmurs against my skin. "How I adore you."

"I love you," I cry out. "I love you all."

"Our queen," he murmurs as his coils wrap tighter around me, helping me fuck him until his lips crash onto mine and we sink into the pleasure.

Our bodies work together until magic and release slam through me.

I barely have time to breathe before I'm gently lifted off and spun.

My face is pressed to the bed, and my legs are kicked apart.

A huge cock spears me.

Krug, my orc.

His hips slap against mine, pummeling me as he snarls promises and loving words. My eyes clash with my king's as he grins at me.

"You are mine. Ours," Krug snarls.

"Yours," I repeat before chanting it.

"Forever," he states. "This pussy is ours forever. I will spend every day in its heat, filling it with my seed."

"Shadows, yes," I whisper until, with a cry, a slow rolling orgasm slides through me and takes him with me, making him roar as he stills.

Cum splashes inside me, and when he pulls out, I feel it begin to drip down my thighs before he cups my pussy and shoves his release back into me, fucking me with his fingers until I collapse.

I am so well used and filled with pleasure, it should be impossible, but I feel Razcorr hesitating.

Turning, I fall to my knees on the floor before my gargoyle as he steps toward me, cupping my chin. "It can wait, my queen. I do not need your body to know I am yours."

"But I want you." I pout greedily as I look up at the beautiful man made of stone, whose heart beats only for me. "So badly."

"And what you want, you shall always get," he whispers before he reaches down and lifts me. I wrap my legs around him as his hands go to my ass.

The others, even my king, give me a shred of privacy as I prepare to claim Razcorr, the last of my mates.

He turns us, pressing me to a wall as he pulls back slightly. With his eyes on me, he tastes my skin, dragging his tongue across it, before he finds my mouth.

He kisses me so softly, it almost makes me cry. My hands slide down his back and chest, exploring him.

I etch him forever into my memory. After all, we have forever to explore.

"Claim me, my mate," I plead into his lips.

I feel his hard as stone cock prod at my entrance. There's no hesitation. He swallows my moan as he finally thrusts into me, claiming me.

His wings spread behind him, and the sight is so hot, I almost come from the imagery alone.

His black eyes stare into mine as I lean back, panting as I clench around his invading cock. He tilts my hips to hit that spot that has me moaning with every thrust. The pleasure is so much, I'm choking. Our bodies come together, and it isn't long before we both tumble over the edge with each other's names on our lips.

Sealed with a kiss as we fade into oblivion.

The darkness claims me, the pleasure too much.

When I come back, I am wrapped around him, his wings fluttering to keep us upright.

Razcorr staggers to the bed and deposits me between my mates, making me chuckle at the shakiness of it.

All of us are spent and sweaty but so satisfied, I couldn't move even if they demanded it.

My heart is filled to the brim.

My body, heart, and soul have been claimed by all of them.

My fingers dance in the moonlight, caressing where I can reach, my crown forgotten to the side.

I close my eyes as their lips touch the bare skin of my back, and upon the moonlight, I send out a wish, a plea, to the magic.

I pray that wherever Kai is now, she finds happiness as powerful as my own.

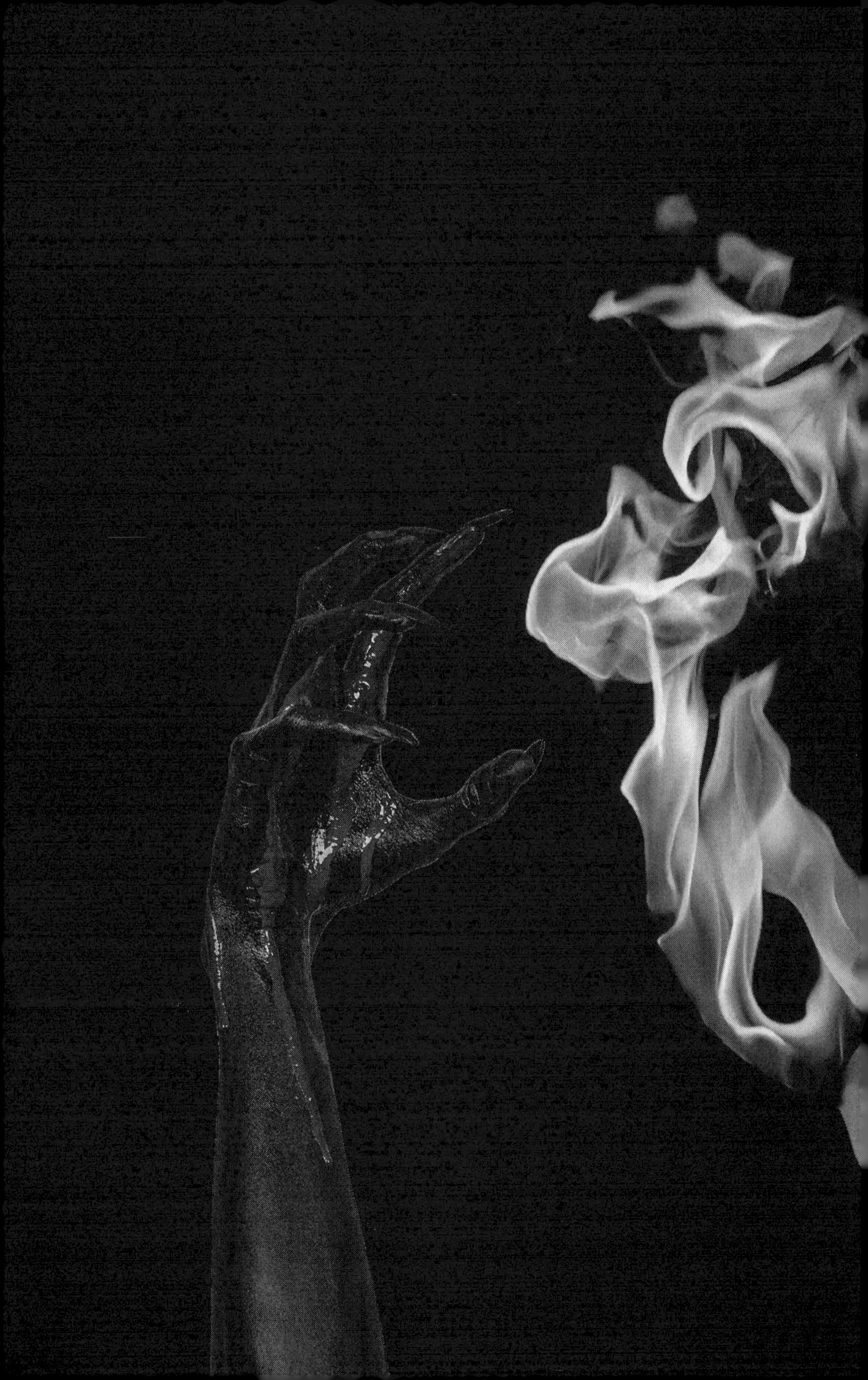

EPILOGUE
BRACKEN

I watch as Goldie trails her fingers along the trinkets at the merchant's table, her eyes alight with happiness in a way that was difficult to bring out for a while. She was mourning, I understand, but I'm glad she's able to be more carefree now and able to walk among the people with nothing but happiness and hope for our future.

It isn't common for a queen to walk among the market, wearing a crown on her head as she searches through the jewelry. Cora insisted on giving back to the people, so each week, no matter the weather, she comes out and purchases from them—food, trinkets, clothing, whatever they sell, she buys. Sometimes, she gives it to children running by. Sometimes, it's for the women. Every so often, she keeps something small for herself.

Today, she's decided to purchase items for each of us.

"Do you think he'll like this one?" Cora asks, holding up a golden chain sporting a rather large jewel. It sparkles in the sunshine that graces the entire realm, catching the light and throwing it around. The merchant looks excited at her interest, and when she asks my opinion, his eyes move over to me, waiting for my answer. There's no fear there, but not because he's not afraid, but because he's a halfling with a talent for jewels.

"Krug does love his jewels," I reply, smiling gently at her. She hasn't picked out something for me, not yet. I suspect she'll try to keep it a secret until she decides to gift it to me.

Smiling gratefully at the merchant, she hands the necklace to him and says, "I'll take it." Her eyes catch on another jewel, a brooch, sitting on the table. It's a glittering twist of wire and small beads that forms the shape of two birds in flight. Carefully, she picks it up before handing it to the merchant. "This too, please."

"Who is that one for?" I ask curiously. It isn't a style she'd choose for any of us.

She smiles at me and takes the parcel from the merchant, nodding her head at his gratitude for her business. "Come," she tells me. "I have one more place to visit."

I trail along behind her, both for protection and companionship, as we move through the city that's grown since the Fracturing of the Shadows, or at least that's what the people have been calling it. Humans, monsters, and halflings live mostly in harmony, rebuilding their world in ways that bring us together. Only those who were from the Gilded Lands struggled in the beginning, but now they know they have no choice. Still, one day, I know there will be someone who will want to fight Cora for creating this peace, and when that day comes, we'll be ready.

I'm not surprised to see the cemetery come into view. Cora spends her time here when she needs to speak, though the gravestone is only a marker and nothing more. Kai's grave sits on a small hill, where the sunshine always gleams. Fresh flowers constantly decorate the grave, a request from Cora.

Although there is a marker, no body lies buried here. In the end, we'd been unable to find Kai's body in the ravine. After weeks of searching, we gave up, assuming something had either gotten to the body first or it had simply been swept somewhere unreachable. Cora mourned not being able to bury her sister, but she has this place now, and she says she feels like Kai can hear her when she talks.

Anything Goldie wants, we give it to her.

I stand back as she moves forward and sets the small brooch on top of the grave, leaving it like an offering for the sister she gave everything for and still lost. Goldie had lost some of her shine before, but it's back now. Still, I know nothing can take away that pain, so I assume the role she needs of me.

Her protector, her jester.

Her love.

"She would have liked it," I say when she comes back up to me.

Smiling gently, she nods. "She would have." Her eyes catch on a different grave, her brows furrowed in confusion. "That's Kai's lover, the one she was planning on marrying."

I follow her gaze and find a small bunch of handpicked flowers sitting on the grave. "He died?"

She leans in. "Apparently so. How sad." She continues to stare at the flowers. "I don't think he had much family to mourn him."

Shrugging, I offer my arm. "At least someone mourns him. That's enough."

Lingering a few seconds longer, she finally threads her arms through mine before reaching into the bag at her hip. Her fingers come out with a wrapped parcel I never saw her purchase.

"Sneaky, sneaky, Goldie," I tease when she offers the package to me.

A mischievous smile curls her lips. "I knew you'd be watching, so I purchased this last week when Nero was with me."

With far more care than I ever intended, I peel open the wrapping to find a golden dagger nestled inside. The hilt sports a large red jewel in the center and a series of smaller jewels in intricate designs.

"It's a blood ruby," she says when I stare at it. "I'm told someone with a connection to blood can feel the power inside it."

Reaching out with my senses, I discover she's correct. My throat goes thick with emotion at the beautiful, thoughtful gift she's given me. "It's perfect, Goldie. I will stab all of your enemies with it and make sure they know whom I'm honoring as I do so."

Her smile brightens. "I love you, my fey."

I tuck the dagger into my belt, displaying it for all to see, and then I pull her into a brutal, sensual kiss. When neither of us can breathe, I break the kiss, only to press my forehead against hers.

"And I love you, Goldie, always and forever, until we both bleed dry."

Even then, it wouldn't be long enough.

It would never be long enough.

～

Nero

The trees feel lush and full beneath my coils in a way they haven't for a long time. The Dead Lands' trees were always sparse and lacking, the rot within them too thick to make them perfect. Now, with magic back in the land and Cora leading the realm, the trees no longer rot.

The world no longer suffers, it thrives, just like us monsters, and it's all because of her.

"How long are you going to slither through the branches?" she calls up, laughing at my clear excitement. It's been so long since I've felt good trees, I can't help myself.

I'm sure she can only catch a glimpse of me every now and then, my pearlescent white scales standing out when the sun catches them. I playfully drop down in front of her so my torso is even with her face, startling her.

"Boo," I tease, my fangs appearing when I smile.

Her answering laughter and the brightness in her eyes makes my stomach flip. I love this human far more than I've loved anything in my life. Cora is glorious, a true queen, who barely understands how important she is not just to her mates, but to the entire realm. Even now, the inhabitants of the new world speak nothing but happy things about their new queen. She's everything a queen should be.

She's everything to me.

"I got you something," she purrs.

Dropping down completely from the tree, I wrap my coils around her, bringing her in close. "Ah, yes, the mysterious gift Bracken said you got each of us. I've been waiting."

Her smile turns into a scowl. "That incessant gossip can't keep a secret."

"In his defense, he didn't tell me what it is, only that you have a gift for me, though I did see his dagger."

She pushes her blonde hair away from her face and smiles at me. "Well, at least there's some surprise then." Pulling a package from her bag, she holds it out in front of her. "For you."

I gently take the package from her hands, making sure not to snatch it like I'd like to. I've never been given a gift before, and my excitement nearly overcomes my manners. Still, I don't realize I'm shaking until her fingers curl around mine affectionately.

"I hope you like it." She worries her bottom lip between her teeth, as if she's nervous about my thoughts.

I'm certain I'll love it no matter what it is, but I can hardly form the words to tell her that. Instead, I carefully unwrap the parcel and stare at the items nestled in the silk. Tiny lilac blue gems, her favorite color, are arranged in two golden settings. I blink at the jewels, realizing she bought me earrings to replace the ones I already wear.

Her mark. Her color.

"Our initials are in the backs of them," she says softly. "See? There's C and an N." I open my mouth to answer, but nothing immediately comes out, and her face falls. "You don't like them."

"I love them," I say hastily, holding them up to the light. "Just as I love you."

I remove the studs I've worn for years and replace them with the newer, more meaningful pair. "How do they look?"

Her eyes crinkle as she takes them in. "Perfect." She stands on her tiptoes and presses a chaste kiss to my lips. "Now, catch me if you can, snake boy."

She takes off running with a giggle, and I stare after her for a few seconds, amazed by my good fortune. I never thought I would find someone like her. I never thought I could be so loved. I touch my fingers to the jewels in my ears before I give a whoop and take off after her into the forest, hunting her once more.

～

Zetros

Her legs kick in the water as I swirl around her, churning up the sea in my kraken form. I am careful not to sweep her too far beneath the waves for fear that I will accidentally drown her, but I know, even if I made that mistake, her magic would kick in and save her. Sometimes, it is easy to forget that my beautiful human is capable of far greater things than most.

She leans back and floats on the surface as my tentacle reaches up and braces her, making sure she doesn't sink. I let her soak for a few minutes before I transform and tread water beside her, letting the salt from the sea soak into my skin. The ocean is no longer as dark as it used to be, and far more inviting now, but there are still dangerous creatures in these waters. Luckily for us, most of them fear me, so we remain unbothered.

I wear the bracelet she gave me around my wrist. The rose gold chain is intricate in its design, but not as much as the tiny kraken charm on it. She laughed as she gave it to me, but I was ecstatic to see a small pearl beside the kraken. I thought of it as representations of us, a way to immortalize us both so that I'll always remember. It's now my most prized possession.

We do not talk, not because we do not want to, but because we relax in companionable silence, letting the sea wash away any troubles.

There sits a pile of clothes on the shore—a pair of pants, some boots, and her pale yellow dress—and on top of it all perches a dainty golden crown.

My heart swells so large, I know I will never be the same without her.

So I will not be.

This is forever.

Forever and always.

~

Krug

Cora the Fearless walks beside me, her chin held high as we walk through my kingdom, the orcs welcoming her like family. That's what she is. Cora is as much a part of the orc kingdom as I am. Each warrior bows their head in respect as we pass, not just to me, but to my queen beside me, and every child stares at her shining skin in awe, giggling at the magic that dances at her feet. Every now and then, she sends out small sparks to amaze them. They are enamored with Cora, and it's easy to see why.

I'm just as enamored with her.

Today is a celebration of the solstice, an important orc event, and Cora had quickly agreed to attend with me. As a king myself, I must still attend to my duties, so my time is split between my kingdom and Cora's castle. We utilize the tunnels, making the trips quicker, but every moment I'm away from her, I yearn for her touch and laughter.

For this event, she has blessed me with the sight of her in traditional orc clothing, the warrior's armor beautiful against her pale skin. Her hair is braided and beaded in a way that tells me she planned this in advance, and the markings painted on her skin proclaim as her the queen she is. Today, no dainty crown sits on her head. Instead, it's a crown fit for an orc queen—a gift from me. Tiny golden bones form the shape, holding a beautiful sapphire in the center.

We reach the square, and I stop us as everyone waits for the moment the celebration will begin. I look down at her at the same moment she glances up at me and smiles, the fierceness in her love making me want to sweep her off her feet and carry her away, where I can have my way with her. For orcs, it's not uncommon for orgies to happen in the streets, but that won't be until later. For now, we start with a feast.

"I have a solstice present for you," she says, her eyes glittering. She passes a package to me and waits for me to open it.

"I assume this is what Bracken told me I would bellow my joy for," I say with a grin, knowing it'll make her scowl that the fey dared to spill a secret.

"That fey is going to get a tongue lashing for gossiping," she grumbles.

My lips curl. "I'm sure he'll like that."

I open the package, and a large, golden chain is revealed. It's simple but intricate. It was clearly made by skilled hands and forged with a creativity I don't possess. It's exactly the kind of jewelry I like, and I stare at it in surprise.

Cora waits expectantly, watching me with eyes that see it all. "You don't have to wear it if it makes you feel...wrong." My warrior is always conscious of the trauma from my past. "But I wanted you to have something from me with you always." She leans in close. "Besides, when I'm riding you, it'll make a great place to grip."

Heat fills me, but in the way of orcs, I don't thank Cora. Instead, I hold the chain in the air above my head. "My queen has gifted me a chain!" I shout loud enough for all those gathered in the square.

Cheers go up at the claiming, at the profound statement that I am spoken for among orcs. With bright eyes, I place the chain around my neck and lift Cora into the air, bringing forth more cheers.

She flushes bright red as they begin to chant.

"Cora the Fearless! Cora the Liberator! Cora the queen!"

"Cora," I murmur, pressing my lips against her. "My warrior queen."

～

RAZCORR

THE LAND below us flashes by as we fly through the air, Cora nestled safely in my arms. We often fly together when we are able to. My mate loves the feel of the wind in her hair and seeing the land beneath her. It's not uncommon for those below us to wave in excitement as we pass, monsters, humans, and halflings alike in awe of their queen.

Just as I'm always in awe.

My mate is everything a queen should be.

She is beautiful, regal, strong, fierce, and powerful.

She's everything I could have ever hoped for in a mate. I even got her handprint chipped into my stone back, a permanent claim that she'd been afraid of because the process is painful. I assured her that all mated gargoyles wear the mark of their mates, and in return, she wears a scar from the barest scratch of my nail along her collarbone, her own mark that the others nearly killed me for.

In the end, only her reassurance that she'd asked for it had kept me alive.

I'm proud of their fierceness—fierce mates for my mate.

She'll never be unprotected. She'll never be alone.

A family I've never known is now mine, and I couldn't be happier.

As we fly through the kingdom, her kingdom, the golden tips on my wings' claws glitter in the sun. She found those tips for me and embedded them with her signature stone, placing her magic inside of them so they pulse with her soul. As I soar to the right, holding her tightly in my arms, I know I've never been happier.

"You are the wind I sail upon," I murmur so she can hear. "The love I never expected."

Looking up at me, she smiles. "And you are the wings I always needed. I love you, gargoyle mine."

I hold her tighter and keep her safe so that she may reign long and forever.

My mate.

My eternity.

My queen.

Grimus

Cora leans over from her throne, her eyes alight with magic, as there is a lull in court duties. We've been sitting on the thrones for hours, listening to the plight of our people, who are struggling. So far, we've heard of a farmer who lost half his harvest to the arachne fey, a jeweler who can't find a supply of diamonds good enough for the new crowns, a past gilded lady who refuses to do any work, and a halfling child who wants to become a scholar, despite the school refusing to allow a halfling girl in. We'd taken care of each and every problem, reassuring the farmer that someone would be out to help, offering the jeweler a stash from the royal jewels, instructing the gilded lady to focus on her skill in art, and making sure the school allows the halfling female to appeal to her ambitions.

Still, even though we're doing good work, it's boring to sit on the throne and wait for more to appear. There are always more problems, always things to address, but at least I'm not alone.

Cora, as she leans in, presses a kiss to my bicep before she sets a large package on my lap.

"What's this?" I ask, staring down at the brown package.

Her eyes sparkle as she gestures for me to open it. "A gift for my king."

Heat fills my eyes at her words, at the way her tone tells me she'll kneel for me later. A queen kneels to no one but her mates, so Cora kneels only for us. Otherwise, we lift her up.

"Why so giving?"

"Can I not just spoil my monsters?" she asks innocently. "Why must there be a special occasion?"

I snort, and a tiny bit of smoke comes out. "Is this you trying to butter me up?"

"Of course." She shrugs. "Anything to spread a little butter."

I lean forward and nip her lip, and in return, she tickles the ring in my nostrils. "Open it." Her excitement tells me it'll be a good gift, one I'll cherish.

Gently, I pull the cord tying the brown paper together before opening it to reveal the largest and most elaborate sword I've ever seen. I stare at it in surprise. The hilt features not only a crown, but a depiction of each of us—a gargoyle, a fey, an orc, a naga, a kraken, and a minotaur all standing with a human. It's our family forever emblazoned on a sword fit for a king.

"You had this made," I rasp out.

Nodding, she reaches forward and strokes a finger lovingly over the minotaur and the jewel embedded for him. "It took longer than I would have liked, but yes."

"I... Thank you." I gaze down at the sword I know will be my prized possession for as long as I live. The temptation to slay an enemy with it is strong, and that's before I even realize there's a bit of her magic infused in the rose quartz centered beneath the carving of her feet. "You put yourself in it."

She presses another kiss to my bicep. "So I'm always with you, no matter what."

With a guttural growl, I cup the back of her neck and jerk her to me, dragging her from her throne to mine, where I kiss her until we're both breathless with desire.

"I accept your gift," I say against her lips. "Just as I accept your heart."

She grins and kisses me again. "Long may we reign," she whispers.

My heart fills until it's nearly bursting as I hold my little human tight while we absorb each other.

"Long may we reign," I repeat.

And so we will.

And so we do.

ABOUT K.A KNIGHT

K.A Knight is an international bestselling indie author trying to get all of the stories and characters out of her head, writing the monsters that you love to hate. She loves reading and devours every book she can get her hands on, and she also has a worrying caffeine addiction.

She leads her double life in a sleepy English town, where she spends her days writing like a crazy person.

Read more at K.A Knight's website or join her Facebook Reader Group.
Sign up for exclusive content and my newsletter here
http://eepurl.com/drLLoj

About Kendra Moreno

Kendra Moreno is secretly a spy but when she's not dealing in secrets and espionage, you can find her writing her latest adventure. She lives in Texas where the summer days will make you melt, and southern charm comes free with every meal. She's a recovering Road Rager (kind of) and slowly overcoming her Star Wars addiction (nope!), and she definitely didn't pass on her addiction to her son (she did). She has one hellhound named Mayhem who got tired of guarding the Gates of Hell and now guards her home against monsters. She's a geek, a mother, a scuba diver, a tyrannosaurus rex, and a wordsmith who sometimes switches out her pen for a sword.

If you see Kendra on the streets, don't worry: you can distract her with talks about Kylo Ren or Loki.
#LokiLives #BringBackBenSolo

To find out more about Kendra, you can check her out on her website or join her
Facebook group, Kendra's World of Wonder.
Sign up for Kendra's Newsletter:
https://mailchi.mp/feb46d2b29ad/babbleandquill

facebook.com/AuthorKendraMoreno

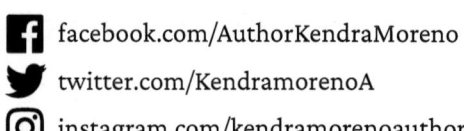

twitter.com/KendramorenoA

instagram.com/kendramorenoauthor

bookbub.com/authors/kendra-moreno

ALSO BY K.A KNIGHT

THEIR CHAMPION SERIES *Dystopian RH*

The Wasteland

The Summit

The Cities

The Nations

Their Champion Coloring Book

Their Champion - the omnibus

The Forgotten

The Lost

The Damned

Their Champion Companion - the omnibus

DAWNBREAKER SERIES *SCI FI RH*

Voyage to Ayama

Dreaming of Ayama

THE LOST COVEN SERIES *PNR RH*

Aurora's Coven

Aurora's Betrayal

HER MONSTERS SERIES *PNR RH*

Rage

Hate

THE FALLEN GODS SERIES *PNR*

PrettyPainful

Pretty Bloody

PrettyStormy

Pretty Wild

Pretty Hot

Pretty Faces

Pretty Spelled

Fallen Gods - the omnibus 1

Fallen Gods - the omnibus 2

FORBIDDEN READS *(STANDALONES)* *CONTEMPORARY*

Daddy's Angel

Stepbrothers' Darling

FORGOTTEN CITY

Monstrous Lies

STANDALONES

IN DEN OF VIPERS' UNIVERSE - CONTEMPORARY

Scarlett Limerence

Nadia's Salvation

Den of Vipers

Gangsters and Guns (Co-Write with Loxley Savage)

CONTEMPORARY

The Standby

Diver's Heart

SCI FI RH

Crown of Stars

AUDIOBOOKS

The Wasteland

The Summit

Rage

Hate

Den of Vipers *(From Podium Audio)*

Gangsters and Guns *(From Podium Audio)*

Daddy's Angel *(From Podium Audio)*

Stepbrothers' Darling *(From Podium Audio)*

Blade of Iris *(From Podium Audio)*

Deadly Affair *(From Podium Audio)*

Stolen Trophy *(From Podium Audio)*

Crown of Stars *(From Podium Audio)*

SHARED WORLD PROJECTS

Blade of Iris - Mafia Wars CONTEMPORARY

CO-AUTHOR PROJECTS - *Erin O'Kane*

HER FREAKS SERIES PNR Dystopian RH

Circus Save Me

Taming The Ringmaster

Walking the Tightrope

Her Freaks Series - the omnibus

STANDALONES

PNR RH

The Hero Complex

Collection of Short Stories

Dark Temptations (contains One Night Only and Circus Saves Christmas)

THE WILD BOYS SERIES *CONTEMPORARY*

The Wild Interview

The Wild Tour

The Wild Finale

The Wild Boys - the omnibus

CO-AUTHOR PROJECTS - *Ivy Fox*

Deadly Love Series *CONTEMPORARY*

Deadly Affair

Deadly Match

Deadly Encounter

CO-AUTHOR PROJECTS - *Kendra Moreno*

STANDALONES

CONTEMPORARY

Stolen Trophy

CO-AUTHOR PROJECTS - *Loxley Savage*

THE FORSAKEN SERIES *SCI FI RH*

Capturing Carmen

Stealing Shiloh

Harboring Harlow

STANDALONES

Gangsters and Guns - IN DEN OF VIPERS' UNIVERSE

OTHER CO-WRITES

Shipwreck Souls *(with Kendra Moreno & Poppy Woods)*

The Horror Emporium *(with Kendra Moreno & Poppy Woods)*

Also by Kendra

Sons Of Wonderland
Book 1 - Mad as a Hatter
Book 2 - Late as a Rabbit
Book 3 - Feral as a Cat
Companion novel - Cruel as a Queen

Daughters Of Neverland
Book 1 - Vicious as a Darling
Book 2 - Fierce As A Tiger Lily
Book 3 - Wicked As A Pixie
Companion Novel - Monstrous As A Croc

The Heirs Of Oz
Book 1 - Heartless as a Tin Man
Book 2 - Empty as a Scarecrow
Book 3 - Cowardly as a Lion
Companion Novel - Vengeful as a Beauty

The Lords of Grimm
Book 1 - Cunning as a Trickster
Book 2 - Bitter as a Captain
Book 3 - Twisted as a Princess
Companion Novel - Hateful as a Sister

Prey Island

Book 1 - Prey Island

Clockwork Almanac

Book 1 - Clockwork Butterfly

Book 2 - Clockwork Octopus

The Valhalla Mechanism

Book 1 - Gears of Mischief

Book 2 - Gears of Thunder

Book 3 - Gears of Ragnarök

Race Games

Book 1 - Blood and Honey

Book 2 - Teeth and Wings

Book 3 - Jewels and Feathers

Stand-alones

Treble Maker

Pharaoh-mones

CO-WRITES

with K.A Knight

Stolen Trophy

Fractured Shadows

with K.A Knight and Poppy Woods

Shipwreck Souls

The Horror Emporium

with Poppy Woods

The Blooming Courts

Book 1 - Resurrect

Book 2 - Sprout

Book 3 - Flourish

Book 4 - Emerge

Book 5 - Blossom

The Dinoverse

(Shared universe with Poppy Woods)

Book 1 – Dances with Raptors by Poppy Woods

Book 2 – Rexes & Robbers by Kendra Moreno

Head Case: A Dark Twist on a Classic